THE ISLE
OF DEVILS

Books by

CRAIG JANACEK

THE FURTHER ADVENTURES OF SHERLOCK HOMES
LIGHT IN THE DARKNESS°
TREASURE TROVE INDEED!^*
THE ASSASSINATION OF SHERLOCK HOLMES

THE DR. WATSON TRILOGY
THE ISLE OF DEVILS
THE GATE OF GOLD
THE RUINS OF SUMMER*

OTHER NOVELS
THE ANGER OF ACHILLES PETERSON
THE OXFORD DECEPTION

§

°Portions previous published in:
The MX Book of New Sherlock Holmes Stories Part I: 1881 to 1889;
David Marcum, Editor; MX Publishing

^Portions previously published in:
The MX Book of New Sherlock Holmes Stories Part IV: 2016 Annual;
David Marcum, Editor; MX Publishing
The MX Book of New Sherlock Holmes Stories Part VI: 2017 Annual;
David Marcum, Editor; MX Publishing
and
Holmes Away from Home: Tales of the Great Hiatus;
David Marcum, Editor; Belanger Books

*Coming soon

THE ISLE OF DEVILS

THE DR. WATSON TRILOGY: BOOK ONE

CRAIG JANACEK

THE ISLE OF DEVILS. Copyright © 2013 by Craig Janacek. All Rights Reserved

Originally published worldwide as an eBook on Amazon.com in 2013

2017 First Trade Paperback Edition

Imprint: Independently published

ISBN: 978-1-52-028543-6

Cover design by Craig Janacek

TO MARGARET

"A love that life could never tire..."

Songs of Travel, XXVI
Robert Louis Stevenson (1850-1894)

CONTENTS

ACKNOWLEDGMENTS

First and foremost, I must give a grateful acknowledgment to Sir Arthur Conan Doyle (1859-1930) for the use of the Sherlock Holmes characters. Without his words, this novel could not have been written. For reference, I consider Leslie S. Klinger's *The New Annotated Sherlock Holmes* (2005 & 2006) to be the definitive edition.

This novel is also deeply tied to the magnificent isle of Bermuda, and I wish to thank all of my Bermudian family and friends who lent their names to this endeavor. A special appreciation is owed to Mark Cordeiro, who went out of his way to ensure my visit to the Globe Hotel (now the National Trust Museum) in St. George's, so that I could pace out the dimensions of the building. Terry Tucker's *Bermuda and the Supernatural* (1968) and Rosemary Jones' *Bermuda: Five Centuries* (2004) were especially helpful when researching Bermuda's history. The first words of this novel were set down in the cedar-paneled library at Bridge House, Southampton Parish, overlooking Ely's Harbor and the famous Somerset Bridge.

Furthermore, I owe debts of gratitude to two great mystery novelists and one historical Japanese legend. The first is Elizabeth Peters (1927-2013), who wrote in 1991: *"I am an admirer of the romances of Sir Henry Rider Haggard. He was a master of a form of fiction that is, alas, seldom produced in these degenerate days; having run out of books to read, I decided to write one myself. It is meant as an affectionate, admiring, and nostalgic tribute."* That sentiment led directly to me attempting the same. The second is to Dame Agatha Christie (1890-1976) whose 1934 masterpiece remains the pinnacle of the form to which I aspire. Finally, this story was also directly inspired by the legend of the Forty-seven Ronin from tale *Chushingura* (1748).

PREFACE:
THE BERMUDA MANUSCRIPT

On the 29th of July, 2009, the British Overseas Territory known officially as 'The Bermudas,' and colloquially as simply 'Bermuda,' celebrated the 400th anniversary of its founding by opening a World Heritage Centre in a long grey building with dark green shutters and the traditional white stepped roof of the island. Formally an 1860 customs warehouse at Penno's Wharf, the new museum celebrated the recognition of the 'Historic Town of St. George and [its] Related Fortifications' by the UNESCO World Heritage committee nine years prior.

Before that time, the proud citizens of Bermuda had long been trying to convince the powers-that-be at UNESCO that the simple fact of the Town of St. George being the oldest continuously inhabited (at least by Europeans) town in the Western Hemisphere should be more than sufficient to merit inclusion in that select list that brought with it renown and (hopefully) tourists. As such, the Bermudians had constructed a temporary World Heritage Display in the old St. Catherine's Fort, located on the northeastern tip of the isle between Achilles Bay and Gates Bay. Once the World Heritage Centre building at Penno's Wharf had been sufficiently renovated, the honored display moved from its temporary domicile in Fort St. Catherine to its new and permanent home. This, of course, left a bit of a glaring hole in the attractions at the aforementioned fort, and as such, the curators of the fort and its associated museum decided to embark on an ambitious renovation of both the previous space, as well as the other areas of the fort that had been more-or-less closed off since it was decommissioned in the late 1950's.

This renovation work progressed at a snail's pace, in no small part due to a chronic lack of funding brought on by an unanticipated lull in tourist revenue following the so-called 'Global Financial Collapse' of the late 2000's. Eventually however the workers stumbled across one small storeroom which was remarkably still crowded with discarded personal effects of the former British Army officers that had been stationed at the fort since the time of its last major reconstruction, which lasted from 1865 to 1878, and which included the creation of the twenty-five foot thick concrete embrasures and casemate which continue to impress visitors unto this day.

The odds-and-ends that were pulled from this room were many and varied. Much of the debris consisted of commonplace items of little interest, such as the remnants of ivory-headed umbrellas, walking sticks, bone and ebony dice, and pipes. There were several rusted flagons and trenchers, and a half-filled bottle of spirits, long-turned into something undrinkable. A deck of mold-riddled whist cards, with the visages of Europe's great royalty on the face cards, was sent off for a conservation effort, as were a small oak barometer and a brass telescope. Several officers' valises and 'mess tines' were found in various states of decay. A rotting fur busby that likely once belonged to some brave soldier was unfortunately deemed beyond possible restoration and was incinerated. A much-rusted but potentially refurbishable Mark I Martini-Henry Rifle c.1871 incited some excitement, for examples of that renowned gun are now relatively rare, and the wooden gunstock was fortuitously carved with the owner's name and regiment. This was earmarked to be sent off to Christie's for auction. Meanwhile, a curious chess-set, the pieces carved to resemble the figures on the two sides of the English War of the Roses, the Yorkists in white and the Lancastrians in red, was referred to Sotheby's. Two busts illustrated the great range of items encountered in that unexpected treasure room. One was a fine marble bust of Athena, apparently of great antiquity and worthy of display in any museum, while the other was a cheap duplicate plaster cast of the famous head of Nelson by the English sculptor Baily, of no real value whatsoever. A few piquant items spoke to the great range of the Empire, which once upon a time the sun never set. This included a remarkably preserved Zulu shield and spear, a lion-skin hearthrug, and a mildewed stuffed tiger-head, clearly trophies of some adventuresome campaigner, while for some time it was thought that a magnificent suit of Japanese armor was the most valuable item in the room.

But it was one of the oldest items, found in the darkest corner of the storeroom, which would ultimately prove to be the most noteworthy. At first glance, it seemed of little import. It was a medium-sized tin box, about nine inches by fourteen inches in dimension, and about four inches thick, of the type once formerly used to contain letters and dispatches. It was very worn and battered, and rusted to the point where the name painted on the lid was almost illegible. The first word 'Capt.' was clearly an abbreviation for 'Captain' and all agreed that the first name appeared to be 'Henry.' Of the last name, literally nothing could be ascertained. Below the name many other letters were missing, but enough remained to hazard a fair guess that Captain Henry had once served in the 99th Infantry Regiment (Duke of Edinburgh). This helped significantly in dating the find, as the 99th Regiment was only stationed in Bermuda from 1880 to 1881.

Opening the box proved to be much harder than anticipated, as the lid had literally been welded shut via the decades of accumulated rust. It was finally determined that the best course of action was to remove the dispatch box to the care of the Bermuda Historical Society on Queen Street in Hamilton. There, careful deliberation was held regarding the safest method by which to remove the aforementioned rust. Standard commercial rust removers were out of the question, of course, as they rely upon either phosphoric or oxalic acid, neither of which was deemed healthy for the papers presumed to be contained within the box. Eventually, the restorers determined that careful applications of white vinegar would be the least harmful method, and several meticulous weeks later, they succeeded in unsealing the box.

To their great disappointment, it was immediately obvious that the contents were heavily damaged by the pervasive damp found on that sub-tropical isle. Nevertheless, the manuscript entombed therein clearly dated from before the turn of the twentieth century, as it was written on one hundred forty-two pages of a decaying but formerly rich royal cream lined foolscap paper sans watermark, with text appearing on only one side in a fading purple-black iron gall ink set down by a broad-pointed quill pen. What then followed was months of painstaking conservation efforts whereby each page was separated from its neighbor with exquisite care. Following this, radiographic analysis aided in determining which words belonged to which sheet, as the ink had completely bled the words into the adjoining pages. This task was further complicated by the fact that the quality of the handwriting varied from sheet to sheet, with some as clear as if the author was printing, while others where the writing was so agitated that it was almost unreadable. The cause of this disrupted writing became more obvious when it was revealed by the author that the majority of the manuscript was written while at sea, with alternating periods of calm and stormy weather, by a man who, at the time, must not have contemplated that it was ever going to be of much practical importance. Eventually, however, these dedicated preservationists were able to read the words set down over one hundred and thirty years ago. And when they realized the monumental significance of their find, they immediately contacted me (due to my past publication history and connections to the island) to be the executor and literary agent for the release of this important episode in history.

I will admit that a palpable thrill ran through my bones when I first received the excited phone call describing their find. But when it became clear who the purported author of this tale was, it became of the utmost importance to verify its authenticity, as the last several decades have literally been littered with purported 're-discoveries' of supposedly 'lost' writings of a man who would be universally hailed as one of the greatest authors of the Victorian Age. Carbon-dating of the paper was of relatively limited use, since the process is still fraught with an uncertainty of approximately plus/minus forty years for samples such as this. While helpful at ruling out a truly modern forgery, it would not debunk one from before 1920, by which time several examples had already sprung into existence. Similarly, the antique iron gall ink had begun its process of corroding the paper, but that characteristic damage could be faked by various clever methods. The provenance of the dispatch box was unassailable, though to a modern scholar, it seemed to be an almost criminal-level neglect that would lead to the abandoning of a manuscript of this extraordinary import in a damp fortress store-room. And yet the author of the manuscript himself would explain this neglect to us, when he later reported that the box's owner, Captain Henry, was "a man of untidy habits – very untidy and careless... who threw away his chances."

Not wanting to make this same mistake with our singular chance, we therefore felt that the most reliable method of authentication was to compare the handwriting of the Bermuda Manuscript (as we began to call it) with those known manuscripts of unquestioned attribution scattered about the globe. Although fifty-six works originally existed, over twenty have been sadly lost to the ravages of time. Most of the remaining thirty-odd treasures are in the hands of exceedingly private collectors with little interest in opening their doors to a scholar of little renown. Fortunately, at least eight are still in the public domain and freely viewable in situ to researchers with sufficient introduction and a carefully controlled appointment. We began with those manuscripts residing in the United States, including the ones at the Houghton Library of Harvard University, the Berg Collection of the New York Public Library, Haverford College in Pennsylvania, and the Lilly Library at Indiana University. The experts at all four institutions were unanimous in their opinion that we were in possession of a genuine work, which raised our level of excitement to an ecstatic pitch. And yet, we tried to temper this emotion by recognizing that more work needed to be done in both the United Kingdom as well as the Continent. We decided to save the toughest authorities for last, and so first traveled to the Bibliotheca Boderiana in Geneva. They were at first skeptical but eventually agreed with the judgment of the American scholars. Even the dons at the British Library were convinced of the veracity of our find, as were the specialists at the Portsmouth City Museum. Only the expert at the National Library of Scotland disagreed and labeled the Bermuda Manuscript a 'clever forgery.' While we obviously would have been happier if we had managed to obtain an undivided degree of support, we felt that in the whole, the burden of proof was on our side. We would release this remarkable tale to the world and await its verdict.

I therefore set before you the earliest known words of one of the greatest authors, not only of the Victorian Era, but perhaps of all of Western Civilization. Although it may at times pale in comparison to the singular vibrancy of some of his later works, when he was composing at the height of his powers, we nevertheless believe it to be an instructive insight into the previously opaque background of one of history's most famous men. For this American edition, I have taken the daring liberty of changing the author's words from his British spelling ('colour', 'sombre', etc.) to one more pleasing to our colonial eyes.

§

CHAPTER I:
THE *SERAPIS*

It is with a muddled mind that I take up my pen to write these words in which I shall record the singular experience I had upon our colonial island of Bermuda. So peculiar was this adventure in its origins, and so dramatic in its details, that I feel that it is worthy of being set down upon paper, even if your eyes are the only ones to ever read it. It will come as no surprise to you that I have long been in the habit of maintaining a diary. Given the far-ranging life that I have led in my short eight and twenty years, I find that scribing my reminiscences assists me to recollect those small details that perhaps grow obscured over the passage of time by those more vivid scenes which are indelibly graven upon my memory. Certainly, however, there is little risk that the extraordinary events I am about to describe will ever be forgotten.

My friends have on occasion accused me of indulging a bad habit of telling stories with the wrong end foremost, and thus I will endeavor to recite what unfolded in due sequence, rather than plunging headways into the matter. I do not wish to waste your time, but I fear that my tale may need a brief preamble. As you are well aware, the twenty-seventh of July, 1880, was a dark time for the British Empire. I saw my own comrades hacked to pieces at Maiwand by the murderous Ghazis. Our defeat during that battle dampened morale significantly, though Ayub Khan lost vast numbers of men in order to gain his small advantage. Many of our men were shut up in Kandahar, until General Frederick Roberts, V.C., made his famous three hundred and fourteen-mile march from Kabul in August, leading to a decisive victory for the Queen's forces.

As for my personal situation, the whole campaign was nothing but a series of misfortunes and disasters. As I futilely huddled over the fallen bodies of my comrades, I too was struck down by a Jezail bullet. This entered my left shoulder, shattering the bone and grazing the subclavian artery. If not for the brave actions of my orderly Murray, I likely would not have ever made it out of there alive. As it was, I managed to acquire yet another piece of ten-rupee lead, this time in my right ankle, during the chaotic retreat across the British lines. Eventually, as part of a great train of other suffering soldiers, my pack-horse led me through a series of deep defiles to the base hospital in Peshawar.

The base hospital was no idyllic sanctuary, however. The wounded were doing quite badly, many dying of lock-jaw, the most horrible death that I know. Fortunately, my surgeon was extremely competent, and fully versed in the Listerian method of antisepsis. With the aid of a hypodermic of morphia and some tightly wrapped carbolized bandages, I was soon on my way to a speedy recovery. However, a small fragment of one of those Jezail bullets was not able to be fully extracted and remains with me today as a permanent souvenir of that terrible day. Despite my own shattered state, I tried my best to bring some measure of comfort to the other men, however false it may be, for I knew that many of those in the beds surrounding me would eventually die. With every sigh of my companions' last breaths, I felt a great pain deep within myself.

The grimness might have eventually overwhelmed me, if not for a flower of beauty that floated in the halls in stark contrast to the Sikh orderlies and stout English matrons. It hardly took a quick eye for color to spot the vision of loveliness that was Violet Devere. In her guise as a nurse, she visited me daily to foment my wounds with a poultice of native medicinal herbs made from the moringa tree. As her smooth hands pressed upon my shoulder and ankle, I will not pretend that my eyes often left her face. Her age was but a year or two over twenty. She was small and dainty, almost ethereal in her figure, but with luxuriant locks of chestnut-tinted hair neatly tied into a long braid. Her deep blue eyes held a hint of timidity, despite the great horrors that they witnessed every day in that hospital, and she had a soothing voice that emanated from her perfectly-shaped mouth. She wore a plain but pretty cerulean frock covered with a white apron in order to protect it from blood and other unpleasantries.

As my strength rallied and her visits passed each day, the struggle within my breast grew ever fiercer. I was well aware that Army regulations expressly forbade any form of intimate liaisons between its officers and those brave women who volunteered their time at the base hospitals. Nor was there any sign from her that she returned any of my interest as she briskly went about her business. I was simply another patient to her. Finally, however, my self-restraint abandoned me, not only due to her remarkable beauty, but also from my natural curiosity over her strange presence in exotic Peshawar. One day she spent additional time working upon my shoulder, where I had foolishly strained the wound while reaching for a novel, inducing a crimson patch to soak through the white linen compress. After days of responding to her in the most cold and distant tones that I could muster, so as not to betray my true emotions, I suddenly asked her if she would take me out onto the hospital's verandah in order to bask in the late afternoon sun.

She looked startled by the suggestion. "I think, sir, that you could manage it by yourself," she replied eventually.

I shrugged my unwounded shoulder sadly. "I have tried to walk about the wards, but met with little success. I believe that my injured leg still requires more nursing before it is ready for such a journey."

Her brows furrowed in thought. "Then I will ask one of the orderlies to push you out there in one of the wheeled-chairs." She began to rise to in order to carry out this plan.

I impetuously reached out a hand and laid it gently upon her dainty white wrist. Something about my recent brush with death made me feel like I needed to live my life more boldly. "Ah, but I would greatly prefer if you would escort me yourself."

She looked down at my hand and considered this. "I do not believe that this would be a wise idea, sir. I will call an orderly."

I unhappily watched her rise and walk away. Later, as I sat in my chair upon the verandah, I gloomily pondered my situation as the sun settled over the arid valley. I remained in place for many hours, brusquely waving away orderlies who attempted to fetch me back to my bed. The night was clear and fine above me. The stars shone cold and bright, while a half-moon bathed the whole scene in a soft, uncertain light. This sterile vision seemed to be a foretelling of my future, which appeared rudderless and forlorn. Despite these dark thoughts, however, when I later returned to my bed I thought that the fresh air had done me some good, and I felt stronger for having made the excursion.

You can imagine my surprise when, the following day, Miss Devere arrived at her usual time and offered to take me out onto the verandah herself. I cautiously inquired as to the alteration in her opinion. "I have carefully considered your suggestion, sir, and decided that you possess a sympathetic face and that there would likely be no harm in conversing with you."

"I am honored, Miss Devere," said I, gravely. "It would give me no keener pleasure."

And so began a steady ritual. My leg grew progressively stronger and yet I hid this fact from all, so as to not disrupt the impetus for our nightly excursions upon the verandah. Much of the time we spent talking, where I learned that she was the niece and ward of her uncle, Major-General Sir Neville Devere, C.B., of the renowned Third Buffs. She had been orphaned at a young age, and her uncle's wife had recently succumbed to the yellow fever, so the good man was at a loss of what to do with a high-spirited young lady. As there were no other close relatives in England, as she grew older, he found that could not simply leave her behind un-chaperoned, and he therefore decided to bring her out to live with him at the base-camp. Unfortunately, Violet's determined nature inherently forbade her from sitting quietly at home all day gossiping with the wives or daughters of the other officers. And so, against the general's better judgment, she persuaded him to allow her to volunteer her assistance in succoring the wounded at the base hospital.

Although Violet had spent the majority of her life at her uncle's estate in Essex, she had quickly adapted to life in the lands of the British Raj. One evening she even showed me the curious pet that she had acquired in Calcutta in order to keep away snakes from her uncle's home. She leaned over to a fabric-lined shutter-topped basket that she had brought with her. I had briefly imagined that it might contain a bit of home-cooked food, as I was rapidly tiring of the food served by the hospital commissary, and my time spent talking of England with Violet had awakened a strong craving for some oysters and grouse. Therefore, I was much surprised when she instead brought forth a beautiful reddish-brown creature, thin and lithe, with the legs of a stoat, a long, thin nose, and a pair of the finest red eyes that I ever saw in an animal's head.

"What is it?" I exclaimed.

"Ricky is a mongoose," she laughingly explained.

As she elaborated, my esteem for her only grew. She was a remarkable woman to brave both the dangers of life upon the frontier and the horrors of a base-camp hospital. I found myself pondering why she chose to spend so much of her precious time with a crippled surgeon of limited means such as myself. I marveled at her lustrous hair, which took on a wonderful golden glow in the slanting rays of the setting sun. On a keen impulse, I reached out my right arm and drew her to my side, where she came without a hint of demurral. And thus, as the cooler air of twilight descended upon us and the days passed into beautiful moonlit nights, our time together was filled less with pleasant talk and more with exquisite moments of silence.

Unfortunately, this happy interlude was not destined to last. Just as I was growing stronger and returning to my prior robust health, I was struck down again, this time by one of the many foul fevers that are so prevalent in the Peshawar valley. As I battled the enteric fever, I had little time for thoughts of romance or my fellow comrades, though it was clear that this particular scourge had affected half of the companies in the area, flooding the poor hospital in which I lay prostrate from the paroxysms of intense cramping. As my hectic temperature rose to over a hundred and four degrees, I found myself growing so dizzy that I could not even rise out of bed in order to evacuate the vileness from my innards in the privacy that a man prefers. I could barely keep in enough liquid to hold body and soul together. Although the doctors were too good to say it to my face, my medical knowledge had not deserted me in spite of my febrile state, and I knew that my life was despaired of. As a further cruel blow, during that time the Third Buffs completed their mission for the Afghan campaign and were mobilized back to England, to be replaced by the Royal Munsters. I was left without even a photograph of her to gaze upon, but was too weak to even give words to my dull despair over Violet's precipitous departure.

Eventually, however, the doctors found a supply of cooling medicine and my naturally vigorous constitution won out over the pestilential flux. As I began to recuperate, I was greatly surprised to be informed that I had a visitor, despite being on the very frontier of the Empire. For a brief moment I imagined that Violet had somehow managed to return to Peshawar, and I transferred myself into the wheeled chair as rapidly as my weakened state would allow. My heart thumped rapidly in my breast as the orderly wheeled me out to the verandah, but this agitated patter stopped abruptly when instead of Violet's petite form, a short man with a frame of white hair confronted me. Two keen brown eyes peered out at me from under tufted white eyebrows, and he was heavily mustached. He was on the long side of fifty, but despite his advancing years, he retained a powerful stature, which lent him an aura of command. The crown above two stars upon his scarlet coat with white facings proclaimed him a Colonel.

"By Jove, Doctor, you look like a man in need of a side of roast," said the man frankly.

My brain was clearly still recovering from its recent bout, as it took me many a long moment before I finally recognized him. "Colonel Hayter! What brings you to Peshawar?" I cried. I was singularly pleased to see that fine old solider in front of me.

"The Berkshires were passing through and I thought I would check to make sure that none of our men were languishing at the base hospital. Imagine my surprise when they told me that you were still here. Why on earth should an old campaigner such as you not have recovered from those Jezail bullets by now?"

His words brought a spasm of pain to my first wound, and I half-consciously rubbed my left shoulder, which I to this day continue to hold in a stiff and unnatural manner. "The Jezails have little to trumpet, Colonel. It is this damned enteric fever."

Edward Hayter snorted in disgust. "Ah, I suspected as much. It's clear as day that you will never recover in these pestilential airs." He turned and gazed out over the valley, every aspect of its flora and dwellings still exotically foreign to my English eyes. "However, I still recall when you plucked that bullet out of my leg and sewed me together so well that I was back on the march within a week. I was not able to show my gratitude at that time, but the moment has come for me to repay my debts. I have arranged for you to recover in more healthy climes. Not a day longer should be lost. Tomorrow morning, you will be transported via *dâk gharrie* to the port at Karachi, where the troopship *Serapis* will convey you to the Cape. I hope that the sea airs will effect the healing these mountain airs were incapable of."

"I am astounded by this, Colonel, and surely unworthy."

"Pshaw, Doctor," he answered warmly, turning back to me. "You are a good man and it has been a great privilege to have served with you, for no matter how short a time. I confess that we hate to lose you. But the Queen's Rules are clear. Two bullets are enough for one man. The medical board has ruled that you have done your duty and you will be most honorably invalided out of the army. You will have nine months of half-pay, during which time you can regain your health before taking up a new position."

"Thank you, Colonel Hayter," said I with emotion.

"I'm not finished, Doctor," said the Colonel. "Since your handiwork was so effective, I have no further use of this Penang-lawyer that I picked up during my time in Malaysia, and then decorated while at Benares. May it serve you well in your recovery." He handed me a fine, thick wooden walking stick, its iron ferule only slightly worn. It had a large lead-weighted irregular bulbous head, intricately inlaid with what appeared to be gold filigree-work.

I was overwhelmed by his generosity. "You are too kind, Colonel. Surely you should keep it."

"On the contrary, Doctor. My little collection of Eastern weapons is complete enough without that stick. And I do not plan to be shot again. I wish you good fortunes upon your return to London."

"And you, Colonel? Where are you headed?"

"Wherever the Queen needs us, I expect. It is a good way to see the world that is for certain. But someday I hope to leave this dusty land, and return to the green embrace of mother England. If you ever find yourself in Surrey, my family's manor is near Reigate. It would bring me great pleasure if you were to honor me with a visit."

"You may count upon it, Colonel." And with that exchange, the Colonel shook my hand and parted from me. I sat there for a moment admiring my new prize. Clutching it in my gaunt right hand, I vowed that emaciation would not hold back my recovery any longer. Eventually, I signaled to an orderly to assist me in returning to my room, as I needed to pack up my small belongings in preparation for the following day's departure.

My best intentions, however, gave way under the strain of the wretched train to Karachi, which was perhaps better suited for transporting animals than recuperating men. By the time we boarded the HMS *Serapis*, I felt as if all of the progress I had made in my recovery had been lost. In addition, the strong south-west monsoon winds of the Arabian Sea brought with them terrible storms that eventually forced the ship to take shelter at the isle of Mauritius. During my outbound journey to Bombay upon the *Crocodile*, rather than rounding the Cape, we had taken the route that led through the glorious Mediterranean and the Suez Canal. There my iron stomach suffered not a twinge, while several of my fellow officers necessitated availing themselves of the convenience of the railings in order to purge themselves. However, I cannot claim any such success upon this tempestuous homeward voyage, and these excursions further weakened me to the point where my fevers relapsed and I could not even bring myself to disembark the ship and sample the pleasures of that lush tropical colony.

Indeed, I have few memories of the trip around the Cape of Good Hope, and no recollection of how I made my way off of the ship. However, I believe it was more of a febrile delirium than anything else, as I do not recall any grey mist swirling before my eyes, and have never fainted in my life. Thus, my first impression of Cape Town was that of a smiling vaguely-familiar face. This belonged to a man about my age of eight and twenty years. He was of a medium height, flaxen-haired and handsome, with steady green eyes. He was clean-shaven, and his mouth had a trace of sensitivity to it. He wore the familiar uniform of an Army doctor.

"By the Lord Harry! You look like you could use a doctor! You are as thin as a lash, and as brown as a nut."

I stared at him in a state of abject confusion, unable to find the words with which to respond to this strange greeting.

"Good morning, old chap!" the man continued with great cheer. "It's wonderful to see you again in this far away land."

"Where am I?" said I, groggily.

"The Military Hospital, Wynberg, Cape Town, of course."

After a significant amount of conscious effort, I finally placed the man.

"Jackson? Reginald Jackson, is that you?"

"Hah!" he chuckled heartily. "I knew it! Nothing sets Hamish back for long. What's a bit of enteric fever to a Netley man?"

"What are you doing here?"

"Well, after you shipped off with the 5th Northumberland Fusiliers, it was my turn. Unfortunately for me, it was then that they discovered the small trifle that I had neglected to inform them upon my completion at the University of London..."

"You have flat feet!" I suddenly exclaimed.

The look of astonishment upon his face told all. "How could you possibly know that, old chap?"

I paused for a moment before I could answer him. "It simply came to me. I recalled the many off-hours that we spent playing cricket. You always preferred to be the bowler, but were never particularly accurate at hitting the wicket. This eventually led me to wonder then why you preferred to bowl. Clearly, it was not because you were the best bowler. Thus, it must have been due to a deficiency as a batsman. And yet, you had a strong arm, and could strike the bowl well. Thus, the problem must have been with your running across the pitch. I then recalled that you had a particular form of running, in which you pronated your feet, rolling your ankles inward and distributing the weight in your foot medially. That led me to conclude that you did this as a natural way to absorb the shock and stress caused by your lack of arches."

"Well, it's a fine piece of reasoning if I don't say so myself! And it's spot on too. Once the sword-holders realized my deficiency, they almost drummed me out of the ranks. But eventually cooler heads prevailed, and the medical board realized that while I may never be a regimental surgeon like you, I could nonetheless still be put to good use in one of these rehabilitation hospitals."

"How has it been?" I inquired politely.

"Well, it is certainly different than treating your average London lady!" Jackson laughed heartily. "There is no dropsy or apoplexy here!"

I shifted in my bed, and noted that I felt much restored. I mentioned this to my friend.

"Ah, yes," he replied. "I gave you several doses of a paregoric while you were out, and it must be taking its effect."

"That is wonderful. I do not know how to thank you."

"No need, no need," he shrugged modestly. "Do you think that I have forgotten the assistance you gave me during our second year at university? In fact," his face brightened, "I am going to do you a turn better. You see we have had a terrible outbreak of erysipelas in the last few days, and have far too many men confined for you to stay here."

I frowned at this unhappy news. "I believe the *Serapis* was continuing on to Portsmouth."

Jackson shook his head gravely. "The *Serapis* has sailed on without you, I'm afraid. Furthermore, where would you go? Did you think that I forgot that you have no kith or kin in England? You would gravitate to London, and that is no place for a man to recuperate. There is far too much excitement on the streets there. You might fall in with dangerous sorts."

I was taken aback by his remonstrance and poor opinion of my character, and I have never been one who could easily hide his emotions.

Jackson laughed again when he saw my stricken face. "I jest, Hamish! But I am serious that I think you would recuperate better in a temperate clime. Fortunately for you, the *Malabar* is leaving in three days for Bermuda. I think you will enjoy it there."

"Bermuda!" I exclaimed happily. "My brother Henry is stationed there!"

"What a propitious coincidence! If you jot down a note to him of your impending arrival, I will ensure that it makes it onto tonight's mail-boat." He took a J pen from his chest pocket and ripped a leaf from his notebook, and then handed them to me.

I took them, and then shook my head in ongoing confusion. "But how can I just go to Bermuda? The medical board..."

"Old chap, I *am* the medical board here in Cape Town." With that Parthian shot, he left me in order to resume his rounds on his other patients, whom he had neglected in order to reminisce with me.

After contemplating this for a short while, I finally acquiesced to his wisdom, and wrote the note, which was duly dispatched. Who was I to complain of a chance to see my brother again after ten long years? Over the next three days I continued to grow stronger, and by the time I was to be discharged to my ship, I was able to amble around the wards with the aid of the colonel's Penang lawyer. On the day of my departure, Jackson kindly took time from his schedule in order to accompany me down to the docks.

"Thank you for everything, Jackson!" I said warmly.

"Of course, old chap! It was my greatest pleasure. I should let you know that I plan to retire soon from this business myself. I have met a nice lady, Miss Olive Sanford, whose father is a captain in the Rhodesian police. We have come to an understanding. She has done me the honor of accepting me as a husband in prospective. Once I can obtain my release, we plan to wed and return to London to start up a civil practice," said he, beaming with joy.

Although my heart ached for Violet, for whom I had once entertained similar thoughts, I nevertheless covered my feelings as best I could and attempted to be happy for my friend. "My congratulations!" cried I, warmly. "That is most splendid news. Then I hope to see you again very soon, when I complete my convalescence. Where should I call upon you? Cavendish Square? Harley Street?"

Jackson laughed. "The citadel of medicine? I am hardly so exalted or so flush with capital as to aim to start up a specialty practice on those hallowed streets. I would have to compete with the likes of Sir Jasper Meek, Penrose Fisher, Sir Leslie Oakshott, or any of the other best men in London. No, I am compelled to buy into an old-established general practice with my brother-in-law, Anstruther. His brass plate can be found in the Paddington district, on Crawford Place. You cannot miss the red lamp that shines outside. I assure you that there are many other excellent practices nearby. You could purchase one yourself and set up your own consulting-room for a reasonable rent and furnishing expenses! In fact, according to Anstruther's last letter, his neighbor old Farquhar is getting on in years and the St. Vitus Dance is preventing him from seeing patients on many days."

"I am not so certain of that, Jackson," said I, my brows knitted. "I think that the public not unnaturally goes on the principle that he who would heal others must himself be whole and looks askance at the curative powers of the doctor whose own case is beyond the reach of his medicines."

"Tut, tut," said he. "You were the best doctor in our class. The public recognize quality. They will advertise your virtues and endeavor to send you every sufferer over whom they have the slightest of influence. You will undoubtedly have clients aplenty."

I nodded my head slowly. "I will think on it. I have not yet decided how I will keep myself occupied once I am fully discharged from the Army." I reached out my hand and shook his heartily.

And with that, I parted from my old colleague, with every intention of calling upon him after my return to London. Within an hour, I was safely ensconced in my new quarters upon the *HMS Malabar*, ready to embark upon yet another chapter in my adventurous life. Only the future could show just how sensational it was to be.

§

CHAPTER II:
THE *MALABAR*

There were certainly no great difficulties in the next stage of my adventure, but I may have been premature in my excitement, as I clearly had little comprehension of the dull monotony that would be the hallmark of that sea voyage. While my time on the *Serapis* was a bit hazy due to the horrible fevers which had wracked my frame, I distinctly recall that we generally hugged the varied coast, which at least allowed for a tableau of some interest. However, once the *Malabar* cleared the great harbor of Cape Town, there was little to look upon, excepting only the never-ending crashing waves of the Atlantic's wide expanse and an occasional great white bird, a gull or an albatross, soaring aloft in the blue heavens.

One incident of mild curiosity occurred at the last moment prior to the ship departing from the jetty at Prince Alfred Basin. I had already settled my limited effects into my shared cabin, and was taking advantage of the warm breeze in order to enjoy a few solitary moments upon the deck. Rather than gazing out into the open water, of which I knew I would soon be seeing a great amount, I was standing at the dockside bulwark admiring the aptly-named Table Mountain backdrop when a commotion broke out at the bottom of the nearby gangplank. A curious man was arguing with Mr. Moore, the boatswain, who I had recently met upon my embarkation. The stranger was a sturdy, middle-sized fellow, some thirty years of age. He had curly blond-hair, with a thin moustache, and hazel eyes that, combined with a strong masculine face, made him appear quite handsome. He was attired in a dark blue pea-jacket with a sage-colored cravat, which gave him a decidedly nautical appearance, though his stride had more of the infantry to it than would be expected in a true sea-man.

He had on well-cut gray trousers and brown leather gaiters that that covered the tops of his elastic-sided boots, and all-in-all seemed a dashing fellow, whose showy dress was in strange contrast with his serious expression. In one hand he carried a Gladstone bag, and with his other he pulled at an Albert chain attached to his gold pocket watch. As they spoke, he glanced at it in an irritated fashion.

Only snatches of their argument upon the jetty floated up to where I stood. It appeared that the man was vigorously attempting to board the ship, while the boatswain was indicating in lower tones that the *Malabar* was a troopship.

"But I must get to Bermuda, and I missed the earlier mail-boat by a fraction of an hour. I cannot wait until next week," the man insisted.

The boatswain continued to block the man's boarding, until the man produced a set of papers from his bag. Mr. Moore perused these documents for a moment, before finally nodding in grudging agreement. He allowed the man to pass, but I noted that Moore did not salute him, as he had upon my boarding earlier that day. I soon lost interest in the matter and saw little of the curiously-hurried fellow upon our voyage.

As for the ship itself, the *HMS Malabar* was a fine vessel. Built only fourteen years ago, her iron hull was painted white like her cousins in the *Euphrates* class, but she seemed slightly smaller than my recollections of the *Serapis*, though the smell of the sails' tarred twine baking in the heat of the midday sun was identical. Since my small cabin felt a little close, and having decided that the best way to recover my strength was to perform at least a modicum of exercise every day, I spent several hours slowly pacing her decks until my limbs were weary and stiff. By this method I eventually determined that the ship was roughly three hundred feet long and just shy of fifty feet in breadth from port to starboard. She could carry up to twelve hundred troops in a state of relative comfort, at least as gauged by a soldier. The *Malabar* was propelled by a single screw to what Master Billy later swore was a speed of fourteen knots. A solitary funnel puffed away the black coal smoke from its trunk engine. The barque-rig sail plan of its three masts supplemented the engine's power from the winds of the Atlantic. A ram bow projected forward from below the waterline, and three small four-pounder guns could be used to repel any undesired attentions. She was named, of course, for the long and narrow coastline of the Indian continent southwest of Bombay, the city where I had disembarked only a few hectic months before. Despite the wounds I had ruefully acquired while on campaign in the East, I still felt that it was a more auspicious appellation than my prior ship, named as it was after a long-forgotten Greco-Egyptian deity.

Our only ports of call during that lonely crossing to Bermuda were at the infamous isle of St. Helena and later at its far less famous sister, Ascension Island. We did not pause long enough at St. Helena for the troops to disembark, so I contented myself with gazing upon the volcanic island's barren coast, and forest-covered center. I attempted to secure a view of Longwood House, the former abode of the world's most famous exile. As far as I knew, the only places in the British Empire that had been given in perpetuity to our rival French government were that house and the nearby Valley of the Willows that had held the former Emperor's tomb for almost twenty years. Unfortunately, Longwood was far too inland for me to view, even with the aid of my excellent field-glass. Nonetheless, this voyage endowed me with the comprehension of the vast tract of ocean that separated St. Helena from any other lands upon the globe. I finally understood why no loyal patriot had ever endeavored to rescue Napoleon and commence a second Hundred Days and Waterloo. All in all, it seemed a far safer locale than Elba, which a strong swimmer could reach in a day's outing from Livorno.

Despite the re-victualing that took place at each isle, after we departed Ascension Island the choice of fare upon the ship grew rapidly worse as we made the long uninterrupted haul from the Old World to the New. The tins of preserved peaches held up fine, but I noted that every day the ship's cook added a progressively greater amount of curry to the mutton, and I began to wonder if we were destined for an outbreak of some deadly flux. Fortunately, by some agent of providence, my fears proved to be in vain.

There were various cabin boys assigned to cover particular areas of the ship, and I became acquainted with one of them, whose missions brought him often within my walking grounds. Although I am certain that he must have possessed a surname, the only appellation I ever caught was a simple Billy. He was a bright lad of four and ten years, whose perpetually smudged face blended with his grey eyes and curly black hair. He would spend the day helping the cook in the galley and carrying the curried mutton to the forecastle, running messages throughout the ship, and scrambling up the rigging whenever a line had become caught. He was a harum-scarum, reckless lad, and some of the feats of acrobatics that he performed high up amongst the sails and spars were simply astonishing. If he owned shoes, I was unaware of it, for I only ever observed his blackened naked feet. Although I could never perceive anything else that was officially out of place with Master Billy's modest uniform, he still somehow managed to affect an air of ragged slouching nonchalance. Only when he was surrounded by his peers, did he make an effort to draw up to his full height, which just barely cleared the others and thereby gave him a sort of unofficial superiority amongst that clan of scarecrows.

One day I asked him how he found himself at sea. "My father thought I was too high-spirited, the doctor prescribed a year at sea, and here I am," replied he, simply.

But he was a fount of information regarding the workings of the ship, as well as its route. As we drew closer to our destination, I began to notice an unpleasant odor drifting off the ocean. I made my way over to the bulwark in order to discover the source of this strange scent, only to find that we were sailing through an enormous patch of a strange brown weed-like substance drifting upon the surface of the waves, which were otherwise a distinctive deep blue color.

"Whatever could that be?" I pondered aloud to myself.

At that very moment Master Billy was scurrying by, and he stopped to answer my rhetorical question. "It's sargassum, Doctor."

I frowned at this strange word, and he read my expression clearly, so he elaborated. "It's a type of seaweed. It congregates in this area of the ocean. It is why we call this the Sargasso Sea, the only 'sea' without a shore in the whole wide world."

I pondered over this information. "I've heard of this area. Is it not dangerous? I've read tales of ships being trapped here..."

Billy laughed delightedly. "Myths, Doctor, myths! It's true that we can have sudden periods without winds in these latitudes, and perhaps before the days of our engines, when sails alone drove our ships, some may have been becalmed here. But the sargassum itself is no match for a ship like the *Malabar*, sir."

"Ah, yes," I flushed with discomfiture that the boy should be so much more knowledgeable than me, an ungenerous reaction since he was in his element, and I out of mine. "I suppose that I have been reading too much Coleridge. 'Water, water everywhere,' and all that," said I, forcing a laugh.

But Billy shook his head again. "Coleridge is not to be trusted, Doctor. The man was an inveterate opium addict. That stuff will drown your life in false dreams."

I started in surprise over these sagacious words from this youthful lad. But in the varied ports of call of this ship, he had likely seen even more of the world than I could lay claim to, and sailors were notorious for their vices. I was glad to see that he had already learned a lesson that had made a slave of many older, but certainly not wiser, men.

Despite Master Billy's warnings about the inherently untrue nature of some literature, I have always been an omnivorous reader, and that long, monotonous voyage was the perfect situation for me to devour several volumes. I first turned my attention to the recent sea story of the American writer William Clark Russell, entitled *The Wreck of the Grosvenor*. Although that wonderful tale of adventure and heroism held fast my attention, from the standpoint of a medical man, I determined that the excitement of reading this dangerous nautical adventure while at sea was a poor restorative for my shaken health. Fortunately, our captain and chief mate in no way resembled the brutes of the tale. I then picked up Mr. Collins' yellow-backed novel *The Moonstone*. I found it to be highly entertaining, despite the preposterous nature of the convoluted plot.

After I quickly exhausted my meager library, I was forced to inquire whether any of my companions aboard were in possession of a spare novel. Once again, my young friend Billy proved his usefulness. He had already taken the pulse of the ship, and through his machinations, I was soon introduced to a short and stout, almost burly man by the name of Major Walter Lomax, formerly of the Eighth Foot. Sadly, like me, he had recently been invalided out of the British Army. Although my shoulder continued to ache terribly from time to time, I counted myself most fortunate when contrasted with my new acquaintance, whose entire lower right leg had been amputated, and replaced by a wooden stump. Despite this grim wound, good humor seemed to always play round his mobile, smiling lips, which peered out from under bushy brown side whiskers and a moustache. He was rather closer to forty than thirty, and this showed in his shock of uncontrolled brown hair that was already a little bald in the center. His eyes were an arresting shade of deep blue, and bespoke of an intense inward life, so alert and responsive they were to every question put to him. His face was brown and weather-beaten, the complexion of a man that had lived many years on campaign, yet still attractive in the strong lines of his brow. He continued to wear his scarlet red coat, with only his black trousers modified to accommodate his injury. I quickly discovered that he had been the assistant to the Regimental Adjutant in charge of all of its organization and administration.

"It is a pleasure to meet a fellow bibliophile, Doctor," said he with a pleasant mellow voice, once he divined the objectives of my mission. "Not all share our passion."

"Indeed," agreed I, heartily. "It is not clear how I became such a bookworm, as my father was not a great reader."

"Well, there we differ," he laughed. "My father is the head-librarian at the London Library in St. James's Square. He sent me off to Cambridge, where I continued to study good books in all departments of knowledge. I admit that there I developed an unhealthy hobby of collecting all sorts of obscure volumes."

"And yet you joined the Army?" I enquired.

"I take it you do not hold to the supposition that a love of knowledge and a love for England are mutually exclusive?"

"Of course not!"

THE ISLE OF DEVILS

"'But dearly was that conquest bought,' as the words go. I had hoped to rise to become the Regimental Adjutant, but that dream has now been cut short, as the case may be." He gestured to his missing limb.

I was a bit taken aback by his grim humor, but pressed on. "And now?"

"I have written to my father, and hold every hope that he can find me a position as a sub-librarian under him. Certainly, after the monsoons and jungles of India, I am greatly longing to see the bright green fields and the hedges of England."

"I share your feelings," I replied. "I myself yearn for the glades of the New Forest or the shingle of Southsea."

"Well until then," said he, shaking off his reverie, "I suspect that my trunk contains at least one book that you have not read, and in which you can engross yourself as we await our eventual embarkation upon the jetties of Portsmouth. So what type of literature are you looking for? Perhaps the essays of Thomas Carlyle collected as *Heroes and Hero Worship*?"

I smiled. "'In books lies the soul of the whole Past Time; the articulate audible voice of the Past, when the body and material substance of it has altogether vanished like a dream,'" I quoted. "No, thank you, I have already studied him at university. I was hoping for something perhaps a tad more exciting."

"'What we become depends on what we read after all of the professors have finished with us. The greatest university of all is a collection of books,'" he quoted back to me. "Ah, I have it then. When faced with a dilemma, there is nothing like Pope's Homer! I have a black-letter edition right here. And it is perfect for our current destination. I have heard that navigating between the treacherous reefs of Bermuda is like sailing between Scylla and Charybdis."

"There are few books that I treasure more," I replied with some warmth. "So many times have I read those words, you might think me a modern Alexander."

"I see," said he, his brows knitted. "You are a difficult one, Doctor. Perhaps if I understood your preferences better? What are the last two books you have read?" Once he heard my reply, his face lit up like a street lantern. "Aha! I think I have just the thing for you. Are you familiar with Poe?"

"Edgar Allen, the American? I did read one of his works once. It was a curious tale about buried pirate treasure."

"Yes," said Lomax, nodding enthusiastically. "*The Gold Bug*! The cipher of Captain Kidd! Brilliant!"

I nodded, smiling at the memory. "It's a clever story to be certain, though I must admit being taken aback by the incomprehensible

American slang."

"Indeed. Then perhaps his stories set in Paris would be a better choice. I have a trio of works here that I am certain you will enjoy. The first is called *The Murders in the Rue Morgue.*"

"That sounds rather gruesome. I do not know if I would enjoy it," I replied.

"Ah," he exclaimed. "It is not as violent as the title might lead you to believe. It is actually a very clever tale about an inspector named Dupin who uses a method of analysis, which he terms 'ratiocination,' to solve an impossible crime."

I raised my eyebrows. "I will admit, that does sound intriguing."

"Oh yes," replied Lomax, with the evident glee of a true bibliophile about to share a special treat. "I am certain that you will enjoy it! And when you are done, if you liked Dupin, I would highly recommend the works of Monsieur Emile Gaboriau about his investigator Lecoq. At least in fiction, the French seem to produce the best detectives." He handed over the slim volume.

I thanked Lomax for his gift and retired to my bunk, where I promptly found myself flipping rapidly through the brilliant tales of Mr. Poe. Whenever the light grew too poor or my eyes protested the strain of reading, I would set my book down and seek out my new friend Lomax for some rounds of *écarté*, backgammon, and draughts. The strained finances that we both found ourselves in prevented any significant wagering, but we still managed to keep the games interesting and formed a bond of union over our common pursuits.

With such diversions, I found that the dull trip passed faster, and I was surprised when one morning I heard a pounding upon the door of my cabin. "Land ho, Doctor!" yelled Master Billy. "We are circling the island and expect to dock within the hour."

Excited to finally see my destination, I quickly performed my ablutions and pulled on my uniform and boots. Grabbing my field-glass and Penang lawyer, I hobbled out onto the deck as fast as my leg would let me and surveyed the majestic scene before. We were approaching what appeared to be the very tip of the island, which was entirely occupied by a massive fortification of pale grey walls that dropped straight down into the sea. The walls were punctuated by two massive projecting bastions topped with massive guns. Within the walls, an enormous two-story Georgian-style white house, with a large verandah with red painted iron railings running around both levels, stood out from all of the smaller buildings. But while the fortifications were impressive, the more thrilling feature of the panorama was the flurry of activity in the harbor. Massive ships of the line bobbed with stately grace upon the waves, their cannon-ports shuttered.

There were dozens in my field of view, many of whom were turned such that I could not make out their names, but I clearly noted the HMS *Northampton*, a Nelson-class armored cruiser, the HMS *Warrior*, an armor-plated, iron-hulled warship, the HMS *Irresistible*, an 80-gun screw-propelled second rate, the HMS *Scorpion*, an ironclad turret ship, the HMS *Vixen*, an armored composite gunboat, and the majestic four-masted iron frigate HMS *Achilles*. Dashing between these dreadnoughts, smaller single-masted cutters ferried troops, supplies, and munitions from the shore to the waiting ships. These lighter ships moved so quickly that I could hardly turn my glass on them before they were gone from my field of view. The only ones whose names I spotted were the *Alicia*, the *Elizabeth*, and the *Karnak*. At least one ship appeared to be an old convict ship adapted for use as a troop transport, and I was suddenly very glad that I was fortunate enough to have sailed on the relatively new and comfortable *Malabar*.

As I took in this tableau, the *Malabar* grew ever closer to its berth. Eventually she began to round a breakwater, clearly intending to draw up directly upon the docks. I finally tore myself from the scene and hobbled back to my cabin in order to finish packing up my valise for my looming disembarkation. At last I could look forward to a peaceful recuperation of my shattered health in a salubrious climate, free of rocking waves, both literal and figurative.

§

CHAPTER III:
THE ISLE OF DEVILS

It soon became clear that my alighting from the *Malabar* was not imminent. I had forgotten that the gangplank of a ship can only accommodate so many men, and not all twelve hundred troops aboard could depart at once. The Navy had, of course, foreseen this complication and the day prior had issued every man a color-coded card that would determine the order in which they should queue up on the deck. Unfortunately, the indigo-hued card that Master Billy had handed me meant that I would be in the last group to leave the ship. I therefore spent the time trying to take stock of my new environs.

The *Malabar* had come to rest in what I determined was the southern of two artificial basins, separated from the open seas by concrete breakwaters. In the northern basin, a sixteen-gun iron screw floating battery was docked. Her prow was pointed at me, so that I could not make out her name, though I later ascertained that it was known the HMS *Terror*, a formidable appellation for such a trifling vessel. Beyond it was a small slip, where a sloop was being loaded with goods that originated from a series of low white-roofed buildings that clearly served as a victualing yard. Iron-hooped barrels were being rolled about with great energy and the cries of the men in action made apparent the great strength of our Empire. Further past the yard was the land-facing portion of the colossal fortification ramparts, certainly no more vulnerable to attack from this route. Directly opposite where the *Malabar* had docked lay a massive two-story grey building with a white roof that was broken by two soaring towers that easily approached a hundred feet in height. I was at first greatly puzzled by the need for two clock-towers so close to each other, until I realized that only the southern tower kept the time, while the northern tower possessed but a single arm that appeared to mark the high tide. I thought this was a clever feature to aid the local sailors in their quest to avoid any treacherous reefs.

Eventually, my reverie was broken by a signal that it was time for me to finally join the queue. I purposefully held back so as to not inconvenience those that moved faster than I, with my wounded leg. I finally reached the bottom of the gangplank, where I was surprised to note a young marine holding a piece of paper with my name plainly written upon it. I indicated to him that I was the man he was looking for and he broke into a relieved smile.

"I am happy to finally see you, Doctor," the marine said. "I was concerned that something amiss had occurred."

"No, I am just moving slowly these days, I am afraid," I replied with as much good cheer as I could muster. "But you have me at a disadvantage..."

"Ah, I am so sorry, Doctor! Midshipman Philip Brewis, Royal Marine Light Infantry, at your service," said he, saluting. He was a moderately tall, stalwart man dressed in the standard Marine blue uniform. He had trim brown hair, and wore regulation side whiskers on his reddened cheeks. His blue eyes were keen with the energy of youth, and I figured him to be no more than his twentieth year.

"Welcome to Ireland Island, home of the North American and West Indies Station, Vice Admiral Sir F. Leopold McClintock commanding," he continued cordially. "Of course, it is better known as the Royal Naval Dockyard, or the Gibraltar of the West. It is the mightiest fortress of the Empire, even more so than Halifax, in Nova Scotia."

"Thank you," I replied. "How long has your short stint on Bermuda been, Midshipman?" I asked him.

"Six months..." he began, and then stopped in puzzled astonishment. "Wait! How did you know that I've not been here long, Doctor?"

"First, the skin of your face is still red, which suggests that you have not had the necessary time to turn the deep brown color that most of us eventually obtain when stationed in the tropics. Furthermore, I had heard that the inhabitants of the colonial islands, especially the older ones like Bermuda, have acquired their own peculiar dialect, and yet you speak like a native to the west of England. Bristol, perhaps?"

The man's face beamed. "Exactly! Ah, Doctor, you cannot know how much I would love to walk the streets of Bristol again. There is a pub on King Street, the Llandoger Trow, with the sweetest barmaid you will ever lay eyes upon. If I can only find my way back home, I plan to make her my wife."

"Well, I wish you and your maid the greatest of happiness,

Midshipman. But perhaps you would care to tell me why you are holding that sign with my name upon it?"

"Ah, my apologies again, Doctor! Your brother sent me."

"Henry?"

"Yes, the captain received your letter warning him of your arrival, and he has arranged for you to recuperate in a local hotel, rather than the base hospital like the other men."

"I am not certain that that is necessary," I stammered, but he interrupted me before I could complete the thought.

"It has all been arranged, Doctor. I will take him to you now, and he can explain further." Eyeing my walking stick, he inquired whether I could stand a short walk. When I indicated that I could, he took my valise and off we went down the quay to the south.

As we walked, I gave free reign to my natural curiosity and asked him about our surroundings. "Tell me about that imposing structure upon the hill, Mr. Brewis."

"Ah, that's the Commissioner's House, Doctor. It's the largest residence in Bermuda. They say that it has over ten thousand square feet, and that its frame is made from case-iron forged in England and shipped here over fifty years ago. The façade is the local limestone, of course."

"And what is this monstrosity that I see before me?" I asked, for we had by now cleared the stern of the *Malabar* and were approaching a truly massive metal structure that appeared to be almost four hundred feet long, and well over a hundred feet in both width and height. It was shaped like a giant 'U' with narrow bridges connecting the two uppermost sides at both ends. Nestled inside it, like a Chinese puzzle-box, was a partially constructed frigate which, while large on its own merits, was dwarfed by the surrounding structure.

"Ah, the pride and joy of the Dockyard!" said Brewis, warmly. "This is the largest floating dock in the world, Doctor. You see, once the rebellious colonies of the Americas broke from Great Britain, the Admiralty determined that we needed a new base to service the ships that ply our remaining lands in the Western Atlantic and the Caribbean. That way they would not be required to go all the way back to England to fit up for repairs. But the docks would need to be very big in order to accommodate the great ships of the line and when the Royal Navy originally began construction here on Ireland Island, they discovered that the local Bermuda limestone was far too porous. Thus, Colonel Clarke suggested that, rather than abandoning this strategic location, ingenuity should be put to work. They therefore approved construction of the floating dock upon the Thames."

"This was built upon the Thames?" said I, incredulously. "It's so

THE ISLE OF DEVILS

enormous! How could they have possibly brought it here?"

"I agree that it is hard to imagine, Doctor. It weighs over eight thousand tons, and it is almost four thousand miles from here to England. And yet, there is little that the greatest navy in the world cannot accomplish," the man said with evident pride. "It was towed by the HMS *Northumberland* and the HMS *Agincourt,* assisted by the HMS *Warrior* and HMS *Black Prince,* while the HMS *Terrible* guided the stern. After thirty-five days of towing, it finally reached its new home here in 1869."

"An amazing tale, Mr. Brewis..." I began to comment before I was suddenly bumped into by a man approaching from the other direction. Fortunately I took the blow upon my healthy right shoulder, and thus was not much inconvenienced.

The man promptly apologized. "I am greatly sorry, sir. I did not see you. I was consumed with anger." His voice was thin, and his breathing was painfully asthmatic.

I took a moment to gaze upon my accidental assailant. He was a pale, sad-faced, but refined-looking man approaching fifty in years, his black hair streaked with grey, and a remarkably smooth skin. He wore a parson's gown and a broad-brimmed hat that was clearly designed to protect him from the sun. "It is no trouble," I replied with reserve.

He looked at me and shook his head. "It will be if you plan to remain on this accursed island for long. I have been unhappily submerged here and very badly treated."

"What is the matter now, Dr. Penny?" Brewis interjected, clearly familiar with the querulous man.

"Oh, Brewis," he sighed. "My tribulations are unceasing. I shall have to close down the library. Can you believe that a man would borrow a volume and then not return it before they left the island for good? That is a sin if you ask me, and he will surely suffer for it. I had hoped for the best, but I clearly must expect the worst in people." With that grim pronouncement, the strange man ambled off.

"Don't mind old Penny, Doctor. He's not quite right, if you catch my drift," he tapped the side of his head for emphasis.

"Ah yes, I have read of such maladies in a monograph published in the *British Medical Journal.*"

"If you say so, Doctor," replied Brewis, non-committedly.

By this time, we had cleared the end of the Floating Dock and passed up a short ramp that led through a set of gates in the outer wall that surrounded the entire Dockyard. We then crossed over a short bridge and down to a rough pier where a small sloop was tied up with two men aboard. Upon our approach, one of the men, dressed in the standard red coat and midnight blue trousers of a British Army soldier, his head capped by a regulation busby, stood up and faced us. His face erupted in a broad smile, and with a start I realized that it was my brother Henry, upon whom I had not laid eyes since he had joined the Army eight years earlier.

"Hamish!" he exclaimed. "I should never have known you under that moustache!"

But I recognized him in a heart-beat, despite the years that had passed. Only two years my senior, Henry and I both strongly resembled our father, for whom he was named. Like myself, he was of a middle-height, though his strong-build and robust shoulders contrasted with my current haggard thinness. He had a square jaw, dark face, and thick neck, with sandy brown hair that receded slightly from the lateral sides of his forehead, and which was tousled in a slightly untidy fashion. His moustache was thicker than my modest one, though they both tapered slightly towards the ends. Only in his eyes did he differ greatly from me, as he had the dark green of our father, while I the light blue of our mother.

"Welcome to the Isle of Devils, brother!" he continued.

"Devils?" I said incredulously. "This happy place?"

"Well, not all have felt as you do. When the Spanish Captain Juan de Bermudez first alighted here in 1505, his sailors refused to go ashore because of the horrible cries that they heard emanating from the trees, cries that they believed could only be coming from devils."

I frowned. "But what were they, Henry?"

My brother laughed. "Birds, Ham, birds. There is a local bird, called the Cahow, which makes an unearthly nighttime screech. On a return trip, Bermudez landed only long enough to sow the island with a dozen hogs in order to provide food for any mariners who unluckily found themselves shipwrecked upon the isles."

I raised my eyebrows. "Boars?" I inquired.

"Now, now, brother. I know from your letters that you have coursed many creatures in many countries, but you are here to rest and recuperate from your wounds and illness. There will be no drawing the cover for you here!"

I nodded deflatedly. "You are right, of course."

"Of course, we are fortunate that the Spanish have always been such cowards, for their loss is the Crown's gain. It's a fine land."

"And what of you, brother?" I enquired. "I have not, of recent, been in a place to receive your letters."

"I have been given command of the stout Fort St. Catherine, on the far opposite end of the island," he replied with a tone of modesty, though I could tell that he was secretly proud of such a responsibility.

"My congratulations," I said warmly.

He shrugged nonchalantly. "It is nothing. But the Fort is as far from

Dockyard as Lands' End to John o' Groats, and if I am to see any of you during your sojourn, I determined that you could not spend your time here. Nor is Fort St. Catherine a good place to recuperate, of course, but close by is the town of St. George's."

"I am certain that I would be fine bunking either here, or at the Fort."

"Nonsense, Ham. It's all been arranged. I think you will like St. George's. Now that the capital has been moved to Hamilton and the war in America is over, it is a quiet place."

"That does sound good," I admitted reluctantly. "My nerves are still rather shaken, and I do not think that my constitution is strong enough yet to stand much noise or excitement."

"Then let us go. Is that all you have, brother?" he queried, motioning to my valise, still in the hands of the helpful Midshipman Brewis.

I nodded. "My experience in camp life has at least had the effect of making me a prompt and ready traveler. My wants are few and simple."

Henry took the valise from Brewis, whose hand I shook before the kind and knowledgeable marine departed. Henry then motioned me to the waiting boat.

For a moment, I balked. "Another boat? I have just gotten off one and you want me to climb aboard another?" I said with wonderment and a hint of dismay.

Henry smiled. "Although Bermuda is only twenty-two miles long, and the charms of the isles are many, the fastest way from here to where you will be staying in St. George's is to take a sloop."

"Not a train?" I queried, hopefully.

"A train? In Bermuda? You must be mad, brother! Wait until you see this island. It is no place for a train." Henry said with finality.

"Ah, perhaps it is for the better," I said. "It is a dangerous occupation, that of a railwayman."

Henry placed my valise into the small boat and then lent me an arm so that I could make my way onboard. Many years ago I may have resented the thought that I needed assistance, but now, older, wiser, and two wounds later, I did not begrudge him that gesture.

Once aboard, Henry introduced me to the captain of the sloop, which was a private vessel called the *Caliber*. He went by the name of Nathaniel Smith. He was a small compact man, but with broad shoulders and a deep chest. He had a round face that was seared with a thousand wrinkles and burned yellow with the sun. His grey eyes were deep set in hollows beneath overhung brows, and were perpetually set in a squint. His shock of hair, beard, and moustache were all white, save that the area around his mouth where they were stained yellow with tobacco smoke from the brier-root pipe that was clenched fast between his lips. He was a taciturn fellow, who had a fair trick of managing to rumble out a few words from between teeth that still clenched the pipe. Only for longer sentences did he deign to remove the pipe, thereby exposing a line of yellow and irregular teeth. His age was nearly impossible to determine; he could easily have been an aged man of forty, or a vigorous man of sixty years.

As Mr. Smith unfurled the sails and the sloop began to back away from the pier, my brother began to describe the island to me. "Bermuda is shaped much like a fishhook. We are currently on the point here at Dockyard. The eye is way over by St. George's, the bend is an area known as Southampton, and the shank runs through several parishes, known as Warwick, Paget, and Smith's. The latter is no relation to our skipper... at least, so he claims. Of course, many a man is related here, since the descendants of those first colonists control much of the land."

Henry pointed to an area of land directly across from our position that appeared to reach out into the water. "That there is Spanish Point, a reminder of the original discoverers of these isles. The legend is that in 1603, six years before Admiral Somers claimed Bermuda for the Crown, a great Spanish treasure fleet was scattered in a storm. One galleon, commanded by a Captain Diego Ramirez, was driven upon the coast of Bermuda. Unlike innumerable other seamen who have met their end in this old death-trap of sailing vessels, and whose ships litter the bottom of the sea, Ramirez managed to avoid the worst of Bermuda's treacherous surge-swept reefs. After three weeks, his men had managed to repair the ship and they sailed away. Before he left, however, he erected a large cross, made from the wonderfully resistant local cedar wood. Supposedly, on it was carved directions for locating drinking water, and the cross lasted so long that this area is still remembered as Spanish Point."

The reticent skipper suddenly intervened. "Wasn't water," he said enigmatically.

My brother frowned. "What's that, my good man?"

Captain Smith shook his head. "Those directions. They weren't to water. They were to the gold that they had to leave behind."

My brother tried to hide his grin. "If the Spanish had to leave treasure behind, why did they never return to claim it?"

"Mayhaps they did. Mayhaps Guv'nor Moore drove them away," the man replied peevishly.

My brother looked as if he were about to challenge the point, when his attention was distracted by another matter. He stopped for a moment and gazed out at our track upon the sea. He leaned back and called up to Mr. Smith. "Where to, skipper?"

"Ah, I'm sorry Captain Henry. I forgot to tell ye. We've got to make a Two Rock Passage. I previously made an arrangement to pick up a gentleman at the Hamilton docks who wishes to go to St. George's."

My brother frowned at this piece of information. "Need I remind you, Mr. Smith, that we are not going to St. George's? We're headed to the Fort."

"Aye, Captain. But to get to St. George's from the Fort, all a man needs do is nip around the end of the isle. And Bob's your uncle."

"And what of the time that this side-trip will cost us? I don't suppose that you were planning to give us a partial refund on our fare."

The man did not appear enthused by this suggestion. "What did you have in mind, Captain?"

"Perhaps your passenger and I should split the fare?"

Smith made a long face. "If that, I would have only taken you."

"My point exactly, Mr. Smith, my point exactly," Henry replied.

The skipper shook his head grudgingly. "I'll tell you what, Captain. We'll take a third from the fare for each of you."

My brother stared at him for a moment, before finally signaling his agreement. Henry then turned his attention back to me. "If you sail between Ireland Island and Spanish Point, as we are doing, you will enter the gap of the fishhook, or what is known as the Great Sound. And tucked into a little corner of the Sound is the harbor belonging to the new capital town of Hamilton. Before we reach there, however, if you turn your gaze over those small islands dotting the Sound, you can see, high on that hill, a white conical structure known as Gibbs Hill Lighthouse. It stands on one of the tallest points of the island, and it is the world's first cast iron lighthouse, built back in 1846."

My brother's narration trailed off as we sailed into Hamilton Harbor proper. Like the area surrounding Dockyard, the waters were thick with ships. However, rather than the Royal Navy vessels that I had witnessed there, we were now surrounded by a plethora of civilian ships of all shapes and sizes. A full-sailed merchant-man was being guided by a tiny pilot boat, presumably to avoid Bermuda's hazardous reefs. Of the ships at anchor, many of the appellations were impossible to make out, but I clearly counted the brig *Hotspur*, its home port listed as Sydney, Australia. There was one old-fashioned, heavy-bowed broad-beamed craft that I judged to be about five hundred tons, and I suspected that she had once been employed in the Chinese tea-trade, but she was turned so that I could not spot her name. There were at least two barques, the *Sophy Anderson*, registered as hailing from Dover, England, and the *Lone Star*, Savannah, Georgia. There were many steamers, including the *Esmeralda*, home port Vitoria, Brazil, and the *Mathida Briggs*, registered to Banda Aceh, Sumatra. A great clipper, the SS *Palmyra*, Cape Town, South Africa, was also resting at anchor, her masts overrun with lascars evidently working upon repairs.

Smith tied up the *Caliber* along a busy quay directly across from a row of brightly-painted two-story commercial establishments which appeared to be an admixture of shops and restaurants. A broad street fronted the buildings, and from it a faint odor of horse dung wafted towards us, a sudden clash from the fresh salt air to which I had become accustomed. A small army of wharf-fingers loaded barrels and crates to and from trading ships also tied up at the waterfront. Up the hill, directly behind the buildings in front of us, I could make out the grey stone single spire of a cathedral. My brother also motioned to the left, where another large white structure stood apparently along the same back street as the cathedral. "That's the Hamilton Hotel. I had thought to have you stay there, since it is by far the finest hotel upon the island. It has twenty-six rooms appointed with every modern luxury. However, it is still far from here to the Fort, so I opted instead to engage a room for you at the smaller and more bucolic Globe Hotel in St. George's."

I nodded my approval at his choice. "That is perfectly all right with me, Henry. A private bed in a room that does not sway back and forth will seem like luxury enough when compared to my poor quarters over the last year. And I am not certain that my pocketbook could withstand the assault of a fine hotel."

At that moment, a man hurried up to the ship, waving his right arm. "Is this the *Caliber*?" he inquired, a trace of an accent apparent upon his lips. He was a tall, handsome man, with keen dark brown eyes. I thought I detected a hint of a former military man in his erect posture. His dark brown hair was slicked back and his moustache suavely waxed. He was exquisitely dressed in a black-frock coat faced with green silk, a black waistcoat, and well-cut pearl-gray trousers. Neat black gaiters protected his leather shoes. Based on his accent, he seemed to me a quick-witted Latin.

He hopped aboard the boat, and after a quick word with Mr. Smith, he turned to us. "Good afternoon, gentlemen. Allow me to introduce myself. My name is Antonio Jose da Paiva Cordeiro. How do you do?"

My brother and I inclined our heads and greeted the newcomer, who sat down across from us. I recognized his name as hailing from Portugal. As the skipper threw off the line and the *Caliber* began to drift away from the dock, I decided to strike up a conversation with the man. "What brings you to Bermuda, Senhor Cordeiro?"

"I am originally from Ponta Delgada, a city on the largest island of what you would term the Azores," he replied. "I am a traveler in wines, what some might vulgarly describe as a merchant. I have heard that the Bermudians are large consumers of rum, but I am hopeful that I can convince them that, while rum is fine for a sailor, a true gentleman will vastly prefer more sophisticated drinks, such as port or Madeira wine. As such, I have recently come out from Oporto aboard the *Norah Creina* to see if I can make headways into this market."

I raised my eyebrows with interest at his story, but by this time the sloop had moved out back into the Great Sound, and the noise of the wind made it impossible to carry on any further conversation with Senhor Cordeiro. My gaze fell upon the tract-less ocean, with no other land visible from this far corner of the world. I allowed my thoughts to drift into pleasant fancies. The spirit of the sea seemed to sink into my soul, its vastness, and its playful charms. When you are aboard a small boat, sailing only by the power of wind, you leave all traces of modern life behind you, which allows you to become conscious of all those that have sailed these same waters before you. It was effortless to imagine forsaking my own age, and if at that moment I had seen a Spanish galleon crest one of the great waves in the far distance to port, I would have felt that its presence here was more natural than my own. I am no antiquarian, but I felt a primeval pull from this small island adrift in the midst of the great Atlantic. My greatest puzzlement was that the Spanish refused to settle these idyllic shores. Did they know something that we had failed to recognize, or had their primitive superstitions been washed away by the march of science and progress? I turned my face to the dashing spray of the sea and wondered what other curiosities I might encounter upon that day.

§

CHAPTER IV:
THE GLOBE HOTEL

The *Caliber* retraced its course back out into the Great Sound, and when it reached Spanish Point, it turned to the east and began to sail along the lovely North Shore of the island. The coastline was composed entirely of tapering limestone cliffs, with green vegetation sprouting from every crevice and which generally ran all the way down to the lapping waters. In some rare spots, curves and hollows in the rock created tiny coves where lovely pink-hued sand gathered to make splendid beaches from which to invitingly plunge into the crystal clear shallow ocean.

Henry leaned forward and yelled to me over the wind. "That is the Admiralty House," he pointed to a large building high upon a wooded bluff. "From there, Vice Admiral Sir Alexander Cochrane planned the invasion and burning of Washington, the United States' capital city, in 1814." Henry smiled roguishly. "But nowadays, it is more famous for the so-called 'Admiral's Cave' down below in Clarence Cove. Over a decade ago, one of our illustrious commanders – I will not besmirch his name – diverted some of the convicts from their assigned task of building the Dockyard in order to dig a cave and series of tunnels there. Ostensibly, it was envisioned to serve as a place to land naval stores and a subterranean shelter for his flagship. But rumors have it that the tunnels were actually intended to function as a discreet method by which a certain lady could access the grounds of the Admiralty House for a secret rendezvous with the Admiral." I raised my eyebrows in response to this scandalous detail, but Henry only laughed. "From what I hear of the Admiral's wife, the expense was entirely justified."

"And you, Henry, have you found a potential mate here among the charming ladies of Bermuda?"

He shook his head violently. "No, the marrying life is not for me. Women have always been your specialty, Ham. I am afraid it will be up to you to carry on the family name."

With this unintentionally-cruel comment, thoughts of Violet Devere flooded back into my brain. My mood turned solemn, but Henry failed to take notice. He pointed again to another stretch of land. "Along there is the Black Watch Well."

"Any relation to the Royal Highlanders?"

"Aye. In 1849, there was a long drought on Bermuda. This island is remarkable in that there is no source of fresh water on the surface. That is the reason for the unique stepped white roofs that you see on every house, which they use to collect rainwater. But in a drought, times grow very hard round here. In that year, the cattle were dying, as people had to reserve every drop of water for themselves. The Governor ordered the soldiers based in Bermuda at the time to seek a fresh water supply for the suffering people of this part of the island. The Black Watch was the first regiment to step forward and they did such a fine job that the well continues to be used to this day. But tell me, brother, did you serve with any Scots regiments in Afghanistan?"

"Of course! I hesitate to make comparisons, but in bravery, they are second to none. It's been many years since our family has treaded the stones of Scotland, but we may hold our heads high with pride."

"Aye, that's been my experience too during my time fighting with the Zulus. Though since then the 99th has not seen much action out here in the middle of the Atlantic, where no country is mad enough to try to invade. Ah, look," Henry pointed at a small island seemingly floating in a shallow brilliant blue sea off the coast of the main-land. "That there is Gibbet Island. No explanation is necessary on how it acquired its name. Beyond it is a small inlet, which passes a small village with the curious name of Flatts. It then opens into a remarkable natural harbor called Harrington Sound. It almost appears to be the crater of some long extinct volcano."

"Why is the fleet based at Ireland Island then?" I queried.

"The cut is too shallow for any large ship of the line. Thanks to the myriad of small isles everywhere, even St. George's Harbor and Castle Harbor have too narrow channels for the most modern ships. The only place for those is at Dockyard." Having exhausted the subject, Henry turned to the future. "Now, when you get to the hotel..."

"I do not believe that I require a hotel, brother. The barracks are more than good enough for me," I interrupted him.

Henry narrowed his eyes and peered at me. "You are the most long-

35

suffering of mortals, Ham! Do not worry. I've fixed up a special price with the innkeeper's assistant. It shouldn't require a significant portion of your pay."

"By thunder!" exclaimed I. "How did you know that I was concerned about the price of the room?"

"When a half-pay surgeon fingers his breast-pocket with a concerned look upon their face, it can only mean one thing. He is concerned about the state of his cheque book."

"So how much am I paying?" I asked, somewhat peevishly.

"A typical room would run you five shillings a day. But I have spoken with Mr. Boyle, and he has agreed to take you in for the lowly rate of only twenty-eight shillings a week. That should leave you with something extra for the horses, eh, Hamish?"

I raised my eyebrows with interest. "Do they have horse racing on Bermuda?"

"They do indeed. We just passed the track at Shelly Bay. The biggest race of the year is called the St. George's Stakes, and a formal ball follows the races. It's nothing compared to the Grand National or the Derby at Epsom Downs, of course, but it is fine enough for the colonies."

"Hmm," I mused aloud. I mentally calculated whether I should risk a little sporting flutter on the turf. Shortly before departing England I had made a tidy sum at Manchester betting upon Isonomy at four to one odds. Even with my discounted rate at the hotel, I still would only have seven shillings, six pence a day. With some good luck, I could supplement that nicely, but without fortune's favor, I could be left in serious straits. As much as I would love to be there at the fall of the flag, the financial implications would need to be taken into careful consideration. I suspected that I could draw through half of my wound pension in a blink of an eye.

Henry nudged me out of my reverie. "We are coming up on a place of great historical significance. One moonlit night, a hundred and five years ago, a group of traitors broke into the magazine at St. George's and stole many barrels of gunpowder. The enterprising rascals rolled them up over the hill and back down the other side to an American ship waiting here in Tobacco Bay." He pointed at a little cove that, on this glorious sunny day, little seemed like a place of great intrigue. "The gunpowder was sailed to America, where the rebels under George Washington used it against our own men at a battle known as Bunker Hill."

Mr. Smith continued to confidently sail the little sloop past this inviting beach, and Henry pointed to another little bay. "There's one for you, Ham. Your man Homer would approve. It's called Achilles Bay. That's where we will dock, right under the ramparts of Fort St. Catherine, the base of the 99th."

As I gazed upon the magnificent walls of the fort, the *Caliber* glided up to a waiting dock. Smith hopped out and tied fast the boat. Henry lifted my valise in one arm, and with the other, helped me navigate my way off the boat, no easy task with my injured leg. Once we were safely on land, Smith and the Portuguese wine-merchant undid the ropes and backed away from the dock. I waved my gratitude to the skipper, and turning back to the fort, I expressed my admiration.

"Aye, it's not bad." Henry replied, a hint of false modesty in his voice. He then smiled broadly. "In fact, she's the finest fort on the isle. We've recently installed the latest in artillery. A sixty-four pounder rifled muzzle loader on a Moncrieff disappearing gun mount. It has a range of four thousand yards! No one will be invading this isle, I can assure you. Of course, no commission is entirely free of problems. Mine is the ghost."

"What?" I spluttered. "You cannot be serious!"

"I assure you that I am, Ham," said he, earnestly. "No one is quite certain where he came from, but the soldiers have jokingly named him George. What is less amusing is their fear of venturing into the lower chambers in groups of less than three."

"Surely you can educate them sufficiently to erase such superstitions?"

"I would, Ham, if I hadn't heard his chanting with my own ears. There has even been talk of bringing in an exorcist."

I was about to protest this outlandish statement, but just then a trap, pulled by a single horse emerged from down a little lane. "Ah, perfect," Henry said. "That will be Robinson. I asked him to take you over to town. From here, it is but a short ride."

"And you, Henry?" I inquired.

"I must return to duty. But never fear, brother. I will take another leave and come over to the hotel some night very soon. We can catch up more then."

"I would enjoy that," I replied warmly, shaking his hand.

Henry placed my valise into the cart and helped me up next to the driver. With a flick of his crop the man whipped up the horse, and away we pulled. Henry waved and called after me. "Don't forget to talk to Boyle! I squared it with him."

Mr. Robinson and his cart turned onto a small road that led back west along the coast, so that I soon got another glimpse of Tobacco Bay. Robinson himself was a small foxy man with a sharp and by no means amiable expression. If he had a first name, it was never spoken. His black curly hair was thickly shot with grey, though I somehow placed him closer to fifty than sixty. His heavy brows and aggressive chin suggested that he would not be a good conversationalist, so I turned my attention to the island's native charm. It was a perfect day, with a bright sun and a few fleecy clouds in the heavens. I was amazed at the abundant foliage that bloomed everywhere. Poinciana, oleander, cedar, agave, and frangipani were but a few of the species that I could recognize, and the air was full of the pleasant smell of the flowers and the moist earth. The colorfully-painted buildings nestled snugly into the surrounding greenery and told of the prosperity of this fair isle. On the limestone walls that lined the road, I noted a profusion of rock lizards sunning themselves in the lingering afternoon. As Robinson turned the trap to the south, the road began to climb a moderate sized hill, and the country roads in this part of the world proved to be of a rather inferior quality to the ones at home, for we lurched and jolted terribly. Suddenly the man spoke. "Capt'n Henry is your brother?"

I replied in the affirmative. He nodded as if this was the answer to something that he had been pondering for some time. "Thought so. You've the same look."

"Indeed. We take after our father."

Robinson was silent for a pace after that. "Good man," he finally said, gruffly.

"Our father?" I asked, rather confused.

He shook his head. "Capt'n Henry."

"Ah yes. I am glad to hear you say so."

With no reply to that, the conversation, such as it was, appeared as if it would flag. By the contortions of his lips and cheeks, Robinson appeared to be working something from his tooth. "The Globe, eh?" said he finally, his monosyllabic tone not betraying whether he had any real interest in my reply.

"Yes, that is where Henry told me I would be staying."

He shrugged. "Not much choice o'er here, I suppose."

I raised my eyebrows. "Is it not a good establishment?"

He shrugged again. "Don't reckon I know, not having ever stayed there."

I frowned in momentary confusion, but a reasonable question suggested itself to me. "Have you ever stayed at a hotel, Mr. Robinson?"

"Can't say that I have. Ain't never left St. Georges. Not much need, I suppose."

I nodded at this rough wisdom, not certain what other response was required.

Robinson smacked his lips again. "Course, it seems like just yesterday that it opened."

"The Globe?" I prodded the taciturn man.

"Aye. After the War Between the States, it became mighty quiet round here. The building wasn't needed for its old purpose no more, and right around then Ralph Foster came back to the island. He rented it, refitted it, and became the first proprietor."

"I believe Henry mentioned a Mr. Boyle. Does he assist Mr. Foster?"

The man shook his head. "That would be right difficult."

I was becoming a bit vexed by his cryptic utterances, but soldiered on. "Why is that, Mr. Robinson?"

"Foster's dead."

"Ah," I said non-committedly, still not very enlightened. "And so who does Mr. Boyle assist, then?"

Here a bit of animation came into Robinson's face. "Mrs. Foster. From what I hear, Boyle assists her with many things."

I frowned. "What do you mean by that, Mr. Robinson?"

He shook his head. "I've said too much. Ain't talked this much in years. You must be a magician, sir, to pry so much out of me."

"I have many talents, Mr. Robinson, but I assure you that magic is not one of them." If it was, I reflected, I might have understood something of what the blasted man was saying.

But the man's lips were truly sealed tight, and we rode the rest of the way in silence, save only for the trotting of his horse's hooves and the crunching of the gravel under the trap's wheels. Fortunately, our sporadic conversation had taken quite some time, and we had already crested the hill and begun our descent. The road improved to a fairly crisp smoothness and we shortly began to pass between a small and ancient cluster of cottages and small shops. It soon became evident that these buildings represented the outskirts of the town of St. George's. Many of the buildings were brightly painted in a kaleidoscope of pastels, with lime, turquoise, lemon, and pink representing but a fraction of the tones. Unfortunately, not a few had fallen into a state of disrepair with their color all stained and streaked with damp and bad weather. Within a few minutes, the horse came to a stand on the busiest thoroughfare of the village, though that was not saying much. Looking up, I found that we were in front of a large three-storied peach-colored building with an enormous white gabled roof, its paint evidently newly applied. Four white chimneys buttressed the north and south sides, and white-framed windows apparently looked out in all four directions from the two lower floors, while a small north-facing opening provided some light to what I presumed was an attic. On all sides, the windows were potentially protected from the elements by stout black shutters, though these were currently thrown open. There was little exterior decoration, save a large sign over the first floor window that read simply: *"GLOBE HOTEL."*

I managed to climb down from the trap without assistance, while

Robinson saw to my valise. I mounted the five steps that led to the small porch in front of the main door, which was propped open by a ruddy brick. I took my valise from Robinson, and handed him two pence for his troubles. He tipped his hat at me and departed mutely. Crossing the threshold into the entryway, where a flight of dark cedar turned its way to the upper level, I faintly heard the rattle of wheels as the trap drove away. Straight ahead, another door led into what appeared to be a dining room with white-washed walls. As I looked about, a striking looking woman approached me with a pleasant smile of welcome. Small lines around her dark eyes pronounced her to be over forty, and though she was a little short and thick for symmetry, her strong, clear-cut face still registered a commanding presence. I suspected that she would have once been considered a great beauty. She was a brunette, with her hair wound up around her head with a green ribbon, and she wore a simple dress made from dove-colored cotton.

"How can I help you, sir?" she asked.

I realized that this must be the proprietress, Mrs. Foster. "I believe that you have a room for me? My name is Doctor..."

As I began to speak she had pursed her lips and shook her head, and finally she interrupted me. "I am sorry, sir, but we are full up."

I stared at her, dumbfounded. This possibility had not crossed my mind. "I see," I finally ventured. "Perhaps there is another inn?"

She shook her head again, a touch of color rising to her wan cheeks. "Not in St. George's. You will have to go back to Hamilton, I am afraid. But come, sir, I can offer you a whisky and soda before your journey." She motioned towards the dining room.

I finally recalled Henry's words. "I am supposed to speak to a Mr. Boyle."

She frowned at this utterance, as if she could hardly find it credible. "Just a minute, sir. Kindly take a seat while you wait. I shall return in an instant." She motioned to an unoccupied table, and then strode off through an adjacent billiard room and then into some sort of private quarters. I pulled up a seat, which gave me a chance to finally stretch out my aching leg after the cramped situations of first the sloop and then the trap. I took a moment to survey the architecture of the unfamiliar building. The dining room was about twenty feet in length and nearly that in width. Besides the door by which I had entered, there were several other exits. A set of wide-open double doors led into the billiard room. Single steps up led to two doors, one of which appeared to guard a ladies sitting room, while the other belonged to one of the guest rooms. Finally, another door to my right led out onto the street. The room was well lit by two large windows, and in the wintertime, a fire could have been made in the fireplace, though it was lying cold and bare on this fine day. The room was filled with tables and chairs, two larger ones set up to seat four, and six smaller ones set for two persons. However, only one other table was occupied at the moment by customers, which consisted of two men seated at the table furthest from the windows. When I entered they had seemed deep in conversation, but my presence seemed to stifle their discussion. I noted that they were an oddly matched pair.

The first was above all else remarkable for his extraordinary height, which I could discern even while he was sitting. His head was topped with lion-like hair, but his sandy whiskers were flecked with the earliest hints of grey, and I judged that his age may have been nearer forty than thirty, though his tremendous vitality made that number irrelevant. He had a splendid masterful forehead over magnetic amber eyes, and his sunbaked skin was so craggy it might have been chiseled in granite. He had massive broad-shoulders, with the limbs and chest of a Hercules. I figured that he must have been sixteen stone of solid bone and muscle. His huge hands looked as if they could bend steel. All in all, he was an imposing, commanding figure, with a natural expression of authority, and my first thought was that he would have looked splendid in an Army uniform, though he was dressed plainly in a simple black-frock coat with a circular malachite pin.

His companion was much smaller, likely below average height, though well-built and freshly complexioned. His age was not more than three or four and thirty, and he possessed a frank, honest face with the brow of a philosopher. His sandy hair was cut short and continued around along his cheeks and chin in a trimmed beard with a slight moustache. He used an eye glass, and I noted that his alert eyes were a piercing shade of blue. He wore a very shiny top hat and a neat suit of dark-grey, with an emerald and black silk cravat.

As I studied them, I noted raised voices coming from the back room where the woman had retreated. One voice was surely hers, while the other had the deep tones of a large man. Shortly thereafter, the owner of that voice appeared. In age he may have been about fifty, I should judge, with a strong-jawed, rugged face, and a grizzled moustache and shock of brown hair, which failed to fully cover a bald shining scalp which shot out from among it. He was a thick-set, burly man, with broad shoulders that were unencumbered by a coat, and he was stripped down to his rolled-up shirtsleeves, clearly having recently been engaged in some physical activity. His grey eyes appeared slightly flustered, but he smiled broadly at me, exposing a line of crooked teeth. "You must be Captain Henry's brother, the doctor! It's a pleasure to meet you, sir. I am Graham Boyle. Your brother secured your room with me, and I am afraid that I forgot to mention it to Mrs. Foster. Don't you worry yourself, sir! If you could just sign the ledger here, please?" He pushed a worn leather book towards me. "Of course we have a room for you. It's our last one, but one of our finest. It is the corner room, upstairs, the Walker Room."

"The Walker Room?" I inquired.

"Ah, named after the previous tenant of the building. Before this was the Globe Hotel, it was the headquarters of Major Norman Walker. He was the agent for the Confederate States of America. From here he oversaw the shipment of war materials from Europe to the Southern States."

I frowned. "I was but a lad back then, but was there not a blockade by the North?"

"Hah!" the man laughed loudly. "Of course there was. But where do you think the best blockade-runners came from?"

"That's enough history, I think, Mr. Boyle." Mrs. Foster had reappeared from the back room and was busying herself with setting up the tables for the dinner service. "Have you even fixed our guest a drink?" She fixed me with a piercing state, and I thought I detected a hint of sulky defiance in her eyes, though what I had done to agitate her was beyond my power of comprehension.

"Oh, I am sorry, sir." Boyle moved over to a sideboard, where he pulled a bottle of whisky from a spirit case and expertly sprayed a bit of soda water into it from a nearby gasogene. He set the glass down in front of me, and I sipped at it contentedly.

"When you are ready, sir, I can show you to your room," continued Boyle.

I nodded. "If you don't mind me taking your glass up with me, then I am prepared to go now."

"Of course, sir!" he grinned at me. "I can bring you another in twenty minutes, if you please. I am certain it has been a long voyage."

I smiled back at his thoughtfulness. "Twenty minutes would suit me well, I think."

"Then after me, sir." He took up my valise and we returned to the entryway. To our right, a fine set of cedar steps curled upwards. Four steps led to a small landing, then a ninety degree turn, with seven more steps before a second landing, and then another turn with four more to the top. I noted that the steps creaked alarmingly as we rose. The area at the top of the stairs was relatively bare other than a small table, and a propped open door which led into what appeared to be a twisting corridor. As we walked, I observed that the floors were lined with coconut matting, which served to brush the accumulated dirt off of my shoes. The halls themselves were very dimly lit and they twisted like a labyrinth.

As if reading my thoughts, Boyle spoke from ahead of me. "I am afraid that there is no electricity upon the island, sir. Even piping for gas lamps is rare over here in old St. George's. You will need to confine yourself to a whale oil lamp, I am afraid." As the corridor twisted and turned to the point where I was becoming a bit uncertain what direction I was facing, Boyle spoke again. "Mr. Foster, bless his soul, wanted to maximize the space for guest rooms when he converted Major Walker's offices to guest rooms. Originally, there were but four large rooms upstairs, and the walls were too critical to the support of the frame to knock down. So Mr. Foster added some new dividing walls and cleverly built this twisting passage to link all of the rooms. There are now eight guest rooms on this floor, plus one below, and room for two more to sleep in the gables."

Finally we arrived at what appeared to be the last door, save one, of the corridor. "Here we go, sir." He fetched a key from his pocket and turned it in the lock. Swinging the door open, he revealed a cozy, well-furnished room. It was shaped like an 'L' and had a low ceiling, but sunlight filtered in from windows on both the north and west walls. Another door must have once connected this room with an adjoining room, but access was completely blocked by a tall dark cedar chest of drawers. There was also a cedar dressing table with a Japanese vase holding a dainty arrangement of hibiscus flowers. A small wickerwork chair tucked under the open west window, from which came the salty scent of the balmy fall air. A great white counter-paned four-poster bed dominated the entry part of the room, and an iron soaking tub completed the furnishings. A square of Wilton carpet covered the wooden floors, while two oil lamps stood on the bedside table.

Boyle surveyed the room for a moment, and then edged past the bed to put my valise down by the chest of drawers. "Aye, it's a bit of a daft design, if you ask me, as there is not such space to get around the bed, but Mr. Foster was working within the constraints of the walls, you see." He rapped his knuckles on one of the walls, as if to prove his point.

"Do not concern yourself, Mr. Boyle. It is a fine room indeed."

The man grimaced. "Unlike the new fancy hotel in Hamilton, there is also no private water-closet, I'm afraid. But we passed one down the hall, which is plainly marked."

I shook my head. "Mr. Boyle, I have just returned from campaign in Afghanistan. I assure you that this room seems like Buckingham Palace itself compared to what I have become accustomed."

He smiled broadly and nodded. "Very good, sir, I understand. Will you be coming down for supper, sir?"

I considered this question for a moment. "I am certain that Mrs. Foster is an excellent cook, but after having spent the last month with over a thousand of her Majesty's finest men aboard a ship that was not overly large, I believe that I am in need of some solitude and rest. Would it be a terrible bother to include some cold cuts of meat and some bread with that second glass, Mr. Boyle?"

"No bother at all, sir. No bother at all." And with that, he let himself out of the room, closing the door behind him.

For a moment, I stood there, gazing at nothing, but luxuriating in the room's privacy and lack of noise. After a month aboard the *Malabar*, I was still surprised to note that the floor was not swaying gently under my feet. I sipped my whisky and soda, and contemplated stretching out upon the bed. My aching shoulder and leg called out for a rest. But the military training in me finally won out, and I rejected that alluring plan in favor of unpacking my valise, knowing that if I had lain down, my eyes would not have seen the light of this day again. I set my drink down upon the bed-stand and threw my valise upon the bed. First, I placed upon the desk my travel-worn and battered tin dispatch-box, my name painted upon the lid, though I suspected that I would receive few letters during my sojourn on this remote island. I reflected that even if Ms. Devere had wanted to write to me, there was little way for her to ascertain my location. Shaking off these melancholy musings, I took out my shaving kit and tooth-brush and set them near the wash basin. Looking at myself in the mirror, I barely recognized the man staring back at me. Little wonder that both Jackson and my brother had difficulties recognizing me! My face was dark and haggard. But underneath the thinness, a hint of my past strong-build was still evident in my square jaw and thick neck. I silently stroked my moustache and contemplated shaving it off. I had first grown it when I joined up at Netley, but now that I was done with the Army, perhaps I should relieve myself of this final vestige? And yet, I knew from the ache in my shoulder that my time with the army would never truly leave me, and I admitted that the moustache looked proper on my face. I resolved to leave it for now.

A knock on the door proved to be the reliable Boyle with another glass and a modest slaver holding the promised cold cuts with some rough bread. I took them from him and thanked him profusely. Snacking upon the morsels, I finished my unpacking and inspection of the room that was to be my home for the next few weeks while my wounds finished healing. The windows looked down onto the kitchen garden and out across a street, though traffic was rare and the noise little and tolerable. Diagonally across from my windows, a set of steep stairs led up to an apparently ancient church. I decided to explore it tomorrow during my tour of the town. All in all, I was not so fastidious to doubt that I could put in a pleasant month here.

Returning to the valise, I lifted out my spare sets of clothing so as to put them away. In so doing, I exposed my five-shot Adams Model Mark III .450 army service revolver and a few cartridges. I contemplated it for a moment, before I finally left it in the otherwise empty valise. I knew that I would have no need for it on this calm isle. Here I would find a simple life and peaceful, healthy routine. Between the sea-air and the sunshine, this respite would do me well. I lifted the almost empty case up on top of the chest of drawers in order to get it out of the way. I noted that it was about the hour when a man gives his first yawn and glances at the clock, so I stretched out my six-foot frame upon the bed, its linen above reproach. It was only then that I noticed that the canopy was made up of an enormous flag consisting of a field of red crossed by two blue lines, each of the four arms dotted with three white stars and a thirteenth in the very center. I could not be absolutely certain, but it appeared to be flag of the now defunct Southern Confederacy. As I closed my eyes, I recalled the suspicious look in Mrs. Foster's eyes and a vague feeling of uneasiness began to steal over me. I wondered what kind of madhouse Henry had gotten me mixed up in?

§

CHAPTER V:
ST. GEORGE'S

The next thing I knew, sunlight was streaming through the panes of the north window. It was the most refreshing sleep I had experienced in many months, and I felt much revitalized. Before I was wounded, I had a military regularity to my waking habits, and generally rose at half-past seven. However, since the shaking of my nerves, I have become extremely lazy and have gotten up at all sorts of ungodly hours. Today was no exception. The clock on the cedar bedside table showed me that it was a quarter-past nine. Although the pangs of my stomach directed me to immediately repair downstairs for sustenance, my military neatness would not allow me to appear without first having fully shaved, moustache excluded, and dressed. I took up my shaving kit and razor, and by the light filtering in through the windows I made a valiant effort to smarten the slovenly whiskers that had broken loose upon my cheeks.

Once I was done, I donned my reserve uniform and tucked my handkerchief into my sleeve. I took up my walking stick and made my way through the twisting, crackling corridor back down to the dining room. I was gratified to find that I was not the only late riser that morn. I noted the pair of mismatched gentleman from the previous afternoon, though they were not sitting together now. Also, perhaps not surprisingly given the lack of other accommodations in St. George's, Senhor Cordeiro, the traveler in wines, was seated at a table with another man who I did not recognize. The latter had a swarthy face, with large, dark, languorous eyes. He maintained a formidable dark, carefully-waxed moustache, which shaded a thin-lipped mouth. Something immediately suggested to me that he was of Italian extraction, and in age, I should have put him a little over thirty, though it was often hard to tell with these Latins. He wore no coat, but his white shirt cuffs were stiff, his chartreuse cravat was impeccably tied, and his grey Harris tweed trousers had crisp lines, the whole effect conferring on him a rather jaunty appearance.

Mr. Boyle noted my descent from the stairs and immediately greeted me.

"Good morning, Doctor. Care to break your fast?" he inquired, as me motioned me to an empty table.

"I would indeed," I replied heartily.

"Some café noir to start, I assume?"

"Yes, certainly."

As he brought over the cup, I took a moment to study my companions in the dining room. In addition to the four men I already noted, there were five more guests at various stages of their repast. Two men sat together at a small table. Like the others currently stopping at this peculiar little hotel, this pair was quite distinctive. Both appeared to be in their early thirties. The first was a rather short, stout man, with a powerful frame. Olive skin and coal-black hair proclaimed his Southern origin, and I decided that he likely hailed from Greece. His face was strong, yet deeply lined in the areas where it was visible, as a large bristling black beard covered much of it. His crinkled hands were half-closed in a way that is distinctive of sailors, and I felt that my diagnosis of his occupation was confirmed after observing his clothing, which appeared to be a rude sailor outfit. A navy pea jacket, clearly of advanced age and wear, lay open over a red-and-black check shirt, while a coarse pistachio-colored scarf was loosely wound around his neck. His legs were covered in dungaree trousers, and heavy boots completed the ensemble. His dark eyes sparkled as he conversed animatedly with his companion. This proved to be a small, wiry man, also with a swarthy complexion that suggested a Mediterranean origin, albeit different than the first gentleman. His hair and eyes were dark, and he was heavily-mustached. Viridian-framed glasses rested on a long curved nose, like the beak of an eagle. He was well but quietly dressed in a dark-gray suit, though the respectable picture was oddly marred by a checkered shepherd's muffler.

At a nearby table an older man sat alone, his appearance proclaiming that he had no wish for the company of his fellow man. He had a sallow face, scored with deep lines, and yellow-shot bilious eyes, like someone who had spent too long in the tropics. His scanty black hair was receding from his high forehead, and his little pointed beard was thickly shot with grey. He was haggard and thin, with bowed shoulders. His nose was thin and projecting, and he wore grey-tinted glasses to protect what I imagined were weak brown eyes from the sun. I placed his age as nearer to sixty than fifty, though honestly it was nigh impossible to tell for certain. He was clad in a suit of grey flannel, and wore a Panama hat, while a cane rested against his table.

But this sinister-appearing man was certainly not the most remarkable creature in the room, for that honor belonged to a woman. Although her age would be rather over forty than under it, she was still tall and queenly, but with a mask-like, pale, aquiline face. Her entire figure was emaciated, but appeared to radiate an inner fire. She had lustrous raven-black hair, and small dark Spanish eyes. She wore a dress of midnight black, made from an excellent silk and decorated with ostrich feathers. She seemed like a grand lady from another era, when Don Quixote still roamed the plains of La Mancha. When she saw me looking in her direction, she reached up behind her head and dropped a thick black veil over her face.

All in all, I thought to myself, the Globe Hotel was the abode of a fascinating mélange of characters. I would never have thought to find on this small island in the middle of the Atlantic Ocean such an assortment of people from around the world. Perhaps Mrs. Foster's establishment was truly worthy of its name. But my observations and ruminations were cut short by the return of Mr. Boyle with my coffee. As he set it down, he smiled at me. "Are you a sporting man, Doctor?" he asked.

"I certainly like to think so," I answered. "Why do you ask?"

The man smiled. "I'll give you a sporting choice then. I can have the kitchen fix you up a good English breakfast of fresh rashers and eggs."

I raised my eyebrows. "And my other option?"

"Well, if you are feeling adventurous, you can have a true Bermudian meal."

"But I do not get to learn the ingredients beforehand?"

"Tut, tut! Where is the adventure in that, Doctor?" he said, smilingly.

I nodded my head vigorously. "All right man, let me have the Bermudian meal."

Boyle beamed. "You will not regret it, sir. In the meantime, would you care to partake of the newspaper while you drink your coffee?"

"Absolutely," I replied. "I am great devotee of reading the paper and digesting the news of the day while simultaneously satiating my hunger."

"I'm afraid that I cannot offer you a London paper, such as *The Times* or *The Daily Telegraph*, but I hope that our poor *Royal Gazette* will sustain you. It doesn't hold a candle, I'm afraid, but it serves us well enough." He handed me a folded paper.

"It will do nicely, I am certain," I said, as I took it from him. "I have had nothing current for many a long month since I shipped out from Netley."

"Anything else, Doctor?" he asked, solicitously.

"Yes, in fact, I do have a question for you. Last night, as I was falling asleep, I could swear that I heard the most unusual whistling song. I was wondering what strange bird made that noise? Was it the Cahow?"

Boyle chuckled loudly. "That was no bird. That was the infamous tree frog."

I raised my eyebrows in skepticism. "I cannot believe that the bell-like singing I heard was a frog."

"Not just a single frog, Doctor. A mighty chorus of tiny frogs, each the size of your thumbnail. No one is certain where they came from, only that they appeared but a few years ago. One theory is that they came from one of the islands in the Lesser Antilles, riding on some imported orchids. Many people think they are a bloody nuisance, making it hard to sleep, though I myself have gotten used to them."

"It is a world of infinite variety in which we live," a new voice said over my shoulder, its timbre weak, as if the man suffered from a terrible case of quinsy.

"Shakespeare, *Antony and Cleopatra,*" I said automatically, as I turned. I was surprised to find sitting behind me the man who I had witnessed in Cape Town boarding the *Malabar* at the last moment.

He stuck out his hand. "George Warburton, at your service."

I shook his hand and introduced myself.

"I am a naturalist by training," he continued, a slight whispering quality to his voice, "and I could not help but overhear your discussion of the elusive *Eleutherodactylus johnstonei.* It is always heard at night, but almost never seen. Quite a treat indeed!"

"Is that why you have come to the island, Mr. Warburton?"

"Well, he laughed, "not just for the tree frogs, of course. After I completed my studies at Cambridge, I obtained a post as a teacher at the Cloister School, near Chesterfield. It is one of the best and most select preparatory schools in England, but I soon found myself growing frustrated and impatient trying to impart any wisdom to the scions of the wealthiest men in England, who cared nothing for my teaching of natural history and even less for my attempts at discipline. I found myself daydreaming of an escape from that daily toil, and setting forth on a grand expedition. Unfortunately, there were no expeditions to be joined at the moment, and while I have a modest income of my own as a bequest from my dear mother, it was certainly far short of what would be required in order to outfit a full expedition as the patron. So, I am on an expedition of one! I have decided to follow in the footsteps of the great HMS *Challenger* expedition that completed but four years ago. While they were focused on probing the depths of the world's oceans, I have turned my attention to the wondrous flora and fauna that exists upon the islands that they visited. It will be a fit complement to their achievements once I have finished. The

Challenger docked in Bermuda in 1873, and so here I am."

"That's quite a story, Mr. Warburton," I replied weakly. "So you are an entomologist?"

"Much more than that, I think!" he laughed softly. "I don't limit myself to one kingdom or phylum, but hope to study all aspects of the varied world."

My medical curiosity was piqued by his fashion of speech. "Are you suffering from tonsillitis, I wonder?"

"Hah! Not presently, Doctor, but I had the quinsy as a child and it left me with this weak throat. But I am perfectly hale now, I assure you. No need for your services!"

"I am happy to hear that," I began, but my train of thought was derailed by the appearance of my morning meal.

Warburton laughed at my evident discomfiture at trying to choose between continuing the conversation, and turning to face my plate. "Don't let me detain you, Doctor, I'm sure we will have more time for conversation later." He turned back to his newspaper, and I was free to devour the food in front of me.

It had been delivered by a little coal-black negress, about thirteen years of age, if I wagered a guess. She flashed a set of bright white teeth at me as she grinned at my amazement of the odd meal she had set down. I will not pretend that I was prepared to eat codfish and potatoes, with a side of bananas, avocado, a boiled egg, and sautéed onions with bacon. But I must admit that I relished every last bite, even mopping it up with a hunk of fresh bread smeared with butter from the dish resting on my table. All in all, it was a satisfying feast. Once it was concluded, I saturated myself with the news of the day, and by the time I pushed my chair back from the table, the rest of the dining room had cleared out.

Boyle looked up from his accounts and hurried over to me. "Are you headed out, Doctor?"

"Indeed. I cannot simply sit around all day. My first instinct is always to do something energetic. Since the weather seems exceptionally genial, I thought I would take a ramble through town."

"Well, since you are recently returned from the East, I likely shouldn't have to warn you about the climate of Bermuda. But it's going to be a hot and humid day."

I shrugged unconcernedly. "After my term of service in full kit under the blazing sun of India and Afghanistan, I have learned to tolerate heat much better than cold. A thermometer of ninety degrees is no hardship."

He nodded sagely. "Still, it is always wise to have an extra swill of water before you head out."

"Thank you, Boyle. That is sensible advice."

"It's my pleasure, Doctor. Here is some of our finest water." He handed me the strangest goblet I have ever witnessed in my life. It was rounded and made of a brown wood-like substance. I hesitated before raising it to my lips.

"You look puzzled, doctor," he said, seriously.

"Whatever is this cup made from?" I spluttered.

"Hah!" he finally laughed. "That is my little joke that I like to play on first time visitors to the isle. It is carved from one of the fruit-shells of a calabash tree, which grow in profusion here. A countryman of yours, a Mister Thomas Moore, wrote poems under one such tree while residing in Bermuda."

"Moore? An Irishman, I think," I said as I took his strange cup and drank the water. "Thank you, Mr. Boyle."

With that I took up my hat and stick and set out for a stroll of the quaint little village of St. George's. I have always been fond of wandering the streets of any town in which I find myself. Not only would a walk be good for the stiffness in my injured leg, but it would give me a chance to watch the ever-changing kaleidoscope of life as it ebbed and flowed through the streets of this small island.

It was a perfect day when I exited the hotel through the dining-room side-entrance onto what I determined was called the Duke of York Street. Turning to my right, I rounded the hotel and strolled down to a small square. It was bounded on three sides by a multitude of two-story brightly-colored buildings, and on the south by the water, where a wooden bridge led over to a trio of small offshore islands. By the bridge, a group of boats were tied up and a significant commotion was disturbing the otherwise tranquil air of the town. I limped my way over to the growing crowd in order to ascertain what was happening.

Despite my good height, the only thing that I could make out at the center of the crowd were two inebriated men standing over a large pale white lump, streaked with black. Even from my distance, I noted a strong fecal smell, which unfortunately reminded me of the uncontrolled loosenings that on occasion transpire upon the battlefield. "Whatever could that be?" I wondered aloud to myself.

I had not expected anyone to answer, but to my surprise a man standing next to me replied. I judged him to be in his late twenties, a small wiry, sunburnt man, with brisk, brown eyes and a trim beard. He wore a bowler hat, a brown frock-coat, and black gaiters over square-toe boots.

"Ambergris," said the man, nodding.

"Truly? Whale vomit? The stuff they use to make perfumes?"

"Aye," the man said. "Two fishermen found it this morning on Horseshoe Bay, and lugged it back here, perhaps hoping to avoid the tax collectors at Hamilton. But they started celebrating too early, and now the whole town knows about it."

"I've heard that it is valuable?" I ventured.

"Valuable? You could say that," said the man dryly. "That there lump looks to be a good forty stone. They might get five thousand sterling for it, if they are smart about things, though the Queen will get her share."

I was staggered by this sum and stared at the man open-mouthed.

"Of course, that little lump is nothing compared to the famous haul of Carter, Waters, and Chard," the man continued.

"Who?"

He raised his eyebrows. "Don't tell me you've never heard of the Three Kings of Bermuda?"

"Not that I can recollect," I admitted.

"Well, it's a bit of an old tale, I suppose." He took a cherry-wood pipe from his pocket and proceeded to light it before continuing. "It goes back to the earliest days of Bermuda, when Sir George Somers had crashed the *Sea Venture* upon its reefs. He managed to rebuild two barks, the *Deliverance* and the *Patience*, out of its timbers supplemented with cedar from the island, and was ready to set forth to complete his mission to the Virginia Colony at Jamestown. Amongst his men were two, Christopher Carter and Edward Waters, who were guilty of capital offences, but before they could be shot, they escaped into the deeper reaches of the isle. Somers departed without them, and upon his return the two criminals convinced a third seaman, Edward Chard, to desert and join them. Thus, for almost two years, until the *Plough* arrived with Governor Moore, these three men 'ruled' Bermuda, sovereigns over no one but themselves! One day, as the legend goes, while searching the rocks for turtles to eat, they came across a great mass of ambergris. It was one of the largest ever known, weighing over eighty pounds. This was worth a great fortune, and if only they had a way to carry it to London or Paris, they truly could have lived like lords. But as it was, they had no way to leave the island until the Governor arrived, and he promptly confiscated the treasure of the three 'kings' for the Somers Isles Company. There was an American who even wrote a little story about the Three Kings." The man finally decided to introduce himself. "By the way, I am Harry Dunkley, the constable of this town."

I grasped his outstretched hand and identified myself in turn. "This looks like a very nice town. It must be a pleasant job, Constable."

"Well, Doctor, it has its moments. To be honest, this post was just established last year, and I'm the first man to hold the job. Before the Police Establishment Act, things were much looser round here, with only part-time men filling the post. Of course, I'll admit that the town is much quieter now that the American war is over. I remember when I was a lad President Lincoln erected his huge naval blockade to strangle Southern supplies, and awoke a great ingenuity in my fellow islanders. There had long been trading ties between us and ports like Wilmington and Charleston. The swift, low-profile steamers of Bermuda refueled here on the run from England and Europe to the Southern ports, eluding Union gunboats. There they picked up 'white gold' to bring back to the hungry textiles mills of Europe."

"White gold?"

"Cotton bales, Doctor. Fortunes were made, lives were lost, and St. George's was the capital of a boisterous time. The streets were awash with woozy sailors duking it out, dolled-up ladies of the night, the enigmatic, the shifty, the straight-laced, and those up to no good. But with the South's eventual surrender fifteen years ago, the boom times were over. Debts and destitution replaced the short-lived surge in the economy."

"Surely it must be utterly peaceful now then? How can one get up to much mischief here?" I inquired.

"You would be surprised. It was only two short years ago that poor Anna Skeeters disappeared. They eventually pulled her body from Chub Cut, tied to a boulder. I suppose it wasn't too hard to pin this upon her husband, since he was a real violent wreck of a man once he got up in his Bibbey."

"Bibbey?" I asked, unfamiliar with the term.

"The curse of the colony! Since time immemorial, mankind has applied an incredible amount of industry to the task of making spirits that will render themselves senseless. Bibbey is the island's version of this strong swill, made from fermenting and distilling the sap of the local Palmetto. Its use has landed my good fellows in the stocks, the pillory, the whipping-post, and of course, gaol. There are laws in Bermuda against the use of the Palmetto for making Bibbey, not only due to its riotous effects, but because it is a valuable plant used for building, thatching, cordage, hats, baskets, and a thousand other necessities."

"A type of whisky, then?"

"More akin to rum," he clarified.

"But the murderer?"

"Ah yes, well, Edward Skeeters eventually confessed to his crime and swung right over yonder on Gallows Island." He pointed to a small island offshore. It was felt that an appropriate tombstone for Mr. Skeeters would be the very stone with which he drowned his wife, and so it was lashed to his body and he was sunk near Moses Island in the Great Sound. It is said that Edward does not rest easy, and on violent nights, when the lightning is flashing, you can sometimes see his spirit leaping upon the rocks of that solitary isle."

I smiled at the conclusion to his tale. "Surely you jest, Constable."

He raised his eyebrows and nodded his head slowly. "There are stranger things in heaven and earth..."

"Shakespeare, *Hamlet*," I immediately answered.

"Indeed." Dunkley nodded. "Well, it's been a pleasure, Doctor. I hope you enjoy your stay at St. George's and that it is a quiet one."

"I am certain it will be. I suspect that this great fortune of ambergris will be the most exciting thing that happens while I am here."

With that we parted and, in high spirits, I made my way back to the square. Passing a two-story building with flanking staircases, which I reckoned to be the Town Hall, I strolled along a small brick-paved lane. This was lined with handsome houses, separated from the street itself by low, sunbaked walls, mottled with lichens and topped with moss, the sort of walls what might have stood for a hundred years. The lane eventually led up a slight incline to a venerable but fine two-story Italianate-style white building. This had two cross-shaped gun slits in the upper floor, and a welcoming-arms staircase leading up to it. A man was resting upon the stairs, clearly a local by his manner of dress. I engaged him in a few moments of conversation, and he informed me that this was the former State House, the oldest stone building on the island, constructed with mortar made from turtle oil and lime. The governor of the time felt that Bermuda had a similar climate to Italy and directed that the building should be completed in that style, hoping to commence a general trend for the isle. However, the poor deluded man forgot that Italy was generally not beset by hurricanes, and thus the flat-topped roofs that flourish in Tuscany simply would not serve in stormy Bermuda. Rain water collected and seeped through the porous limestone blocks of the roof, and ensured that all future houses on the isle would adopt the curious white-stepped roof now typical of the charming island architecture. Once the capital moved to Hamilton in 1815, there was no real use for a State House in St. George's and thus the entire building was rented out to the Scottish Freemasons for the absurd sum of one peppercorn per year.

I thanked the man for the history lesson and then continued on my way, angling down to the crooked Duke of York Street. Wishing to inspect the church that I had spied from the window of my room, I turned to the left and headed in its direction. Once there, it was a significant climb up a set of some thirty or so brick steps to the admirable grey and white church itself. Since the full heat of the day was upon us, I had hoped to escape it temporarily in the cool that is usually found in an old church, but to my dismay the building was shut up tight. I therefore determined to find some shade in the graveyard that wrapped around the back of the church, and therefore followed the path off to my left. I was immediately struck by both the age of the graves, as well as the terrible power of the weather of this land, for many of the gravestones had been completely eroded, the names of their occupants lost to the ravages of time.

I eventually found a bench tucked under a massive tree and availed myself of its comforts to rest my leg, which had begun to throb mercilessly. Ignoring the pain, I surveyed my surroundings, and though some might call them morbid, in the bright light of day they seemed to me to radiate a sense of peace. I continued to bask in the sun and I found myself silently thanking Jackson, who had so kindly engineered my respite here. I decided that I was quite pleased with this little island of ancient comfort. My thoughts drifted and I am uncertain how long exactly I remained on that bench, when I was finally stirred from my rest by the sound of approaching voices. At first the words were indistinct, but as they drew closer, I was certain that I heard the word 'doctor,' which of course attracted my attention.

"Well, when it's over, he can finally rest," a voice said, a hint of a slight foreign accent upon on his tongue.

"That will be a joyous day," a British voice replied warmly.

And then the owners of the voices strolled into my view from a small lane that led into the back of the graveyard. I have a quick eye for faces and given the smallness of the town, I was not surprised to note two of my fellow lodgers at the Globe Hotel. The second voice obviously belonged to the Herculean man that I had encountered the previous evening, while the first had plainly emanated from the Italian that had been eating with Senhor Cordeiro this very morning. Upon seeing me, they immediately ceased their conversation. Both men wore hats against the brightness of the sun, and it may have been a trick of the shadows on their faces, but neither appeared pleased to see me sitting in the graveyard. If indeed such emotions had been present, they were quickly replaced by pleasant, non-committal smiles. Both men tipped their hats at me as they passed by my bench, but neither spoke again. I noted that the giant man walked with a hint of a limp, which told my surgeon's eyes that he was suffering from a wounded knee.

After they had passed from my view around the east end of the church, I decided that I had spent enough time resting my leg and resumed my walk. By coincidence, I followed the path that the two men had taken, since I had yet to explore in that direction. But I did not overtake them, as my attention was soon distracted by one of the larger gravestones in the yard, its relative newness plainly evident by the fact that the carved words were still clear. They read:

IN MEMORY OF DOCTOR C. RYAN, PRINCIPAL MEDICAL OFFICER TO HIS MAJESTY'S FORCES, WHO FELL ONE OF

THE FIRST VICTIMS TO THE EPIDEMIC FEVER OF 1819, IN THE BLOOM OF LIFE.

I paused and rubbed my throbbing left shoulder. A myriad of thoughts washed over me. I was grateful that I had escaped Maiwand with but the two wounds, my life intact. At the same time, I reflected on the grim toll that the spread of the glory of the British Empire took upon its brave lads. When they survived their wounds, they still might be struck down by a fever, as I had almost been. And despite all the learning of our age, many doctors still paid the ultimate price for their intimate treatment of their pestilential patients.

I shook my head at these somber thoughts and decided that tea-time was nigh. That was certain to lift my spirits. I therefore turned my steps back to the Globe Hotel, and upon entering the dining-room from the side entrance, I was heartened to see a kettle boiling furiously on the spirit lamp. We may have been over three thousand miles from London, but as long as the sun shone, our English traditions would remain. Mrs. Foster clearly ran a tight ship at her hotel.

When the good lady had brought me my cup, in order to make conversation, I asked her how the hotel had come by its name.

She paused and raised a hand to cover her mouth. A hint of sadness appeared in her eyes. After a pause, she lowered her hand and replied. "My husband Ralph decided upon the name. Like myself, he was born in Bermuda, but he always wanted to be an actor. There was no call for such a thing on this small isle, and he dreamed of one day moving to London and taking to the stage. But eventually, the fires of youth died down, as they always do, and he abandoned that thought in favor of something much more practical. Any yet, whenever given the chance, a glimmer of his first love would occasionally break forth, and so he named his hotel after the greatest theater in the world. By so doing, it was almost as if every moment that he spent within these walls, he was actually far away in Southwark, walking its timbers. When he passed, I kept the name to honor his memory."

"I am sorry to have raised a painful subject, madam."

She smiled bravely, and dabbed at her eyes with a kerchief. "There is no blame, Doctor. You could not have known. And it was a long time ago."

"This hotel is hardly the only Bermudian connection with Shakespeare, of course!" a voice interjected, with the queer accent of one who hailed from one of our colonies in the Pacific. I had spent enough time in Australia as a lad to recognize this tone anywhere I encountered it.

I turned from Mrs. Foster to discover that the Herculean man had descended from the stairs and was entering the dining room. He smiled at me, and held out his hand. "Bruce Sims, at your service."

After my reply, he continued. "I am sorry that I did not greet you sooner. It seems like I was occupied at every opportunity that we encountered each other."

"Think nothing of it, Mr. Sims. You were saying about Shakespeare...?" I prompted him.

"Ah yes," he replied. "Well, as you may know, Shakespeare based his great play *The Tempest* upon the wreck of the *Sea Venture* in 1609, as detailed in William Strachey's report. As such, this is the actual island of the sorcerer Prospero and the devil Caliban. In fact, there is a great cave over near Castle Harbor that is named after Prospero. Steps lead down to a deep saltwater lake that fills much of the cave, with magnificent stalactites hanging down overhead. In reality, it was likely discovered by Sir George Somers when he was first exploring the isles, but it pleases the imagination to think of the great sorcerer still dwelling there."

I smiled at this fanciful tale from the leonine giant before me. "I have heard of the *Sea Venture* wreck before, but I also understand that Mr. Strachey's report was not published until long after Shakespeare had died. I have read that it was the wreck of the *Edward Bonaventure* upon these reefs in 1593 that was the actual source for the story."

Sims frowned. "I was unaware of those details, Doctor." He then brightened. "But it does not diminish the Shakespeare connection to the isles."

"I concur. Though I have heard Mr. Emerson doubts whether the merchant of Stratford could truly have written the plays ascribed to him."

"What?!?" the man appeared truly astonished.

The rest of the evening was agreeably passed in a great debate with my new acquaintance Mr. Sims. He was a very interesting man. He knew hardly any books, and so was unfamiliar with the questionable attributes of the First Folio and its authorship, but he had travelled far and had seen much of the world, which he could describe in meticulous detail. His especial passion was for the theater, and was most proud of his accomplishment of having seen a performance of every single one of Shakespeare's thirty-seven plays. He even took in a rare staging of *The Two Noble Kinsmen* in Narbonne just for good measure. During this process he had evidently become intimately acquainted with more than one actress in the process, though as a gentleman, he refused to identify them by name. Nonetheless, I feel as if I held my line well. Even the unusual dinner that was eventually served to us could not shake my satisfaction with the day. Rather than a traditional English dinner, I found myself eating a buffet of foods that appeared to have recently been a fathom or more under the ocean. It started with chowder made from an unidentified fish, which in a pleasant surprise was flavored with a sauce made from sherry peppers and rum. Following this was a shark hash and a mussel pie. Washing this hearty meal down was an excellent bottle of Montrachet, which appeared to be fresh off the boat from Marseilles.

After dinner I parted from my new friend, and took a brief stroll back out into the quiet square to enjoy a pipe prior to retiring. How sweet and wholesome the town looked in the fading light. The sun was beginning to sink behind the western hills, where it turned the wispy clouds a riot of scarlet and purple. The gently lapping waters of the harbor in front of me were tinged with a luminous quicksilver where they caught the evening light. The glories of the still seascape in the slanting rays of twilight were more than sufficient to compose a fitting end to a lovely day. I was sunk in the deepest thoughts. If all of my subsequent days on this isle could be so tranquil, I feared I might never leave.

§

CHAPTER VI:
THE HEART OF THE ISLAND

My first act upon awakening the next morning was to open the shades of my room. It was an ideal early fall day, with a light blue sky flecked with little fleecy white clouds drifting across from the west. The sun was shining very brightly, and I knew that we were to have more magnificent weather which would surely work wonders on restoring a man's depleted energy. After repeating the ablutions of the previous morn, I donned my one civilian suit and repaired downstairs for another repast and time spent perusing the *Royal Gazette*. As usual, I had awoken late, and as I descended the creaking cedar stairs, from the noise emanating from the dining room, I perceived that it was near-fully occupied. However, in the entry room at the bottom of the stairs, Mrs. Foster was speaking softly but earnestly with two individuals apparently new to the clientele of the hotel.

"Mrs. Foster," a man's voice was saying, with something of a French accent, "I am most displeased. Lucy and I are supposed to have our own rooms." As I moved downwards, the man's features came into view. In age I judged him to be in his early thirties, with a clean-shaven, smart, keen face. There was perhaps something sensitive or weak about his mouth, though it may have been a trick of my imagination, as he seemed an alert fellow. In height he was middle-sized, with firm, though not overly broad shoulders. A thin black cord held golden pince-nez to be used for his grey eyes, which matched his dark hair. His dress was somber and quiet, a black frock-coat, dark trousers, and a touch of color about his olive-colored neck tie.

"Monsieur Dubois, I am well aware of the plan. I assure you that this alteration was not my design, but was foisted upon us..." Mrs. Foster broke off as she saw me descending the stairs. She appeared much flustered.

"And how do you propose to fix this situation..." the man continued, until his companion put her delicate hand upon his arm and stilled his angry voice. I am not much for hyperbole, but I think I will not be amiss in claiming that this individual was one of the loveliest young women that I have ever seen in my life. She was very young, not much into her majority, but possessed of a remarkable poise that hinted at a refined and sensitive nature. I have a quick eye for color, and she was awash in it. A wealth of fiery red hair sat above a bright, quick face, lightly freckled like a plover's egg, with the exquisite dainty pink bloom of the French rose. She had brilliant green eyes and an exquisite mouth with a delicately rounded chin. The rich coils of her luxuriant hair were held back by a pale blue ribbon, and her ears were adorned with small round gold earrings. She wore a sage-colored gown made of some sort of *mousseline de soie*, a thin silk-like material similar to muslin, with a touch of fluffy forest green chiffon at her neck and wrists, and her feet were clad in white satin shoes. All in all, she was a striking looking woman, tall and graceful, with a slim flame-like perfect figure and she took my breath away.

When she spoke, her voice was melodic and pleasing. "Hector, do not fret. All will be well. We will simply have to share a room."

Both Mrs. Foster and Hector seemed taken aback by this idea, but any further discussion on the matter was lost to me, as I politely nodded and made my way past them into the dining room. Mrs. Foster greeted me distractedly as I went by.

Ready to take my breakfast, I shook off my distraction at the site of the beautiful Madame Dubois, and I sat at a table with the two men with whom I was familiar, Mr. Sims and Senhor Cordeiro. The third man at the table with us was Mr. Sims' conversant from the evening I had checked into the hotel, who proved to be a fellow physician by the name of Leos Nemcek. Due to his unusual name and slight trace of an accent, I knew that he must trace his ancestors to somewhere on the Continent, and with cautious inquiries, I discovered that he hailed from Prague. Despite the fact that I was very newly acquainted with my table-mates, our conversation was broad-ranging and stimulating that morning. One highlight was a fantastic description by Dr. Nemcek of the exploits of a certain Tycho Brahe, an astronomer at the court of Rudolph II in Prague. To this day I wonder if he fabricated the stories of the golden nose and the moose. From there, we turned to a discussion of the importance of the Copernican System and the great Renaissance polymath who created it in the face of all established teachings. Only by observation alone can progress be made! Eventually, however, all of the scrambled eggs and ham had been dispatched, and the men separately took their leave from the table. I sat there alone for a moment and contemplated my agenda for the day. The proximity of the hotel to the ocean had given me an idea.

Mr. Boyle approached my table and inquired whether there was anything else I required. He seemed like a knowledgeable man, so I put my question to him.

"I was deliberating trying to engage a boat captain to take me out upon the water. As long as he has a spare rod, reel, and spoon-bait, I could occupy myself for many hours trying to catch some jack."

But Boyle dashed my hopes with a grim shake of his head. "I think not, Doctor. The fishermen tell me that they feel a squall coming on, and they aim to bring in all they can today before their boats need be drawn ashore for a few days. They won't want to be burdened by a stranger, no matter how skilled or well-intentioned."

"A squall?" said I, the disbelief plain in my voice. I glanced out the window to confirm my prior estimation of the day. "That seems unlikely."

But Boyle only shook his head. "Not today, that is for certain, but I've learned not to question some of the old dogs that ply these waters. They say there was a red sky this morning."

"Well then," said I dejectedly, "what sights would you recommend I endeavor to take in today, Mr. Boyle?"

"What did you do yesterday?" he inquired politely.

After I explained my previous ramblings, he pursed his lips and thought for a moment. Finally he said, "I think the new church under construction is quite a sight, Doctor. You could also hire a four-wheeler to take you around the island."

"No, thank you, Mr. Boyle. The intention of my respite on Bermuda is to regain my strength, which I shall never do if I am carted around by a horse. I will walk."

"As you will, Doctor. Then the church is the thing, though it is situated up the hill towards Fort St. Catherine, and will be quite a hike."

"Ah, yes. I recall the church now. I saw it briefly as I rode in with Mr. Robinson the other day. It is not quite finished, correct?"

"That's the one. We began building it six years ago in order to replace old St. Peter's Church across the way there," he waved towards the window. "I expect that it will be finished very soon. And it will be magnificent."

"So be it." I declared, and pushed my chair back from the table. Taking up my hat and Penang lawyer, I strode out the side door into the street named after the Duke of York. I followed it towards the east, and turned onto the street that I recalled led up and over the hill back to Fort St. Catherine. As I began my climb, I passed a small alley where I heard the distinctive clanging of a printing press at work. Across from this was a good-sized park, with towering palm trees shading a beautiful stretch of lawn. The garden was enclosed by an aging wall constructed of what I had come to recognize as the local grey limestone, held together by a rough mortar. As I walked along the narrow, cobbled road, inhaling the fresh morning air, and rejoicing in the music of the birds and the soft rustle of the breeze through the leaves of the trees, I congratulated myself on my choice of outing.

Pressing on, I eventually began to spy the central tower of the unfinished church in the distance. Even though the morning was not far along, I paused for a moment to remove my hat and wipe the sweat from my brow with my handkerchief. Suddenly, I realized that my leg was aching ferociously, and I was beginning to regret my bold words at the breakfast table. Clearly I was not as far along in the recuperative process as I had optimistically hoped. For a moment I feared that my health was irretrievably ruined. Then I shook off that morbid thought, and realized that I simply had prematurely exerted myself before my condition could return to its natural vigor. Until then, I needed to set less lofty goals. I determined to return to the shade of the recently-passed garden and take refuge there for a moment in order to rest.

I retraced my steps all the way back to Duke of York Street in an endeavor to locate the entrance to the garden, and found the downwards slope to be much more conducive to my poor leg. I finally found a gate by which I could access the area and soon found myself on a small landing that overlooked the lawn proper, where several benches lined a meandering gravel path. An old pedestalled sundial sat in the middle of the path near a previously unrecognized second entrance to the garden. The whole effect was so soothing and restful that it was welcome to my somewhat exhausted body. In that deeply peaceful atmosphere, I could hopefully forget the face of the exquisite Madame Dubois, which kept intruding into my brain. The landing was unprotected from the sun, and so I descended the short flight of stairs into the garden itself. Before I could make my way over to one of the shady benches, a peculiar sight tucked against the south wall caught my notice. I have always been naturally curious, even at the expense of my own well-being. My brother once called me foolhardy, and I suppose that this overly-harsh term was not completely undeserving. Certainly, the promise of adventure has always held a fascination for me.

The object of my attention proved to be a plain sarcophagus, whitewashed on the sides with a featureless grey slab of stone on top. Grey painted bricks formed an archway and wall above it, and partly protected the tomb from the elements, though its stone was already weather-stained and lichen-blotched. Set into those bricks was a white marble slab that explained why such an object was found outside of a church or graveyard:

NEAR THIS SPOT
WAS INTERRED IN THE YEAR 1610
THE HEART OF THE HEROIC ADMIRAL
SIR GEORGE SOMERS KT.
WHO NOBLY SACRIFICED HIS LIFE
TO CARRY SUCCOUR
TO THE INFANT AND STRUGGLING PLANTATION
NOW
THE STATE OF VIRGINIA.
TO PRESERVE HIS FAME FOR FUTURE AGES
NEAR THE SCENE OF HIS MEMORABLE
SHIPWRECK OF 1609
THE GOVERNOR AND COMMANDER IN CHIEF
OF THIS COLONY FOR THE TIME BEING
CAUSED THIS TABLE TO BE ERECTED
1876

I must admit that I was moved by this saga of a great hero. I reverentially laid my hand upon the stone slab and silently pondered what stirrings of the soul led a man to rise to the heights of human triumphs, so that his name would never be forgotten to the annals of history.

"'The proper study of Mankind is Man,'" a woman's voice suddenly pierced my reverie. I turned about suddenly, only to discover the stunning woman that I had encountered only just this morning in the hotel's entryway and whose face had never left my mind's eye. She had put on a thin mantle and a bonnet, which protected her fair face from the full glare of the sun, but had the unfortunate effect of partially obscuring her lustrous red hair. She had also donned elbow-length white gloves, and carried a trim little hand-bag of crocodile skin and silver.

"I beg your pardon?" I finally stammered.

"Pope," she said simply. "Alexander Pope?" she elaborated slightly, raising her eyebrows, after witnessing what I can only imagine was a completely blank look upon my face.

"Yes. I am familiar with his works," I finally replied. "But I am at a loss as to what Pope has to do with anything?"

"You were contemplating the final resting place of Somers' heart. Since he died over two hundred years ago, even if you happened to be directly related to Sir George, you cannot possibly have been specifically grieving his passing. Thus I assumed that you were engaged in a more profound introspection of the nature of man, and Pope seemed germane. Only by studying the exploits of the great men - and women, mind you - can we ourselves be elevated to perform a momentous deed," she concluded, smiling broadly.

"I believe that you may have just read my mind. I stand flabbergasted."

"It was nothing. You have a very expressive face. I am Lucy, by the way." She held out her hand in a very manly fashion. From this action and her distinctive accent, I could only assume that she was an American, which was surprising, since her husband was clearly French.

"A pleasure to meet you, Madame Dubois," I said and introduced myself in turn.

A wary expression entered her dazzling green eyes. "Do I know you, sir?"

I laughed. "No, I simply heard Mrs. Foster call your husband by that name as I descended the stairs this morning."

"Ah," the wariness disappeared, "you are very observant."

"No more so than yourself. As you said, 'the proper study...'" I let the sentence trail off.

"*Touché*," she nodded her head. "So tell me, sir, do the deeds of Sir George inspire you?"

"How can they not?" I replied. "Of course, Somers is but one of many brave men upon whom the bedrock of the British Empire was laid. Even today, great men walk amongst us. Take General Gordon for example."

"Chinese Gordon?"

I frowned. "I'm not certain that he cares for that sobriquet. It is true that he made his military reputation in China as the head of the Ever Victorious Army, a band of Chinese soldiers led by European officers, who put down the much larger forces of the Taiping Rebellion. But I think he is more to be admired for his work in the Sudan suppressing the slave trade."

"I will grant you that," she conceded.

"And you, Madame Dubois? You said that women were also capable of great deeds. Which woman inspires you?"

"I am partial to Boudica," she said.

I raised my eyebrows at this statement.

"You disapprove, sir?" she said.

"Not at all," I shook my head. "It is simply that I was not expecting such a violent example. I had simply presumed you would reference someone more gentle; Florence Nightingale, for example."

She inclined her head. "It is a valid point." She pursed her lips, apparently lost in thought. "We do so glorify the warriors of this world, often forgetting that bravery takes many forms, and you need not set foot on a battlefield to prove it," she said seriously.

"They also serve who only stand and wait."

The frown vanished from her forehead, and she smiled broadly at me.

"Milton. Exactly! You know both your history and your literature, sir. Tell me, what else do you enjoy reading?"

"Recently I have appreciated the works of Collins, Poe, and Gaboriau."

"Ah, said she, a hint of disdain in her voice. "I don't take much stock of them. They were smartly written, I suppose, and have some small talent, I grant you, but nothing worthy of significant attention. Perhaps someday an author will emerge who will shake the very foundation of modern fiction, but I have yet to read him." She paused and stared intently into my eyes. Then she seemed to make a decision. "Will you walk with me, sir?" she said, as she offered me her arm.

I suddenly realized the precariousness of my position. "Ah, Madame Dubois, I am not certain that..."

She laughed at my obvious discomfort. "Do not fear, sir. I won't bite. And please call me Lucy."

"I assure you, Madame Dubois, that I am not worried about myself. Your husband..." I trailed off, the implications clear.

She smiled. "Hector? Do not worry about Hector. I promise you that he will not be the slightest bit concerned if I spend a few moments with a respectable gentleman in a highly public locale." She looked down on her outstretched arm. "You are a gentleman, are you not? Would you forsake me?"

I drew in a deep breath as I realized that I had little choice. I took her arm, careful to not make any more contact with her slender body than absolutely necessary. As I did so, I absently noted a small black ink stain on the inner aspect of her right glove. Once she had secured my arm, she led me back along one of the gravel paths towards the larger part of the garden. At her touch, it seemed as if all of my senses were heightened. The sun was shining very brightly, and yet there was an exhilarating crispness in the air, which set an edge to a man's energy.

"Tell me about yourself, sir," said Madame Dubois, as we sauntered through the garden.

"It's a simple story, really," I said awkwardly, not overly comfortable discussing my life with someone I had just met, no matter how entrancing she may be. "I was born twenty-eight years ago in Edinburgh, Scotland. But I have few memories of my ancestral home, as my father moved our family to the Australia Colonies when I was less than a year of age, and my brother Henry but a boy of three."

"Why?" she inquired softly.

"You are likely too young to recall what happened in Australia in 1851. John Dunlop discovered gold there, and by November a cataract of that precious metal was pouring from the hills. Wherever gold is found, you will soon find a swarm of men seeking their fortune, and my father was no different. Within a few months, more than fifty thousand people, gathered from every nation on the globe, were on the diggings."

"I know a little of this phenomenon, Doctor," smiled the lady, faintly. "My father was about to become a young man in Philadelphia, when gold was found at Sutter's Mill. Within a few years, like so many others, he rushed to California. There he met my mother, and eventually I was born in San Francisco."

"Ah, it is amazing that a little metal can so greatly shape the course of our lives."

"Indeed," she agreed. "But I interrupted your tale. Please continue."

"Well, I am told that we traveled on a boat of the Adelaide-Southampton line, but my dear mother did not survive the voyage. My father was not an overly-affectionate man, so my brother Henry and I raised each other. Whether my father was too late, too unlucky, or too scrupulous, he failed to acquire any significant fortune. There was no 'Welcome Nugget' for him. But he was modestly prosperous, and once my brother was thirteen, my father realized that the two of us were becoming rather wild in the freer, less conventional atmosphere of South Australia. He determined that we lads could not obtain a sufficient education in the colonies, so Henry was sent back to England to board at Winchester College at the old English capital, while I followed two years later. I will never forget how he put his hand on my shoulder as we parted; giving me his blessing before I went out into what he knew to be a cold, cruel world. It was the last time I would ever see him. I had always meant to make the passage back, but it always seemed like something arose that made it impossible, such as my medical training. And now, of course, I have little reason to go back to Australia."

"That is a sad story, Doctor. Do you have no fond memories of your childhood?"

I contemplated this question for a moment. "My school days were mighty fine. I spent my days learning everything I could, and my nights making every mischief we could devise. Those were good years for old number thirty-one." I smiled fondly at the reminiscence.

"Thirty-one?"

"My school number, used by the tutors to identify me amongst the other boys."

"Ah, I thought perhaps those were the number of hearts you broke. Surely not all of your time was spent in boy-hood pranks? There must have been more than a few girls who fell for your handsome visage?"

"Ah," stammered I, staring at her in stupid surprise. "I.... do not know what you mean." I was completely at a loss of how to respond to her provocative words.

But she merely laughed gaily. "So why did you become a doctor?" she asked lightly.

I reflected upon this most personal question. In many circumstances, such a probe would have been considered rude, but I knew that Americans were frequently not as constrained by social circumstances as those of us who consider England home. "I suppose it was the loss of my mother. I had a great anger that I had no clear memories of her, and I vowed to try my best to prevent such a loss for others."

Now it was Lucy's turn to grow serious. "And do you think that anyone can really affect the fates in such a fashion, Doctor?"

"Perhaps not, perhaps it is hubris. But such were my thoughts when I left Winchester in order to attend the University of London. During that time, I served as a surgeon at St. Bart's Hospital. With my dresser Stamford, we dealt with many gruesome wounds..."

"Dresser?" Lucy interrupted me to inquire.

"Ah, a term we use for a surgeon's assistant," I explained.

"Of course, please continue."

"Well, after I obtained my M.D. I realized that it was not easy for a man without kith and kin to set up practice for himself. And so I decided to follow in my brother's footsteps by joining the Army. I did a residency at the Royal Military Hospital at Netley, near Southampton, where I saw men arriving on the incoming hospital ships from all parts of the Empire. And then I myself was shipped out to India. Upon landing in Bombay, I was attached to the Fifth Northumberland Fusiliers as an Assistant Surgeon and saw service in India and eventually Afghanistan. I was eventually transferred to the Berkshires Regiment, where I encountered some action around Candahar."

"Oh my, I am so sorry, Doctor."

"For what?" I inquired.

"For my earlier words about warriors and bravery. I did not know that you had been in the Army. I certainly did not intend to disparage your service."

"I never thought you did, Madame Dubois," I smiled reassuringly at her. "Well, it was a rough-and-tumble work. And then a few months later, and several ounces of lead heavier, I found myself here."

She smiled. "I suspect that it was not quite so simple as all that. Your modesty becomes you, Doctor."

"Not at all," said I, shaking my head.

By this time, we had exhausted the paths of the garden and had climbed up a set of sloping steps that led to the rear gate. From there, we turned to the left and followed a small alley back to the street that led up to the unfinished church. Not wanting to repeat my failure from this morning, especially while escorting Madame Dubois, I steered us back down towards the main square and the harbor. Lucy herself was silent for a few moments, before she inquired. "And what do you think of war, Doctor?"

"War?" I responded, a bit surprised by this change in subject. "In what sense?"

"Do you think it serves a purpose?" she asked seriously.

I thought about this question for a moment. "I suppose that I have never really considered this. Certainly, it is hard for someone like me, unconnected with the corridors of power, to fully understand why countries must occasionally exert force to settle international questions."

She shook her head angrily. "Well, I think that war is a preposterous way of settling a dispute."

I was taken aback by her presumptive opinion. "What makes you think that, Madame Dubois?"

"The waste," she said strongly, her lips set and eyes sparkling. "The useless waste of so many innocent lives lost. Young men, who know no better, blindly following fools, far removed from the killing grounds, their lives unscathed, and their uniforms pristine." Her hands were clenched with deep emotion.

"But think of the great gallantry so often found in the midst of a violent struggle."

"Gallantry is a man's preoccupation. For those left behind, parents, spouses, children, it is a cold comfort from the horror of being left alone."

I was stunned. I had never considered it from that point of view. It was if she had turned my whole world upside down, and I struggled to make sense of my feelings. "You speak as if you had firsthand experience of this, Madame Dubois."

By this time, we had reached the King's Square, and she paused to look out into the distance over the calm waters. Finally, she nodded her head sadly. "My father was a patriotic man. When our great country dissolved into its Civil War, he did not care that the action was taking place far from our home in California. He joined a regiment that headed east to fight against the Southern Secessionists. He was a brave soldier – gallant, if you will – and survived many actions, including the bloody Battle of Antietam. But he eventually died defending a stone wall on the field of Gettysburg from the charge of General Pickett."

"You have my most sincere condolences, Madame," said I, with a quiet voice. "I did not mean to bring up painful memories."

She took out a lacy handkerchief from her handbag and dabbed at her eyes. She then smiled tightly at me, her upset features perhaps even more alluring, if such a thing was possible. "Do not worry, Doctor. I was the one who raised the subject. And please call me Lucy."

I shook my head. "I'm afraid that I cannot do that, Madame Dubois."

She sighed, and I thought I detected a hint of sadness in her eyes. "So tell me, what is your philosophy of life, Doctor?"

"My philosophy of life?" said I, perplexed.

"Yes, how do you see the world? What is its meaning?"

I shook my head in undisguised wonder. "No one has ever asked me such a thing before."

"And is that a bad thing?" said she, imperturbably.

"Of course not! But to date my path has mainly led me along the rougher side of life. From the cries of pain echoing in the hallways of a London hospital, to the equally miserable agonies of a dusty battlefield. Such philosophy has not come within my horizon at all."

She shook her head skeptically. "Come now, Doctor, that is an absolute fabrication if I have ever heard one. You may have been born a man of action, but that does not mean that the pursuits of the mind and the heart are not equally within your *métier.*"

I shrugged my shoulder. "I simply have never had to put this into words. I suppose that I find life to be formidable yet eminently worthwhile. And in one man's story you can often find a microcosm of the whole. We are constantly reaching for answers, and often times our grasp falls short and closes on nothing but empty air, but that does not mean that we should ever stop striving to know our purpose on this great ball of matter."

She smiled demurely. "Ah, Doctor, if you had not told me otherwise, I would have thought you a poet."

I found myself again growing warm and flustered. "It is just that I do not wish for my existence to ever become either comfortless or meaningless, so I keep seeking."

She stopped and looked into my eyes. I found myself falling into them. "And where do you think that a man can find both comfort and meaning?"

"Ah," I stammered again, trying to break free from her entrancing gaze, "I suppose that many find it in their work, especially when such work brings succor or happiness to another."

Again she shook her head, but this time with a hint of sadness. "And here I thought that you might say that you could find it in love."

Her words took my breath away for an instant. I was uncertain how to respond. A wondrous subtle thing is love, but why would it strike me here of all places in the world, and why would it be this woman, who was forever unattainable, bound to another? But any further words that I might have spoken were lost, as my attention was suddenly drawn to another commotion occurring in a spot very close to the prior day's ambergris-induced excitement. However, something felt different about today's crowd, which seemed more agitated than animated.

Abruptly, a voice called out in great anxiety. "A doctor! Someone fetch a doctor!"

Without a further thought for my companion, I leapt into action as fast as my leg would carry me. I hobbled across the square and used my walking stick to try to part the crowd before me. Despite my best efforts, I still ended up knocking my injured shoulder against another man and the sudden intense pain almost knocked the wind of out me. I finally managed to croak of words as loudly as I could. "Make way! I am a doctor!"

A path through the crowd separated and I was finally able to see the source of the problem. A small boy, no more than ten years of age, was lying still upon the cobbles, his face swollen and slate-colored, his lips a purplish-blue. His hair and clothes were soaking wet, immediately suggesting to me that he had been submerged for a considerable time. I bent over the lad and examined him. His pulse was feeble and intermittent, and no breaths appeared to emanate from him. I quickly turned him over and cradled his chest in the crook of my right arm, as well as I could with the stiffness of my wound still troubling me. With my left hand, I proceeded to strike the boy's back with not inconsiderable force. The first blow failed to produce an effect, and a woman nearby gasped at my actions, which must have seemed outlandish, but I pressed on. The second blow accomplished my goal, as the boy proceeded to cough and expel a great deal of seawater from his lungs and stomach. It made quite a mess upon the cobbles, but I could tell that it was having an effect by the little shivering of his eyelids which showed a thin white slit of ball beneath. After one more blow and another purging of his lungs, I turned him back over and laid him down. I placed my finger back upon his neck's thready pulse, where the stream of life trickled thin and small. But soon I could tell that both his pulse and breathing were growing stronger. To augment their recovery, I raised and sank his arms until he was drawing a series of long, natural breaths. However, I could not ascertain if I had been successful in removing all of the water, and I cursed my lack of foresight. Before I shipped out of England, I had at all times carried a stethoscope with me secreted in my top hat, but as I was in Bermuda to recuperate, it had never occurred to me to bring it with me that day. Fortunately, the lad soon rolled onto his side under his own power, blanched and ghastly, but plainly on the mend with the inherent vigor of youth. I contemplated accelerating his recovery by sending someone for a splash of brandy, but ultimately decided that the boy would be fine without. When he finally opened his still-vacant blue eyes, in which a tiny spark of reason had returned, I had the satisfaction of knowing that my hand had drawn him back from that dark valley in which all paths meet.

I rose and spoke to the anxious surrounding crowd. "It has been touch-and-go with him, but he'll live now. He simply needs some time and rest." A series of congratulations and painful backslaps from the crowd followed this pronouncement, but my sole interest was in ascertaining the location of my abandoned companion. I soon spotted her standing in the shade underneath the porch of a nearby building. She was staring at me with the most peculiar look in her bewitching green eyes.

I slowly made my way over to her and inclined my head slightly. "I apologize for abandoning you, Madame."

A brilliant smile spread across her face as she shook her head. "That was not abandonment, Doctor. That was true gallantry." She then lifted on her toes, leaned forward, and gave me a kiss on my cheek. "You are a brave man."

I was thunderstruck. "It was nothing, Madame," I stammered. "My bravest moment must have come shortly after I arrived in India. I rose one morning only to found a shower in my swamp adder."

She laughed delightedly. "You are a complicated man, Doctor. I do hope to converse more with you soon." And with that ambiguous statement, she turned and strode back in the direction of the Globe Hotel, the frangipani scent of her perfume lingering in my nostrils.

As I watched her saunter away, I pondered the absurd racing of my heart. I was an army surgeon with a weak leg and a weaker bank account, but even more importantly, she was a married woman. Despite the rapport that had been established between us, I vowed to banish all thoughts of her from my brain.

I slowly followed in her wake back to the hotel, only to discover upon my arrival that she must have already retired upstairs to her room. I felt vaguely disappointed not to see her again, but also relieved that I would not have to test my resolve so soon. I sat down in the dining room intending to partake in a light lunch. Boyle entered from the back rooms and raised his eyebrows at my disheveled appearance. My suit had been stained with water spots during my treatment of the nearly-drowned lad, and was quite a sight.

"Good afternoon, Doctor. So it's true."

"What's true?" asked I, confused.

"That you brought little Benji Trimingham back to life."

I snorted. "Nothing of the sort. It was just a simple matter of some water removal from his lungs."

"Well, that's not what they are saying, Doctor," replied Boyle. "They are saying that the lad was dead, and that you restored him. They are calling you a miracle worker."

I shook my head ardently. "Not true at all! Who is spreading such a tall tale? This happened but ten minutes ago!"

"Remember that this is a small town on a small island, where everyone knows each other's business. News travels fast around here, especially something so moving an anecdote as a resurrection."

I frowned at the man. "Please assure me, Mr. Boyle, that you will strive to correct future versions of this tale. I tell you that the boy still had a pulse when I reached him."

He raised his hands in mock defense. "Of course, Doctor, of course." His expression suddenly changed. "Ah, in the excitement, I almost forgot to tell you. A messenger came over the hill to let you know that your brother has secured a few hours of leave, and intends to pay you a visit this evening."

I smiled broadly at this welcome news, and even more at the peculiar plate of food he set before me, whose outlandish appearance helped drive all distracting thoughts from my brain. It was an oblong roll consisting of charred bread, presumably wrapped around some inner filling. Mr. Boyle finally explained that it was filled with a stewed lamb and was known as a *roti*. He had learned the trick of it from a visiting trader from the island of Grenada in the southern Caribbean. I soon found that it possessed an excellent flavor and subsequently devoured my luncheon with a ravenous gusto. This was all washed down with an admirable Beaune, which proved to have hailed from the *Clos des Ursules* vineyard some dozen years prior. However, my morning exertions had proved to be too much for my weakened constitution, and after lunch I was too tired to even begin to contemplate returning to the afternoon heat outside. Instead, I repaired to the soothing cool of my room and stretched out upon the bed, endeavoring to get a couple of hours' rest. At first it seemed a useless attempt. My mind had been much excited by all that had occurred. Every time that I closed my eyelids, I saw before me a vision of a woman's freckled face capped with lustrous red hair. I felt as if her green eyes penetrated to my soul. I would not be boasting if I claimed an experience of women which extends over many nations and three separate continents. And yet, none have left me as confused as the fascinating Madame Lucy Dubois.

§

CHAPTER VII:
PIERCING THE VEIL

I awoke from my rest feeling exceptionally relaxed. For a moment, I could not feel any pain coming from either my shoulder or ankle and I luxuriated in that glorious sensation. Then I moved, and the reality of my wounds came crashing down upon me. Glancing at the clock, I realized that I had nodded off for several hours and that Henry would likely be calling soon for supper. I changed back into one of my service uniforms, setting my seawater-stained suit out for a cleaning. I then made my walk back downstairs, barely noticing the creaking step, through the fortuitously-deserted dining room and into the billiard room. In order to glean additional funds when the number of overnight travelers was low, Mrs. Foster opened the ground floor of her establishment as a sort of restaurant and gentleman's club. As a woman herself, she was not neglectful of the gentler sex, and a ladies' parlor also opened off the dining room, though I had not yet attempted to penetrate that lair. Instead, I hobbled up to the bar in the billiard room, where I found Mr. Boyle polishing glasses.

"What can I do you for, Doctor?" he inquired, solicitously.

"No sign of my brother yet?"

"No sir, though I reckon he'll be by soon. Care for a drink while you wait?"

I nodded. "I think that would be just fine."

"Another whisky and soda?"

"Do you have anything more unique to the island? Constable Dunkley was telling me about something called 'Bibbey,' I believe."

Boyle looked aghast. "This is a reputable establishment, Doctor! Bibbey is a swill served from the back of someone's carriage house." Then the man got a curious shine in his eyes. "Ah, but if you want something unique, I may have just the thing for you." He reached under the bar and brought out a small white bottle, and then grabbed a small stemmed glass with his other hand. Twisting off the cap, he poured a small amount of a clear liqueur into the glass. Sliding it over to me, he said, "Give that a try, Doctor."

I picked it up and sipped a small amount of the strange smelling drink. A hint of bitter oranges washed down my throat. "What is it?"

"It's called curaçao. It's made in the Dutch Antilles, and I have a sailing man that brings me a few bottles from time to time."

I tried another sip, and decided that I liked it. "Well, it is certainly exotic." But I was spared any further thought on the subject by the arrival of my brother through the side door of the hotel.

"Ham!" he called out.

I rose to greet him, and was surprised to find that he was not alone. He was accompanied by both another army officer, as well as a white-and-tan bull-pup. The man was tall, with a spare frame and a middle-height. He appeared about my age, placing him a few years behind Henry. This fit with the lieutenant bars on his uniform, which I recognized as having the same facings as Henry's 99th Regiment. His blond hair was rather unruly, though this effect was tempered by his rubicund clean-shaven face, and he possessed curiously penetrating light blue eyes. He had a large smile on his face as he held out his hand. "William Thurston at your service, sir! It's a real pleasure to finally meet you, Doctor. Captain Henry has told me a great deal about your exploits and I am most eager to hear more of them for myself."

"I'm afraid there's not much to tell..." I began, before Henry interrupted.

"Now, don't be modest, brother. I did receive your letters after all. I expect a full report over drinks."

"All right," I laughed, "I will be properly boastful, I promise. But first tell me who this little guy is?" asked I, bending down to rub the bull-pup's head.

"Hah! I thought you might like him, Ham. He's our new regimental mascot after we had to recently put down the old bull terrier for uncontrollably freezing onto the ankles of strangers. But you must guess this guy's name."

I frowned. "How could I possibly guess the name of a dog, Henry? The possibilities must be nearly infinite."

"Not nearly so bad as that! I assure you that the name was not chosen at random."

I continued to frown. "If not at random, then you must have used some physical feature of the pup to guide your choice," I reasoned slowly.

"Spot on!" Thurston laughed.

I stared at the lop-eared pup, and he in turn obediently gazed back at me. He had a funny patch upon the top of his head that gave him an appearance of baldness, and this was further accentuated by tufts of white hair was stuck out by his ears. He also had a humorous tendency to lift one shaggy eyebrow higher than the other, which suggested that he was questioning you. Unbidden a name arose in my head, but I rejected it as being far too absurd. Henry, however, must have seen my expression change and motioned for me to speak.

"Well," I stammered, "I had a thought..."

"Out with it!" my brother commanded.

"I suppose he does look a bit like Gladstone..."

Both my brother and Thurston broke out into a gale of laughter at this pronouncement. Thurston proceeded to reach into his pocket and pull out a shilling, which he good-naturedly handed over to Henry. "You were right, sir!" he said, continuing to laugh. "First guess."

I was mildly shocked. "Henry, please do not tell me that you named your dog after the Prime Minister of England."

Continuing to laugh, Henry responded. "In all fairness, Ham, he wasn't the Prime Minister at the time. Disraeli was."

I shook my head at his inappropriate mirth. "And the bet?"

"Thurston did not believe me when I said that you would guess it in one try. But I had great faith in your powers of observation."

"One shilling is hardly great faith," said I, dryly.

He smiled. "One can never be too careful, brother."

With that sage pronouncement, we settled down at one of the dining room tables for dinner. Mrs. Foster appeared from the kitchen holding plates containing a type of fish. Setting them down in front of us, Henry exclaimed, "Rockfish maw! You have exceeded all my expectations, Mrs. Foster."

But the proprietress seemed immune to Henry's charms. "I'm glad you approve, Captain," she said briskly before vanishing again into the kitchen.

Henry did not seem to notice, so intent was he upon the plate in front of him. "We don't get food like this at the fort mess, eh, Thurston?" Sensing my unfamiliarly, he explained. "Rockfish is a type of grouper native to these waters. The stomach is stuffed with a dressing of forcemeat and simmered slowly upon the stove. Properly prepared, it can be a wonder."

I soon found that Henry was right with his praise. Our meal was a merry one. Once I had consumed enough of the fish, I realized that poor Gladstone had not partaken, and I filched a lump of sugar from the tea service to seal our alliance. He gave me a shrill whine of excitement, proving that he was a good-natured pup, and I smiled affectionately at him. "Perhaps he will prove to be as brave as Bobbie of the 66th Foot."

"Who is that, Doctor?" Thurston asked.

"Ah, the regimental dog of the brigade I was attached to at Maiwand. She was present at the final stand of the Eleven, and escaped wounded to Candahar. The few survivors of the regiment were returned to England, where Bobbie was presented a campaign medal by the Queen herself."

"That's a great story, Ham," my brother said. "Now that you've done so well with the dog, tell me whom Thurston looks like."

I studied him for a moment, and then I knew whom Henry was thinking of. "Mr. Hilton Soames, our old instructor at Winchester!"

"Exactly!" my brother laughed. "You really are sharp today. Thurston does look exactly like a younger version of old Soames, though of course, the lieutenant here has a much less nervous and excitable temperament."

"I would hope so!" I said fervently.

"Whatever happened to good old Soames?" Henry asked me.

I shrugged. "Last I heard he had moved up in the world from a boy's public school. He became a tutor and lecturer at the College of St. Luke's, Oxford. But what about you, lieutenant?" said I, changing the topic. "Where are you from?"

Thurston shrugged modestly. "There's not too much to tell. I am from Horsham in Sussex originally. My family has a small estate there, near where Percy Bysshe Shelley was born. My elder brother was due to inherit, so after finishing my schooling I decided to join up. I trained at Woolwich Arsenal, and was then attached to the 99th, in order to replace losses suffered in South Africa. As a reward for their service, the 99th was stationed here in Bermuda, but I'm afraid that it's rather dull for me, since I've never had the opportunity to see any action."

"Be careful what you wish for, Lieutenant. It may come true," I cautioned him. "A battle may seem like a glamorous thing until you actually see your friends' bloody entrails spilled on the dusty ground, hear their last shrieking cries of pain, or feel the bite of hot lead entering your body."

My brother cut off my tale of horror. "Come now, Ham, don't scare the lad. If you do not wish speak of Maiwand, at least regale us with an anecdote of adventure. Surely something interesting must have occurred as you traipsed across the Indian subcontinent?"

I nodded and smiled at the image that immediately entered my mind. "Well, there was one night worthy of a recounting. After I arrived in India, I discovered that my corps had proceeded without me. With a group of fellow officers in the same situation, we followed in their footsteps through the mountain passes. I was often of the habit of staying up later than my companions, so that after most of the lights of our camp had been extinguished, I could enjoy the incredible views of the stars in the thin mountain air. On one of those nights, I lay awake in my tent, my mind racing with thoughts that I wanted to set down upon paper, but could not seem to bring to order. By this time it was the dead of night, and the camp was utterly quiet. Imagine my surprise when the flap of my tent was slowly pulled back. My first thought was that some native must have slipped past the watchful eyes of the pickets in order to avail himself of some easy-to-carry loot. By that notion was quickly disabused when I plainly heard the sound of a low growl emanating from my intruder. In a flash, I reached out for my double-barreled musket, which I always kept immediately next to my roll. I lifted it and fired as quickly as possible, so as to avoid becoming the meal for some great beast. Obviously, the blast awoke the entire camp, who rushed to my tent to find out the meaning of the uproar. As lamps were lit and the excitement died down, a survey of the ground in front of my tent was undertaken. To my chagrin, there was no animal sprawled out there, and at first I was accused of startling at shadows, like a neophyte subaltern on his first campaign. Although the commotion of the milling soldiers had obliterated most tracks, finally a paw-print was located, which served to exonerate me from such charges. However, one older man, who was widely known as a great hunter, proclaimed that the reason why my musket failed to take down the beast was not in fact due to my poor aim. Or rather, it was because I aimed far too high for the beast in question. My shot likely 'would have taken down a full-grown tiger,' he declared, 'but not the little cub that had left that tiny print!'"

My brother and Thurston laughed uncontrollably at my moving tale. "That will teach the little beast not to look for snacks in the midst of a British Army camp!" Henry declared. "Though I suspect that he was more interested in your rations than your side."

Thurston nodded agreeably. "No harm done then, Doctor."

"No harm, sir?" said I, with mock crossness. "Tell that to my poor shredded tent flap! Fortunately, my skill in sewing up the wounds of men translates well into the repair of canvas or I would have had a drafty tent for many months."

By the time my reminiscence was finished, Mr. Boyle had returned in order to clear our plates and to fill our glasses from a fine bottle of Imperial Tokay. We then pulled out our pipes.

"Are you still smoking your Arcadia mixture?" Henry asked me.

"No," I replied. "I've gotten in the habit of smoking 'ships.'"

"That naval tobacco?" Henry scoffed. "It's hardly pure. It has traces of cocoa in it!"

"I know, but I ran out of the Arcadia on my way to Bombay, and it was all the sailors had to loan me."

"You'll kick that foul habit soon, I expect," Henry proclaimed. "Father always said that nothing beat Arcadia."

I nodded sadly at the thought of our departed father. "True enough. Have you any word from the authorities in Melbourne?" I inquired, changing the topic to our father's recent passing.

"Yes, they assured me that he was laid to rest with honor and forwarded on to me the most personal of his possessions and his accumulated wealth, which was unfortunately scant. I do, however, have his watch here." He reached into his coat pockets and pulled out a gold pocket watch, handing it to me.

I stared at the object in my hand. On the surface, it appeared like nothing so much as a fine fifty-guinea piece of jewelry, dated 1844, its pristine case recently cleaned. But as I turned it over, I ran my fingers over the 'H.W.' carved into the back, and felt an immediate connection with my father. For a moment, I could picture the watch as it once lay comfortably in his strong hand, and it was as if that watch was a direct link to the tangible past.

My brother must have seen the expression on my face. "Keep it, Ham," said he, kindly.

I shook my head and handed it back to him. "No, we keep with tradition. It must go to the eldest son."

He took it back with some reservation and slipped it back into his coat pocket, where I heard it clink against some coins or keys. "I will see that you get it someday."

I shook my head again. "It should go to your son."

Henry laughed. "Ah, I doubt that I will be so fortunate! Even if I survive all that the British Army throws at me, I've never been much inclined to take a wife. No, you may still inherit father's watch yet, Ham."

Thurston suddenly slammed down his glass upon the table. "What do you say to a round of billiards, Doctor?"

I shook my head. "I've not much skill at that. Especially now, with my left arm so stiff."

"Practice makes perfect, Doctor, practice makes perfect. Come now, just a game between gentlemen for pure sport. No money involved."

Henry seemed affronted by this suggestion. "Where is the fun in that, Thurston? My brother is not so poor that he cannot afford a small wager. Come, Ham, you must still hold a few of the Queen's shillings?"

I reluctantly agreed. "But unless Henry plans to sit out, we will need a fourth."

We glanced around the dining room. By this time, most of my fellow lodgers had already finished their suppers and had retired. To be honest, I had taken little note of them, so engaged was I in the conversation with my brother and Thurston. I was pleased to note that I was completely unaware whether Madame Dubois had even entered the dining room that night.

"Well, those two appear too thick in discussion to be bothered," Henry noted, indicating the pair of swarthy fellows that I recalled from my breakfast the previous morn.

"And I cannot say that I like the look of that one," Thurston pointed to the bilious man, who sat alone in the darkest corner of the room. In fact, I had yet to see that remarkable individual conversing with anyone. A solitary creature indeed!

"Then, here's our man," I said as the man with the languorous eyes entered the room. I stood up as he passed by our table to draw his attention. "Sir, it is a pleasure to meet you," said I, introducing myself.

A smile cracked his Latinate face, and his manner was effusive. "Good evening, Doctor. I am Dario Aicardi." I noted again that his English was touched with a slight lisp, confirming his foreign origin.

"Where are you from, Signore Aicardi?"

"Milano. I am a painter, and have come to Bermuda in order to capture the exquisite light as it reflects off the brightly colored buildings. Where else can you find such unique structures, all capped in white, like the dwellings of Paradise?"

"Indeed," I agreed with him. "And do you play billiards, Signore? We find ourselves in need of a fourth." I introduced my brother and Thurston.

"I would be honored to join you gentlemen," said he, agreeably.

The four of us repaired from the dining room to the adjoining billiard room, where Mr. Boyle was manning the bar. I paired with my brother against Aicardi and Thurston, hoping that my brother's skills would hide my shortcomings, both in terms of experience as well as agility.

"Let me remind everyone of the rules," Thurston announced as he took up one of the cues. "There are three balls, two cues in white, and one object in red. A winning hazard is potting the object ball, worth three points, or the opposing team's cue for two points. A losing hazard is potting one's own cue. Two-ball cannons are scored if you strike both the object ball and the opponent's cue ball on the same shot. Each person shall take two shots per game. High score wins the game. First team to three games takes all. Shall we call it three shillings each for the pot?"

We all agreed on the wager and began. Henry took the first shot and softly reminded me of the tricks of the game. "Don't forget to put chalk between your left forefinger and thumb to steady the cue."

Thurston overhead this and commented upon Henry's tip. "I myself have gotten into the habit of wearing gloves while playing billiards to prevent getting chalk upon my hands."

With this congenial banter, the games passed rapidly. Although I like to think that I held my own, especially considering the state of my left arm, Henry and I eventually fell two games to three to Thurston and Aicardi, as the latter proved to possess a deadly accuracy.

After the Italian had scored a two-ball cannon that won the final game, he graciously took his leave of our trio. Henry then indicated that it was time for him and Thurston to return to the fort. Henry picked up the faithful pup Gladstone, who had sat quietly through our games, but now whined in mild distress.

"It has been a great pleasure to meet you, Doctor," Thurston said.

"And you as well, Lieutenant. What are your plans?"

"I expect that I will be in the 99th for some time. My father believes that I need to prove my mettle, and if so, then I will be fit to inherit from my mother's brother, when he finally shuffles off that mortal coil. Once that happens, I will be free to get my discharge papers and return to London. I plan to invest my inheritance in some property, perhaps in South Africa now that the war is over there, and live the life of a gentleman. You will then find me at the United Service Club on Pall Mall. It's a wonderful place. In the upper billiard-room there is a magnificent painting of the Battle of Trafalgar, the frame of which was made of wood from the timbers of the *Victory*. Please drop by and see me, Doctor."

"It does sound quite pleasant," I granted. "I will plan to take you up on your handsome offer."

"Excellent!" he replied, shaking my hand enthusiastically.

I turned to Henry. "I hope to see you again soon, brother."

"Count upon it, Ham," said he, warmly.

With that exchange the two men and Gladstone exited the hotel. I watched them through the window for a moment and then turned into the dining room, intending to retire to my room after a long and pleasant, but less-than-restful, day. As I strode through the room towards the stairs, I noted that the Mediterranean-appearing gentlemen had vanished, and for a moment I thought the room deserted. Then I heard the strike of a wax vesta. Looking over into the dark corner, I spied the bilious man lighting a small cheroot. Soon a plume of blue smoke curled up from him.

He noted me looking at him, and suddenly addressed me. "Would you care for a glass of port, Doctor?" There was a trace of an accent upon his words, but I could not immediately place it.

Not wanting to appear rude, I agreed, though my instincts suggested that I should steer clear of this sinister-appearing man. Time had not improved his appearance, and he wore the same grey flannel suit that I recalled from the previous morn, only more rumpled. He took off his tinted glasses to peer at me and I swore that his eyes shone with a sinister light.

"I am afraid that you have me at a disadvantage, sir. How did you know that I was a physician?"

"I have ears, Doctor. And I use them."

I licked my lips, strangely nervous. "I see."

"Boyle!" the man suddenly called out, the cheroot still clamped between his curiously animal teeth. "A glass and some port!"

The innkeeper's assistant promptly appeared with a sparkling glass and a bottle of Warre's port from 1870, which he set down gingerly in front of me. "As you wish, Mister Dumas," said he, quickly backing away.

Dumas, as he was apparently named, unstopped the port and poured me a bumper. I sipped some and found it quite good, but noticed that he was not drinking.

"Dumas, no relation to the author?" I finally inquired.

"No," he replied, monosyllabically, shooting a suspicious look at me. He stared me in the eyes for a moment, and then finally asked. "Where did you say that you served, Doctor?"

"Afghanistan," replied I, with equal brevity.

"What unit?"

"The Fifth Northumberland Fusiliers."

"Did you see action?"

"Maiwand."

"A great conflict..."

But I interrupted him. "And you, sir? What do you do?"

"I am an investor."

"What do you invest in?"

"Investments," said he, tersely.

A feeling of revulsion, and something akin to fear, had begun to rise within me at the strange responses of this jaundiced man. I had heard enough of his speech to definitively determine that he was French, but I became impatient with his game, and rose to leave. "Thank you for the drink, Monsieur."

"Sit down, Doctor," said he, sharply. "I need a professional consultation about two matters."

My natural curiosity was now raised, and I reluctantly lowered myself back into the seat. "Certainly, sir. However I may be of service. What is the first matter?"

"What is your opinion about spiritualism?"

"Spiritualism?" I replied slowly, thinking about the subject. "Piercing the veil between life and death."

"Exactly!"

"That is the realm of charlatans, not men of science such as myself. I thought you were going to consult me regarding a medical condition?"

"And what if I told you that I had proof?"

"Proof of what, sir?"

"The spirits calling to us from beyond the veil that shrouds death. Tell me, Doctor, have you heard of automatic writing?"

"The process by which a writer produces words without a conscious awareness of what he or she is writing?"

"Indeed. I believe it is the work of spirits taking control of the medium's hand."

"Frauds," I scoffed.

"And if they were to write something that they could not possibly know of?"

"Clever frauds," I countered.

"I tell you, Doctor, that I visited a medium in New York who wrote something that only one living being – me! – knows."

"And why did you visit this medium in the first place?" I inquired.

"That is not relevant to the discussion at hand," he snapped.

"I still would suspect that you are the victim of fraud."

"This is not a fraud, Doctor," the man said, morosely. "I am being stalked by a ghost."

"Stalked? How so?"

"He is trying to poison me!"

I was astonished. "Why would you think that?"

"Every drink that I am served smells of bitter almonds."

I stared, aghast, at my partially-drunk glass of port. He noted my alarm. "Do not fear, Doctor. I am not drinking, hence you are safe. I do not drink anything that I have not personally inspected."

"I see..." said I, though I plainly did not. "I am afraid that I fail to understand how I can assist you."

"Although I control my intake of liquids carefully, I still require sustenance. And that is much more difficult to monitor. So, I ask if you are an authority on the assorted poisons used by mankind?"

"I have the ordinary knowledge of the educated medical man," I replied, with some stiffness. "Do you wish me to provide you with an antidote to Prussic Acid? I have heard that you can inhale the vapors of crushed amyl nitrate pearls..."

"Bah," he scowled, waving me off but becoming quite garrulous in his angered state. "I know all about the pearls. I go nowhere without them. No, I fear that my ghost is far too clever for that. He must know by now that I am prepared for cyanide. He was widely traveled. What if he recalls the properties of strychnine or worse, of aqua tofana? It is odorless and tasteless. How will I see it coming?"

"You cannot, sir, unless you measure everything you ingest with the Marsh test, which is not a very practical solution. Nor is there a reliable anecdote to arsenic, though I have heard that garlic may provide some protection."

"Yes, yes," said Dumas, irritably. "I know of all this. But I have devised a better solution to countering the effects of the '*poudre de succession.*' Tell me, Doctor, do you not sometime use arsenic to treat your patients?"

"Of course," remarked I, with some coldness, for I was repelled by his suggestion which appeared to imply that physicians were no different than poisoners. "Fowler's solution is an important part of the treatment of malaria and other personal problems that a gentleman may sometimes acquire."

"But here is my question for you, Doctor. Does it always work?"

"Of course not. While the science of medicine progresses every year, it is still very much an imperfect art. Some fail to respond."

"And do not some respond for a time, and then fail?"

"Yes," I agreed, cautiously.

"Why?" inquired he, pointedly.

I thought about this for a moment. "I suppose their ailment must grow resistant to the dose."

"Exactly!" said Dumas excitedly. "And if the body can become resistant to a small dose of arsenic, can it not then tolerate a larger dose?"

"Ah," said I, finally understanding where the discussion was headed, "you speak of Mithridatism. Of course that tactic eventually proven unsuccessful for Mithridates, the King of Pontus, who having been defeated by Pompey, tried to commit suicide using poison but failed because of his built-up immunity, and so had to resort to having a mercenary run him through with his sword."

Half of Dumas' mouth curled up with a cruel grin. "Do not fear, Doctor. I have no plans of running myself through. What I wish to know is what dose to begin with, and how rapidly to escalate?"

"I am afraid that I do not have that knowledge readily available. My instructors at Netley must not have felt it was a matter that would arise frequently upon campaign," said I dryly.

He seemed oblivious to my attempted humor. "Can you find it in the literature of toxicology?" said the man, anxiously.

"Yes, I am certain I could, if the local hospital is sufficiently supplied with the necessary texts, though it would take a few days."

"The sooner the better, Doctor. I will pay you well. I wish to embark on the program at once, before he learns a new tactic."

I licked my lips, suddenly nervous. "There is one thing that I do not understand. If it is truly a ghost that plagues you, why does he use poison? Does he not have more supernatural tactics at his disposal?"

He stared at me unhappily. "You mock me, sir. You do not have to believe in order to aid me. What of your Hippocratic Oath?"

"I did not say that I would not assist you, Monsieur Dumas. But perhaps it would help me to understand if I knew why this ghost tormented you so?"

Dumas suddenly rose from his seat, his face turning livid with fear and his yellow eyes blazing with fury. He violently waved his cane in my face. "That is none of your damned business!" And with no other words of leave-taking, he stormed out of the room and up the creaking stairs, leaving me sitting alone in the darkening dining room. There goes a man in mortal dread of something or somebody, I thought. Despite the lingering heat of the day, for a moment I thought I felt a cold breeze pass through the room which sent a brief chill right down my back. After my long, strange day, I could almost imagine that the tales of ghosts and devils upon this isle were all too real.

§

CHAPTER VIII:
THE DARKENING SKY

After the excitements of the day, I retired to my chambers with a glass of warm milk and a biscuit to try to calm my overwrought nerves. I was quickly between the sheets with every intention of indulging my laziness and sleeping to a late hour. Shaking off the lurid imaginings of Monsieur Dumas, I quickly found myself in dreamland, where the sweet face of Lucy Dubois seemed to look down upon me. However, these fond visions were soon dashed by the rise of a fierce howling wind. This awoke me on multiple occasions throughout the night as it rattled the shutters that protected the glass panes of my windows. After tossing restlessly, eventually I gave up hope of sleep and rose to peer out of the window that looked down into the side garden. I noted that the morning was so wild that the leaves were being stripped from the tree that graced that yard. I heard no other sounds emanating from the other parts of the hotel. Glancing at my pocket watch, I found that it was but a few minutes after six o'clock, and it was little wonder that no one else was stirring on this foul day.

Both my shoulder and ankle throbbed mercilessly, and I knew that it was futile to consider going back to sleep. Unfortunately, I had no willow bark extract in my kit, and thus little hope of dulling the persistent pain brought on by this sudden turn in the weather. I listlessly lay back down upon the bed for a few minutes more and watched the tepid pale light slowly filter through the shutters. I wondered lazily what Lucy was doing at that very moment. Was she thinking of me? I tried to banish the distressing thought that she might be locked in the embrace of her husband. Eventually, I rose for good and dressed deliberately. I shaved at an even more turgid pace, slowed by the pain in my shoulder, which made it very difficult to raise my arm across my face. I decided not to add more light in order to inspect my handiwork, as I suspected that it would leave me less than satisfied. I descended to breakfast in somewhat of a depressed spirit, for today I found myself easily impressed by my decidedly tempestuous surroundings.

On the contrary, I soon found that some of my dining companions appeared affected by a particularly bright and joyous mood, which I found somewhat sinister given the nature of the day. Although by this time, I had met all of that morning's dining room occupants, namely Mr. Sims, Signore Aicardi, Senhor Cordeiro, and Dr. Nemcek, I decided to take a solitary table for myself. Mr. Boyle came over to inquire what I wished to eat, and this time, I brusquely refused anything adventurous. I asked for two plain hard-boiled eggs, lightly salted, and some toast to go with my coffee.

It was at that moment that Monsieur and Madame Dubois entered the room. Fortunately, they took a table as far from me as possible, and I desperately interested myself in that morning's *Royal Gazette*. I did everything in my power to avoid looking into her entrancing eyes, though at times, I seemed to feel them lingering upon me. Although with some force of will I could just barely avoid her lovely face falling into the range of my vision, taking away that sense only seemed to make the others more acute. I fancied that I could smell her frangipani perfume from across the room. And I could certainly hear the lilt of her melodious voice as she ordered a simple breakfast that maddingly mirrored my own. Her husband on the other hand, futilely attempted to order a type of cake that he termed a 'waffle.' Unfortunately for him, neither Mr. Boyle, nor the summoned Mrs. Foster, admitted to knowing how to create such a substance. She offered to make a crepe instead, which he coolly rebuffed, finally settling for Mr. Boyle's suggestion of a Bermudian breakfast. I suspected that he little knew exactly what that meant and I devoutly wished that I dared to raise my eyes to witness the look upon his face when it arrived.

Mr. Boyle finally turned his full attention upon me, thereby distracting me from what was taking place at the Dubois' table. "What did you have in store for today, Doctor?"

I shook my head. "I'm not certain, Mr. Boyle. What does the barometer read?"

"Well," he said, thoughtfully. "The glass is reading twenty-seven, and the mercury is falling. I suspect that it will turn to rain very soon."

I rubbed my throbbing shoulder. "So, just a usual storm then?"

Boyle pursed his lips. "Well, now that you mention it, Doctor, the shark's oil suggests that we may be in for a bit of a blow before the day is done."

I frowned at his near-incomprehensible speech. "Shark's oil? A 'blow?' I am afraid that I am not following you, Mr. Boyle."

"Ah, you see, if you catch a puppy shark between June and September during either a full or waning moon, you can cut out its liver and hang it in the sun. This draws out the oil, which is then collected in a sealed bottle. If you hang it outside, you can rightly see if a blow is coming or not. On a fair day, such as yesterday, the oil is as clear as the sky. But it turns cloudy when stormy weather is on its way."

"And today?" I prompted him.

"It's as white as milk."

"Which portends?"

"A hurricane!"

I was dumbfounded. "Are you serious, Mr. Boyle? Is it not too late for hurricane season?"

"Well, you are correct, Doctor, that most hurricanes occur from August to October. But in some years we have seen them as early as the first of June, and as late as the end of November. This autumn has been a very stormy one, and there has been a long succession of northerly gales."

"If that is the case, then how do ships know when to sail?"

"Then don't always. Just last year the steamer *Lartington* went down on the reefs northwest of Dockyard. An unfortunate accident, though all survived."

"Aren't they all unfortunate accidents?" I inquired.

"Well, nowadays, that is probably the case, thanks to the lighthouse on Gibbs Hill, which has really curtailed the activities of the wreckers."

"Wreckers?"

"Aye," he nodded, cleverly. "You see, Doctor, in days past, some of the inhabitants of our more remote parishes, such as Sandys and Southampton, used to engage in a rather illicit trade. They would wait until the night of a strong storm, and then descend to a point along the coast where the offshore reefs were thickest. A mule would be driven back-and-forth along the beach with a lantern tied around its neck. The up-and-down motion of the light resembled that of a wave-tossed vessel and would lead unsuspecting mariners to think that they were further from shore than the actual situation. The following morn, the gang of wreckers would head out in their small boats to the reef-caught vessel and strip it clean of all its valuables."

"That is terrible!" I protested.

"Aye, though as I said, it's a bit of a historical curiosity at this point, most of the wreckers having gone legitimate, as the lighthouse on Gibbs Hill gave the lie to their deception."

Just then, a particularly strong gust of wind rattled the windows. I turned to look outside, where the day continued to be wild and tempestuous, with the wind screaming past the hotel and the rain starting to fall. A single cab was splashing its way down Duke of York Street, but the town otherwise seemed deserted. I was heartily glad of the fire blazing behind the grill, as it brought a measure of comfort to the room which contrasted strongly with the weather outdoors.

When I turned back, Boyle had wandered off, but his place had been taken by Mrs. Foster. She looked at me sagaciously. "It's not much of a day for venturing outside. Perhaps you should rest yourself in one of my easy chairs in the billiards room, Doctor? The hotel has a nice selection of books that you might be interested in. We can put a pillow beneath your leg..."

After another glance at the darkening sky, the wind whistling shrilly down the long street, her words seemed wise. I had no mackintosh, and did not wish to become soaked. Furthermore, I had experienced plenty of adventure on my jaunt around town the day prior. I therefore gave in to my inherent languor and curled up in the recesses of the billiard-room's velvet-lined armchair, but not until after selecting another novel from her small collection.

On the *Malabar*, as well as during my recuperation in the base hospital, I had abundant time to read, but my sociable nature often led me to seek out either good conversation or games of chance with my fellow soldiers. Here in the Globe Hotel, with Henry rather unlikely to visit today, I was surrounded by strangers from every land, none of whom were soldiers, and my inclination for conversation was limited. Therefore, I delved deeply into the pages of my new novel, *The Mystery of Edwin Drood*, by the late Mr. Charles Dickens, which was more than sufficient to absorb all of my attention for the next several hours.

Although I was vaguely aware of hearing the rain pattering against the windows, the next thing that I was clearly conscious of was Mrs. Foster delivering a pot of tea in a Derby china set. "What happened to the luncheon?" I inquired.

"You missed it, Doctor," she explained. "I tried to catch your attention, but you were too engrossed in your book. It is now already four o'clock. If you go any longer, it will be time for high tea!"

I shook my head in amazement. "No wonder I feel so ravenous!"

"Well, only some sandwiches for you now. I'll be fixing up some amberjack for supper, which you will not want to miss."

As she excused herself, I finally rose from my armchair. Although the rest had likely performed long-term wonders for my wounds, the period of immobility stiffened my ankle, and it was with a pronounced limp that I walked over to the window to look through the blurred panes onto the deserted street. Outside the wind howled, and the rain beat fiercely against the shutters. Given the lack of street lamps on the island, with every building shuttered tight, nothing illuminated the muddy road. Even clad in the thickest of overcoats, galoshes, and every other aid that mankind has invented to fight the weather, only a madman would dare brave the elements on this night. Certainly, I have lived through my fair share of mighty storms, some so powerful that it seemed as if great London itself was but one of the molehills that dot the fields before their awesome power. But here, perched on a small island, mere yards from the sea itself, I was most conscious of the huge elemental forces that comprised the iron grip of Nature.

I returned to my novel, but my concentration had been broken, and I was now constantly distracted by the ever-strengthening howls of the wind, which began to provoke eerie noises from the fireplace. Eventually, one by one my fellow travelers all descended to the bar in the billiard room, and I was forced to set aside Mr. Dickens so as to not appear rude. Although I was very eager to discover the identity of Drood's murderer, as fate would have it, many months would pass before I found the time to return to that novel. My eyes were immediately drawn to Lucy Dubois, who was enveloped in a black-sequined dinner-dress. Seldom have I seen so graceful a figure, so womanly a presence, and so beautiful a face. I tried to turn away, but I was acutely aware that whenever I, more than once, glanced in her direction found that she was looking at me with a great intensity.

"I think that weather like this calls for a drink," exclaimed Mr. Warburton, as he sidled up to the bar. "Where is Mr. Boyle?"

Mrs. Foster was not present, but we heard her voice emanate from the rear corridor. "He's gone home to ensure that his own house is properly boarded up."

I looked over at my previous vantage point, only to find that Mr. Boyle must have sealed all of the Globe's windows before he left. Until this storm spent its fury, we were essentially trapped in the hotel.

"Do you mind if I pour a few drinks then, Mrs. Foster?" Mr. Sims called out.

"Go right ahead," we heard her reply.

Sims thus took a place behind the bar and began to pour some gin and tonics.

Monsieur Dubois stopped Sims from making one for him. "Not for me, Bruce. I once had a terrible reaction to a gin and tonic. I broke out with these terrible purple spots all over my body."

"Ah, cocktail purpura," exclaimed Dr. Nemcek. "Wouldn't you agree,

Doctor," said he, turning to me.

"Absolutely," I concurred with his diagnosis.

"And what is that, Doctor?" asked Madame Dubois.

I forced myself not to stammer as I looked into her entrancing eyes. "You see, one of the great scourges of the British Empire is the pestilential malaria we find in India and so many other tropical areas. The medicinal quinine is an effective preventative so the medical board decided to add it to carbonated water. But the resulting tonic is rather bitter, and thus our soldiers began to add gin to make it more palatable. Unfortunately, rare people have an idiosyncratic reaction to the quinine, which causes great bruises, or purpura, to break out upon their skin. It's rather harmless, but not very attractive, and sufferers are counseled to avoid tonic water in the future."

"In that case, I recommend some rum, Hector," said Mr. Sims, pulling out a bottle. "This stuff appears locally made."

"Yes," said Senhor Cordeiro, the traveler in wines. "That, mate, is the famous Bermuda Black Seal rum. It is a particularly dark, full-bodied elixir which was originally found only in barrels, but enough people asked for smaller quantities that the makers decided to start bottling it. However, since new glass bottles are scarce on the island, they decided to salvage discarded champagne bottles from the officer's mess. After filling them with rum, the bottles are sealed with a black wax, hence the name."

"And for those of us that do not drink alcohol?" interjected the Spanish lady, whose name I had still not caught. Her tone was imperious, though I thought I detected a hint of nerves.

Dr. Nemcek spoke up. "In that case, I recommend a simple mixture of hot water and a lemon. It does wonders to warm the spirits on a night like this. I will ask Mrs. Foster to prepare you some."

The lady inclined her head gratefully as the Doctor slipped from the room. Monsieur Dumas also declined to drink and sat silently in one of the corners. After everyone else was settled with a drink, the conversation died down. With the lack of voices, the violent sounds of the storm were magnified as the wind screamed and rattled against the windows.

"Lucy, would you favor us with a song?" Signore Aicardi suddenly asked.

She initially demurred, but others joined in with their encouragements, and eventually her husband was dispatched to their room upstairs. He returned with a violin case, which Lucy opened and gently lifted the violin to her shoulder, pausing for a moment to think. She began by playing some low, dreamy melodious air, and for a moment it was as if the storm had vanished and I was floating peacefully upon a soft sea of sound. Eventually, she looked up and addressed the hushed crowd. "How about a

Song without Words?" she asked, rhetorically. Bending her chin to the rest, she raised the bow to the strings. As the tender notes began to permeate my brain, I recognized the work of Mendelssohn. Although I knew it had been written for the piano, she managed to transform it into a piece for the violin. I marveled at the talent that it took to accomplish this feat. As a rule, I had little enthusiasm for German music, for I found it too introspective. I generally prefer the grand music being made by the English composer Sullivan, or a good Scotch air. But this music was like a treat for the gods, a perfect blend of sweetness, delicacy, and harmony. As I sat there, enthralled by the beauty of both her playing and her face, a tumult of emotions struggled in my breast. I could scarcely credit the sentiments that I possessed for a married woman. While she played, she generally kept her eyes closed, but once she opened them and they thrillingly fixed upon me. For a moment, I thought that perhaps she sensed – and possibly shared – my feelings. But of course, an impassable barrier separated us.

The next several hours were a general blur. I vaguely recall that she played a moving rendition of what I later learned was Offenbach's new *Bacarolle,* and this was followed by some long-drawn, wailing notes that composed one of the most haunting of tunes I have ever heard. I never learned the name, nor have ever heard it again, but its sounds have never left my brain. I know that eventually supper was served, a brace of a local bird that tasted exactly like grouse, and washed down with a fine Château Lafite. Outside the storm continued to rage, with rain splashing and pattering against the boarded windows. Although I made light conversation with my companions, and learned the names of those few I had previously not met, my thoughts constantly turned to Lucy. More than once our eyes met across the room, and it was never hers that broke off that distant contact. I wish I knew what to make of her. At one point in time, I had considered the fair sex to be one of my areas of expertise, but I now knew that supposition to be a grand delusion.

Eventually Mrs. Foster had cleared the tables, and once again a lull settled upon the conversation. The great shrieking of the wind forced us to raise our minds for an instant from the routine of life, and to recognize the presence of those terrible raw forces which shriek at mankind through the bars of his civilization, like untamed beasts in a cage. These thoughts eventually drove most of the guests to retire to their rooms, including, to my relief, Monsieur and Madame Dubois. I would no longer be forced to gaze upon her comely face. But having spent most of the day in the arm-chair, I was little tired, and knew that the great noise of the storm would prevent me from falling asleep. I dreaded the idea of being alone in my room with only my thoughts of Lucy to torment me though the long night.

Thus I resolved to remain downstairs for as long as possible. Fortunately, three of my companions also showed no inclination to retire, and Senhor Cordeiro suggested a game of whist. I readily agreed, as did Mr. Sims. After a few moments hesitation, as if he suspected a trap at every turn, even in something as innocuous as a card game, the normally-taciturn Monsieur Dumas acquiesced to be the final member of the *partie carrée*.

Dumas proved to be a cautious but excellent partner and the game progressed to our advantage. My hand was constantly full of color cards, while Cordeiro seemed to draw nothing but the smallest of the small. In order to make it more interesting, we had determined in advance to allow a small gentleman's sum to ride on the outcome of the game, and it appeared likely that we would prove victorious after we achieved a small slam in two games running, so as to take the first rubber. At least an hour ticked by, with the team of Cordeiro and Sims steadily losing most tricks to the finesse of Dumas and I.

Dumas became steadily more talkative as his fortunes improved, though it would be an overstatement to call him garrulous. Of course, any English gentleman knows that it is strictly against the rules to comment on the cards you were dealt in any way. One should not remark about one's good fortune or bad fortune until the final score is tallied. But the misanthropic Dumas did not appear to understand such courtesies, and after one deal, he smiled cruelly. "When the other fellow has all the trumps, it saves time to throw down your hand."

"Hang it all!" swore Sims. "You have the most incredible luck, sir, while I've had a nasty facer! All this losing is making me thirsty. I need another drink." He began to rise.

"We cannot keep raiding Mrs. Foster's bottles," pointed out Senhor Cordeiro.

Sims paused. "Damn again! You are right. But I know just the solution. I have the perfect bottle for a night like this in my room."

"As do I," Cordeiro rejoined. "This storm seems like it could be another Deluge. And if the world is about to end, I will not let this bottle go to waste!"

Realizing that another drink would perhaps be nice before trying to retire to the solitude of my thoughts, I spoke up. "Perhaps you gentlemen could both collect your bottles and Monsieur Dumas and I will decide which one is the superior?"

Sims smiled. "Good idea, Doctor."

Sims bounded up the stairs, while Senhor Cordeiro passed into his room on the ground floor. Dumas and I remained at the table, unable to contribute anything to the competition. Dumas had relapsed into a moody silence. The man's unforthcoming nature precluded any attempts at conversation, and he appeared content to silently smoke his cheroot while awaiting their return. The wild night had not abated. The wind was still howling outside, and the rain was beating and splashing against the windows. At times I felt as if the building itself was going to blow down. Seldom have I found my temperament so affected by my environs, but my surmise is that even a man with nerves of steel would have been shaken by that terrible night. My companion, his reticence to speak making him seem like nothing so much as a giant carrion crow, was not lightening the mood of the room. Fortunately, it was not long before Sims and Cordeiro were back.

Senhor Cordeiro was the first to present his bottle, which had a curiously rounded bottom and was protected by a wicker-like coating. "This is the finest bottle of my collection, which is, as a whole, absolutely first-rate. This is a Bual Madeira from 1789. As you may know, the wines of Madeira are unique in all the world. Since our islands were a regular port-of-call of ships travelling to the East Indies, we were often required to supply these ships with casks of wine. But the earliest ones had an unfortunate tendency to spoil at sea. And so, we began to add a small amount of distilled cane sugar alcohol in order to stabilize the wines. After a long, hot, rocking sea voyage, the wine would transform into something different, something special. However, sailing casks of wine solely for the purpose of heating and aging is a costly venture. Therefore, nowadays most Madeira wine is made by storing the wine in a special room, which we call an *estufa*, where the natural heat of the island's intense sunlight produces, over a period of several years, a similar effect. But very rarely, you can still find a bottle made in the old fashion, *a vinho da roda*, a wine that has made a trip round the globe. And it is truly magical. This is what I propose that we drink tonight." He puffed his chest proudly, with the air of a true *bon vivant*.

I was highly impressed and doubted that Mr. Sims's wine could match such an impressive pedigree. Nevertheless, Sims looked confident as he held up his slightly dusty amber-colored bottle. "I cannot claim to come from a land that makes such magnificent wines, though I would say that my countrymen are starting to change that. But what I propose to drink tonight is not from Australia; rather it is from the home of great wines – France. Some might call this a claret, but do not mistake this for some of the cheap raisin-wines exported by one of the *fraudeurs* of Marseilles now that the vineyards of Bordeaux have been devastated by the *phylloxera* plague. This wine may not be as quite as old as Antonio's, but the grapes were picked in 1811 in one of the greatest of the *premier cru* vineyards, Chateau d'Yquem. And 1811 was not just another year for Bordeaux wines. For that year the Great Comet Flaugergues passed overhead!"

At this mysterious pronouncement, Senhor Cordeiro audibly grunted in surprise.

"Yes," Sims continued, "this is a comet vintage from the greatest Sauternes vineyard in the world. The comet's passage transformed what is normally a splendid wine into something wonderfully robust, something exceptional. I won two bottles of this extraordinary wine in a bet with a good friend. One bottle I drank with him, as a consolation for his loss. The other I have carried with me on my travels, always wondering when something momentous enough would occur to justify opening it. I suspect that the end of the world, or at least our deaths in this hurricane, would suffice."

I was flabbergasted. "Gentlemen, how do you expect me to choose? It would be like choosing between Homer and Shakespeare! They are both magnificent bottles, and I would be greatly honored to drink either with you."

If the fourth person at our table was equally impressed, he certainly did a masterful job of concealing it. Dumas studied the bottles, and the men holding them, carefully. Finally, he broke his silence. "I generally do not drink with strangers."

Sims looked as affronted as I felt. "What are you suggesting, sir? You are happy to play cards with us and take our money, but you are not willing to drink my wine? So be it then! More for us!"

Dumas weathered this verbal assault impassively. "You misunderstand me, Mr. Sims. As long as you fine gentlemen are prepared to drink before me, I will try your wine. It is, as you say, an exceptional vintage from the only land that can make wine."

As I said this, I recalled the previous night's conversation about poisons, and understood the reason, however unjustifiably paranoid, for his rudeness. On the other hand, Senhor Cordeiro stiffened at this pronouncement. "Perhaps I misunderstood you, sir?"

Dumas turned his vulture-like stare upon the Portuguese gentleman. "No, I think not. What you hold there is not wine. It is fortified pig swill. I would rather drink piss."

Cordeiro turned white with chagrin and surprise. For a moment, I thought that Cordeiro was going to leap across the table and strike the Frenchman. But finally he restrained his temper. "This is intolerable, sir! I came here to share with you a treasure, not to be insulted as if I were a beggar." He turned to Sims and I. "Good night, Mr. Sims, Doctor," said he, with a clenched jaw. "Enjoy your wine. But I will not share a glass with that foul brute." He turned and strode off to his ground floor room.

Dumas mutely watched him go, while the pleas of Mr. Sims and I went unheeded. Finally, Dumas turned to Sims and nodded to the bottle in his hand. "Well, are we going to drink it?" said he, imperturbably.

From the interplay of emotions across his face, Sims appeared to be considering a withdrawal of his generous offer due to Dumas' discourteous behavior, but he apparently decided to remain polite. "Of course," he finally said, "let me find a corkscrew."

When Sims returned it was with Mrs. Foster in tow. She plainly was frazzled and harried by the absence of Mr. Boyle on this tumultuous night, but she bore it well. She produced a corkscrew from a pocket in her apron. "I only keep one in the house, and that one on my person, so as to ensure that I know exactly which of my bottles is being opened," she explained.

"This one did not come from your cellar, Mrs. Foster, but you are welcome to enjoy it with us," said Sims, handing it to her.

Mrs. Foster inspected the dusty bottle and nodded her head gratefully. "This is no common vintage, sir. Perhaps I will try some, but only a sip. I must keep my wits about me, in case the storm worsens." She went to work upon the cork, and when she drew it out, it was long and deeply stained. She first poured it into a decanter, and the golden liquid that issued forth briefly seemed to brighten the room.

Sims had collected four glasses from the bar, and Mrs. Foster poured a generous amount into three of them, and then a dram into her glass. Each one contained a small amount of beeswing. Sims picked up his glass and looked at the three of us. "Gentlemen, and a Lady of course, I hereby propose that we drink to Aeolus. May he turn his wrath from us." He then took a long swallow of his wine.

"To Aeolus," I echoed and also rose the glass to my lips. It was an appropriate salute, as what entered my mouth could only be described as the nectar of the gods. It was as if liquid sunshine had been bottled, and I drank deeply from my glass.

Mrs. Foster sipped from her small amount, and only then did Monsieur Dumas deign to try a taste. I watched his face as he did so, and for a moment, the guarded scowl that had seemed a permanent feature melted away, to be replaced by pure rapture. "Rather fine," was his sole gruff comment, which I felt did the glorious wine a grave disservice.

Mrs. Foster soon left us to our silent contemplation of that bottled bliss, and the three of us ensured that not a drop would be wasted. As the imbibing continued, I finally found myself growing tired, as if we had drunk to Morpheus instead. How exactly I got back to my room that night is a matter of purest speculation, but at least I did not lose sleep ruminating over the matter of Madame Lucy Dubois.

§

CHAPTER IX:
MURDER!

When I awoke the next morning, I was in a state of complete confusion. Several factors accounted for this, the first of which was the strange absence of sound. I was not able to quite deduce why this seemed so unusual until I recalled the incredible storm, with its shrieking winds, that we had just endured. I could barely credit the possibility that such a monster had run its course. Secondly, I felt like I was in an absolute stupor. I believe that I would not be boasting if I claimed that I had experience of wines and spirits which extended over many nations, but nothing had ever affected me like that comet vintage.

I rolled over to look at my pocket-watch and was astounded to discover that it was a quarter past eleven o'clock! This was so inconceivable that I staggered over to the window and threw up the shade. The stormy night had been followed by a glorious day, with the sun high in the sky. I blinked at the bright light in stupefaction, for even at the peak of one of my lazy spells I have been generally quite regular in my habits. I do not recall ever sleeping so late, and I could not fathom the cause of this torpor. However, when I finally managed to stagger over to the wash basin and gazed in the mirror hanging above it, the reason was made both crystal clear and hopelessly obscured. For my pupils were but tiny pin-points of darkness in the center of the enormous blue irises. As a medical man, I knew that only opium, or one of its derivatives, produces such an effect!

My first thought was to check my wallet, which I found to be relatively barren, but no more so than was typical for a half-pay surgeon. I had not been robbed. Then why had someone drugged me? It was a complete mystery.

I rapidly threw on my clothes and was ready in a few minutes to make my way downstairs, desperately hoping for both a café noir and some answers. When I entered the dining room, I found Mrs. Foster and Mr. Sims in deep conversation. The only other individuals present in the room were Mr. Aristides Delopolous, his Grecian name betraying his homeland, and Mr. Mehmet Nazim Bey, a Turkish engineer. I had only met them the prior evening during the gathering after Madame Dubois' violin playing, but I recalled also observing them talking together in the dining room on my first morning at the Globe Hotel.

When she saw me enter, Mrs. Foster turned to me. "I noted your irregularity at meals, Doctor. I was about to knock on your door. Mr. Sims just appeared and asked for a late breakfast, and I thought it would be easier if I made it for two."

Sims laughed. "I suspect that most of us slept late once the storm passed. I for one slept as deeply as if I had taken a large dose of castor oil."

Mrs. Foster nodded. "Yes, though you and the Doctor are the last of them to awaken."

My brow furrowed as I gazed at them, for Sims' blue eyes clearly showed the same miniscule pupils that I possessed. "I must confess that I don't recall sleeping so soundly since they took the Jezail bullet out of my shoulder, and treated me afterword with morphine."

Sims appeared puzzled. "Are you suggesting that we were under the influence of some drug, Doctor?"

"I am."

"But how?" he queried.

"It must have been in the claret."

"Impossible," he scoffed. "I brought the claret."

"But where else could it have been for both of us to feel the same effects?" I asked him.

"But Mrs. Foster also drank some of the wine," protested Sims.

"It was but a small sip after opening it," said Mrs. Foster slowly. "But I must say, gentlemen, that I did sleep especially soundly last night and awoke much later than usual this morning."

"You see, Mr. Sims. The claret must have been drugged," I concluded.

"If we were drugged, it could have been something put in the glasses either before or after the wine was poured," pointed out Sims.

"If that's the case, then there were only three of us at the table last night," I said. "You, Monsieur Dumas, and myself. Are you suggesting that Monsieur Dumas drugged us? To what possible end?"

"How should I know what that madman was thinking? But let's ask him," he looked around, as if expecting to find the Frenchman in the dining room. "Well, where is Dumas?" asked Sims, his question directed at Mrs. Foster.

The innkeeper shrugged. "Mr. Dumas has some eccentric habits. He usually awakens before dawn and leaves the hotel before I can even make him some breakfast. He eats so little that I have wondered how it can even keep life in one. I never saw him this morning, and so I assume that he departed before I awakened."

I shook my head. "Not if he drank the same drugged wine that we did."

"Then he must still be in his room," declared Sims.

"Shall we find out?" I suggested.

The three of us climbed the stairs, followed by both Mr. Delopolous and Mr. Bey, whose curiosity had clearly been awakened by our conversation. I discovered that Monsieur Dumas' room was the one at the very end of the twisting corridor, immediately past my own. Sims knocked vigorously at the man's door, but there was no answer. He knocked again, and called out. "Dumas! Open the door!"

There were still no sounds emanating from the man's room and my companions looked confounded by the next step. Finally, Mr. Delopolous spoke up with an accented voice and a raise of his eyebrows. "Perhaps we should open the door? He may be ill."

"Good idea," said I. "Mrs. Foster, you must have duplicate keys?"

"Of course," she replied. She drew a ring of keys from her apron and, after a moment's selection, slipped one into the keyhole. The key turned with a sharp metallic snap, but the door refused to open. "He must have barred it from the inside."

"Then we will have to force our way in!" exclaimed Sims. "Step back, Elizabeth!" He threw the entire weight of his Herculean frame against the stout door, which held after the first blow.

"Put your shoulder to it!" I cried. And indeed the second blow was too much for the door. It gave way before his great strength, as one hinge snapped, then the other, and down came the door with a crash. Sims staggered into the room, but then drew up with an incoherent exclamation. None of us in the hallway could see past his enormous shoulders to spy the cause of his alarm.

"Doctor!" he said urgently. "Get in here!"

I pushed past him, and was thunderstruck by the appalling sight before me. In the middle of the bed lay the stretched-out figure of Dumas, his mouth horribly agape, and his body encircled by a ghastly crimson halo of blood that stained the white bed-sheets which had been drawn up to his neck. It gave even my hardened nerves a shudder to look at him. But two things made this sight even more grotesque. The first was that the man's eyes were covered by a pair of silver coins. The later was that two letters –

"E" and "M" – were painted upon his forehead in blood. These stood out in vivid relief upon his lard-colored skin.

My attention was diverted from what was clearly Dumas' corpse by the sound of a gasp from Mrs. Foster. Her face turned deadly white, her eyes rolled upwards and she collapsed to the floor behind me in a dead faint before anyone could catch her. I turned around and leapt to her aid, since Dumas was beyond such. "Fetch some brandy!" I commanded the dazed Mr. Delopolous, who rallied and dashed downstairs. Meanwhile, I propped her head, its face as white as chalk, under my rolled up jacket, for certainly the pillows on Dumas' bed would never be usable again. I contemplated the propriety of loosening the collar of her high gown amidst a group of relative strangers. Fortunately, I was spared such a decision by the speedy return of Mr. Delopolous with the brandy. I poured a bit down her throat, and she began to revive. "There! There!" said I, soothingly. "That was quite a shock."

"I am alright now, Doctor," she said, a tinge of color beginning to return to her bloodless cheeks. She forced a shamefaced smile. "What has happened?"

"I am afraid that Monsieur Dumas is dead," I explained. "The cause is not yet clear."

"You must send for Constable Dunkley."

"Excellent idea," said I, turning to Mr. Bey, who seemed to be the master of himself and his emotions, unfazed by the tableau before him. "Would you be so kind as to step out to locate him?"

"I will do my best," he replied calmly before departing.

Since Mrs. Foster appeared to be recovering, I turned my attention back to the corpse, wondering if the nature of the injuries might not reveal something to my medical instincts. His duvet was drawn up, so I gently reached and turned it down. I found that Dumas was clad only in his long purple night-dress, his knobby ankles and ungainly feet protruding starkly from beneath it. The gown was once fine, but now in great need of repair, as it sported multiple holes, clearly made by bullets. It was only then that I became conscious of a faint hint of gunpowder still lingering in the air of the room. I looked about and soon discovered the likely cause of those holes, as a Colt Single Action Revolver lay on the nightstand beside a guttered bedroom candle. Of course I refrained from handling it, not wanting not contaminate any of the evidence. I stood there, rather perplexed about the next step, as one glance was more than sufficient to show that the man was clearly beyond any aid that I could offer. Fortunately, my indecisive state was soon interrupted by the out-of-breath appearance of my acquaintance from two days earlier, Constable Dunkley. He was dressed similarly to our prior encounter though today he carried a brown wide-awake in his hand.

"Well, that one's a deader," he said unceremoniously, obviously un-rattled by the sight. Notwithstanding this callous remark, he immediately took up the case with a great deal of energy. He drew out a memorandum book and pen from his breast pocket and began to take notes. "Now who touched what?" he glared at Sims, Mrs. Foster, and I, the only three people to have entered the fatal room.

"Mrs. Foster and I touched nothing," replied Sims. "Only the doctor..."

I threw up my hands to ward off his glare. "I was only doing my duty and ensuring that he was in fact expired."

Dunkley nodded grudgingly. "Fair enough, Doctor. Now tell me, how long has he been dead for?"

I considered this inquiry. "I am not certain that I am fully qualified to answer that question, Constable. You must have a coroner..."

"Rubbish!" said he, waving off my suggestion. "By the time old man Tucker gets here from Hamilton whoever shot this man will be halfway to Virginia. You've been around a dead man or two, I suspect, Doctor, so just give it to me straight."

Reluctantly, I nodded. "I should say that he has been dead about ten hours, judging by the rigidity of the muscles. But, as you likely know, many things can affect the period of *rigor mortis* and hence that estimate."

Dunkley pulled out his pocket-watch and consulted it. "Still, we'll take it as a reasonable starting point. Even if you are off by an hour that places the murder as occurring sometime between midnight and two o'clock. That was right at the height of the storm, so whoever did this was almost certainly a resident of the hotel. Elizabeth," he said, turning to Mrs. Foster, "has anyone checked out this morning?"

"No," she replied. "Not officially. I suppose it is possible that someone left without paying their bill."

"We can only hope so!" exclaimed Dunkley.

I frowned in non-comprehension. "But that means that the murderer would have gotten away."

Dunkley chuckled. "Not in the slightest, Doctor. Lest you forget, this is an island! The only way someone is getting off Bermuda is via a boat, and no boats are running yet this morning while the sea recovers from last night's tempest. Once the hue-and-cry is raised over him, it would be a short trip to the rope for any man who has fled this hotel. No, the only purpose served by someone running would be to sign their own confession of guilt. We can only hope that whoever did this foul deed is so obtuse. Now let's figure out the exact time of death." He reached up and rapped on the wall to his right. "Elizabeth, who is staying in the adjoining room? There were how many gunshots? Six? Seven? Too many to sleep through, that's for certain."

Mrs. Foster glanced at me uncertainly. "That would be the Doctor's room, Constable," she replied hesitantly.

Dunkley's bushy brown eyebrows shot up as he turned to me. "Well, Doctor?"

I felt my brow furrowing. "I am afraid that I did sleep through it."

Dunkley looked skeptical. "You must be a powerfully deep sleeper, sir."

"I am afraid that my slumber was not natural."

"I am not certain that I am following you, Doctor. Are you a consumer of laudanum?"

I shook my head. "No, I rarely take any medications myself. But last night, I was under the influence of some powerful drug, and not intentionally, I assure you."

"Drugged!" Dunkley exclaimed. "By who?"

"That is what we were trying to ascertain when we were rousting Mr. Dumas here. I had thought that perhaps it was him."

"And what made you think that?"

I explained to Dunkley the sharing of the comet vintage the prior evening. As I concluded, he looked around at Mrs. Foster, Mr. Sims, and I with silent astonishment.

Uncertain of the reason for his reticence, I ventured to ask a question. "Was there any point that I did not make clear?"

He shook his head. "Not at all, Doctor. Your statement is extraordinarily lucid. Well, that certainly is a major clue. If we can ascertain who drugged you, then we have our murderer."

I nodded slowly. "I suppose that what you say is probably true. It's unlikely that we have both a murderer and a wine-bottle druggist under this roof."

"You misunderstand me, Doctor," said Dunkley, shaking his head. "I was not implying that this was an unlikely coincidence. It is obvious that these events were directly related. You see, the murderer was not trying to drug you and Mr. Sims. His aim was Mr. Dumas here. Look," said he, pointing at the bedclothes, where some black powder appeared mixed in with the blood. "The powder-blackening demonstrates that the shots were fired from close range. Mr. Dumas was drugged to ensure that the murderer could get close to him. You were simply a bystander in the process."

Dunkley stopped and looked around the room. "Below us is the billiard-room, so no one would have heard shots there." He looked up at the ceiling. "What about the garret, Elizabeth? Who is staying up there?"

Mrs. Foster glanced out into the hall, where Mr. Delopolous and Mr. Bey continued to loiter. "Those gentlemen," she replied. "But they could not have heard anything, for the slope of the roof is such that the garret room does not extend much over this room. And the noise of the storm would have been loudest up there."

The two gentlemen in the hallway hastened to assure the Constable that Mrs. Foster's assessment was correct. They had heard nothing unusual in the night but the winds and the rains.

Dunkley shook his head. "Then what about the room across the hall?" he asked, pointing out the door. "Who is in there?"

Mrs. Foster nodded at the huge man in the room with us. "Mr. Sims."

Dunkley snorted. "So, anyone who might have heard anything over the noise of the storm was passed out in a drugged stupor?" said he, incredulously. "This will be harder than I thought. Still, our man will be one of the guests, so we should be able to narrow down the list of suspects quickly." His gaze swept the chamber of death, and I mirrored his behavior, noticing for the first time that it was a near square, much smaller than my L-shaped room.

In so doing, something caught my eye over by the window. I stepped over towards it, and discovered a puddle of water on the floor. I then glanced out of the window and was surprised by what I found there. "I am not so certain about that, Constable."

"What do you mean?"

I indicated the puddle. "We had to force the door, since it was barred from the inside. So the murderer did not flee through the hotel. He must have left through the window, hence the puddle."

Dunkley considered this and tested the window, which he found to be unlocked. "That would not have been easy," he mused. "It was quite a storm last night."

"Ah, but they were aided by that," said I, pointing out the window, where a ladder rested against the frame of the hotel directly under Mr. Dumas' room. At the bottom was the hotel's rear garden.

"By Jove!" exclaimed Dunkley. "Still, they could have simply re-entered the hotel through the garden door and returned to their room."

Mrs. Foster shook her head violently. "That's not possible. I do a round of the building every night to lock up. I test that door every night, along with all of the others. No one entered this hotel last night."

"Lock or bar?" inquired Dunkley.

"Both," she replied.

Dunkley nodded approvingly. "Excellent. Locks can be picked. Therefore, I agree that no one entered this hotel last night, except possibly through this window. I will need to take an inventory of this room and then interview the guests. I must find out if any of them knew Mr. Dumas and can shed light on who would want to kill him."

"I can set up the downstairs ladies' parlor for your use," volunteered Mrs. Foster.

Dunkley nodded his agreement. "That will serve nicely. I will be down in a minute."

Mrs. Foster and Mr. Sims turned to leave the room. I was about to follow them when Dunkley spoke again. "Hold a minute, Doctor." Mrs. Foster closed the door behind her to shut off the terrible scene from the other guests.

"Sir?" I inquired.

"Doctor, I would be much obliged if you would deign to assist me."

"With the body? Of course."

He shook his head. "More than just the body, Doctor. You have sharp eyes, as evidenced by the puddle. I am going to need your help in questioning the guests. We shall see if you can spot any inconsistencies in their stories that I might miss."

"But Constable," I protested, "surely I too am a suspect. How can you trust me?"

He smiled for the first time since our encounter on the town square and I was reminded that he was, at my best guess, no older than me. "There are at least four reasons why I do not think that you are the murderer, Doctor. Would you like me to list them?"

I raised my eyebrows.

"First, you volunteered yourself as a suspect. Few guilty men are cool enough to do that. Second, the evidence that you were drugged has been verified not only by Mr. Sims, who I do not know, but also by Mrs. Foster, who I've known all my life. Third, as a medical man, I am certain that you could have devised a less noisy end for Mr. Dumas. Why take the risk that someone would hear the shots? Fourth, you were recently wounded in Afghanistan and were posted here for medical recuperation. It would take a very devious man to engineer that type of posting, and thus I suspect that you are on Bermuda by pure chance alone. And whatever the reason for Mr. Dumas' killing, this is not the work of a random murderer."

"You do not you think it was a robbery then?"

Dunkley shook his head violently. "No. Absolutely not. I don't even have to search his room to know that nothing was stolen from him." He pointed at Dumas' head. "A thief does not leave behind two pieces-of-eight upon a dead man's eyes. Nor does he write letters in blood upon a dead man's forehead."

As I contemplated the dead man, something stuck me as odd about the letters, whose vivid red color had not yet begun to oxidize like the rest of his spilled rust-colored blood. I leaned over and touched a small corner of the letter "M." A bit of the color came away on my index finger, and I realized what was so unusual. "This is not blood," I exclaimed. "This is paint."

Dunkley's dark brown eyes peered at me, as he pursed his lips and shook his head. "These are deep waters, Doctor. Deep waters."

§

CHAPTER X:
A TANGLED SKEIN

Breaking the ominous silence, Constable Dunkley cleared his throat. "Can I rely upon you, Doctor?"

Between my wounds and my recent illness, I may have been only a pale shadow of myself, but I fancy that I have always been a man of action, and I rose to the occasion. "Most certainly," I replied, simply. "I am your man."

"Capital! Our first task should be to inventory the room." He tapped his official notebook and then began to scribble down thoughts. "First, the items of the room itself. There is the gun, of course, presumably the murder weapon."

I frowned in confusion. "Why 'presumably?' Do you doubt it? Surely you are not hypothesizing the presence of a second pistol when this one is staring us in the face? I have not yet attempted to extract one of the bullets, but it would little surprise me to discover that the caliber corresponds to that weapon."

"No," said the constable, shaking his head slowly. "But there is a major problem with this weapon. How many bullet holes do you count in this body, Doctor?"

"Seven," replied I, with confidence.

He grinned sardonically. "That is the problem. You see, the Colt is chambered for only six rounds. So either someone shot Mr. Dumas six times, paused to reload the cylinder, and then shot him once more, or there is a second gun." He picked up the heavy gun and shook out the cartridges. "Empty."

I was perplexed by this development. "Neither seems very plausible. Six shots were certainly more than enough to kill the man, especially at such short range. So why reload? But if you had a pair of pistols and used both in a moment of anger, why take only one away with you?"

"Agreed," replied Dunkley. "A cold-blooded business, that is for certain. Is there a method to this madness? I do not know what to make of it, but we shall file it away as our first clue. The second is, of course, the ladder."

"Which does not tell us much."

"No," he agreed, "but we can inspect the ground beneath the window. If we are lucky we will find a footprint in the mud. Next, we come to the man's possessions."

He began to inspect the contents of the bed-stand. On it rested a silver watch with a gold chain. Dunkley picked it up and turned it over. "Barraud's of London, but not numbered. Not much help there. They make too many watches to help us. And there is no personalized inscription," said he, with a hint of disappointment.

"He told me his given name was Gustave, so surely it would only say 'G.D.'"

Dunkley shook his head again. "You are forgetting the initials on his forehead, Doctor. What do you suppose that they stand for?"

"I really couldn't say. Perhaps it is the mark of some secret society?"

He pursed his lips as if to consider this possibility. "Perhaps. But I am more inclined to the hypothesis that it stands for a name. Since our killer likely was not foolish enough to leave his own initials, I suspect that this may be the true initials of our murdered man."

"So, 'Gustave Dumas' was nothing but a *nom-de-plume?*" I asked, intrigued.

Dunkley moved on to the dressing table and began going through the litter of personal effects and other *débris*. He studied the man's identity papers carefully. "Well," said he, finally, "if it's a forgery, it's a damn good one. Our dead man certainly appears to be none other than Gustave Dumas from Rouen, Normandy. He has been on the go a lot recently. Most recently New York, and before that, all about the Continent. The Dacre Hotel, London. The Hôtel du Louvre, Paris. The Hôtel Dulong, Lyon. The Hôtel National, Lausanne. Copenhagen, Strasbourg, Odessa, Luxembourg, Buda-Pesth. A well-travelled man, our Mr. Dumas," he concluded, finishing his flipping through the man's travel documents. The constable quickly examined a box of wax vestas and some cheroots, and then picked up a small cigar holder made from some light green stone. "Now this is interesting. What do you make of this, Doctor?"

I circled the bed in order to get a better look at it. "Ah, I've seen something like this before. An officer who had served in China had something quite similar. It's made of jade."

"A *very* well-travelled man, our Mr. Dumas, or whatever his real name is," observed Dunkley. He emptied out a pouch of sealskin, which contained a dozen gold sovereigns and about twenty fifty-pound notes of the Bank of England, held together by an India-rubber band, which was more than a year's pay for someone like myself. "And not lacking for money, either," he noted pointedly.

An aluminum pencil-case and a disarranged pile of papers also lay scattered about the tabletop, and Dunkley began to scrutinize them. They appeared to be receipted accounts, written in a crabbed foreign hand. "The question is whether Mr. Dumas was a slovenly man, or whether his murderer scattered these papers. And of course, who knows if any have been taken. I will have to study these a bit, Doctor. Perhaps they will tell us exactly who Mr. Dumas was. Hmmm," he paused, "these appear to be list of Stock Exchange Securities and South American railway bonds."

I took some of the papers from him and looked them over. "I would have to examine the lists, but if my memory serves, most of these have seen heavy losses in the last few years."

"Ah, now look at this!" he exclaimed, handing me one of the papers.

It appeared to be a receipt for a deposit at the bank of Cox & Co. at 16 Charing Cross, London. "This is one of the most reputable banks in all of England," said I. "Certainly if I had anything of value to my name, I would deposit it there. But the description of exactly what he deposited is maddingly unclear."

"I agree," said Dunkley, dejectedly.

Just then a smeared and partially-torn newspaper clipping fluttered out of the pile. It looked as if it had once been crumpled up and then smoothed out again. I picked it up and read though it quickly:

ATLANTA CONSTITUTION

October 4, 1880

MURDER AT THE BATTLE HOUSE HOTEL

Mr. Fabian LaRue, born 1835 in New Orleans, Louisiana, was found shot to death in his hotel room in Mobile, Alabama. Mr. LaRue was a one-time resident of Atlanta and had served under General P. G. T. Beauregard at the Battle of Shiloh. After the War, he hired his services in many far-flung locales, but often returned to Atlanta, where he was a popular fixture in the Postbellum social scene. At this time, the police are still actively investigating and have no suspects in the murder of this former Dixie hero.

I showed it to the constable. "I wonder why Monsieur Dumas was so interested in this particular article that he saw fit to save it?"

Dunkley nodded. "This is an excellent question, Doctor. Notice that the two men, LaRue and Dumas, were both shot to death in a hotel. These crimes are too similar to be a coincidence."

He was about to turn his attention to the rest of the room when I stooped down to pluck a piece of paper that had slipped behind the table. This proved to be quite different from the others. Rather than the methodical receipts, this was a crudely-scrawled letter. It was written with a violet-tinted lead-pencil on a half-sheet of cheap, thin slate-gray-tinted notepaper without watermark. It was headed "October 31," and beneath this were the following enigmatical lines:

Sir,

You will be pleased to note that everything has been arranged per your specifications. I trust that your communications with Captain R. have confirmed that the items are still in situ at the place of the barrel?

- B

"What do you make of this, Doctor?" Dunkley asked with evident puzzlement.

"The penmanship is at great odds with the tone of the letter," I said. "The writing is hardly legible, as if the man was barely literate, and yet he freely uses a Latin term. It reads as though it were an appointment. Very strange," I concluded, glancing up from the message to find the constable pensively stroking his trim beard.

"Perhaps it was an educated man attempting to disguise his hand. But it is indisputably the hand of a man, don't you think?"

I nodded. "Yes, a man with the initial 'B.'"

"Are you aware of any of the guests with such an initial?" inquired Dunkley.

I tried to recall the names of all of my fellow lodgers. "Yes, there are two. One is Mr. Sims, whose given name is 'Bruce.' The second is Mr. Bey, the man who fetched you. Of course, Mr. Sims drank from the same wine bottle as me and Dumas, so he could not possibly have been in a fit state to murder anyone."

"How can you be certain that he actually drank the wine? Perhaps he only pretended to?" hypothesized Dunkley.

"I may not recall the end of the night, but I do clearly remember him drinking deeply from the first glass. And I do not know how he could have faked the constricted pupils that I witnessed this morning."

"Hmmm," Dunkley appeared to be pondering this bit of information. "So, the first 'B' does not appear to be a suspect, but what about the second? Mr. Bey seemed like a cool customer, not overly distraught by the sight of a dead man."

"Not everyone is," I pointed out. "Especially if they have been around one before."

"True," admitted Dunkley. "Though we will need to determine where Mr. Bey has seen so much death. And we will need a sample of every man's handwriting."

"Everyone's?" said I, surprised.

"Of course, Doctor. If Mr. Dumas can fake his name, as I suspect he did, so can any of Mrs. Foster's guests."

Dunkley moved over to a portmanteau that rested upon a little stand, and proceeded to unpack and inspect the dead man's travelling bag. From the very top, he drew forth a pair of large light brown canvas work-gloves, heavily stained with something black. "Ah!" Dunkley exclaimed. "Well, we shall not need to inspect the hands of your fellow lodgers."

I frowned in relative incomprehension. "I'm not certain that I understand, Constable."

"Look at these black stains, Doctor. This is clearly gunpowder. And more gunpowder than one shot would produce. But seven shots from the Colt? Yes, that could produce this amount of staining. Our murderer clearly wore these gloves to avoid the development of incriminating powder stains on his hands."

"But they were in Dumas' bag. Surely they could belong to him? He could have used them for target practice."

Dunkley shook his head. "I think not, Doctor. Look at the size of these gloves. Compare them to the dead man's hands. Do you think that he would have owned gloves that size?"

Taking the gloves from him, I quickly ascertained that he was correct. The gloves were huge. Only a very large man would have hands big enough to call for gloves like this. "But the only man who has hands this size is Mister...." my voice trailed off, wonderingly.

"Sims," said Dunkley, finishing my thought. "Yes, very interesting indeed. Either Mr. Sims has a remarkable tolerance for whatever drug you both ingested, or someone very much wants us to believe that Mr. Sims is the guilty party. Remember, Doctor, that the gloves were left here for us to find. They could have very easily been taken away and secreted somewhere in the hotel. Our murderer would have had time this morning to smuggle them out for destruction or burying or dropping in the ocean." He placed the gloves into his evidence bag and turned his attention back to the portmanteau.

"Ah, yes, here is another interesting item," said Dunkley. It was another piece of paper, but in stark contrast to the other note. This held but two words, written with a broad-pointed pen in an indelible ink on a sheet of fine thick blue-tinted stationary. The blocky handwriting showed no similarity to either Dumas' crabbed notes, or the illegible scrawl of the unknown 'Mr. B.' The constable held it up to the light to show the watermark, which read 'Scott, Phil.' Dunkley nodded in satisfaction. "American paper," he concluded. But the words made little sense. The first was 'MOREAU,' while the second was 'ÉMERAUDE.' "What do you make of this, Doctor?"

I shook my head in complete mystification. "Moreau is a French painter. Perhaps it is a reference to a painting?"

"I don't see how that is relevant," said Dunkley. "Now this is most unusual," he said. He held up a three-inch circular piece of bronze, most carefully wrapped in some fine Eastern silk. On it was an equestrian portrait of a soldier, who appeared to be the American General Washington. He was surrounded by an intricate wreath of cotton, tobacco, sugarcane, corn, wheat, and rice. Around the edges were inscribed the words:

> **THE CONFEDERATE STATES OF AMERICA**
> **22 FEBRUARY 1862**
> **DEO VINDICE**

"What is it?" I asked wonderingly.

Dunkley shook his head. "A seal of some sort. And a dangerous item, proclaiming loyalty to a vanquished nation. I would not be surprised if this was a motive for his death, especially since the other murdered man in the newspaper was also involved with the Confederacy."

The only other item of note in the luggage was a solid-frame, double-action revolver, with a fluted cylinder and blued finish, and which I recognized as a MAS 1874 pistol common in the French army. The remainder of the man's clothes appeared unremarkable. Dunkley hefted the man's handsome cane. "Hmmm," he mused, "this is no ordinary cane. You should feel its weight, Doctor. It appears to have been fortified with lead. He fidgeted with the cane for a moment, and then it made a clicking noise. With a sudden movement, Dunkley separated the cane into two sections, an external sheath and a short but wickedly-sharp sword. "Hah!

Hardly the cane for a gentlemanly stroll about town! This is a formidable weapon. I wonder what Mr. Dumas had to fear."

"He clearly knew that his life was in danger." I quickly briefed the constable on my conversation with Dumas two nights prior.

"Very interesting, Doctor," he mused. "Very interesting, indeed! Here we have a man who feared both assassins bearing weapons and ghosts pouring poison. And yet he fell prey to both attacks in one night. Very careless."

"I doubt that he ever imagined that his murderer would be so reckless as to poison multiple innocent bystanders. He must have felt safe enough to drink the comet vintage with us. Normally, I believe that he only drank from his own bottle."

"Yes, indeed," agreed Dunkley. "And that leads us to this." He indicated the final possession of note in the room, a green bottle on the dressing table. It was a French long-neck flowerpot-shaped bottle, with very thick walls of a dark grass green color and a blistery inclusion at the bottom. The seal proclaimed that the bottle contained a fifty-year-old Calvados from Normandy. "The cork is still in place," he noted, "and the bottle is full and very heavy. Dumas must have been saving this one for a special occasion."

"I am not certain how that helps us, Constable."

Dunkley pursed his lips and shook his head in a perturbed fashion. "I am not certain either, Doctor. But I don't like this case at all. It is a real snorter."

"It seems to be that there are plenty of clues, you should have no problem tracking down the murderer and quickly making an arrest." said I, consolingly.

"That is the very problem, Doctor. This would appear to be my red-letter day. But there are far too many clues in this room. How are we to distinguish the essential from the rubbish? Look at this body," he pointed. "What do you make of it?"

I turned my full attention to the body and pondered of what use I may be to the constable. Might not the nature of the injuries reveal something to my medical instincts? But the cause of death was quite plain. Seven gunshots were not a subtle finding. There were the mysterious painted letters on his forehead, of course, and the strange coins on his eyes. But what could it all indicate? I cudgeled my brain to find some possible explanation. What a tissue of mysteries and improbabilities the whole thing was! "I have no plausible explanation, Constable," I finally admitted.

"It seems to me that the coins are a clear sign to one of the guests. Is this not a payment to enter the underworld? And is not one of the guests a Greek? Mr. Delopolous, I believe is his name?"

I shook my head. "I'm sorry, Constable, but that is a false conclusion. Charon's obol was a coin that the Greeks placed into the mouths of their deceased relatives and friends so that they could pay the ferryman to take them across the rivers Styx and Acheron, and thence hopefully to the fields of Elysium. The Greeks did not place the coin on the eyes, nor would they have done it for a bitter enemy, which presumably Dumas was, or he would not have been murdered in the first place."

Dunkley pursed his lips as he considered this information. Finally, he nodded slowly. "That is fine reasoning, Doctor. So Mr. Delopolous is not our suspect. But perhaps our murderer does not possess as fine a Classical education as yourself? Perhaps he was trying to throw suspicion towards the Greek, expecting that I would think this was a Greek custom?"

I agreed that this was a plausible hypothesis. "One thing that bothers me is that Dumas' pistol was clear across the room, as was his sword cane. He seemed too paranoid to make such a mistake."

"But he was drugged, Doctor," pointed out the constable.

"True, but I think Dumas would have things arranged in advance. Aha!" exclaimed I, carefully reaching under the pillow beneath his head and extracting a unique jack-knife. The blade was about six inches long, and the black ebony handle was inscribed with yet another set of mysterious initials: "L.E." and a well-worn symbol that looked like a flame arising from a ring:

"What is it?" exclaimed Dunkley.

I shook my head in confusion. "I do not know."

"Very interesting, Doctor. To what society did our Mr. Dumas belong, I wonder? And then there is this." He pointed to a red stain on the far side of the bed. The sheets had become saturated with blood and a few spots had clearly dripped onto the floor. But the spots had been smeared by someone stepping upon them. "Look at that bloodstain. The pattern is most unusual. I am at a loss to explain what type of shoe has a sole that leaves such a featureless print."

I stared at the smudge of blood for a moment before responding. "What if it's not a shoe? A soft-soled bed-slipper might make such a mark."

Dunkley laughed. "That's brilliant, Doctor! Of course you are right, but that only muddles things further," said he, shaking his head in despair. "Think of the picture that we are compiling: Mr. B drugs at least two innocents to get at his mark, and then climbs up a ladder to Dumas' room in his bed-slippers during a terrible storm. 'Mr. B' then proceeds to don a pair of giant gloves, shoot the mark seven times – which required a re-load of the pistol! – all the time trusting his great fortune that the two men whose rooms were close enough to hear the gunshots just so happened to be the ones that were bystanders in his drugging scheme. 'Mr. B' then places two coins on Dumas' eyes, writes two letters on his forehead in paint, neglects to steal any gold sovereigns or bank-notes, and departs again via the window in his blood-stained slippers. Who would believe such a tale? It's outlandish!"

I could not argue with his assessment of the situation, and only shook my head in bewildered commiseration. I finally corrected him on one part of his narrative. "It's not absolutely certain that the murderer came in via the window. Only that he left that way. It's still possible that he came in through the main door, with some sort of lock-picking tool, and then bolted it behind him in order to have time to initiate his escape in the event that the gunshots awoke the hotel."

Dunkley finally shook off his dark musings. "That is a good point, Doctor," he nodded. "Well, there is little else to glean here, I think. Let's repair downstairs and examine the ladder in the garden. After that we can begin to question the other guests."

We closed the door behind us as best we could given the damage done to it by Mr. Sims' giant frame and I led the way as we twisted through the corridor back to the staircase. When we reached the landing, I was about to descend, when Dunkley stopped me with a hand on my shoulder. "Hold a minute, Doctor. What do you make of this?"

I looked over at a small side table nestled against the cedar railing that separated the open staircase from the landing. On it rested a copy of the prior day's *Royal Gazette* and a handful of small glass shards of varied colors. I failed to see what had attracted his attention. "What is it?"

"The glass. I did not notice it in my haste to reach the dead man's room. Was it there when you passed through this morning?"

I stared at the pieces of glass, which summed to a total nine and were a mixture of mostly deep green shards, with two that were a lighter blue color. I wracked my brain to try to remember. "I'm sorry, Constable, but I cannot recall. On my way down, I was still rather befuddled by the drug, and on our way up, we were in a rush to confront Mr. Dumas. But I don't understand the significance of the shards. Was something broken here?"

He shook his head. "No, Doctor. Look at those worn edges. This glass was not recently broken. This is sea-glass."

"Sea-glass?" I inquired.

"As I am certain that you know by now, Bermuda is ringed by treacherous reefs which have spelled the end of many a ship. When those ships go down, so does their cargo, including many glass bottles. Over time, most of those bottles break apart. Then the sand etches the pieces and the waves tumble them about until they obtain this uniquely smooth shape and color."

"But what do they have to do with anything?" I protested.

"Perhaps nothing," shrugged Dunkley. "But why are they here? Nothing about this murder makes any sense, and I don't like things that are out of place. We will need to ascertain if anyone knows how this sea-glass appeared here. As you said, the murderer could have entered Dumas' room via the corridor. Did the mysterious Mr. B leave this sea-glass behind? And if so, why?"

I shook my head again in confusion and began to descend the creaking staircase, a thought entered my mind. "One thing is for certain, Constable, whoever killed Dumas was not staying in the downstairs bedchamber."

"Why do you say that, Doctor?"

"Climbing these stairs would be nigh impossible without awakening all of the inhabitants of the closest rooms."

Dunkley appeared to consider this. "That is an interesting observation, Doctor. I must ponder that one. As far as I can tell, no one in this hotel could have killed Dumas. And yet the man is indisputably dead, and not by his own hand. It is our job to find out who the person is that could – and had a reason to – kill the man, creating such a bizarre spectacle in his wake."

§

CHAPTER XI:
THE EVIDENCE OF THE PROPRIETRESS

W ith a befogged mind, I finished descending the stairs, only to
find Mrs. Foster waiting for us in the entryway with a look
upon her face that indicated either extreme agitation or
excitement.

"I have discovered something, Harry!" exclaimed the lady, and
addressing Constable Dunkley by his given name, clearly forgetting in her
eagerness that he was present on official business.

"What is it, Elizabeth?" he responded in kind.

Rather than immediately answering him, she led us into the dining
room and indicated the dark iron fireplace. "I found it in there, when I
was cleaning out the ashes from last night's fire," she explained. I recalled
that during the prior evening a splendid log fire had blazed behind the
iron screen throughout the long night in order to help ward off the chill
from the great storm. "It must have slipped through the dog-grate, and
therefore was not fully consumed." She pointed to a small object lying
before the fireplace that I had originally assumed was a large un-burnt
wooden cinder.

Dunkley bent down to examine it. "What is it?" I finally exclaimed.

"It is badly burned, so it is impossible to tell for certain, but I believe
that it is the remnants of a Turkish slipper," said he, looking at me
meaningfully.

I immediately realized that this could have been what the murderer
wore when he stepped in the drops of blood. "Is there a bloodstain?" I
inquired.

He shook his head. "If there was, it's gone now. But Doctor, there is
only *one* slipper."

The implications of his words finally dawned on me. "If he only
burned one slipper, we can find the match. And if we find the match, we

will have found the murderer," said I excitedly. "Unless the other one was completely consumed, of course," I concluded, trying to tamp down my enthusiasm for the hunt.

"Indeed, Doctor," the constable nodded. "But there are more difficulties. Remember our scenario. In the hypothesis that we have constructed, the murderer fled via the window, not through this room. If he did not flee via the window, then how was the door barred? If he did flee through the window, why in the world would he come all the way down here to burn a slipper after he had already killed Dumas? He could have disposed of the slipper anywhere in St. George's. He could have tied it to a rock and sunk it in the ocean!" He shook his head again. "It's damn odd!"

I silently agreed. In fact, between the drugging of my wine the prior night and the muddle of the investigation, my brain felt like it was swimming in treacle.

"Well, if he did flee via the window, he must have stepped in the garden," continued Dunkley. "Let us see what we can make out." He stood up while adding the burnt slipper to his bag of evidence.

I followed Dunkley and Mrs. Foster through the billiard-room and into the corridor that led to the rear entrance. Three doors led off the corridor, and two were closed, but they were plainly marked with signs. The one closest to the billiard-room door was simply labeled: "Private." I assumed it led to Mrs. Foster's chambers, and I calculated that it likely lay directly below Dumas' room. The next door was propped open by a lead weight and I could see that the kitchen lay beyond. The far door in the corridor was labeled: "To Garret." We stepped out the rear door and entered the garden, which was divided from Duke of York Street by a low wall. The garden was shaded by a large tree that I thought might be some American variety of sycamore, and a pleasant wooden bench completely encircled it. Snug against the building to our left lay a raised square with a black lid, which I realized must lead to an underground rainwater cistern. Immediately outside the door and beneath the bench, the ground was paved with bricks, but the rest of the garden grounds were simple dirt paths winding between the vegetable beds, now saturated by the recent rain. The ladder leading to Dumas' window was set in the middle of one of those beds. Upon further inspection, the ladder itself appeared to be quite ancient, and I thought that it was a miracle that anyone could descend it without breaking at least one rung. Clearly the man who used it was not heavy. Before we moved any further out into the garden, Dunkley held out his arm to block the way. "No further, please. Now, Elizabeth, have you been out here today?"

She sniffed derisively. "Constable Dunkley, do you honestly think that I could have entered my own garden and not noticed that damned ladder? Look at it! It's smashing the lettuce!"

Dunkley nodded. "Good..."

"Good!" she exclaimed. "Maybe for you, but I have a dead man in one of my rooms and a wrecked garden down here!"

Dunkley tried to recall his words. "Calm down, Elizabeth. I was simply noting that you will not have obscured any footprints. Why don't you take a minute for yourself, and then join us in the parlor?"

She glared at him, but strode away without a word. Dunkley raised his eyebrows and shot me a look that seemed to say: 'women... they are a mystery.' I, of course, silently agreed with him. Turning back to the garden, Dunkley carefully made his way over to the base of the ladder and bent down to observe the marks in the moist soil. I remained in my place in order to avoid causing any confusion.

After a few minutes, Dunkley shook his head in exasperation. "I cannot tell anything conclusive, Doctor. Certainly someone passed along this path at some point last night to place the ladder, but it appears that he kept to the border which lines the vegetable beds, likely in order to avoid leaving a track. And his path away from the ladder is even harder to distinguish. I do not see anything resembling a distinct footprint. Oh well, with the pouring rain and blowing winds from last night's great storm, it was never very likely that we'd find anything in the nature of a distinct impression that would help us with this cipher." He stood up and rejoined me at the doorway. "Let us adjourn to the parlor, Doctor."

We retraced our steps and soon found ourselves stepping up into a warmly-decorated room with a gorgeous cedar-beam ceiling. An east-facing window cast light upon the handsome space, which held a Japanese cabinet, a comfortable cedar settee, an old-fashioned upholstered chaise-lounge, and several velvet-lines easy-chairs. A small writing desk with a fine surface of red-leather was tucked under the window. A fine carpet of amber and green covered the center of the room, so soft and so thick that the foot sank pleasantly into it, like a bed of moss. It was surrounded by highly-polished squares that made up the wood flooring. Unlike the billiard-room, there was absolutely no smell of tobacco in the air. Rather the converse held true in this refuge of the ladies, and I could almost imagine that Lucy Dubois' frangipani scent still lingered in the room. The constable seemed to little notice these details and strode over to one of chairs across from the settee. I followed his lead and sat down in the other chair.

"Who should I send in first, Harry?" asked Mrs. Foster.

But instead of answering her, Dunkley motioned to the settee. "Please sit down for a moment, Elizabeth."

She frowned and I imagined that a shade appeared to drop over her eyes. But she obeyed him. "Am I a suspect, Constable Dunkley?" she said stiffly.

"Now, now, Elizabeth, of course not," he replied with a chuckle. "I just wanted to get a lay of the land. I've spent many a night in your billiard-room, but I've had little call before today to ever venture upstairs in your fine establishment."

"Have all of the guests been accounted for?" I interjected.

"Yes, they all returned for their midday meal," she nodded.

"Well, that's a shame," said Dunkley. "No one is going to make this easy on us, eh, Doctor? Elizabeth, please inform them that no one is to leave the hotel again without my permission. I will need to question everyone first."

"Perhaps we should start by determining the situation of everyone who spent the night in the hotel?" said I. "I propose that we draw a map to aid our investigation."

"That's a capital idea, Doctor," exclaimed Dunkley. "What say you, Elizabeth? Can you help us?"

"Of course," she replied. She stood up and moved over to the desk, where all of the accoutrements of writing could be found, including a variety of pens and pencils, a blotting pad, a block of purple wax and a small sealing-wax knife with an ivory handle and a stiff blade. Sitting down in the chair, she took out several sheets of foolscap and began to sketch a rough plan of the place. The constable and I stood up and looked over her shoulder as she drew, and as the rooms began to unfold we started to acquire a general idea of the position of all of the guests of the hotel. When the two pages were complete, Dunkley and I returned to the arm-chairs in order to study them, which I here reproduce:

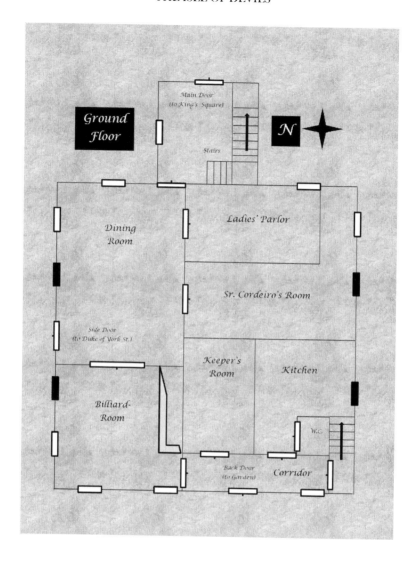

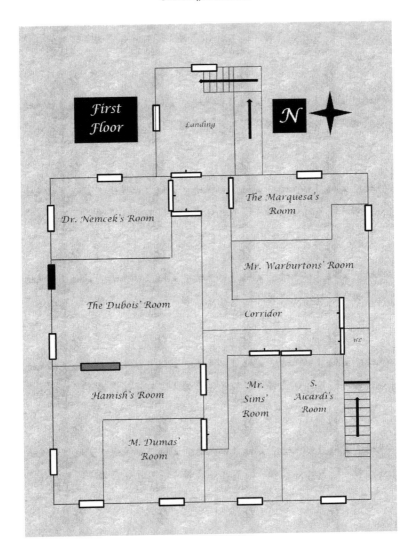

"It's a bit rough, of course," Mrs. Foster said with apparent modesty, for I found them to be quite well done. "It deals with the most essential points, including who is staying in the various rooms. I did not draw the garret floor, as it is simply a large room running from north to south, with the two windows that you have seen from the street and sharp sides that fit under the slope of the roof. I am happy to show it to you, if you would like, Harry. It is currently occupied by Mr. Bey and Mr. Delopolous, the two gentlemen that you have already met this morning."

As I studied the map, I realized that only Senhor Cordeiro had a room on the ground floor, immediately next to the parlor in which we sat and opening directly into the dining room. All of the remaining guests were lodged in the cleverly laid-out quarters of the first floor.

"If that will be all, gentlemen, I can call the first guest," said Mrs. Foster, as she began to rise.

"A moment, if you will, Mrs. Foster," I stilled her. "I have a few questions."

She stiffened and then turned to the constable with an inquiring look. But he only nodded. "I've asked the doctor to aid in the investigation. So please answer his questions. You've nothing to worry about, Elizabeth. By god, how long have I known you?"

"All your life, Harry," she said, unconsciously smoothing her hair. "I remember when you were just a sniveling little boy, always filthy..."

"Yes, yes," he interrupted her. "What were your questions, Doctor?"

"Only a few routine things, of course, Mrs. Foster," said I, reassuringly. "First of all, you've already demonstrated that you possess duplicate keys to all of the rooms...."

"I have to!" she interrupted. "It is the standard practice at a hotel! Ask anyone! How else do you let the girl in to clean the rooms, or open it when a guest has misplaced their key?"

"Now, now, Elizabeth," Dunkley said. "The doctor is not accusing you of anything, are you, Doctor?"

"Of course not. I was merely trying to establish where the duplicate keys are kept."

"Ah, that's an excellent question, Doctor," said Dunkley, approvingly. "Did the murderer enter via the corridor or via the window? If the former, then he must be one of the guests, since the outside doors were barred."

Mrs. Foster was shaking her head. "No one ever has possession of these keys other than me or occasionally Mr. Boyle, who as you know, was securing his own home last night. I kept them on my person all of last night."

"Even while you slept?" I inquired.

"Yes."

"But you also imbibed some of the drugged wine," I pointed out. "Someone could have taken them off you while you slept."

She shook her head again. "Not possible, Doctor. I am a single woman running a hotel by myself. Much of the time, my only guests are men. I have learned to take precautions. My room is barred at night. I may have slept more deeply than usual, but no man got through my door."

"And you are certain that you barred it last night?" I persisted. "I for one can barely recall how I made my way back to my room."

"I am certain. I did not indulge to the degree that you did, Doctor," she said dryly, a hint of accusation in her tone.

I decided to abandon that line of questioning. "Do you have a dark lantern, Mrs. Foster?" I asked instead.

She frowned. "Of course."

"And where do you keep it?"

"We have several. There is one behind the bar, and one in the kitchen. Why?" she asked, with a suspicious tone in her voice.

"If the murderer came from inside the hotel, then he would have needed a way to move through the corridor without attracting much attention," I explained. "A candle would shed too much light. But a dark lantern would be the perfect way to illuminate his path. It's a common thieves' tool."

"It's a common tool of anyone who lives in a windy place, Doctor," Mrs. Foster lashed out. "Or did you not notice the storm last night?" The sarcasm was plain in her voice. "If you ever have to venture out in a storm like that, you too will need a lantern with a sliding shield! And I thought we established that the murderer did not come from within the hotel? He may have picked the lock on Mr. Dumas' door, but if he left via the window, he did not return! And all of my guests are still here!"

"We need to explore all of the possibilities, Elizabeth," said Dunkley, calmly. "Surely you can see that?"

She was visibly calmed by his words. "Of course, Harry. Any other questions, Doctor?"

"What are your opinions about the War Between the States, Mrs. Foster?"

She frowned. "In what way, Doctor?"

"Were you in favor of one side?"

"No." she said simply.

"Really, madam?" I said with gentle disbelief. "You had no opinion whatsoever?"

"It was not our war," she shrugged. "We profited by it, of course. My father was a cotton broker, so the war was good for us. When it ended, things would have turned tough if he had not been wise with his money. So, you could say that I was in favor of neither side winning."

"That's rather cruel. Think of the young men that died."

"It was not our war," she repeated. "We did not tell them to start it. We had no way to end it. Why would we refrain from profiting from it?"

"Then why, may I ask, do you have a large Confederate flag in my bedchamber?"

She laughed delightedly. "Is that what you are concerned about?" She looked over at the constable. "Harry, you might need to educate your assistant here about the history of our good isle before he will be of much use to you!"

Dunkley looked chagrined. "Doctor, you see, before Ralph Foster bought this building, the upstairs was rented to one Major Norman S. Walker."

Mrs. Foster took up the tale. "Major Walker was a graduate of the West Point military academy and a close friend of Jefferson Davis, the President of the Confederacy. He was appointed to supervise the Confederate Ordnance Bureau's operations in Bermuda, and arrived here in 1863. The rooms above you served as the headquarters for the efforts to run the North's shipping blockade. I freely confess that I became friends with his wife Georgiana. She was a lovely woman, widely read, and the mother of three adorable children. She made their home a meeting place for Southerners visiting the island en route to England, and hosted some wonderful dinners and parties. So, yes, Doctor, I admit that I certainly hoped that Georgiana's family and friends would come through the war unscathed."

"And the bed?" I inquired.

"Hah! That was Georgiana's idea. When she was expecting her fourth child, she insisted that a flag be raised to form the canopy of her four-poster bed. She told me that: 'even if my child could not be born in the South, he would still be born under the Confederate flag.' And when the Walkers left the island, Georgiana insisted that we take her beautiful bed, and it still graces your room, in her memory."

"Has she passed?"

"Oh no, she is well. She and Major Walker lived in England for many years after the war ended, but recently returned to Virginia. But I doubt that they will ever return to live in Bermuda and I miss her greatly."

"And your husband never fought in the American Civil War?"

"Ralph? No!" she said laughingly.

At this point, the constable frowned. "I thought that Ralph did fight somewhere when he was off the island?"

She shook her head violently. "Your memory fails you, Harry. Though tis' natural, as you were but a lad then. Ralph left Bermuda in 1864 to take up acting in London. The war in America was all but over by then. I can promise you that Ralph did not fight in the American Civil War."

She said it with such conviction that it was difficult to doubt her. "I am sorry if I broach a painful subject, but how did your husband die, Mrs. Foster?"

She gazed pensively out of the window. "When Ralph realized that he lacked the talent to be an actor, he returned to Bermuda. We married in 1867, and he first rented the Globe. It was to be out great endeavor together. But he died the following year from the yellow fever."

"My condolences, madam." I paused for a moment. "I have just one more question." I turned to the constable. "Do you have the note from Dumas' room?" He took it from where he had folded it into his notepad and handed it to the proprietress. "Do you recognize this handwriting? Perhaps from the hotel ledger? Could it have been written by one of the current guests?"

She took the paper and gazed at it for a moment, her eyes narrowing. Finally she handed it back to Dunkley. "No, I do not believe that this was written by one of our guests. But I can fetch the ledger if you would like to inspect it?"

He nodded. "That would be lovely. Thank you, Elizabeth. And while you are doing that, if you would be so kind as to ask Mr. Sims to step in here?"

She rose briskly from her seat and made her way to the door. Just as she was about to step out, another question entered my mind. "Have you ever been to France, Mrs. Foster?" I called out.

She suddenly stopped and turned to look at me. "France?" her voice lifted. "No, of course not."

"And yet you know how to cook crepes?" I wondered aloud.

I imagined that she hesitated for a moment. "I learned it from a guest many years ago. A French lady, Madame Dantes, stayed here for a week and was shocked at the limits of my culinary talents. She graciously agreed to teach me some of her skills, and I find that they come in handy with many of my guests from the Continent. Why do you ask?"

I shook my head. "No reason. Just curious, I suppose."

"Anything else then?" she inquired sharply.

Dunkley looked at me, but I could only shake my head. "No, I think that will be all for now, Elizabeth. Thank you," said he.

After she closed the door behind her, Dunkley turned to me with a troubled frown. "What are you thinking, Doctor? You cannot possibly suspect Elizabeth Foster! She has lived in Bermuda her entire life! What possible motive could she have for suddenly deciding to murder one of her guests?"

I shook my head. "I suspect no one and everyone right now, Constable. Because I do not have a history with her, as you do, I am free of prejudices. Some of her actions and words seem suspect, but I agree that she has no conceivable motive. Let's say no more until we have had a chance to question some of the other guests."

§

CHAPTER XII:
THE EVIDENCE OF THE AUSTRALIAN RUGBY-PLAYER

While awaiting the first guest, Constable Dunkley arose and requisitioned a few pieces of paper and a J pen from the writing desk. He had barely resumed his seat when a rap upon the door was quickly followed by the entrance of Mr. Boyle, carrying a great tray of food. At the sight of it, I immediately realized that I was famished and I was touched by this thoughtful gesture. The constable and I snatched a hurried luncheon before the arrival of Mr. Sims into our appropriated interrogation room.

I have already described the extraordinary appearance of Mr. Sims in these pages, so suffice it to say that his great height was especially apparent as he briefly towered over us before sinking into the settee. His massive frame made that piece of furniture appear like a child's chair. As on the day of my arrival at the Globe, he was plainly dressed in a black-frock coat. He turned the full force of his magnetic amber eyes upon us, and raised his sandy eyebrows high upon his masterful forehead. "Constable, Doctor, how can I be of assistance?"

"May I see your identification papers, sir?" asked Dunkley, politely.

Sims drew them from his coat pocket and handed them over for the constable's inspection. "You are Bruce Arthur Sims, born 1840, resident of Sydney, Australia?"

"I am."

"Did you grow up there?" I interjected.

"I did."

"I too spent my childhood in Australia, when my father went prospecting near Melbourne," said I, attempting to establish a rapport with the man.

Sims grimaced. "Unfortunately, my father did not journey to Australia by choice. I will be honest with you, gentlemen, so that you do not think that I am trying to hide anything. He was transported."

I wish that I could report that I hid my surprise well, but I am certain that my astonishment was plain. He clearly saw the brief twitching of my eyebrows. He leaned back into the settee and ran his fingers through his leonine mane of hair. "I am not proud to call my father a convict. But his crime was a common one. One winter day he was caught poaching a deer from a nobleman's estate. His mother was ill and he thought that some fresh meat would help her recover. A more lenient judge may have considered the extenuating circumstances. But my father had dreadful ill-luck and drew one of the harshest magistrates on the bench. At least he was not hung outright, as might have been the case in an earlier decade. He was loaded on a ship with over two hundred so-called felons, ranging from mere boys like him, guilty of only the most minor offences, to hardened rapists and murderers. Chained between decks in the hold of a rat-gutted, beetle-ridden coaster, he must have felt as if he was riding in a moldy old coffin. Treated like animals, many failed to survive the voyage. But my father had an iron constitution and upon finally landing at Botany Bay he served his seven years of hard labor without complaint. When he finally obtained his Certificate of Freedom, his family in England was no more. Rather than return to the land that had treated him so harshly, he chose to remain as a settler in Australia."

"I am truly sorry to hear that," said I.

The man shrugged his massive shoulders. "It is ancient history now, Doctor. My father has passed, and Australia is the only home that I have known."

Dunkley finally spoke up. "Would you be so kind to write a few words for me?" He slid the paper and pen across the low Japanese tea table that separated us from Mr. Sims.

Sims picked up the pen. "What would you like me to write?"

"How about the phrase: 'you will be pleased to note?'" said Dunkley casually, as if the words had just entered his head. "And then your signature, of course."

Sims took up the pen in his massive left paw and quickly wrote out the requested words. Dunkley picked up the paper and studied it for a moment, before carefully folding it and placing it in his memorandum book. "You have large hands, Mr. Sims," he observed.

"I think they are rather proportionate to my frame," replied Sims, stiffly. "What of it?"

Dunkley reached into his wide-awake and drew forth the powder-stained gloves. "Have you ever seen these gloves before?"

Sims' eyes widened at the sight of the gloves. "I have indeed! They are mine," he answered frankly. "Where did you find them?"

Dunkley seemed a bit taken aback at the ease of this confession. "You admit that these are your gloves?"

Sims narrowed his eyes and studied the constable. "I freely admit that these gloves belong to me. But they went missing two days ago. I have not seen them since."

"Where did you misplace them?" asked Dunkley, suspiciously.

"I had been walking early one morning in the graveyard across the way, as I have been wont to do of late, when I sat down upon a bench to meditate. The day had begun rather cool, so I had with me my top-coat and gloves. As I sat there, the sun's rays began to warm me, and I quickly shed those outer layers. I distinctly recall setting the gloves upon the bench next to me. Eventually, my leg began to tighten, so I rose to examine the reason for why the graveyard is separated into various parts by walls. When my curiosity had been settled, I returned to the bench to collect my coat and gloves. Imagine my surprise when the coat was there, but the gloves were missing! I looked around, but no living soul was in sight, and I could not recollect hearing anyone approach while I was away from the bench. As you must know, Constable, the graveyard is not that large."

"Why did you not report it to the police at the time, Mr. Sims?" asked Dunkley, with a serious mien.

The giant snorted, the sound of which brought back thoughts of last night's storm, so massive was his granite-like nose. "I thought it was a prank. Who would go to all of the trouble to steal a pair of worthless gloves, gloves so large as to fit very few men, and ignore the much more valuable top-coat? No self-respecting thief would do such a thing. I figured the gloves would turn up eventually. And so they have," he concluded, motioning to the pair in Dunkley's hands.

"And so they have indeed, Mr. Sims," replied Dunkley. "They have turned up in the luggage of Mr. Dumas, and as you can plainly see, they are heavily stained with gunpowder. I suspect that our murderer wore these gloves while he shot Mr. Dumas in order to avoid marking his hands."

"By Jove!" Sims exclaimed with violent agitation, and he slammed his palm down upon the table. "Someone is trying to frame me! Do I look stupid enough to shoot a man and then leave my gloves at the scene of the crime? Not to mention that I was three sheets to the wind last night from whatever was put into my wine. You cannot possibly think that I did it!"

"I am not certain, Mr. Sims," replied Dunkley, calmly. "The good Doctor here tells me that you were certainly drugged last night. Yet it was your wine that put Mr. Dumas to sleep. And it was your gloves that protected the hands that shot the pistol. You interest me very much, Mr. Sims."

Sims looked Dunkley in the eyes. "I tell you that I slept more deeply last night than I have in a dozen years. After we concluded our game of whist, I was in no shape to have left my bedchambers last night." He spoke with a deep conviction. If he was lying to us, then I judged that he was a magnificent deceiver.

Dunkley appeared as convinced as myself. He was silent for a moment, and he appeared to be collecting his thoughts. "What brought you to Bermuda, Mr. Sims?" he finally asked.

"I am here to recuperate."

"From what?" I inquired.

"Perhaps I have neglected to mention that I am a three-quarter for the Rugby Club that we founded at Sydney University in 1864."

"Ah," I said, raising my eyebrows with sudden comprehension, his great frame very similar to that of some of the other long, slab-sided, loose-limbed men that I could recall opposing.

Sims looked at me with interest. "Have you ever played rugby, Doctor?"

"Indeed," I replied. "I once lined-up at pivot for the Blackheath Club."

"That is a prestigious Club, Doctor. Did they not draw up the original rules for the game back in 1863?"

"I believe that is correct, Mr. Sims, though it was before my time, and I have never had much of a head for dates."

"Well, in any case, to play for a Club of that caliber requires both great skill and excellent endurance."

"Before I injured my *tendo Achillis*, I was reckoned fleet of foot," replied I, modestly.

"I too know something about injuries from our sport. That is how I did in my knee. We were playing a team of lads from the university in Cambridge, Massachusetts, when I suddenly felt like I slipped my right knee-cap."

"May I examine it?" I inquired. The man assented by rolling up the right leg of his trousers. I leaned across the table to feel the capsular space and the motion of the knee for a few minutes before finally giving my opinion. "Your medial collateral ligament, I believe."

"Yes, that's what exactly what Dr. Holmes said," replied Sims.

"Dr. Holmes? Not Oliver Wendell Holmes?" I queried.

"Yes, that was his name. I still have his card in my room, in fact. He was a rather tiny old man who had come out to see us take on the Harvard lads. He was therefore immediately at my side when I collapsed. Do you know him?"

"Not in person, of course, but by reputation. He is one of the great reformers of modern medicine, and a gifted writer to boot. *The Autocrat at the Breakfast Table,* for example."

"Ah," nodded Sims, reflectively. "He did seem surprised when I failed to recognize his name. But I've never been one for books, of course."

"Too bad," I mused, shaking my head. "I would have loved to have met the great man myself. I've often been tempted to take up the pen myself, especially with my injuries accumulating. In fact, I once injured my own medial collateral when Big Bob Ferguson, the three-quarter for Richmond, threw me over the ropes at the Old Deer Park. Like me, you should heal in about ten to twelve weeks, if you stay off it."

"Yes, that's what Dr. Holmes said too. Though I've never taken well to inactivity. At first, I thought I could shave some of that time by recuperating on board the ship to England where my Club was headed next. But I soon found that walking on the wave-tossed decks caused even more harm. I cannot bear to stay off my feet entirely, so I disembarked at Hamilton in order to allow my knee to heal fully before re-joining my Club. The hotels over yonder were prohibitively expensive, so I made my way to this quiet little stretch of the island. At least it was quiet until a dead man turned up in the room next to mine!"

"And what will you do once your injuries become insurmountable?" I inquired. "Rugby is a young man's sport."

Sims leaned back and took a woven pouch from his coat-pocket. At first I thought that he was going to take a pinch of snuff, but instead he removed a small nip of green leaves and slipped it between his teeth and gums. "That is the exact question that I was pondering the other morning in the graveyard. Intimations of mortality, if you will. For many years, my natural gifts have allowed me to absorb a fearful number of injuries. But even the strongest constitution is not proof against the ravages of time. I will soon have to hang up my cleats for good. To be honest, though I would love to re-join my Club in their tour of England and Ireland, I may not physically be able. This knee injury could be the proverbial drop that made the cup run over. But I've never played rugby for money. I have a small annuity, as well as some stock invested at Mawson's. I've always played for the sheer sport of the game, which is the best and soundest thing in the world. That is what I will miss the most. The camaraderie of a group of individuals striving towards a common goal, through both good times and bad. When it is finally over, I suppose that I will have to reinvent my life."

A silence descended upon the three of us as we considered his words. Finally, the constable broke the silence, appropriately as he was both the youngest of us and the least damaged. "Did you know the dead man, Mr. Sims?"

He shook his head and intensely looked Dunkley in the eyes. "I swear to you, Constable, on the grave of my father, that until last night's game of whist I had never spoken to the man before."

Once again, I was absolutely convinced of his veracity. "How about any of the other guests?"

He shrugged and shook his head. "Can't say that I have."

"You certainly seemed intent on a conversation with Dr. Nemcek when I first arrived at the Globe. And then later I noted you walking with Signore Aicardi in the graveyard. Are you certain that you are not prior acquaintances?"

Sims snorted again and then laughed. "Honestly, Doctor. If I only spoke to people that I am familiar with, then I would never meet anyone new! As I told you before, I have never been one to spend time reading. I enjoy nothing so much as a good conversation. Both Dr. Nemcek and Mr. Aicardi are very interesting individuals. As you are yourself, Doctor. I think we had a nice talk the other day about Mr. Shakespeare and his plays. Does that mean that we have once met? Perhaps in a scrum?" concluded Sims, a tone of sarcasm evident in his voice.

"I think that will be all, Mr. Sims," said Dunkley. "Can you please ask Mrs. Foster to send in Mr. Cordeiro?"

As the man unlimbered his giant frame from the settee, he once again towered over us for a moment before moving towards the door. "Good day, gentlemen, and good luck in solving this case. I for one would be most curious to know who drugged me."

Once the door was closed behind him, Dunkley turned to me. "Well, that's a fine specimen of manhood, I think. And he seemed brutally honest. It's a rare man that would admit to being the son of a convict."

I nodded. "That's true. But did you notice the leaves that he was chewing on?"

"Yes, what were they? Some form of strange Australian tobacco?"

"I think not. I am not aware of a green chewing tobacco. Unless I am greatly mistaken, those were the leaves of the coca plant."

Dunkley frowned. "I'm not familiar with those, Doctor."

"Chewing coca leaves increases nervous energy, removes drowsiness, enlivens the spirits, and enables the user to bear great hardships with apparent ease and impunity."

"Are you saying that Mr. Sims could have been immune to the effects of the drug in the wine? That the coca leaves would have prevented drowsiness, but left the effect upon his pupils so that he appeared as affected as you and Dumas?" asked Dunkley, pointedly.

I shook my head in confusion. "I do not know for certain, but I think it is a possibility, at least."

"Damn! Perhaps Sims is our man after all. It would be diabolically clever to willingly take the drug as a means to get at Dumas, while simultaneously diverting suspicion from himself."

"There is only one problem with that theory, Constable. I don't believe that any amount of coca leaves would have allowed a giant like Sims to descend that flimsy ladder in the midst of a raging storm. He is not faking that knee injury, and the ladder simply would not have born his weight."

§

CHAPTER XIII:
THE EVIDENCE OF THE PORTUGUESE WINE
MERCHANT

As we pondered the enigmas raised by the questioning of Mr. Sims, a polite rap upon the door signaled the arrival of the next guest. Constable Dunkley called out for the man to enter. As Senhor Cordeiro bounded into the room, I struggled to think of anything suspicious in his behavior since our first meeting upon the *Caliber*. As I have previously mentioned in these pages, Cordeiro was a tall man, approaching six feet three inches in height, though his relatively slender build made him appear much lither than the gigantic Sims. He was fastidiously dressed in a Norfolk jacket and knickerbockers, with the knee-length breeches worn by sportsmen. He had a cloth cap perched upon his head, and not a hair was out of place either there or from his dark brown waxed moustache. He crisply stopped before the settee and awaited an invitation to sit, which was promptly forthcoming from the constable's wave.

Dunkley stared at the man, as if trying to take his measure. He was clearly a different specimen than the bold, outspoken Mr. Sims. Dunkley would need all of his skills to glean any useful information from this suave Latin. "I am Constable Dunkley. As I am certain that you have heard by now, from either Mrs. Foster or the other guests, a man by the name of Gustave Dumas was murdered in this hotel last night. Who exactly carried out this deed is not yet clear, and thus, it is my duty to question each of the guests. Your papers, please."

Cordeiro drew them from his breast-pocket and handed them over. After a cursory inspection, Dunkley began the inquiry in the same fashion as he had with the Australian rugby-player. "You are Mr. Antonio Jose da Paiva Cordeiro, born 1846, resident of Oporto, Portugal?"

"*Sim*, that is, yes. Correct, mate."

"But you were born on the Azores, I believe you told me?" I interjected.

Cordeiro narrowed his eyes as he glanced at me. "You have a good memory, Doctor. That is true. I am from the Azores, but my business is much easier to run from the mainland, so I spend most of my time there. Unfortunately, the wines of my island home, as opposed to those of our neighbors in Madeira, are sadly underappreciated. Many British gentlemen and ladies travel to Madeira to experience the sun so often lacking in your home island, Doctor. And Madeira is a fine choice, of course, much superior to Cairo or the Riviera. But those few that are fortunate or wise enough to visit the Azores are treated to a unique sight, a remarkable geometrical pattern of long linear walls from and parallel to the rocky shore. The walls were built from irregular weather-worn black basalt stones, and are divided into thousands of small plots of land with no potential for arable cultivation. But the walls protect from the wind and seawater, and provide support for the vines, so that wonderfully hardy grapes may grow there to become bold wines."

Dunkley did not seem overly impressed with this description. "So you are a wine merchant?" he grunted.

Cordeiro drew himself up a bit straighter. "I prefer the term, 'traveler in wines.' I have the enviable task of journeying to some of the greatest vineyards in Iberia and its far-flung islands, as well as the old growths of Bordeaux, Burgundy, and the Rhone Valley. There I sample some of the most magnificent vintages, and decide which of them merits inclusion in my list of worthies for importation to my clients in Portugal, or exportation to my friends abroad."

Dunkley perked up during this statement. "So, do you travel to France often, Mr. Cordeiro?"

The man shrugged. "Of course. Although we have great wines in Portugal and Spain, the *terroir* is different in France, and many a man craves diversity."

"Have you ever met Mr. Dumas before in one of your travels to France?"

Cordeiro shook his head. "Not that I can recall. Clearly the man was French. Such manners the French have. Were it not for their superb wines, I would have nothing to do with them. Where did you say that he was from?"

"Rouen, Normandy."

Cordeiro shrugged again. "They do not make wine in Normandy, mate, only Calvados," said he, simply, as if that was all that needed to be said.

"So, you did not know Mr. Dumas?" said Dunkley, persistently.

"I have told you. I have never met the man."

"And yet," Dunkley probed, "you were willing to share with him your best bottle of wine last night?"

Cordeiro turned and gazed at me, as if he suspected that I was the source of this information, which was in fact the case. "I am sorry, Constable, but am I a suspect in this man's murder?"

"Absolutely. Excepting only the doctor here, who I have asked to assist me with the case, I have not ruled out anyone's possible involvement."

"I see," said Cordeiro slowly, clearly pondering this information. "I wonder, perhaps, if I should then first be inquiring for the services of a solicitor before I answer any more questions?"

Dunkley chuckled. "Now, now, Mr. Cordeiro, I am just getting the lay of the land with some harmless enquiries. I think only a guilty man would need a solicitor for something like this. Now about that wine from last night," drawled Dunkley, in an off-handed manner.

Cordeiro nodded slowly. "As you may have heard, the call for another bottle of wine last night was raised by Mr. Sims. As the storm progressed, I was reminded of a great storm that I experienced as a child. Although my home lies on the other side of the Atlantic, every decade or so a hurricane manages to acquire enough force to cross over and inflict damage upon our isle. On one terrible night, the walls of the nearby warehouse collapsed and brought down the floor into the cellar, where several great vats were shattered. An entire harvest worth of wine trickled between the flagstones before anyone was the wiser, and without anything to sell, everyone in the village went hungry that winter. As the sound of the terrible winds brought back these memories last night, I realized what a shame it would be to let that magnificent bottle of Madeira go to waste. I am certain that the Doctor has told you that it was a truly special wine. It is too bad that the brute did not choose it, or perhaps he would still be alive."

Was the man actually suggesting that he had shot Dumas in a fit of rage over the snub of his bottle, I wondered? "Why do you say that?" inquired Dunkley, intently.

But Cordeiro shrugged again nonchalantly. "Mr. Sims informed me that his bottle had been drugged. I would say that Mr. Dumas chose most poorly."

Dunkley nodded grimly at the obvious truth in those words. "Indeed. And why are you visiting our island?"

"I have made no secret of it. I am trying to break the hold of rum upon this island and open up a new locale to which I may export some of the great wines of Iberia."

"I hate to inform you about this news, Mr. Cordeiro," said Dunkley, "but St. George's is no longer the center of Bermuda. You should be in Hamilton."

Cordeiro shook his head in response. "No, I am afraid that is not possible, mate. I have not the clout of a great claret importer, such as Westhouse & Marbank. The Goslings brothers made sure that no hotel in that town would give me a bed. They have tremendous power locally and are not afraid to use it to keep away a competitor. But I think St. George's is rather perfect. Is your town not known for its history of running goods to the American South? Where else on this island would my 'contraband' foreign wines find so much favor?"

Dunkley nodded again. "Indeed. Perhaps you would do me the favor of providing a copy of your handwriting," said he, changing the subject by pushing the paper and pen across the table.

"The same phrase as is written here, mate?" inquired Cordeiro, referring to what Mr. Sims had written.

"If you please." Once Cordeiro was done, the constable inspected it. From the look upon his face, I could tell that it was no more of a match than Mr. Sims' hand had been. "And your room, Mr. Cordeiro? It is the one immediately next to us?" said he, pointing to the room upon the map that Mrs. Foster had drawn.

"You've got it, mate."

"Did you request the sole bedchambers on the ground floor, Mr. Cordeiro?"

He shrugged. "No. It is simply where Mrs. Foster put me. Any room would have been alright with me. My needs are not great."

Dunkley looked down at Cordeiro's feet, which were clad in a pair of rubber-soled tennis shoes. "I noticed that you wear very quiet shoes, Mr. Cordeiro. Have you been upstairs in the hotel yet?"

Cordeiro licked his lips. "I've had no reason to go upstairs, mate. These shoes are the best for playing lawn tennis. I had hoped to find a court today in order to obtain some exercise."

"So you are a player of *Sphairistike*, Senhor Cordeiro?" said I, finally added something to the questioning.

He snorted. "Come now, Doctor, only Major Wingfield calls it by that ridiculous name. Everyone else terms it lawn tennis, which is sufficient to distinguish it from the royal tennis that they play indoors."

"And are you any good?" I persisted.

"Aye, mate. I'm not half-bad. I've even played a bit in your homeland, at a little private club southwest of London, in the town of Wimbledon."

"The All England Croquet and Lawn Tennis Club? You did not play in the Championship tournament?" said I, dubiously.

"In fact, I did, mate," said the man, without a trace of modesty. "Not the first year, of course. But I almost won the second year, which was just two years ago. I lost to the eventual champion in the semi-finals."

"Really?" said I, raising an eyebrow questioningly. I fancy that I am a sporting man, and when my injuries prevent my own participation, I follow the endeavors of others with great interest. If Senhor Cordeiro was bluffing, I was certain to call him on it. "I've forgotten," I pretended, "who was the first Gentleman's Singles champion?"

"That old bore, Spencer Gore, or course," responded Cordeiro at once. "He thrashed William Marshall (6-1, 6-2, 6-4). But it was not much of a feat. There were only twenty-two entrants, and the final game was postponed for four days due to rain, so he had plenty of time to rest. He took home the prize of twelve guineas and a silver cup, but was not much enamored of the game. In fact, I believe that he called it a 'monotonous game compared with others.'"

"And your year?" said I weakly, as it was now clear that the man was telling the truth, but I was forced to politely inquire.

"In 1878, Gore failed to defend his title when he lost to Frank Hadow in the finals (7-5, 6-1, 9-7). Hadow possessed a devastating weapon, which he termed the 'lob,' and it thwarted all of us who came across it. I've now added it to my own repertoire, of course, but at the time I was defenseless and Hadow eviscerated me (6-1, 6-3, 7-5)."

"What about last year? I hear that Hadow refused to defend his title?"

"That is true. Of course, he had only played the year prior as he happened to be in London whilst on holiday from his coffee plantation in Ceylon. When he was asked if he was going to return, he reportedly retorted, 'No sir. It's a sissy's game played with a soft ball.' I disagree of course, but I developed a terrible pain in the socket of my shoulder last year that knocked me out of returning. I'm afraid that the doctors have been unable to do much about it other than counsel rest. It is just now starting to return to normal, but I've already missed this year's tournament as well. Hopefully by next year I will be ready to mount another challenge."

Dunkley was bristled by the track that this conversation had taken and gruffly interrupted us. "Thank you very much, Mr. Cordeiro. You've gotten us side-tracked with your interesting anecdotes. I would ask that you cancel your plans for locating a tennis lawn and remain at the hotel for the time being."

"For how long, mate?"

"Until I have had time to question all of the guests, and have the murderer in custody," retorted the constable, severely.

Senhor Cordeiro was immediately contrite. "Of course, Constable."

With a nod of his head, Dunkley indicated that the man could leave. He gracefully rose from the settee and made his way towards the door. Before he could reach it, however, I called out one last question. "What happened to the bottle of Madeira?"

"Excuse me?" said Cordeiro, plainly confused.

"The bottle of Madeira that we almost drank last night, if Monsieur Dumas had so chosen. What did you do with it?"

"Ah," he paused for a moment. "Well, you see, mate, I was so angry that I went to my room and drank it myself."

"The entire bottle?"

He shrugged. "I would never waste a drop of a wine so magnificent."

"Thank you, Senhor. That was my last question."

Cordeiro tipped his cap to us and departed. Dunkley and I sat in silence for a moment digesting what we had learned. Finally, the constable spoke. "Well, Doctor, what do you think now of your theory that the person in the downstairs chamber could not be the murderer? I suspect that Mr. Cordeiro and his tennis shoes could have silently climbed those stairs."

I nodded my agreement with this conclusion.

"But, of course," Dunkley continued, "he had little motive for the killing. I can't imagine that Dumas' insult of his wine was enough to provoke such a brutal murder. No, I think we can rule out Mr. Cordeiro. What is it, Doctor? You look troubled."

I shrugged off my suspicions. "It is nothing. Who are we going to interrogate next?"

"I have been pondering that very question. Tell me, Doctor, when Mrs. Foster opened Mr. Sims' bottle of wine, did you notice how it was sealed?"

"Yes," I nodded. "It was corked, of course, and the cork covered in a yellow wax."

"Did you notice any signs of tampering?"

"No, but I admit that I was not on the watch for such a thing."

"And yet, as you have told me, Mr. Dumas was! He inspected every bottle that he drank from, did he not, fearing poison?"

"Yes," I agreed.

"And so, if the original wax had been stripped, and the cork temporarily removed in order to introduce the laudanum, the wax must have been expertly reapplied, or Dumas would have noticed."

I nodded slowly, thinking it through. "That appears to be a safe deduction."

"But this bottle belonged to Mr. Sims, and was kept in his room. Who would have had the time to do such a thing? Only Mr. Sims! No one else would have dared to spend that much time in his room. The other explanation is that someone stole the bottle from his room, drugged it, repaired the wax, and then re-burgled Sims' room in order to replace it?"

"That sounds absurd," said I, shaking my head.

"I agree. So where does that leave us? Back to Mr. Sims."

I continued to shake my head. "Even if Sims could have fought off the effects of the laudanum sufficiently in order to leave his room and aim a gun, which for the record I highly doubt despite the possible aid of the coca leaves, I remain convinced that a man of his size and with his injured knee could never have climbed that ladder. Sims is innocent," I concluded firmly.

"Then how did the laudanum get into the bottle of wine?" asked Dunkley.

For several minutes I silently pondered this question. I tried to imagine how I would have accomplished such a feat, if I had been the murderer. And then an inspiration appeared in my brain. "I can think of a way to introduce the laudanum quickly, while leaving almost no trace upon the wax."

"How?" inquired Dunkley, eagerly.

"We have already determined that the murderer is skilled in the art of picking locks, since that must be how he entered Monsieur Dumas' room. If the murderer first broke into Mr. Sims' room, he could have used a hypodermic syringe to inject the laudanum through the wax and the cork into the wine. A small hole would have remained in the wax, but a quick application of a candle could have melted the hole out of existence. The resulting imperfection would have been so small that Dumas could have easily missed it."

"That is brilliant, Doctor," said Dunkley, without a trace of mockery in his voice. "It would take a cool hand to go and do that, but it is possible."

"And it would have been a very fast procedure. A bold man could have done it in less than a minute. They could have even been listening to our conversation below from the upper landing and raced to Sims' room when it became clear that Dumas intended to join him in a drink."

"So anyone lodging in a room upon the first floor would be a possible suspect."

"Indeed," remarked I, looking at Mrs. Foster's map. "That includes Signore Aicardi, Mr. Warburton, Monsieur Dubois, and Dr. Nemcek."

"Do not forget Mrs. Dubois and the Marquesa, Doctor."

"A woman?" said I. "Surely not."

"Whatever the motive was for last night's murder, it was plainly a crime of passion. There is no other explanation for the number of gunshots, when one or two would have been sufficient. And where there is passion, I always suspect a woman may be involved."

"Well, at least we can safely say that the Marquesa is not fit enough to carry out such a bold plan."

"Perhaps," nodded Dunkley. "Perhaps. But if your theory is correct, Doctor, I think we can narrow down the suspects even more. I can think of only one person, other than you, who is likely to possess a hypodermic needle."

"Dr. Nemcek," I said.

"Indeed," agreed the constable. "I think it is time to pay the Doctor a visit, rather than the other way around, wouldn't you say?"

§

CHAPTER XIV:
THE EVIDENCE OF THE BOHEMIAN PHYSICIAN

Constable Dunkley and I rose from our chairs and decamped from the parlor. Exiting into the dining room, we found most of the guests of the hotel gathered there. Clearly, the constable's instructions had been obeyed and no one was venturing far from the scene of the crime. Everyone looked at him with anxiety plainly stamped on their faces. My eyes involuntarily sought out Madame Dubois and found that she was looking at me with a long, questioning gaze. An absurd gush of hope rushed to my heart that she might share my feelings.

"Dr. Nemcek?" called out Dunkley.

"Yes?" replied my fellow physician. As he rose from his seat, I recalled when I had first seen this brother medico. Nemcek had been speaking intimately with Mr. Sims in this very room when I arrived at the Globe, though he had now removed the jacket from his neat suit and his top hat was nowhere to be seen. Despite the casual appearance of his dress, his person was still immaculately groomed.

"Doctor," continued Dunkley, "we would like to talk with you in your room."

"Certainly, sir." If the man was discomforted by this thought, he hid it well. "It is upstairs."

"Yes, the first on the right, I know," said Dunkley, who had plainly memorized Mrs. Foster's map. "I will lead the way, if you don't mind."

Nemcek and I followed the constable up the creaking stairs. As we reached the upper landing, Dunkley rounded upon the doctor. "Tell me, Dr. Nemcek, are you a heavy sleeper?"

The man looked surprised by the question, but quickly recovered. "No, absolutely not. Years of being roused in the middle of the night for medical emergencies have habituated me to waking at the slightest sound."

"Have you noticed that these stairs tend to make loud noises when you walk upon them?"

"Of course, sir. The door to my room is not heavy, and I can certainly tell when someone is climbing the stairs."

"Even during the night?" probed Dunkley.

"Absolutely," replied Nemcek.

"And last night? Did anyone climb the stairs after you retired?"

The doctor nodded. "Yes, there were three sets of steps, all together, about midnight."

"How do you know it was at midnight?"

Nemcek shrugged nonchalantly. "I was still awake reading a recent edition of *The Lancet*. I glanced at my watch when I heard the steps, as I thought they were rather late."

"And after those three?" said Dunkley, persistently.

Nemcek shook his head. "Nothing."

"You are certain of it?"

"Yes," said the doctor, calmly.

"If you are such a light sleeper, Doctor, then why did you not hear the seven gunshots that rang out last night?"

Nemcek pursed his lips and shook his head again. "There are several walls between my room and that of the deceased. Surely these muffled the noise sufficiently enough as to cause me to confuse the shots with the sound of the booming thunder. You do agree, Constable, that the thunder was particularly loud last night?"

Dunkley failed to answer this rhetorical question and instead indicated for Nemcek to open the door to his room. Once that task had been accomplished, the three of us entered only to find the small space a bit cramped. Dunkley indicated that Dr. Nemcek should sit on his bed, while he and I stood. "Your papers, sir?"

Dr. Nemcek handed them over as requested. After a brief perusal, Dunkley looked up. "Leoš Nemcek, born 1847. You are a citizen of Austria-Hungary?"

"*Ano,* yes," he replied tightly.

"From Prague?"

"Indeed. I am a Bohemian."

I frowned and entered the interrogation. "I had always assumed that a Bohemian was one of the free-spirited artists that haunt the Montmartre district of Paris."

The man laughed deeply, flashing a golden filling as he did so. "Very amusing, Doctor," said he, suavely. "I am afraid that you have read a bit too much of Thackeray's *Vanity Fair.* No, I must admit that I do not fully comprehend how those artists appropriated our name, but I am a

Bohemian in the truest sense of the word. The lands of my ancestors have been distinct since the ninth century."

"Are they not simply a Germanic nation?" interjected Dunkley.

"*Mit der dummheit kämpfen götter selbst vergebens*," muttered Nemcek.

"What was that?" said Dunkley, sharply.

"Nothing," replied Nemcek, plainly equivocating and obviously not suspecting that I was fully versed in my Schiller and well-conversant in German. I decided that the quotation was not very kind to the constable. 'Against stupidity the gods themselves contend in vain,' indeed!

"So it is Slavonic then?" continued Dunkley.

"Yes, the Bohemians are part of the western Slavs," answered Nemcek, calmly, his irritation now apparently under control.

"But as an Austro-Hungarian, are not the French your natural rivals?" persisted Dunkley.

Nemcek smirked. "Hardly, Constable. The French may be vying with the Empire that rules Bohemia, but they are not my enemies. In fact, I took my medical degree in France."

"Where?" I inquired.

"Montpellier," the man replied with the name of one of France's finest universities. "I studied there under Dr. Ainstree."

"France, eh?" interjected Dunkley. "So you must have been familiar with Mr. Dumas?"

Nemcek shrugged his shoulders. "Honestly, Constable, I had never met the man before my arrival upon your fair island. France is a big land, you know. And Montpellier is tucked down in the far south."

"And why are you visiting Bermuda, Doctor?" continued Dunkley.

Nemcek took off his glasses and used a piece of chamois leather to polish them as he replied. "I found that I no longer wished to live under the Austrian yoke, so I left Prague," he explained. "After I completed my schooling, I initially spent some time in London with one of my uncles on my mother's side, by the name of Antonín Dvořák. He keeps a large general store on the Commercial Road, and deals in items from the old country. Do you know the store, Doctor?"

I admitted that it was unfamiliar to me. "I'm afraid that is Whitechapel. Royal London Hospital territory. My haunts were near the University by Russell Square and by St. Bart's in Smithfield."

"Yes, well, I found that my medical skills were not in great demand in London, as the British tend to want to be treated by one of their own," continued Nemcek. "In correspondence with one of my cousins, Rudolph, he put forward that no such prejudices exist in America, so I am joining him there in Chicago. I had entrusted my belongings to the

Aberdeen Shipping Company, which ultimately proved to be an unwise choice. Everything was delayed at Cherbourg, and rather than arrive in the chaos of New York without my trunks, I thought it wise to delay for a few days upon this fair isle."

"Chicago is a rough town, Doctor," interjected Dunkley. "It is filled with gangs of dangerous crooks."

"Ah yes, I have heard as much. Fortunately, I have prepared myself."

Dunkley's eyebrows rose. "You have a pistol?" he inquired.

"Of course," said Nemcek, off-handedly. "We Czechs invented them, back during the Hussite Wars, and a true Czech would never be without one in today's dangerous world. You gentlemen may find it interesting that the word 'pistol' is, in fact, the only word in the English language derived from the Czech."

"Indeed," said Dunkley dryly, apparently uninterested. "May I see it?" he asked.

"Certainly." Nemcek arose from his perch on the bed and moved to where his valise rested under the north window.

Before he could open it, however, Dunkley stopped him. "If you don't mind, Doctor, I would prefer to open it myself?"

Dr. Nemcek raised his hands in acquiescence. "But of course."

Dunkley set the valise on the bed and flipped it open. Inside laid a quaint carved wooden pistol box. He drew this forth and opened it to reveal a six-shot open-framed revolver, loaded via a hinged gate on the right side of the frame, through which empty cartridges were ejected via a rod running along the barrel. "Ah, this is a Lefaucheux M1858, is it not?"

"That is correct. You know your guns, Constable."

"It does not appear to have been recently fired," noted Dunkley.

"No," agreed Nemcek. "I fortunately have had little need."

"It is a French gun," insinuated Dunkley.

Nemcek shrugged. "Yes, you could view it in that fashion, since Monsieur Lefaucheux was of course French. But I believe that his pistol design was very popular. Models were purchased by half the nations of Europe and both the Confederate and Federal forces in the American Civil War."

"Si vis pacem para bellum," I interjected, suddenly.

Nemcek glanced at me. "Exactly, Doctor. I would not say that I am in favor of war, or any form of violence for that matter, but I do believe in being prepared."

I concluded from this little test that his Latin was excellent, as I would expect from any medical man. He certainly seemed authentic. But there was another method to test this, and that was to examine his satchel. The constable was clearly thinking along the same lines.

"And your medical bag, sir?" said Dunkley.

Dr. Nemcek handed over the satchel, which was a folding piece of nice brown leather with a silver clasp. From it Dunkley proceeded to extract various medical instruments, which by their worn nature were clearly the property of a busy physician. Amongst the other items in the bag were a cannula, some clamps, a phial of iodoform, some nitrate of silver, cotton wadding, and numerous carbolized bandages. Dunkley was plainly not interested these items or Nemcek's stethoscope, and he tossed them aside onto the bed. He paused abruptly when he brought forth an ebony-handled knife with a very delicate inflexible blade marked Evans & Co., London. Its tip was guarded by a cork. "Now this is an interesting weapon, Doctor. I suspect that you could make a deep incision with this and leave barely a trace."

I shook my head. "I don't think so, Constable. That is what we call a cataract knife. It is quite fine and used only for precise surgeries. It could not possibly be used as a weapon."

"Unless the victim was asleep, perhaps drugged?" proposed Dunkley.

"Well, yes, I suppose that is possible" I agreed, reluctantly.

Nemcek grew warm and interrupted us. "Gentlemen! I must protest. I have already heard from Mr. Sims that the Frenchman was shot. Why are you so interested in my knife? Do you not have one too, Doctor?"

Before I could answer, Dunkley shook his head. "I am not really interested in the knife, Doctor. I am interested in this." With a flourish, Dunkley drew a neat red goatskin gilded morocco case from the bag. Flicking open its hook, he flipped the lid to reveal a hypodermic syringe. He lifted the syringe from the case with nervous fingers and brought it up to his eyes for closer inspection. He touched the sharp tip with his finger and experimented with plunging the tiny piston. He measured the length of the needle, which plainly was sufficiently longer than that of a typical wine-bottle cork. "It appears to be clean."

Nemcek shrugged. "Of course, I have had little need for it recently."

"Then how do you explain these?" said Dunkley, holding up a pair of empty phials that he had removed from the satchel.

"Many ladies onboard the vessel with me suffered from seasickness during the passage to Bermuda. I have found that a low dose of morphia is often helpful in alleviating these symptoms."

Dunkley turned and looked at me. "I agree with Dr. Nemcek," I volunteered.

Dunkley snorted in exasperation. "Well then, Doctor, are you acquainted with any of the other guests of the Globe?"

"Certainly," he nodded.

"You are?" I asked, surprised.

"Of course," continued the man. "I've conversed with every person staying here, some more than others, Mr. Sims for example. And I've had little to say to the Marquesa, I suppose, but..."

"What I meant was: 'did you know any of the other guests before your arrival upon Bermuda?'" said Dunkley, interrupting him.

"Oh no, definitely not," replied Nemcek, assuredly.

Dunkley pursed his lips. "May we have a copy of your handwriting then, Doctor?" He fished the note already written upon by Sims and Cordeiro out of his breast-pocket. "Just the same as the others, if you please."

Nemcek took the paper over to a small writing desk and carefully wrote out the prescribed phrase with a somewhat archaic nib pen. When complete, he picked it up and blew on the paper to assist in the drying process before handing it back to Dunkley. The inspector examined the paper and nodded to himself, before folding it up and replacing it in his pocket.

"That will be all for now, Dr. Nemcek." With a nod to me, Dunkley exited the doctor's room. He paused for a moment upon the upper landing and glanced at me as if to ascertain my opinion, which I obligingly provided.

"I have no doubt that he is a skilled physician. Therefore more than anyone else in the hotel he possesses the skill to add the optimal amount of laudanum to Sims' bottle of wine that would permit the taste of it to pass undetected, and yet successfully stupefy all who drank from the bottle. And, of course, he had several empty phials."

"But you are not convinced?" probed Dunkley.

I shook my head. "No, I am not. Yes, he trained in France and owns a French pistol. Thus it is certainly possible that he knew Dumas. But I still do not see a motive. For a physician to violate his Hippocratic Oath – 'I will not give a deadly drug to anybody' – would be a grave offense."

Dunkley snorted. "It certainly was 'grave' enough for Dumas! You are too trusting, Doctor. History is unfortunately replete with physicians who have ignored their oath and committed the most foul of deeds. Dr. Webster of Harvard, for example."

"Yes," nodded I, in sad agreement, "I suppose that you are correct. We must keep Dr. Nemcek on the list of suspects. Whom do you plan to question next?"

Dunkley shook his head. "The most solid clue that we have is the burned Turkish slipper. Which of the guests strikes you as being the most likely to own such a slipper?"

I frowned in bafflement. "I suppose anyone could own a pair of Turkish slippers."

"But are they not uncommon? I suspect that the most likely person to own something from Turkey would be someone from that country."

"Ah, Mr. Bey, then?" said I, finally following his train of thought.

"Yes," he nodded. "Mr. Bey."

§

CHAPTER XV:
THE EVIDENCE OF THE TURKISH ENGINEER

Constable Dunkley and I made our way back down the creaking staircase to the dining room, where we found the assembled guests anxiously awaiting us. Dunkley surveyed the crowd before calling out, "Mr. Bey, if you would be so kind as to step into the parlor."

Bey rose from his place at one of the tables and followed us quietly into our appropriated room of interrogation. As the three of us settled into our placed in the parlor, Bey in the settee facing us, I took his measure. He was a small, wiry man with the swarthy complexion typical of his countrymen. His hair and eyes were dark, yet he wore a sardonic grin that animated his eyes in such a way so as to instill a sense of companionship in all whom he beheld. His eyes were covered by grey-framed rounded glasses that imparted a scholarly air to his bearing. These rested upon his great curved nose, which in turn presided over his heavy moustache. He wore the same neat dark-grey suit that I had noted the first morning after my arrival, as well as his odd checked shepherd's muffler. The only new piece of ornamentation was a silver necklace from which dangled a glass pendant with a series of concentric circles, first a deep blue outer rim, then white, then a lighter shade of blue, and finally a central black area, the combination of which greatly reminded me of a staring eye. If I thought to learn something profound from this inspection, however, I was greatly mistaken. The man and his passions were still a complete mystery to me.

"Your papers, please," said Dunkley, beginning the inquiry.

Similar to the actions of our other guests, Bey's documents were rapidly provided without debate. Dunkley peered at them. "You are Mr. Mehmet Nazim Bey, born 1846 in Istanbul, Ottoman Empire?"

"*Evet*, yes, that is correct," replied Bey in perfect English, but with enough of an accent to place him as a foreigner.

"And you are an engineer?"

"Yes. I specialize in locomotives. They are the future of transportation."

Dunkley snorted. "Not in Bermuda!"

Bey shrugged. "Perhaps not. It is too small. But in larger countries they have become essential."

"As an engineer, you must be familiar with many tools?" said Dunkley, probingly.

Bey's eyebrows rose questioningly at this odd tack. "Of course."

"If we were to search your luggage would we happen to find a tension wrench, a pick, a hook, or a rake?"

Bey's mouth tightened as Dunkley pronounced this list. "Sir, those are not the tools of a railway engineer," replied Bey heatedly. "They are the components of a pick-set. I am neither a locksmith, nor a burglar, and I would encourage you to examine my room immediately if you think otherwise."

Dunkley nodded. "Perhaps we will, sir, perhaps we will. But tell me, why have you left Turkey, Mr. Bey?"

"Are you aware of the current political situation in the Ottoman Empire, Constable?"

Dunkley shook his head. "No, I am not."

Bey shook his head, as if annoyed by ignorance of the constable. From his breast-pocket, he pulled out a pipe carved from a white stone, clearly meerschaum, and clapped it unlit between his teeth. "Then please allow me to enlighten you. Four years ago, Abdul-Hamid II assumed the throne after his brother, Murad V, suffered a mental breakdown. Abdul-Hamid is a cruel despot, who relies upon censorship and his secret police to keep the populace in line. Two years ago he dismissed the Parliament and suspended the constitution. Like a spider in his lair, he rules from the seclusion of his palace. Someday soon he will be deposed. But until that time, Turkey is no place for a man who seeks to use his brain and live in the modern world."

"And where have you gone since then?"

"I have moved about seeking work. I was in Cairo for a time. From there I went to Paris briefly, then on to Greenwich, where I apprenticed for the firm of Venner and Matheson. Finally I went to London, where I worked for Mr. Stephenson's Institution of Mechanical Engineers. The stamps on my passport should tell the story, I think."

"So why are you in Bermuda? There is no locomotive here."

"It is a stop-over. The great railways of Europe are essentially complete. I realized that I was no longer content to merely maintain what others had built. I wished to be on the frontier, where the rails were first being laid down. There is only one place that fits that description: the western United States. So I am headed there to find a position, hopefully with the Central Pacific Railroad Company. However, I realized that the western deserts will be a harsh place, so I decided to briefly indulge myself in this veritable oasis of pleasure before I continued with the final leg of my voyage."

"I have a question, if I may," I interjected.

Dunkley nodded, so I pressed on. "When we broke down the door to Dumas' room, there were five of us present. Mr. Sims, Mr. Delopolous, and I were quite shaken by what we found. Mrs. Foster was so upset that she fainted. You alone appeared calm and collected. Some might suggest that is because you were already aware of what we would find behind that door?"

Bey grinned sardonically. "Really, Doctor? You may have been shaken for a moment, but you rapidly sprang into action to first examine Dumas' body and then tend to the stricken Mrs. Foster. Why do you think that is?"

"Unfortunately, I have seen my share of dead men before, both during my medical training and then on the battlefields of Afghanistan. My nerves have been hardened."

"Exactly," responded Bey with a flourish of his hands.

"Are you saying that you were a soldier, Mr. Bey?"

"Not at all. But the railway profession is hardly a safe one. I have seen some terrible injuries in my time at the scenes of railway smashes. Limbs hacked from bodies, so that only red spongy surfaces remain. Whole bodies so mangled that you could hardly tell that it was even a man, and not some mute beast. As you say, eventually your nerves become hardened. Although the discovery of a dead man was certainly a surprise, he looked rather peaceful compared to some of the sights that I have seen."

I nodded slowly. "I would agree with that assessment."

Bey continued. "Doctor, I noticed that you are suffering from a recent injury. I highly recommend a stint in a Turkish bath. It is highly restorative."

This was a suggestion that I had not previously considered. "Have they one in Bermuda?"

Bey shook his head. "Alas, no. Not that I have found. But if you were to return to London, you will find many there. I recommend Urquhart's or Nevill's. Either will give you a fresh starting-point, a cleanser of your system."

"Thank you for that counsel, Mr. Bey. I may seek one out upon my return."

Dunkley interrupted this tangential exchange. "I was noticing your evil eye, Mr. Bey," said the constable, indicating the man's necklace. "Do you intend harm to someone?"

Bey raised his hand to the pendant. "Ah, you refer to my *nazarlık*. This is no weapon, Constable, it is a ward. It fends off negative energy from jealous gazes."

"But it is Turkish, is it not?"

Bey shrugged. "Of course. So is the *hookah* you will find in my attaché. But neither is responsible for the death of Mr. Dumas."

Dunkley reached into his bag and pulled forth the burnt slipper. "Tell me, Mr. Bey, is this your slipper?"

"No," he rapidly replied.

Dunkley's eyebrows rose. "How can you be so certain? Surely you must own a pair of Turkish slippers?"

"Of course I do. I own a pair very similar to those. They are in my room now. Perhaps you would care to see them?" said he, gesturing to the door.

"A man can own two pairs of slippers," observed Dunkley.

Bey smiled. "I am a poor engineer, Constable, not the Sultan of Turkey. I do not travel with giant chests and trains of servants. One pair of slippers is all that I could manage to fit in my simple luggage."

"But we have only your word for that. Perhaps you would care to try it on?"

"And if I did, what would that prove?" scoffed Bey. "That I have the same size foot as a thousand other men upon this island? This is not *La Cenerentola!*"

Dunkley frowned. "I do not follow you."

Bey shook his head exasperatedly. "The opera by Rossini, how do you call it in English... Cinderella!"

Dunkley pursed his lips, perhaps unwilling to admit his ignorance of the stage. "But you admit that they are Turkish slippers?"

"In fact, Constable, I do not," replied Bey. "I believe that what you are holding is a Persian slipper."

Dunkley frowned again. "Are they not the same?"

"Not at all!" said the man, heatedly. "The Ottoman Empire never conquered the Persians. Thus, our traditions differ. While both slippers have a pointed toe, the style of embroidery is vastly dissimilar."

"I see," said Dunkley dryly, the skepticism plain in his voice. "And tell, Mr. Bey, were you previously acquainted with any of the other guests of the Globe, including the dead man?"

"No, I have never seen Dumas before in my life." His tone was emphatic.

"But you are sharing the garret room with Mr. Delopolous, are you not?" said Dunkley, consulting Mrs. Foster's map.

Bey shrugged. "I am not yet employed by the Central Pacific Railroad, Constable, and it is still a long journey to California. I must be careful with my funds, so as to not exhaust them prematurely. The garret room was the cheapest accommodation offered by Mrs. Foster, and I have never been averse to boarding with others."

Dunkley grunted unhappily at this reasonable response, and switched gears, asking Bey to write the same statement as the others. After inspecting the man's handwriting, Dunkley dismissed him. Bey rose from the settee and, with a very courteous air, nodded his head to us before passing out through the door.

"What do you think, Doctor?" said Dunkley, irritably.

I shook my head. "All of his answers appeared very reasonable. I admit that the slipper is a potential link to him, but without the missing half of the pair, it is hardly conclusive. He has no apparent motive, and since he shared a room, his companion will likely be able to offer him an alibi."

"He admitted to being in Paris for some time. He could have met Dumas there."

"True, but if everyone who has ever visited Paris is a suspect, then our list will be long indeed."

"I suppose that you are correct, Doctor. Well, let us check out his alibi then. I think Mr. Delopolous should be next."

§

CHAPTER XVI:
THE EVIDENCE OF THE GREEK PUGILIST

Dunkley rose from his seat and walked over to the door. Opening it, he peered into the packed dining room. "Mr. Delopolous, would you join us, please?

The man arose and followed Dunkley back into the parlor. As he sat down, I studied his appearance. He was a short, stout man, with a powerful frame. If his name was not enough of a clue, his olive skin and coal-black hair were completely consistent with his proclaimed country of origin. As I had noted previously, his face was strong yet deeply lined in the areas where it was visible, for a large bristling black beard covered much of it. His ears were remarkable for a peculiar flattening and thickening, and the right had a distinctive mark that suggested it had once been pierced for an earring, was no longer present. When I first laid eyes upon the man I had thought that his dark eyes sparkled animatedly, but now they appeared hooded with dread. I watched his crinkled hands, which he nervously clenched in a spasmodic fashion. His clothes were the same he wore every time I had seen him; the old navy pea jacket over a red-and-black check shirt, with a coarse red scarf was loosely wound around his neck, and denim trousers slipped into heavy boots. If he owned another outfit, I had yet to lay eyes on it.

Dunkley commenced the questioning in his typical fashion. Delopolous rummaged in his coat pocket for a moment, and then handed his identity papers over to the constable. Dunkley looked at them for a moment before asking, "You are Aristides Delopolous, born 1846, Athens, Kingdom of Greece?"

The man made a sort of hiccoughing noise in his throat before answering. "No."

Dunkley eyebrows shot upwards. "No?"

The man stammered to correct himself. "I mean, yes, my name is Aristides Delopolous, but I was not born in Athens."

"Then why does your passport make this claim?" asked Dunkley severely.

"I was actually born in Iraklion, Crete."

"I still fail to see why you have falsified your passport, sir!"

Immediately the answer came to me. "Crete is not part of Greece, Constable," I interjected. "It is under the control of the Ottoman Empire."

Delopolous nodded angrily. "We are Greeks in our hearts. Someday we will break free from their yoke and join our countrymen."

"So, this entire passport is falsified!" exclaimed Dunkley.

Delopolous shook his head vigorously. "Not entirely, sir. My mother is from Athens. She is a Kratides, a proud clan hailing from the capital. From her, I claim my citizenship as a Greek."

"It is highly irregular, Mr. Delopolous!"

"Yes, sir, that is why I wanted to bring it to your attention immediately. If you were to check upon my background, I did not want you to think that I was being dishonest with you."

Dunkley nodded reluctantly. "That was wise. I am still considering whether I need to report you to the authorities at Hamilton. You entered our country under false pretenses."

"Whatever you think is best, sir. I will accept your judgment. It is true that I refuse to admit to being a citizen of the Ottoman Empire. But I am not a murderer," said the man, passionately.

"I don't recall saying that you were, Mr. Delopolous," replied Dunkley, evenly.

"Isn't that why you are questioning everyone in the hotel? Are we not all suspects?"

"Perhaps," replied Dunkley, calmly. "Or perhaps I already know the identity of the murderer, but wish to have all of the evidence in place for my report."

"You do?" said the man, his eyes opening wide. "One of the guests?" he asked breathlessly.

"Perhaps," answered Dunkley, nodding. "Perhaps. Tell me, Mr. Delopolous, did your bunk-mate in the garret, Mr. Bey, ever leave your room last night?"

The man seemed to consider this question. "No, I do not believe so."

"What about whilst you slept? Could you swear that he did not leave between midnight and two in the morning?"

"On a normal night, I would not be able to say, as I am an extremely sound sleeper. It used to be a jest amongst my shipmates that once in my hammock only the watch bell could ever wake me during the night. I would not startle even if the ship was fetched up on a reef. But last night I lay awake, for my lumbago was bothering me too much to sleep. It was not until very late, around four in the morning, when I finally fell asleep. He may have left after that, but not before."

"I see," said Dunkley, plainly dejected at the thought that at least one suspect appeared to have an iron-clad alibi. "And what is your occupation, Mr. Delopolous?"

The man shrugged. "I have done many things in my life. For many years I was a sailor. Eventually I grew weary of picking my salt meat out of the harness cask and I jumped ship in Dantzig, never looking back. Recently, I have earned my keep by engaging in the sport of gentlemen."

"Boxing?" exclaimed I, dubiously.

He nodded vigorously. "You do not have to be tall to be a successful boxer, Doctor. You must be quick and strong. I am both. I was once light-weight champion of New York City. Furthermore, your Marquess of Queensbury may have codified the modern British rules, but we Greeks invented the sport... *pygmachia*, we call it. Towards the end of the *Iliad*, Homer depicts boxing as one of the funeral contests held in honor of the fallen Patroclus. And of course, it was part of the original Games at Olympia, which some are now trying to revive in Athens. So no country produces superior pugilists to those of Greece."

"Your English is excellent, Mr. Delopolous," I continued. "Have you spent time in England?"

He shook his head. "Sadly, no. A few days at Portsmouth during a revictalling, but nothing more. Fortunately, my cousin spent some time at one of your universities, Oxford, I believe it was. He was highly sought after by the students there for tutoring in Greek, which is essential to the examination required for certain scholarships. He was a natural linguist, and upon his return home, he would work with me, my brothers, and my cousins, to ensure that we all had a firm grasp of your tongue, in case we ever found ourselves in an English-speaking country. Sadly, most of my family never truly picked it up, but I share his ability to acquire foreign languages easily. Although he eventually moved to London to serve as a guide and interpreter, I've never lost the skill."

"And what other languages do you speak, Mr. Delopolous? French perhaps?" interjected the constable.

"*Oui*," said the man, nodding. "My ships often called at Marseilles. And the lingua franca is widely spoken across the globe. Of course, I have acquired a fluency with it over the years."

"And Mr. Dumas? Were you familiar with him?"

"I believe that I spoke to him once, a few days ago. I had ordered a brandy from Mr. Boyle, and Dumas made a disparaging remark about it.

We argued briefly about the best aperitif, but he didn't appear interested in my opinion, so I moved on to more gracious conversations. It was hardly memorable, and nothing worth killing the man over."

"So, prior to your stay at the Globe, you had never met the man before?"

"That is correct."

"I see," said Dunkley, dubiously. "And what brought you to Bermuda, Mr. Delopolous?"

"I am on my way back to Athens, after a recent bout in New York against a young buck from Newhaven called Murderous Mathews. Although I was ultimately victorious, my opponent was a brute, and in addition to losing my right incisor, I have been suffering from lumbago ever since. Although I was once a sailor, I have lost my sea legs and the ship travel, with it shifting decks, provoked unpleasant waves of pain. Therefore, I decided to disembark here and rest until my muscles had a chance to heal."

"May I have you write out a phrase for me, sir?" inquired the constable, pushing a piece of paper towards him.

"Certainly," said Delopolous, leaning forward to quickly scratch out the same phrase as the others. "Will there be anything more?"

"Not for tonight," replied Dunkley. "But please remain at the hotel for now. We may have more questions in the morning."

Delopolous nodded his acquiescence and rose smoothly from the settee. Once the door had closed behind him, the constable turned to me. "What do you make of him, Doctor?"

I shrugged my shoulders. "Like most of the other guests, his story seems eminently reasonable."

"And yet, if there was one man capable of descending that ladder during the storm, I believe that a sailor would be the most obvious," said Dunkley.

"But what about his lumbago?" I protested.

"You are too trusting, Doctor. Did you see him grimace when he rose from his seat? Did you see him groan when he leaned forward to write? No! Does that sound like a man with lumbago?"

"You believe he is malingering?" said I, somewhat shocked.

"Why not? And you saw his denim trousers... the favorite dress of the sailor due to its fast drying properties. If he wore denim during his excursion upon the ladder, it would be more than dry by now."

"Well, that certainly sounds plausible," I admitted slowly. But as I considered this possibility, I began to doubt it. I finally shook my head. "No, I will not put stock in that theory. Even if your conjecture is true, it would have required nerves of steel. And of all of the guests, Mr.

Delopolous and Mr. Bey have the best alibis, for it is highly unlikely that either could have left the garret without the other knowing. It is either one of the guests that we previously questioned, or one of those still remaining on the list."

Dunkley nodded agreeably. "Yes, you are likely correct, Doctor. I think it is too late to do any further interviews tonight. Let us both ponder what we have seen and heard today, and perhaps things will be clearer in the bright light of the morn." He stood up, and I made to follow him, albeit more slowly, as a wave of fresh pain shot up my not-yet fully recuperated leg.

Dunkley opened the door leading to the dining room where the guests still congregated, buzzing like an overturned bee-hive. At his appearance, the sounds of conversation died away. Looking over his shoulder I saw many anxious faces peering back at him. Like birds to a lighthouse, my eyes were drawn to her and I found that only one gaze did not appear to be turned on the constable. A glint from those brilliant green eyes was like a spark from a flint. She utterly captivated me. If Madame Lucy Dubois was troubled by the murder that occurred in such close proximity, her lightly freckled brow failed to show it. I looked away before I lost my senses in those eyes and became carried away by the will-o'-the wisps of my imagination.

Dunkley addressed the crowd in a carrying voice, despite the relatively small size of the room. "Ladies and gentlemen, for those of you that had the patience to submit to our enquiries today, I thank you for your cooperation. For those of you that we have yet to question, namely Mr. Warburton, Mr. Aicardi, Mr. and Mrs. Dubois, and Marquesa Garcia Ramirez, rest assured that we will take your statements in the morning. Furthermore, until the investigation is complete, I must ask all of you to remain at the Globe. If you need fresh air, you may take a short walk within the immediate confines of St. George's, but please do not stray more than a few minutes from the hotel, so that you can be recalled if needed for further questioning. Please do not even consider attempting to leave the island. I will be informing all of the port authorities and ship's captains of your names and descriptions, with orders that you are confined to Bermuda until this investigation has been properly concluded."

As soon as it was clear that his speech was concluded the crowd erupted in protest. So rapidly did everyone speak that it was difficult to parse out the source of the individual complaints. Some apparently had plans to leave Bermuda for appointments elsewhere, either in Europe or the Americas. Others appeared to have no specific arrangements but simply objected to being treated like a suspect. Perhaps the most reasonable complaint came from a visibly upset Mr. Warburton. "Now see here, Constable. You propose to leave us in a hotel with someone who you suspect of being a murderer? What is to stop him from killing again tonight?"

Dunkley shook his head. "I believe that everyone in this room is safe. The slaying of Mr. Dumas was not a random act of some madman. Someone had a specific motive for seeing him dead. The rest of you should be in no danger."

Warburton did not appear satisfied by this answer. "But what if one of us that you have not yet questioned possesses critical information that the murderer does not wish to have revealed? That would seem to be motive enough. Spending another night in this hotel is like living on top of a volcano!"

At this terrible suggestion, the Marquesa sank down into a chair, visibly upset. Madame Dubois immediately went to her side and began to provide whispered comfort. Dunkley meanwhile licked his lips and pondered this for a moment. "Do you possess such information, Mr. Warburton? It would have been better if you had volunteered this earlier."

Warburton quickly shook his head. "No, no. I do not know anything of use. It was purely hypothetical. But who knows what twisted beliefs lurk in the mind of a murderer? Just because I do not think that I know anything useful, does not guarantee that the murderer also considers it prudent to let us live."

Dunkley smiled sardonically. "If anyone who has yet to be questioned would like to do so now, I would be happy to talk with them. However, by your logic Mr. Warburton, no one is truly safe, for even those that have already been interviewed may still possess some unrevealed piece of information that turns out to be a critical clue. Fortunately for you, the murderer cannot kill everyone in the hotel without making his identity crystal clear."

Warburton's brow knit even further at this pronouncement. "And how do you propose that we remain safe until you determine who he is?"

"I would lock your door," replied the constable, dryly.

Warburton shook his head. "I heard from Mr. Bey that Dumas' door was locked. And yet little good it did him. The murderer still found a way in!"

"If you are that concerned, then I would recommend that you also bar the door and lock the window. Now, does anyone else have anything that they would like to report tonight?" He paused for a moment, but was met with only silence. "No? Then I bid you good-night. I think we will start with you tomorrow, Mr. Warburton. Shall we say eight o'clock here in the parlor? Doctor, I trust that you will join us?"

I murmured my agreement, and bid Constable Dunkley a pleasant evening. He replied in a similar vein, though I doubted that I would find much peace that night. Between the conflict of emotions in my breast and the tumult of questions in my brain, I was completely out of sorts. The crowd began to disperse, and I stood by the door leading to the stairs, lost in deep contemplation. I was jolted from this state by the feeling of someone brushing against my arm. I looked up suddenly, but only caught a glimpse of Madame Dubois mounting the stairs, her light green gown trailing behind her. For a moment, as the stairs turned the corner, I thought I saw her briefly glance downwards towards me, and a half smile curled up one corner of her mouth. And then she was lost from view, but the dwindling *frou-frou* of her skirts rustled in my ears and the frangipani scent of her perfume lingered in my nose as I pondered her intentions. Fortunately, my attention was soon focused upon the arrival of my brother Henry, who bounded through the front door of the hotel.

"Ham!" he exclaimed. "What the devil is going on here? I can't seem to leave you alone, brother, without you getting into some sort of adventure! First, you acquire all of that Jezail lead, and then a man is shot to death in the room next to you! What's next? A rendezvous with royalty? Now tell me all about it!"

The two of us repaired to a nearby table, where Mrs. Foster brought me the supper that I had missed, as well as two glasses and a Venetian carafe filled with an excellent Chianti. We spoke in low voices, and paused whenever someone drew near, but eventually I divulged everything that I knew about the case.

When I was finished, Henry sat back with a sigh. He nodded toward the door. "Come outside, brother." The two of us pushed back from the table and taking our hats, we ambled out to King's Square. All was sweet and mellow and peaceful in the golden evening light, such a contrast to the physical turmoil inside the hotel, and the emotional turmoil in my breast. "What a mess, Ham! I've never seen anything like it. Since the War Between the States ended, St. George's has been such a quiet place. This is shocking. What do you make of it? Have you formed any definite conceptions as to who is responsible?"

I shook my head. "I admit that I am at a loss. Everyone that we have talked to today has an excellent story for why they are in Bermuda, and none have a good reason why they would want to kill Dumas. Although there were many clues in his room, they do not appear to point towards anyone in particular. Perhaps our questioning of the remainder of the guests tomorrow will shed some light upon the subject."

Henry nodded. "I would wager that the old Spanish lady did it."

My eyebrows rose in surprise. "Whatever makes you think that?"

He shrugged. "There is something morbid, something Gothic, about the whole death-scene that you described. She fits that mold the best, with her black dress and veil. Mark my words, she will have some dark secret in her past. The Spanish are a nation of sinister folk!"

I shook my head. "I am certain that you are wrong, brother. The Spanish have passionate blood, but you paint with too broad a stroke when you assign an entire race to villainy."

Henry nodded amiably. "Perhaps you are right, Ham. Only time will tell. I hope Dunkley gets to the bottom of this soon. He's a good man, if a bit unimaginative. It's a good thing that he has you by his side. Perhaps you will see a spark where all is dark to him. I'm certain that your imagination is plenty active, courtesy of all those yellow-backed novels that you read."

I cocked my head. "I cannot tell if you mean that as a compliment or an insult, brother."

"If you catch the murderer, consider it a compliment. If not, the latter," said he, laughing.

I snorted. "I will do my best to assist the constable, if only to prevent a terrible falling out between us! Tell me, brother, do they still permit dueling here in the colonies?"

"Hah! Sorry, old chap, but the same laws apply here as in mother England. No duels since 1815, I'm afraid. You will just have to catch the chap that offed poor Dumas to avoid a quarrel."

"Speaking of that, I have a favor to ask of you, Henry. I met a librarian over at Dockyard, when I first arrived. His name was Shilling, I think. Do you know him?"

Henry frowned at first, and then laughed. "You must mean old man Penny. Yes, of course, I know the old complainer."

"Could you send him a telegram? I want him to identify something for me."

"What is it?"

I described the flame-arising-from-a-ring symbol that we had found on the jack-knife in Dumas' room. "It must mean something. I want him to tell me what it is."

Henry nodded. "Certainly, brother. If anyone on this island can figure that out, it would be Dr. Penny. He's a bit odd, but still sharp as a tack. I will send your enquiry off tonight from Fort George. It's a bit of a detour from my way back to Fort St. Catherine but, Ham, you will appreciate the name of the road that the Fort lies off – the Khyber Pass." He motioned off to the west, where the sky's last red streaks had faded away and night had settled upon the white roofs. A few faint stars were gleaming in what was still a violent sky. "Not far from where you convalesced in Peshawar, if I recall my geography correctly," he concluded.

I nodded. "That's correct, brother." But I didn't elaborate. My mind was elsewhere. Henry's reminder of the base hospital brought with it thoughts of Miss Violet Devere. I gloomily wondered where she had gone. Did she still think of me? Or had she moved on to some dashing officer with a strong pair of legs and a stronger bank account than I? Worse yet, if she still cared for me, was my foolish attraction to the married Madame Lucy Dubois a terrible betrayal of Violet? I felt as if I had marked my zero-point.

Henry obviously could sense my inner turmoil and bade me farewell for the night. I staggered back into the hotel and upstairs, scarcely more aware of my surroundings than I had been during the previous drugged evening. I retired to my room, where I vaguely noted that the light of the moon was shining brightly through the windows. Falling into a brown study, I plunged furiously into the latest treatise upon the utility of bone marrow examination for the diagnosis of blood cell proliferations. For a few moments I thought that I was successful at purging my mind of all thoughts of her smile, the sweet tones of her voice, the strange mystery that overhung all. But who was it that I tried to forget... Violet or Lucy?

§

CHAPTER XVII:
THE EVIDENCE OF THE ENGLISH NATURALIST

The day was just breaking when I awoke the following morning, and I was amazed to see sunlight streaming through my window shade. The day before had been such a chaotic blur that I never fully realized that the terrible storm of two nights prior was but a distant memory and the natural glorious sunshine of the island had returned. I recalled lying awake, tossing and tumbling half the night, brooding over the strange problem in which I had become inexorably enmeshed. I devised a dozen theories, each of which was more impossible than the last and all of which had fled from my brain when the first beams of sunlight began to penetrate my eyelids. I shifted, and the monograph that I had been reading in bed fell from my chest. I suddenly recalled my duty of the morning, namely to assist Constable Dunkley in the examination of the remaining guests. It was a task that I had little stomach for, since one of those yet to be questioned was Madame Lucy Dubois, and I wondered how I was to face her, with her eyes lingering upon me the entire time.

However, I have never been one to shirk my responsibilities, and I swung out of bed and began to prepare for the day. I reached into the chest of drawers to remove my suit for the day, when I startled back as if bit by a swamp adder. I noted that my clothes appeared more untidy than usual. Not that I am in the least bit prim, but the rough-and-tumble work in Afghanistan has made me rather more lax than befits a medical man. Nonetheless, it was not the disarray of my garments that shocked me. For there in my drawer, lying calmly next to my own clothes, was a red heelless Persian slipper made of the finest velvet. My mind whirled at the wonderment of how it had found its way into my room, and what its presence could possibly mean. I determined to show it to the constable immediately in hopes that he could puzzle it out. In the meantime, however, I decided that carrying the slipper through the hotel for all to see was a poor idea and I tucked it back into the drawer from which it came.

As soon as I was ready, I made my way back through the twisting hall and down the stairs. Upon entering the dining room, I happened to catch glimpse of Boyle carrying a withered potted plant out of Senhor Cordeiro's room. "What ails, Mr. Boyle?"

He looked up with a start. "Ah, good morning to you, Doctor. Nothing ails, as far as I know."

"It seems to me that the sorry specimen in your arms would disagree," said I, motioning to the dead plant.

"Hah," he laughed heartily. "I'm afraid that this patient is past your powers of resurrection, Doctor, even knowing what you did for little Benji a few days back."

He seemed at ease, but a queer glint in his eye caught my attention and induced me to continue the conversation. "What do you think happened to it?"

"Don't reckon I know. Funny things, plants. When you don't want them to grow, there is no getting rid of them, like the weeds in our vegetable garden. And when you want them to grow..." he trailed off and looked significantly at the plant, which I recognized as a variety of orchid.

Something rang false in his explanation, for the climate of Bermuda seemed conducive to the growth of virtually all plants. "Hmmm," I replied. "May I take a look at it?"

"Of course, Doctor," said he, with a hint of a stammer, setting the pot down upon the nearest table.

A quick glance at the rare and precious former bloom itself confirmed Boyle's surmise that it was dead. But something in the soil caught my eye. I had once read an elementary book on botany and, since my memory is like a steel trap, the words seemed fresh in my brain. I knew that a careful balance of the acidic and alkaline in the soil was crucial to the health of a flowering plant. But mixed in with the usual brown dirt were some small red specks, almost crystalline in nature. I pinched a small amount between my thumb and index finger and rubbed them together, trying to ascertain where I had seen something like this before. The answer seemed to elude me, like a will-o-the-wisp.

"Mr. Boyle, where did this soil come from?"

He adopted a surprised look and shrugged his shoulders. "The back garden, I believe. We will have to ask Mrs. Foster to be certain."

However, before I could explore this topic any further the side door opened and Constable Dunkley entered the room nodding his good mornings to us. "Come now, Doctor," said he, with a hint of peevishness.

"Have you become a naturalist too? I thought instead you were about to help me question such a man?"

I straightened up and addressed him as if he were my superior officer. "I await your command, Constable."

"Excellent," he replied, pulling out his pocket watch and glancing at the time. "Boyle, would you please summon Mr. Warburton? It appears that he is running late."

"Certainly, sir. I won't be but a minute." He scooped up the pot containing the dead orchid and rapidly mounted the stairs.

I finally registered the fact that Mr. Warburton was not prompt for our appointment and a sudden horror descended upon me. "Good heavens, Constable! Do you think Mr. Warburton was murdered last night? He feared as much!"

His brows knitted. "Nonsense, doctor. The man simply overslept. You will see in a minute."

"I hope you are correct, Constable," I replied with emotion. "I trust that there is not a madman loose in this hotel. Ah, that reminds me! You will never guess what I found in my room this morning?" said I, explaining my discovery of the Persian slipper.

When I had concluded my short tale, Dunkley appeared very disturbed. "I cannot fathom what this means, Doctor. Why would someone do such a thing?"

"And how?"

He shook his head. "That would not be too difficult. We have already hypothesized that the murderer is in possession of either a set of duplicate keys or is a skilled lock-picker. For how else would he have drugged Mr. Sims' wine? But why would he want to call attention to himself in such a fashion? What could he possibly stand to gain? It is like the flamboyant touch of the coins on Dumas' eyes or the initials on his forehead."

"I think that he must be mad."

"No, that is too easy an explanation, Doctor. There is a deep intelligence lurking behind these crimes. Perhaps he feared that we were about to search all of the rooms and could not dispose of it in any other fashion? Still, that does not explain why..." Whatever else the constable planned to say was lost when he noted that Mr. Warburton was finally descending the stairs. "Ah, sir, did you forget about us?"

"You have my sincerest apologies, Constable. I do not know how to explain it. My clock has been accurate for so many years, only to fail me on this morn," said he, pulling out a fine pocket-watch attached by a gold Albert chain and gazing at it sadly.

"That is alright, Mr. Warburton. Perhaps you only forgot to wind it last night amongst all of the excitement?"

The man nodded absently. "Perhaps you are correct, though I have been through more dire straits than last night without forgetting..."

"Such as when?" interjected the constable.

Warburton looked up at him and frowned. "Ah, well," he laughed, "anyone who has sailed across the Atlantic has faced at least one restless night when a strong squall is blowing, wouldn't you agree, Constable?"

Dunkley shook his head. "I would not know, sir. I was born on the island and have never left. Come now, sir, let us repair to the parlor for our discussion." He spread out his hand as if to indicate that Warburton should enter first.

Once the three of us had settled into our respective positions upon the chairs and settee, Dunkley asked to see the man's papers. I used this time to study Warburton's features again. He was a sturdy, middle-sized fellow, with curly blond-hair and a thin moustache. His hazel eyes seemed confident, and he had a strong handsome face. He was attired in the same dark blue pea-jacket with a green cravat that he wore when I first saw him. He had on well-cut gray trousers, brown leather gaiters that covered the tops of his elastic-sided boots, and a straw hat. After inspecting the papers for a moment, Dunkley finally looked up at the man. "You are Mr. George Warburton, born 1847 in Cheshire, England?"

"I am, sir," he answered, with his slight whispering voice.

"And where was your last residence?"

"The Langham Hotel, London."

"I see," said the constable. "Would you be so kind as to write this phrase for me and sign it?" Dunkley pushed the piece of paper with the other guests' writing upon it towards him. When Warburton had completed this request, Dunkley glanced at it and then continued his questions. "And can you tell me your business here in Bermuda?"

"Ah, well, as I explained to this gentleman several days ago," said he, inclining his head in my direction, "I am a naturalist. I was inspired by the voyage of the HMS *Challenger*, whose findings have become the very foundation for the whole field of oceanography. Although I realize that on my own I will never be able to accomplish a feat as great, I believe that their focus on the oceans left many gaps in our understanding of the flora and fauna of the locales that they visited, including here in Bermuda. Once I have completed my voyage, I hope to write a great treatise on the subject. I've even decided upon a title: *'Challenges in Natural History, With Some Observations on the Infinite Variety of Life.'* What do you think?"

Dunkley grunted noncommittally. "Very nice, I'm sure."

Before he could go on, I interjected a question of my own. "I noted, Mr. Warburton, that you travelled here from Cape Town aboard the *Malabar*?"

If he was surprised by this question, he covered it well. "Ah, I wondered if you were also aboard that ship, Doctor. But there were enough soldiers aboard that I am afraid that I do not remember you. To my enormous regret, I spent much of the voyage in my cabin. I have never been one for sea voyages, and I was ill a great deal of the time."

"What I am curious about, sir, is that the *Malabar* is a troopship," I explained. "How is that you were able to take passage aboard it? Are you a member of the Queen's forces?"

Warburton's look turned serious. "Ah, well, that is a long story."

Dunkley seemed interested in the direction that this line of questioning was taking. "We have time, sir."

Warburton sighed deeply. "No, I have never served the Queen. But my father did, in the Crimea. You may have heard of him, Doctor? Colonel Trelawney Warburton, V.C."

I furrowed my brow. "Yes, the name seems very familiar, though I cannot immediately place it."

"He was part of the 17th Lancers at Balaclava," said Warburton, quietly.

I immediately understood. "The Light Brigade," I breathed, a touch of awe in my voice.

"Indeed," said Warburton, nodding sadly. "He was one of the few fortunate enough to survive the charge into the Valley of Death, though it broke him utterly. He has never been the same since, and he grows worse with every passing year. Of all ruins, that of a noble mind is the most deplorable. Once a great and kind man, my father is now a semi-invalid, and not a pleasant man with whom to live, capable of considerable violence and vindictiveness. My sainted mother could not bear it any longer, and I am certain that is the reason they found her drowned body in the lake upon our estate, for she was an excellent swimmer. If truth be told gentlemen, one reason why I decided to leave England was to put as much space between my father and I as possible."

"So you decided not to follow his footsteps into the army because of how you saw it affect your father's health?" I persisted.

He shook his head before replying. "No, I am afraid that they would not have had me in any case. You see, I am afraid that my father is now quite mad, and his symptoms were apparent long before he was forced to leave the service. It is only because of his great protector that he was allowed an honorable discharge. As fate would have it, during the retreat from that terrible valley he helped a wounded man back behind our lines.

That man would prove to be the son of the mighty Lord Balmoral, who has ever since looked out for my family. He advised me that any attempt of mine to join the service would only stir up unfortunate memories, and that I should look elsewhere for my occupation."

"I fail to follow how that allowed you on the *Malabar*?" I continued.

"Ah, Lord Balmoral has kindly provided me with papers that permit me to request the aid of Her Majesty's forces during my voyage around the globe. I utilized these to enable my passage on board the ship."

I nodded. "I understand, but why were you so anxious to arrive in Bermuda? It is almost as if you had an appointment here? Someone that you did not want to miss?"

"Hah!" he laughed, though I thought I detected an anxious note to it. "No, nothing of the sort, but I had already thoroughly exhausted my exploration of the fauna of Cape Town, and did not wish to waste any further days there. Though, I must admit that the behaviors of the Chachma baboons were fascinating. You see, when a male baboon..."

"Yes, that is very interesting, Mr. Warburton," said Constable Dunkley, interrupting the man before he could discourse any further on baboons. "But let us come back to the more recent past. On the day prior to our little storm, did you leave St. George's?"

Warburton nodded vigorously. "Indeed, I went looking for the *Pterodroma cahow*, also known as the Bermuda Petrel, but more simply called the Cahow."

"The Cahow is extinct, Mr. Warburton," said the constable, dryly.

"Ah, that is the common supposition," replied the man, excitedly. "There has not been a Cahow captured since 1627. However, I have been talking with the natives of St. David's Island. There are rumors of sightings in Castle Harbor, only at night of course, and nothing confirmed, but what else could make such eerie cries other than the reputed devils of the poor superstitious Spanish sailors? My hypothesis is that they might be nesting upon the island they call Nonsuch. The Cahow nests on the ground, you know, and if they still exist, they could only be on an island on which no human feet commonly tread, not to mention there must be an absence of destructive cats, dogs, hogs, and rats. Imagine if I could actually find a Cahow after two hundred and fifty years!" His voice continued to rise in a fevered pitch. "It would be like the reappearance of Lazarus from his tomb. I would become famous throughout the world, and it would guarantee my acceptance into the Royal Society."

"And yet," the constable continued, "Last night, after I left the Globe, I spent some time talking to the inhabitants of St. George's. And I have the testimony of Mr. Butterfield, a local fisherman, that he saw you walking along the beach at Alexandria's Battery yesterday. If you were looking for Cahows, you were in the wrong location all together."

Warburton appeared to pause for a moment. "Ah, yes. Well, you cannot leave any stone unturned, I always say. Due to the roughness of the waters that morn, no one would ferry me across Castle Harbor. Not wanting to waste the day simply because of a little storm, I decided to seek out *Malaclemys terrapin*, or the Diamond-Back Terrapin, which, as you must know, Constable, is native to Bermuda. I thought that the beaches might be the place to start looking..."

"Yes, yes," interrupted Dunkley. "And do you claim any acquaintance with the murdered man?"

Warburton shook his head vigorously. "No, the man was an uninformed brute. A few days ago, over breakfast I attempted to explain to him the various qualities of *Juniperus bermudiana*, the glorious Bermuda Cedar tree, but all he wanted to know was whether there was anything to the science of dowsing."

I frowned at this unusual interest of Monsieur Dumas, who in my prior experience was only interested in trying to preserve his own skin, though ultimately, he failed terribly at that task. "Dowsing? For water?"

Warburton shook his head. "That is what he claimed, Doctor, though his replies were maddingly vague. If you want my opinion, I would say that he was more interested in using it to search for buried treasure."

Now it was Dunkley's turn to frown. "Is that possible?"

Warburton appeared to briefly consider this and then shrugged. "The science is incomplete. I suppose that it is conceivable that certain men have enhanced talents in this regard."

Dunkley nodded vaguely while staring down at his hands, obviously thinking. Finally, he looked over at me. "Anything to add, Doctor?"

"I do have one question. Your inheritance from your mother. Where is it deposited?"

Warburton shrugged. "It is at one of the best banks in England, of course. The City and Suburban Bank, Bloomsbury Branch, are my agents. Why do you ask?"

I shook my head. "No reason."

The constable clearly understood the purpose for my inquiry however and diverted the naturalist from this topic. "Do you have anything else to add, Mr. Warburton?"

"I do not believe so. If I may ask, when do you hope to solve the murder of Monsieur Dumas, Constable? I would very much like to renew my search for the Cahow once you have lifted the restrictions upon our travel."

"Soon, Mr. Warburton, soon. In fact, I hope to conclude this case tonight."

"Truly?" said Warburton, his eyebrows rising. "I will be most interested, Constable."

"Until then, sir, would you please see if Mr. Aicardi is outside? If so, kindly send him in. If not, pray ask Boyle to track him down."

"Certainly, sir," replied Warburton, rising from the settee. He gave us a stately bow and departed.

"What do you think, Doctor?" said Dunkley, turning to me.

I shook my head in wonderment. "Do you truly believe that you can unravel this mystery tonight? It still seems impossibly convoluted to my mind. And every person we question only adds to the confusion."

"On the contrary, Doctor," Dunkley said, "although he may not have known it, I believe that Mr. Warburton just gave us an important clue. You see...." But any further elaboration was cut short by a knock upon the door, followed rapidly by the dramatic entrance of Signore Aicardi. He thrust the door back, and exclaimed, "Gentlemen, I know who did it!"

§

CHAPTER XVIII:
THE EVIDENCE OF THE ITALIAN PAINTER

"W hat?!?" I spluttered, giving a violent start.

"Yes, it came to me in a flash of inspiration," exclaimed Aicardi. "You see, I was working upon a painting out in the square. It was of a young man and his lady friend who were about to depart from the dock in a small boat. The lady lounged in a light blue dress with a white bonnet. The mustached man wore a shirt and pants all of white, and his head was topped by a straw hat with a blue band, not unlike the one worn by Mr. Warburton on occasion. Suddenly, I realized that my depiction of the scene, although beautiful and true to what lay before my eyes, was far too similar to a painting done by the Frenchman Édouard Manet just six years ago. As I despairingly sponged and scraped the paint from the canvas, forever blurring the image, my thoughts turned to another painting by Manet, also of a man wearing a white shirt. But this man lay sprawled backwards upon his bed, his shirt stained with a bloody red wound caused by a shot from the gun in his hand. He called it *'The Suicide.'* I believe that Dumas met his fate by his own hands!"

I shook my head in disappointment at this proposed theory. "I assure you, Signore Aicardi, that if you had witnessed the scene in Monsieur Dumas' room, you would understand that it was incompatible with a suicide. And I know from conversing with him that the man was terrified of dying."

"Ah, but perhaps he was already too far along that path which leads to unknown shores? Did you not witness the sallow color of his face? Trust me, sir, for I have painted a thousand faces. That was the face of a sick man. Whether he had malaria or a wasting cancer, I leave to the diagnosis of a physician. But I believe that he was angry with the lot that fate had dealt him and decided to take his revenge upon the world. Rather than bravely facing his end, he decided to take someone with him. Perhaps he did not even care who turned out to be his victim, as long as someone received the blame! And so he did away with himself in such a clever fashion that the police would be forced to indict someone for the crime. By this method, that old cruel spirit of Dumas would accomplish something previously thought impossible... he would commit murder of that innocent victim from beyond the grave!"

Constable Dunkley shook his head. "That is an interesting theory, Mr. Aicardi. I assure you that I will take it into consideration. Now if you will be so kind as to be seated," said he, motioning to the settee before us. Once the man had acceded to the constable's request, I was given a chance to again study my billiards opponent from three nights prior. Aicardi possessed a swarthy face, with large, dark, languorous eyes that I suspected women would find very handsome. His face was framed by dark, curly hair that matched his formidable dark, carefully-waxed moustache over a thin-lipped mouth. As with my prior encounters, he wore no coat, but this time his shirt cuffs and grey Harris tweed trousers were spotted with a varied hue of paint colors. Dunkley promptly began his usual line of questioning after examining the man's papers. You are Dario Aicardi, born 1845 in Milano, the Kingdom of Italy?"

"I am, sir," the man agreed.

"And would you please write out this phrase for me?" Dunkley repeated the instructions that he had used with the previous guests. As Aicardi wrote, my eyes were drawn to a large splotch of red paint that smeared the tip of his index finger. It looked stunningly similar to the color of the paint used to mark Dumas' forehead.

"That is an interesting shade of red, Signore Aicardi," I commented, motioning to his finger. "Almost the color of blood, do you not think?"

"Ah, yes, this is a rare shade. I have to send away to my cousin Pietro Goldini, who runs a restaurant in London, in order to obtain a supply for me. It is made by an English manufacturer named Brickfall. And I agree, Doctor, that there is no other shade like it to suggest the fresh spill of blood."

"But I thought that you were painting a boating scene this morning?"

I may have imagined it, but I thought that Aicardi's eyes tightened a bit at this question. "You have an excellent ability to picture a setting, Doctor. It is true that when I had my epiphany about Dumas I had just removed that boating scene from my canvas, but then my eye was struck by the sight of a young girl leaning a bike up against a vivid red building in the square. None of the other colors in my paint-box were quite right, so I was forced to use the Brickfall *sang* instead."

"I would like to see that picture," I remarked. "But do you not use a brush? Why is your finger so red?"

He smiled broadly. "Brushes are quickly becoming passé, Doctor, as the new guard of artists throw off the shackles of convention and use whatever tools seem most capable of expressing the true nature of the scene."

"So your work resembles that of Corot or Bouguereau from the modern French school, rather than one of your Renaissance countrymen, such as Raphael?"

Aicardi's eyebrows rose in surprise. "You know your art, Doctor. I think that every artist likes to believe that their style is completely original. But of course that is not true. We are always borrowing from the past, mingling it with our own unique tint, and *voilà*, your own style emerges. I would say that I have been most heavily influenced by Greuze and Vernet. But again, my style is all my own. The pigments are set out for the artist who has only to blend them into the expression of his own soul."

"And have you been successful financially?"

He chuckled heartily. "Alas, no. To date, it is all art for art's sake, sadly. But someday I hope to have at least one of my paintings hanging in one of the great Bond Street picture galleries."

"If you want to attract customers at a London gallery, you may need to cater to their tastes. Something along the lines of Kneller or Reynolds would be preferable, I think." I paused, deciding that a change in tack was required. "You are in excellent physical condition for an artist, Signore. In my experience, when they are not painting or writing most artists have a great fondness for tobacco, spirits, and even stronger stimuli, to the detriment of their health. In fact, I initially mistook you for a member of the army."

"Hah!" Aicardi laughed. "No, alas, I chose not to take up arms with Garibaldi as he fought to weld Italia together. But I am a devotee of your English sport of singlestick. As you must know, Doctor, the vigorous thrust-and-parry work keeps a man in top shape."

"This is very fascinating," interjected the constable in a tone that suggested nothing of the kind, "but why have you come to Bermuda, Mr. Aicardi?"

Aicardi frowned. "But that is what we have been talking about!" he replied animatedly. "I have come to paint the glorious seascapes and the colorful, white-topped buildings. The combination is unique to this place."

"I see," said Dunkley, dryly. "And did you know Mr. Dumas before coming here?"

Aicardi shook his head violently. "No, I had never laid eyes upon that man before. And you may believe me when I say it, for what artist could possibly forget that terrible visage, so cruel and vulturine?"

"That is the second time that you used the word 'cruel' to describe him," I noted. "It is an unusual term to describe a man that you had never met before."

"Ah, of course I met him upon my arrival at the hotel, and it only took a few words for me to plumb the depths of his shriveled soul. You see, his face was so unique that I asked if he would sit for a portrait. I will not repeat the foul terms that he threw back in my face at such an innocent request. No, gentlemen, I had no need to speak with him again to determine if 'cruel' was the proper term for that creature."

"And the other guests?" I persisted. "Did you know any of them before coming to Bermuda?"

Aicardi shrugged. "No."

"And yet, two nights ago you asked Madame Dubois to perform a song. How did you know that she played the violin?"

"Ah!" the man said with a confiding smile. "You are a man, Doctor. Surely you have noted that she is an attractive woman? There is a spirituality about her face that I find comes from being inspired by the glory of music. And the lady is obviously cultured, Doctor. What cultured lady of your acquaintance does not possess at least some modicum of musical talent, either with an instrument or her voice? As you must recall, sir, the night was dreadful, and the storm threatened to tear down the very walls around us. I feared that the ladies would become nervous at the terrible noise of the winds. As an artist, I know that once I become enraptured in my work, nothing can transport me from it. All worries and concerns disappear into the canvas. I had hoped that music would do the same for her."

I nodded slowly, thinking about this seemingly reasonable answer. "However, I also overheard you in deep conversation with Mr. Sims four days back. What was it that you said? Something about 'when it's over, he can finally rest?'"

This time I sensed that Aicardi's laugh was more forced. "Ah, Mr. Sims and I had gotten into a pleasant conversation about a serial novel that we have both been reading by Mr. Collins, and we hoped to reach the end of it soon, as we are both very curious to know how he plans to conclude the story. We were speculating that it must be an exhausting task to write a serial, each chapter having to be produced by a deadline, and hoped that Mr. Collins could take a well-deserved rest once it is over. There is something to be said for the serial novel form, I suppose, but I have always been too impatient for it. I prefer to read the entire story in one fell swoop, such as is done in Beeton's Christmas Annual or Lippincott's Monthly Magazine..."

"Yes, yes," said Dunkley, interrupting us, "let us refocus on the task at hand. Have you ever heard of a *qua tofana*, Mr. Aicardi?"

Aicardi's face took on the visage of a man repulsed. "That is the weapon of Neapolitans and of women. It is not something that a gentleman from Milano knows much about."

"And what if I told you that Mr. Dumas' was killed by it?"

"Truly?" said Aicardi with great surprise. "I had heard that he was shot?"

"Perhaps he was shot only to hide the fact that he was poisoned?" responded Dunkley, raising one eyebrow suggestively.

"Then I would suggest that you focus your investigation, in the absence of any Neapolitans in the hotel, upon the women," replied Aicardi, simply.

"I will do so," retorted Dunkley in turn. "Now, other than your hypothesis about Dumas' self-murder, is there anything else that you would like to tell us?"

Aicardi appeared to consider this. "Yes, in fact there is. I believe that there is a real possibility that this hotel is haunted."

Dunkley's eyebrows shot upwards. "Would you care to explain?"

"Indeed. It was your question about the Brickfall *sang* red that brought this incident back to my mind. You see, a painter's pigments are part of himself. Without them, we cannot create. We are unmanned. And so, we pay exquisite attention to our supply of paints. I monitor them every day, and yet, two days ago, I noted that the jar of *sang* was missing from my paint-box. I searched everywhere in my room, though I knew that I had not misplaced it. I even asked Mrs. Foster if she or the maid-servant who cleans the rooms could have taken it. But all without success. It had mysteriously vanished."

"I thought you said that you just used it this morning to paint a building?" I queried.

"I did. You see, Doctor, when I came downstairs yesterday morning, imagine my surprise at finding my little jar of red paint sitting on the bar in the billiard-room. I know for a fact that I did not put it there. And no one else could have had access to it or would have had a reason to take and return it, except for a mischievous spirit that can pass through locked doors. There are many old buildings in Italia that possess such phantoms. I suspect that the same must be possible in Bermuda."

"That is another interesting theory, Mr. Aicardi," said the constable, dryly. "Thank you for your assistance. You've been very helpful."

"Not at all, gentlemen. Please do not hesitate to ask if you have other concerns. As they say in my country, '*E quindi uscimmo a riveder le stelle.*'"

"What was that?" asked Dunkley, a frown forming on his brow.

"It is something we say when we hope that an event comes to a happy conclusion, as I do with your investigation. Good day," said he, rising and bowing before departing.

Once the door shut, Dunkley turned to me. "What was all that about, Doctor?"

I shrugged my shoulders. "I am not certain. My Italian is limited. The final word seemed familiar, however, since much of Italian is derived from Latin. In that tongue, the word for star is '*stella.*' It is not too much of a supposition to think that '*stelle*' is the same word."

"Star? What could that possibly mean? I tell you, Doctor, that this Italian is a shady character. He had too many convenient excuses, if you ask me. Do you think that he could be a member of the Mafia, the Carbonari, or the Camorra? That would explain much. The brutal killing. The macabre style of Dumas' death bed."

I nodded slowly. "I suppose that it is possible. But it is solely a hypothesis. We have no proof."

"Not yet, not yet. But perhaps we will by the end of the day," said Dunkley, coyly.

"Truly?" I said with great surprise. "What have you learned?"

"Nothing definitive. And nothing that you have not heard. But I have thought long and hard about how these stories fit together and a possibility is starting to form in my mind."

"I will endeavor to do the same. Hopefully we arrive at the same conclusion. Now who should we see next?" I asked.

"I think we should take Mr. Aicardi's advice. He suggested that we talk with the women. Let us see what the old Spanish lady can tell us."

§

CHAPTER XIX:
THE EVIDENCE OF THE SPANISH MARQUESA

Constable Dunkley and I agreed that it would be more appropriate for us to formally visit the Marquesa in her room rather than ask her to attend us in the parlor. As such, we decamped from our places and emerged back into the dining room. There we encountered Mrs. Foster, who was setting tables for the upcoming lunch service.

"Ah, Elizabeth," said the constable happily. "Would you be so kind as to inform the Spanish lady that we will be calling upon her in a few moments?"

"Certainly, Harry," replied the proprietress. Quitting her task, she proceeded up the stairs to deliver his message.

"Now, Doctor," said Dunkley quietly, "we must proceed with great tact. If I read her correctly, a proud old lady like her can become easily offended by the wrong questions and clam up like an oyster."

"I will follow your lead, of course," I replied. I pondered whether I should share with the constable my brother's theory about the Marquesa's potential guilt. Fortunately, the rapid return of Mrs. Foster down the stairs forestalled me from spreading any baseless slander.

"She will see you immediately," reported Mrs. Foster.

"Excellent!" replied the constable. "Come, Doctor."

We mounted the stairs until we reached the landing. From there we entered the twisting passage where, per Mrs. Foster's map, the first door on the left promised to lead to the Marquesa's room. The constable knocked on the door with a loud and authoritative tap. This was promptly rewarded by a thickly-accented voice within that bade us enter.

Twisting the handle, the constable swung the door back, and found the Marquesa calmly staring at us from behind her veil. She rested in the only armchair in the room. As we entered, she set aside a black leather-bound book, and turned her frank, searching dark eyes upon us. "Come in, gentlemen," said she, gesturing to the ground in front of her with an overmatching dignity that compelled obedience. For a brief moment, I imagined that she expected us to kneel before her. Her demeanor was regal, and I did not doubt that the blood of the masterful Conquistadors flowed in her veins. Eventually, I realized that she was inviting us to stand before her, as the room had no other place to sit other than the bed or the already occupied chair.

Dunkley formally introduced us and the purpose of our visit, to which she merely nodded. "May I see your papers, Madame?"

Her eyes narrowed and she made no immediate move to carry out his request. "You may address me as 'Marquesa,' for my husband's people have been part of the nobility of Valencia for generations." Despite her accent, her English was flawless. "If you harbor republican notions and do not wish to use my hereditary title, then the proper form of address for a Spanish lady is 'Senora.' The French use 'Madame.' I do not."

"I see," replied the constable, tightly. "My apologies, Marquesa."

She smiled grimly at her verbal victory, and then reached over to her bedside table for her papers. She handed these to Constable Dunkley with great reverence, as if they were a copy of the Magna Carta itself.

Dunkley inspected the papers for a moment, and while so doing, I studied the lady again. She was one of the few guests with whom I had virtually no interactions to date, and thus appeared to my eyes to be a great mystery. This enigma was accentuated by her tall and queenly figure, which made her appear to be speaking down to us as if from a dais, notwithstanding the fact that we literally towered over her seated position. Through her veil, I faintly made out that her face possessed a pale mask-like quality which only highlighted the emaciation of her figure. Despite the translucent quality of her skin she seemed to radiate an inner fire. Her hair was lustrous and raven-black, framing her piercing small dark Spanish eyes. Although she was now but a black-eyes shadow of her former self and no longer in the flower of youth, I had little doubt that she was once a celebrated beauty. She wore a dress nearly identical to, if not the same as, the one in which I always encountered her. It was made of an excellent midnight black silk, though the once-noted ostrich feathers were missing from this particular gown. Instead, her neck was encircled by some old Spanish jewelry made from silver and curiously-cut diamonds.

Eventually, the constable looked up from the papers and said, "You are the Marquesa Dolores Garcia Ramirez, born 1837..."

"A woman does not like to be reminded of her age, Constable," she interrupted him.

"Ah, my apologies, Marquesa," stammered Dunkley. He seemed at a loss of how to proceed.

After his two false starts, I decided that I must take the reins of the exchange. "Is Dolores a common name in Spain, Marquesa?"

She smiled wanly. "Indeed, Doctor. Do you know the meaning of the name?" She paused a moment for me to respond, but I decided to allow her to dictate the flow of the conversation and remained silent. "No? Surely you must know your Latin? It stems from the same root as your English word 'dolorous.' It means 'sorrows.' It is an appropriate name for so many of my fellow countrywomen."

"And yourself?" I inquired. "Does it describe you?"

She made a sound that in a less elegant person could have been mistaken for a snort of amusement. "Oh, yes! I have worn these widow weeds for thirteen years, Doctor. And I will never put them aside, for Diego was the best husband that a women could ever hope for. He was taken from me far too young, before he could grace me with a child to carry on his name. Instead, the line will die with me."

"Is that him?" I asked, indicating a famed picture that rested on her bedside table. It showed a lithe man of about thirty, with dark eyes, immaculately-flowing black hair and a perfectly waxed moustache. He wore a military uniform that I did not immediately recognize.

She glanced over at the picture and reached out to take it. She looked at it for a moment and then clenched it to her bosom. "Yes," she replied simply.

"Was he a soldier?"

She bowed her head for a moment and then drew out a handkerchief to dab at her damp eyes. Finally she looked up at me and responded. "Indeed. Diego served in the King's Own Immemorial 1st Infantry Regiment, Spanish Army, which is considered by historians to be the oldest armed unit in the world."

"And did he fall in battle?"

Her face contracted as if in pain and her mouth set into a grim line. "Doctor, some inquiries are offensive. I do not wish to talk about this subject any more. It is too painful to me. Perhaps for some the passage of thirteen years serves to dull the ache, but for me, each day that I live without him is worse than the one that it followed. Do you have any questions that are pertinent to your investigation?"

"I am saddened for your loss, Marquesa. I too know something of the terrible cost of war." I found myself absently rubbing my wounded shoulder. "May I ask where you last resided, Marquesa?"

"Most recently I was at the Hotel Escurial in Madrid. Before that I had summered at Davos Platz, in Switzerland. Why do you ask?"

For the moment I ignored her question. "I noticed that you do not travel with a maidservant? I find that a tad unusual for a lady of your station, Marquesa, unless these things are handled in a different way in Spain?"

She narrowed her eyes and glared at me. "She displeased me. I dismissed her."

"I see," said I, non-committally. "It is simply that this is an unusual hotel in which to find a Spanish Marquesa. It is a bit homely. I would have thought that you would have preferred to spend your layover in Bermuda at the posh Hamilton Hotel."

The Marquesa pursed her lips and glanced back and forth between me and the constable. "Gentlemen, will you give me your word of honor that what I am about to tell you never leaves this room?"

I immediately acquiesced, but Dunkley shook his head. "I am afraid that I cannot do that, Marquesa, if it touches upon this case."

"I assure you that it does not," said the lady grimly.

"Then you have my word," replied Dunkley.

She paused for a moment, as if to gather her strength. "Gentlemen, I will take you fully into my confidence. I am ashamed to admit that the Garcia Ramirez estate, while ancient in its nobility, is no longer financially solvent. For some time after my husband's death a sufficient endowment had allowed me to live in a style befitting our name. However, I now find that matters have changed for the worse, and I have been forced to diminish my staff, as well as the comforts that I take. That is the true reason that I dismissed my maidservant. That is why I am not staying at the Hamilton Hotel. And that is why I am travelling to Florida. I plan to live in its charming climate with my sister and her husband."

I was unsure of how to respond appropriately to this display of embarrassing confidence. My colleague, however, appeared to possess less qualms. "What about the jewels around your neck? Couldn't you sell those?"

Her free hand flew to her diamond necklace and she shook her head violently. Her eyes hardened. "These were a wedding present from my husband, Constable. They are a part of me, as if they were attached to my skin. They shall be taken from me only when the last breath has left this body." The passion in her voice was unmistakable.

The constable appeared to wither under this assault, and I determined that it would be appropriate to divert the flow of the questioning. My eyes travelled about her room until they alighted upon a framed portrait of a man resting upon the dressing table. It clearly belonged to her and was not part of the regular furnishings of the place. The man had a distinguished face, with incisive deep blue eyes beneath dark brown hair touched with grey about the temples. He wore a red coat decorated with the insignia of a British Field Marshall. Like any true Englishman, I immediately recognized the Duke of Wellington. "I must say, Marquesa, that I am surprised to find a picture of Sir Arthur Wellesley in your chamber."

She did not bother to turn around. "I always travel with it. Besides my husband, I like to look upon a great man every night before I sleep. I draw strength from it."

"But he is an Englishman?"

"Bah," said she, dismissively. "I care not for where he was born. I care about what he did. He marched into Spain with but a handful of men and swept the perfidious French back past the Pyrenees."

"You do not care for the French, Marquesa?" I inquired, my eyebrows rising.

She smiled grimly at me. "Ah, I see, Doctor. You are clever. Yes, I freely admit that I possess an animosity for the French as a whole. But no more so than is typical for any Spaniard after what they have done to our country. Do you know Goya? He depicts it well. The question is whether that is sufficient motive to snuff out a single Frenchman's life?" She paused and stared us in the eyes, first myself and then the constable, before continuing. "The answer is 'no.' My ill feelings are not directly at any one individual, such as the unfortunate Monsieur Dumas, but merely against the entire mass of them, which is too great an enemy for these frail arms to take on." She held up her arms as if to demonstrate her weakness, before re-clutching the portrait of her husband.

"Not to mention that the other Frenchman is still hale and hearty, as far as we know," interposed the constable.

She straightened up and narrowed her eyes to peer at him. "What do you mean?"

"Mr. Dubois," explained Dunkley. "I've not heard that he had any misfortunes during the night."

"Ah, yes, exactly," said she, appearing to slump a bit. "If Monsieur Dubois is still breathing, then I think you must discount any theories that Dumas was assassinated because of his nationality."

"So who do you think killed Monsieur Dumas, Marquesa?" I asked.

"You ask the wrong question, Doctor. Not a 'who' but a 'what!'"

I furrowed my brow. "I am afraid that I am not following you, Senora."

"The door was locked from the inside, was it not? What kind of man could accomplish such a thing? But a vengeful spirit..." her voice trailed off as her eyebrows lifted suggestively.

"Are you implying that Monsieur Dumas was killed by a ghost?"

"It is the only explanation!"

If I have one quality upon earth, it is common sense, and nothing will persuade me to believe in such a thing. "I am not certain that I am prepared to accept a supernatural explanation," said I, tactfully. "The world seems large enough without including that element. The advance of science is sweeping away the primitive superstitions of the past."

She glared at me. "Scoff if you want, Doctor, but your doubt does not abrogate their existence. I know in my heart of hearts that there is a realm in which the answers of science are helpless. From the minute I checked in, I have felt the presence of a ghost in this very building. But better than that... I have actually witnessed one! Late last night, I left my room and began to walk down the hall. I tried to walk as silently as possible given the coconut matting on the floor, but it is impossible to move without making at least a modicum of noise. You can therefore imagine my surprise when I saw someone advancing towards me, though my ears heard nothing. And then I realized that I could see her far too clearly given the darkness of the passage, as if she glimmered in her own emitted light. She wore only a bone white gown, but it was her face which held my gaze. She was deadly pale – never have I seen a figure so white. I knew then that she was not of this world, for only a ghost could look like that. Within seconds the temperature dropped at least fifteen degrees and the hairs on my arms stood erect. It sent a chill to my heart. The only sound was my frightened breathing as she stopped and stared at me. And then, in an instant, she was gone. The hall became warm again, but I elected to forsake the call of nature and rapidly returned to my room for the rest of the night. Though the lock on the door gave me little comfort, and I remained awake until dawn's rosy rays brightened my window."

I glanced at the constable skeptically, but to my surprise he appeared to take her story seriously. Nevertheless, I shook my head. "But why would a Bermudian ghost feel vengeance against Monsieur Dumas specifically? Why have the remaining guests been left unharmed?"

"A ghost does not need a reason, Doctor! Reason is the instrument of the living, not the dead. The worst of them hate anything with blood flowing through its veins. But I sensed that this particular ghost may not be so capricious. Perhaps she only sought out a victim who was most similar to the one who wronged her in life? As a woman, I was left untouched, but who knows what secrets lay buried in Monsieur Dumas' past? Certainly many an innocent woman has been hanged near this very spot!"

The constable shook his head, "Those were witches, I am afraid."

"Bah!" she scoffed. "One man's witch is another man's wise-woman. Constable, can you be certain that justice was done in every case?"

Dunkley failed to meet her eyes. "No, of course not! It was a long time ago. The last hanging of a witch in Bermuda happened over one hundred fifty years ago."

"And what does a spirit care for the clocks of the living?" replied the Marquesa dismissively. "If only I had known how thick this island was with spirits, I would have brought Jimson weed with me to protect my room. They cannot abide the smell."

I frowned at this pronouncement, "Jimson weed? I have read of this. Its consumption is highly hallucinogenic and poisonous."

"So?" was her haughty reply, as if she did not mind being tangentially accused of being a poisoner. "Did he die of poison then? Was that before or after the seven gunshots?"

I nodded reluctantly at the apparent truth to that statement. I decided to try one last approach at a broadside. "Marquesa, I was wondering what currency you are travelling with?"

She stared at me for a moment before replying. "Are you asking, Doctor, if the silver *reales* that you found on the dead man's eyes belonged to me?"

I nodded, impressed by her acumen. "How did you know about the *reales*, Marquesa?"

"This is a small hotel, Doctor," she scoffed. "People talk. As for your *reales*, I would have to see them to be certain."

Dunkley reluctantly reached into his satchel where he had secreted the evidence of the case and brought out the coins.

"May I?" she asked, awaiting the constable's nod before taking the coins from his hand. She studied them for a moment and then handed them back. "The answer is 'no.' They do not belong to me. They are the coins of a different era, when the Spanish Fleet still ruled the Caribbean, before our colonies were lost. More than fifty years ago. No one uses coins such as these now."

"Thank you, Marquesa," said I, turning to my colleague, "Constable, do you have any other questions for the Marquesa?" I wondered if he was going to ask for a sample of her handwriting, though it seemed obvious that the mysterious note in Dumas' room could only have been penned by a masculine hand.

Evidently he agreed with me, as he forsook any attempt to do so. "No," he stammered, apparently overwhelmed by either her aristocratic bearing or her ghostly tale. "Thank you for your assistance, Marquesa."

Her only reply was a dismissive nod, and we silently backed our way out of the room. When we had regained the landing, we both paused and emitted long sighs.

The constable snorted in exasperation. "I don't know what to think anymore, Doctor. All of these tales of ghosts and spirits, I feel like we have stumbled into a Grimm's fairy tale."

While there was something eerie and ghost-like about the Marquesa, I resolutely shook my head. "I refuse to find credence in a supernatural explanation. No ghost fired a revolver into Monsieur Dumas. No ghost wrote in paint upon his forehead or placed those coins upon his eyes."

He appeared to pull himself together. "Yes, I suppose you are right, Doctor." And then he said the words that I had been dreading all morning. "Well, we might as well continue with the female guests. Let us talk next to the American lady, Mrs. Lucy Dubois."

§

CHAPTER XX:
THE EVIDENCE OF THE AMERICAN LADY

I had known that this moment was inevitable, but that did not make it any easier to face. Nonetheless, I am capable of putting up with many hardships, and so I put on my bravest face. "I agree. Do you think that we should question her in the presence or absence of her husband?"

Dunkley shrugged. "If they are culpable, they have had sufficient time in which to coordinate their stories, but I still think that we shall have higher odds for a moment of unguarded honesty if we talk with them separately."

"The parlor then?"

The constable nodded and we decamped back downstairs. We found that the dining room was temporarily deserted, so Dunkley went in search of Mrs. Foster. During his absence, I attempted to explore my emotions. I knew that my attraction to Lucy was an impossible infatuation. It went against every fiber of my being. And yet her appeal was almost magnetic, as if I had no more say in the matter than the needle of a compass did when it was drawn to the north. Fortunately, this introspection did not last long, as Dunkley and Mrs. Foster returned promptly.

"Come, Doctor, we will await her in the parlor, while Elizabeth requests her presence."

The two of us settled into our usual chairs, and while we waited I explained that I already had some interactions with Madame Dubois where I had learned about the death of her father. Dunkley nodded at this information, but did not have a chance to comment, for within a few minutes a knock had sounded upon the door. The door then swung open and Lucy entered. It may have been a trick of the light behind her, which framed her face, but I could have sworn that I saw a halo gleaming about her unbound lustrous red hair.

"Pray take a seat, Mrs. Dubois," said the constable.

My senses drank her in as she gracefully established herself upon the settee. Her green eyes were shining this morning, and her lips parted, a pink flush upon her lightly freckled cheeks. Her frangipani perfume was pleasingly subtle. She was dressed in a gown of a white diaphanous material, with the smallest touch of emerald green at the neck and waist. It was a simple dress, without the cluster of fanciful touches that many women use to distract from the plainness of their features. Instead, her remarkable beauty shone like a beacon in this small room. Then she smiled shyly, and I was reminded of her great youth.

"Good morning, gentlemen," said she, opening the conversation, her melodious voice a balm for my soul. "Where I come from, we don't like to beat around the bush, so I will just come out and say it. I have been conversing with the other guests that you have questioned. I know you are hoping that I will suddenly confess everything to you, but I am afraid that nothing is further from the truth. I swear to you, upon all that I hold sacred, that I've never met Monsieur Dumas before I arrived upon Bermuda, and in fact, I never even said a word to the man before his death. His countenance was not one that invited pleasant conversation." Her eyes turned to me as she said this, and I imagined that she silently added, '*unlike what we shared in the garden.*'

"Yes, that's very well, but you understand that we still have to question you, as we have done with everyone else who was staying at the Globe when Dumas was killed," replied Dunkley. "You may know something without even realizing it."

She shrugged, almost gaily. "Why of course, Constable. Fire away, I have nothing to hide. I have never been questioned by the police before. I expect it may prove to be a fascinating experience. Though," she said, looking about the pleasant little parlor, "the atmosphere leaves much to be desired. I had imagined something rather danker, perhaps with some rats scurrying in the darkest corner? And maybe the slow dripping of water? This settee is terribly comfortable. Are you certain that you do not need to tie me to a chair?" she concluded, a mischievous smile breaking out upon her face.

I couldn't help but laugh, to which the constable threw me a sour look. "There will hopefully be no need for that," said he, without a trace of humor in his voice. "Do not forget, Madame, that a man was viciously murdered two nights ago not twenty feet from where you slept. May I see your papers?"

"Certainly, Constable," she replied more soberly. "I apologize if I made light of the situation." She promptly removed her documents from her handbag and handed them over.

Dunkley inspected them for a moment and then looked up. "You are Mrs. Lucy Dubois, *née* Harrier, born 1860 in San Francisco, California?"

"That is correct."

"And your father's name was?"

"Iain. Iain Harrier."

"Was he born in 'Frisco?"

Her brow furrowed slightly. "I have never been fond of that hideous shortening of the name of my fair city, Constable."

"My apologies, Madame," said he, bowing his head slightly.

"Apology accepted," she smiled and the crease in her forehead vanished as quickly as it had come. "The answer to your question is 'no.' He was born in the north of England, Durham I believe. My grandparents had him late in life. His older sister, who I have never met, remained behind when they immigrated to Philadelphia in the eastern United States. But when he was a young man, almost still a boy really, the great Californian gold rush commenced, and like so many others he chased his dreams westward."

"So he was a miner?"

"Yes, amongst many other things. He had many loose partnerships over the years, and it seemed like his partners were always successful in their pursuits, unlike so many others, whose dreams died in those hills. First there was Mr. Doran, now said to be the richest man on the Pacific Slope. For a while he worked with Senator Neil Gibson, who has now become known as the 'Gold King,' though my father never much liked the man's manners. My father never had their level of success, of course, but it was moving in the Senator's company that he met my mother."

"And your mother, does she still reside in San Francisco?"

A hint of tears formed in the corners of her eyes. "No," she replied tightly. "She was carried off two years ago from diphtheria. I am now alone in the world."

"Excepting your husband, of course," replied Dunkley.

Lucy's eyes briefly darted to mine, "Yes, yes, of course. Hector is a great comfort to me."

"How did you meet Mr. Dubois?"

"Hector was engaged in some business in the city. As you may know, he is a lawyer and was sent out from Paris by his firm to draw up some contracts with the gold companies in San Francisco. He was invited to one of the balls that I was attending, and he was bold enough to ask me to dance. We got along splendidly and decided that there was no sense in waiting."

Dunkley's eyebrows rose. "Truly, you married in San Francisco? What about Mr. Dubois' relatives?"

"That is where we are going now, to meet his family in Paris. I must admit that I am a tad nervous, though Hector assures me that I have no reason to be." During this whole exchange, she held the constable's gaze, and never once looked in my direction.

"The Doctor here tells me that your father, Iain Harrier, fought on the side of the Union in the American Civil War?"

Lucy's eyes darted over to me, as if to gauge what else from our garden conversation I had shared with the constable. "That is true," she said tightly.

"And he died in one of the great battles?"

"Yes," was her simple reply, as if she did not trust herself to say anything more.

"You must have been very young?"

She nodded. "I was. But I have an excellent memory, Constable. The calming sound of his voice, the gentle strength of his arms, has never left me." After those words her reserve broke and a sob escaped her lips. She extracted a handkerchief from her bag and dabbed at her eyes.

The constable gave her a moment to gather herself and then continued. "Would you be surprised, Madame, if I told you that the murdered man had fought on the side of the Confederacy?"

Her eyebrows rose in surprise "A Frenchman fighting for the South? You must be mistaken, Constable. The French were neutral during our terrible war."

"Officially, yes," said the constable, nodding. "But the Emperor, Napoleon III, had both economic interests and territorial ambitions that led him to support the Confederacy. For one, the Union blockade led to a *'famine du coton,'* that crippled the textile industries of Normandy, from where Mr. Dumas hailed. Secondly, do not forget that the French planned to create a new empire in Mexico, which would have been easier with a splintered and weakened nation to their north, rather than a strong United States."

It may have been my imagination, but her eyes appeared to tighten at this piece of information.

If the constable noted this, he gave no indication and continued on. "Not all of the Emperor's ministers concurred with this, however, and under pressure from the British, the French ultimately concluded that a Confederate defeat was close. Therefore they eventually abandoned any efforts to aid the South. But the French certainly had observers on the ground and it is possible that, until very close to the end of the war, some of them actively aided the Confederates. We have evidence to suggest that Mr. Dumas could have been one of them."

Lucy continued to look skeptical of this. "And if he was?" she shrugged.

"Then perhaps you killed him to avenge your father?" suggested the constable.

To my surprise, she laughed bitterly at the constable. "Constable Dunkley, can you possibly be serious? General Lee led over thirty-thousand men into Antietam, and over twenty-thousand survived. Are you proposing that I have a dastardly plan to hunt down and murder twenty-thousand men? That may take me quite a while!"

I was equally taken aback by the constable's response, for I had thought him rather lacking in humor. But he laughed in grim agreement at this suggestion of Lucy's, and then he turned to me. "You have been awful quiet, Doctor. Do you have any questions for Mrs. Dubois?"

My mind was a blank, as it often was in her presence. But I had enough of my wits about me to realize that complete silence on my part would look suspicious in the eyes of the constable, especially considering the significant part that I had played in the inquiry of the other guests. Finally, something came to me, though it was a trivial matter with certainly nothing to do with our case. "I do have one question. When I first met you three days ago, Madame Dubois, I noted a small ink stain on the right sleeve of your gown. I was wondering how that occurred?"

To my surprise, she seemed taken aback by the question, and no answer was immediately forthcoming. Eventually she composed herself, "You are most observant, Doctor. Only one man in a thousand would notice such a trifle," she replied. After this, she paused for a moment, as if hesitating before completing her thoughts.

But Dunkley was too impatient to allow her to finish. "Come now, Doctor. Do you have any questions that pertain to the case, and not the lady's attire?"

I nodded again. "Yes, I have one more. When you first arrived at the Globe Hotel, I overheard your husband's conversation with Mrs. Foster. He seemed quite upset that the two of you would have to share a room," I choked up a bit at this painful thought, but pressed on through it. "I can assure you, Madame, that if you were my wife, the opposite would be true. I could never bear to let you leave my side."

It may have been my overactive imagination again, but I thought I saw a hint of tears appear in the corners of her eyes. She sat quietly, staring back at me, but made no attempt to respond.

Dunkley simply frowned, plainly unaware of the undercurrents in the room. "Was there a question in there, Doctor?"

"Yes," said I, my heart heavy with sadness at our impossible situation, "I thought this was an odd behavior for a newly wedded couple. Do you have an explanation, Madame?"

She licked her lips, and then finally replied. "Indeed. You see, Doctor, Hector is a raucous sleeper. The passages of his nostrils are not straight and he makes a terrible sound when he sleeps. As a physician, you must know of what I speak. This noise makes it difficult for me to rest, and so Hector kindly attempts to sleep apart from me, whenever possible." She glanced over at the constable. "Once we discovered that the two rooms that we reserved had become one, we contemplated changing our accommodations to the Hamilton Hotel. But ultimately, I decided that the attractions of St. George's were too great to forbear," her gaze swung back to me and our eyes locked. "And thus we remain here, despite the troubled sleep that has plagued me for the last three nights."

"And so you plan to depart as soon as this investigation is concluded," I asked heavily.

Her lips pursed together tightly. "That is correct, unless we are stranded here by another hurricane. 'Alas, the storm is come again! I will here shroud till the dregs of the storm be past.'"

I recognized her final words as lines from Shakespeare. Either she was an accomplished actor and a deep conspirator, or she was the most glorious creature I would ever meet.

"Thank you very much for your time, Mrs. Dubois," said the constable, concluding the interview. "If you would be so kind as to send your husband in to see us next?"

"Of course, Constable," she replied while looking at him. And then one last time her gaze swung back to me. "Anything for you."

She rose gracefully from the settee, smoothed out the creases in her dress, and then quietly glided from the room. My eyes never left her tall, slim figure, until the door closed firmly behind her, as if it was snuffing out all the hopes of my heart.

§

CHAPTER XXI:
THE EVIDENCE OF THE FRENCH SOLICITOR

I sat there, blankly staring at the closed door, my mind a tumult of thoughts and emotions. I sensed that Constable Dunkley was saying something to me, but I failed to register it. Eventually however, my trance was lifted by a sharp rap upon the door, followed promptly by the appearance of Monsieur Dubois.

I glared with ill-concealed dislike at the man, with his clean-shaven, smart, alert face. My brain knew it was not his fault that he had married Lucy before I ever had the opportunity to meet her, but my heart could not be reconciled to the man. It was perhaps this base feeling that led to me once again suspect something sensitive or weak about his mouth. His black hair and grey eyes seemed to me unbecoming in their inexorable darkness. I compared him to me in height and in breadth and found him lacking. I silently mocked the golden pince-nez that lay on a thin black cord around his neck. Even his dress bothered me, for it was far too somber and quiet, with its black frock-coat, dark trousers, lacking even a touch of color about the grey neck tie. It was as if he expected that he would be attending a funeral. He carried a small case in his hand, which he set next to the table before lowerig himself into the settee with an unconcerned ease that I found distasteful. He took a tortoise-shell box from his pocket and took a pinch of snuff.

"*Bonjour*, gentlemen, how may I help you?" said the man with a broad smile that disclosed perfectly white teeth. "I shall be happy to give you any information in my power. *L'homme n'est rien, l'oeuvre tout.*"

To prove to the man that he had no greater facility for languages, I responded in kind, "*Bonjour, Monsieur. Battre le fer pendant qu'il est chaud.*"

The man's immaculately groomed eyebrows rose in surprise. "Your French is excellent, Doctor."

"As is your English, sir," I rejoined, with as much pleasantness as I was able to inject into my tone.

"May I see your papers, sir?" asked Constable Dunkley, irritably. He was clearly not happy to be excluded from the conversation thus far.

"*D'accord*," replied the Frenchman, reaching into his coat pocket and handing them to the constable.

After studying them for a longer time than usual, Dunkley looked up. "You are Mr. Hector Dubois, born 1849 in Nîmes, France?"

"*Oui*, that is correct."

"These are replacement papers, sir," said Dunkley, suggestively, waving them about.

A set of tiny lines appeared about Dubois' eyes as he narrowed them at the constable. "Yes, what of it?"

"Replacement papers are often found when a man is attempting to conceal his identity," Dunkley said evenly.

"Ah," replied Dubois, "I see your concern, Constable. But they are also required when a man's original set is lost. There was a great fire at the Palace Hotel, where I was staying in San Francisco, sir, and everything was destroyed. I had not the foresight to store my identity papers in the safe, where they might have survived. Fortunately, I was able to wire to my employers in Paris, who left instructions with the Bank of California to credit me enough money to enable my homecoming to France. But I was forced to have a new set of temporary papers made for me in San Francisco until I can make the crossing and have an official set re-issued."

"I see," replied Dunkley in a tone that suggested nothing of the kind. "And I am certain that your wife can confirm these details?"

Dubois shrugged. "But of course."

"Naturally," Dunkley nodded. "And may I ask you to write out a phrase for me?" He pushed the piece of paper and a J pen across the intervening table.

Dubois sat motionless, failing to pick up the pen. "Why?"

"Come now, Mr. Dubois," said the constable testily, "you can plainly see from the paper in front of you that the other guests all complied with my request. As the last one questioned, I am not clear what your objection could be?"

"I have none," said the man, shaking his head, and laughing with perhaps a forced jollity. "It is simply the habitual caution of my profession. A man's signature is a powerful tool. It is not to be laid down lightly. But you are correct, Constable, that I can see no harm in acceding to this simple request." He picked up the pen and wrote the phrase with a composed air. Even from where I sat, with the writing upside down, I could plainly tell that his elegant hand had nothing in common with the rude letters that we had found in Dumas' room. Once he had finished, he set down the pen and pushed the paper back to Dunkley.

"Thank you, sir," said the constable, placing the paper in his satchel. "You mentioned your profession. I believe that your wife reported that you are a solicitor?"

"Yes, that is correct. I am an *avocat*, trained at the Sorbonne."

"And how did you know Mr. Dumas?"

The man's eyebrows shot upwards in great surprise. "I am not certain how you formed the impression that I knew Mr. Dumas, Constable, but I can assure you that I never met the man before the day that I set foot in this hotel!"

"Come now, sir," protested Dunkley. "Do you mean to tell me that you did not know the man? You are both French!"

Dubois laughed in amazement. "Constable, while it may be possible on an island as small as Bermuda to be acquainted with every last soul, France is another matter entirely. The vastness of the country, the varied terrain, the insular nature of the various provinces does not lend itself to such familiarity as you seem to suppose. He hailed from Normandy, I believe, and I have little to do with that region. I spoke to him briefly on the day of our arrival, but I found the implications of his words distasteful. My impression is that he was an odious man. *Un véritable sauvage.* The world may be better off without him."

"I see," said the constable crossly. "So you have nothing to tell us of the man's death?"

"I did not say that, Constable. In fact, I discovered something of exceptional importance this very morn."

Dunkley leaned forward with sudden eagerness. "Yes, what is it?"

"You see, gentlemen, I am a denizen of one of the greatest cities in the world. I require the noise, the activity, the vitality of a metropolitan area to sustain me. I wither in the quiet provinces, and the closeness of this small island is a thousand-fold worse. Gentlemen, there are areas where you can actually stand and see the ocean on both sides!" He shuddered visibly. "I would rather be onboard a boat. At least there you have the sensation that you are progressing towards your final destination. Here I feel trapped, like a caged cock. It is as if I have *la fièvre roche*, a 'rock fever,' which can only be relieved by setting foot upon a solid continent."

"If you knew that you would dislike it so much, why did you come to little St. George's?" inquired the constable irritably. "At least Hamilton has the semblance of a city."

Dubois nodded, as if he anticipated this question. "I did so at the request of my wife. It was one of her little fancies that, at the time, I was happy to humor. She longed for a peaceful repose before the final crossing of the Atlantic, and I am certain, gentlemen," he glanced over at me, "that you understand that I can refuse her nothing."

Dunkley shook his head crossly, "What in the blazes does this have to do with Mr. Dumas' murder?"

"A thousand pardons, Constable," said the man contritely, "I was just coming to that. You see, in order to relieve the *ennui* born out of our confinement in this town, I decided to engage in my sport of choice." He hesitated for a moment, and pulled a handkerchief from his sleeve in order to wipe the sweat from his forehead. "Is it hot in here, gentlemen? The closeness of the humid air in this room is affecting me."

Dunkley glared at him, and then turned to me. "Would you be so kind as to open the window, Doctor?"

I complied with alacrity and regained my seat, eager to hear what Monsieur Dubois was apparently reluctant to reveal. He licked his lips and his eyes darted back and forth between us, as if to gauge our sympathy upon our faces. I doubt that he encountered much. "What I am about to say, Constable, appears at first glance to be somewhat incriminating. I briefly entertained the idea of keeping this from you, but I was certain that it would come out if you determined to search our rooms, and I ultimately decided that it would be best if I volunteered this information freely." He took a deep breath. "You see, gentlemen, I had heard from the other guests that a pistol had been found by Monsieur Dumas' bedside, but it never dawned on me to ask a critical question: 'What was the model?'" He paused and looked at us, expectantly.

Dunkley frowned. He hesitated for a moment, as if to contemplate the wisdom of sharing this fact with the man. Finally, he said simply, "It was a Colt single action revolver."

The man sighed deeply, as if he had been holding his breath while awaiting this information. "That is what I was afraid of." He reached down and lifted the case that he had entered with. Setting it upon the table, he spun a set of combination locks and threw back the lid. Inside, we found two depressions molded into a purple velvet-lined padding. In one of the depressions lay the duplicate of the six-chambered pistol that we had encountered upon Dumas' nightstand. The other was empty.

Dunkley and I stared at the case, and I am certain that his brain resounded with as many questions as my own. Before we could voice them, however, Dubois continued.

"You see, gentlemen, I always carry a brace of pistols with me when I travel, as one can never be too careful. There are places in the western United States where the arm of the law has never reached. And yet, they are primarily for sport, to be used in target shooting. Therefore, I have always kept them carefully locked up, so as to prevent any unfortunate accidents from occurring. Until this morning, when I decided to do some pistol practice in the open-air, I had no reason to check to see if they were still both safe in their case."

"Even last night, when you knew that a murderer still roamed free in this hotel?" interjected the constable sharply.

"You assured us, sir, that we were perfectly safe. I took you at your word," replied Dubois with equal heat. "And yet now I see that the sanctity of my room has been violated, and my possessions ransacked and stolen."

Dunkley leaned forward and inspected the lock on the box. "Yes, there are many scratches here, as if the lock had been forced," he concluded. He gazed sternly into Dubois' eyes. "However, that effect would also be easy to fabricate."

The man's lips pursed together angrily. "That is the second time, Constable, that you have accused me of dishonesty. It is an unfamiliar sensation to me, and I find that I do not care for it. At another time and place, one such accusation would be grounds for me to seek satisfaction. Do you mean to arrest me, sir?"

Dunkley held up his hands in a conciliatory manner. "Now, now, sir. Take it easy. You must understand that it is my job to suspect everyone in this building until the murderer has been caught."

Dubois visibly calmed, but he raised an eyebrow questioningly. "Everyone excepting the Doctor here, it seems."

Now was my turn to grow offended. "What do you imply, sir?" said I, heatedly.

He shrugged nonchalantly. "Only that I believe that you have no official *locus standi* in this investigation? And you hold a privileged position, sir. You performed the post-mortem examination, even before the constable's arrival, from what I hear. You have been present at the questioning of every guest, able to steer the conversation in the direction of your choosing. In short, you have *carte blanche.* If I was a murderer, it would be the exact arrangement that I would covet. How could I ever be suspected?" His eyebrows rose suggestively.

I started to rise in anger out of my seat, but the constable's hand upon my shoulder restrained me. "*Touché*, I think is the word in your tongue, is that not correct, sir?" said Dunkley.

Dubois merely smiled grimly and nodded.

"Do you have any other theory, besides the guilt of the doctor here, as to who shot Mr. Dumas?" continued the constable in a reasonable tone of voice.

The Frenchman shrugged again. "We have a saying that seems apt. '*Le mauvais goût mène au crime.*' Perhaps he found himself so odious that he shot himself?"

"Seven times?" I scoffed.

He turned to me and looked me straight in the eyes. "He was most odious."

Against my better judgment, a smile cracked my lips. There was a grain of macabre wit to the man. I shook my head in bewilderment, for this did not seem like the kind of absurdity that would amuse the Lucy that I had come to know. I have never been accused of having an overly-developed sense of humor, but I greatly wondered what had attracted her to him? Was she simply tired of being alone in the world after her mother passed on? And yet, a lady as exquisite as Lucy would have had her pick of eager suitors even if she had not a farthing to her name. Why this man?

Dunkley shook me out of my reverie, "Very well, Mr. Dubois, if you have nothing else?"

The man licked his lips. "I was wondering, Constable, if you knew whether I might eventually get my pistol back?"

Dunkley pursed his lips and nodded slowly. "Certainly, Mr. Dubois. There will be no need for the evidence of the case once it has been solved. Any effects will be either be destroyed or returned to their rightful owners... presuming that you are innocent, of course."

Dubois laughed easily. "Yes, of course. I have no such concerns, Constable. I am certain you will catch the man soon, and the rest of us may be on our way." He closed the half-full pistol case and stood up. He bowed slightly to us. "*Au revoir*, gentlemen."

He strode to the door and opened it, but just as he was about to depart, Dunkley called out his Parthian shot. "Mr. Dubois, please be so kind as to let Mrs. Foster know to assemble the guests after dinner, say seven o'clock. The doctor and I will present our conclusion to the crime at that time."

§

CHAPTER XXII:
THE LIST OF EVIDENCE

Dubois' eyebrows rose in great surprise. "Truly? I will be certain to convey your message. I must admit that I find myself anxious to hear your solution." He paused, but when it became apparent that nothing further was forthcoming from either of us, the man departed with a respectful nod.

Once the door was closed, I turned to Dunkley with what must have been an equal amount of astonishment in my eyes. "Constable, dinner is but a few hours away! How can we possibly come to a conclusion in such a short amount of time?"

He shook his head. "I don't know, Doctor. But it must be done. The guests have begun to complain to their consulates about missing their scheduled boats. Governor Beckwith has become involved, and this morning I received instructions from Mayor Hyland that we cannot detain the guests past tonight. On the morn, the suspects in this case will be allowed to depart this island, and once they are gone I am afraid that the case will never be solved. No, we must bring it to close tonight," said Dunkley with a heavy finality.

"But where are we to start?" I asked, baffled and disheartened. I felt that we had reached a dead wall built across every path with which we tried to approach the truth.

"Come now, Doctor, take heart. We have heard their words. Now we must parse them and try to determine if someone was lying to us."

"Such as?"

"For example, did you note, Doctor, that Mr. Dubois was not the first guest to try to convince us that Dumas committed self-murder?"

I nodded slowly. "Yes, Signore Aicardi suggested the same."

"It is as if they want us to take the easy way out. To conclude that he killed himself and let them go scot free. But of course this was no suicide. It was a very deeply planned and cold-blooded murder."

"Are you implying that Monsieur Dubois and Signore Aicardi are in cahoots?"

Dunkley shrugged his shoulders. "Perhaps, Doctor, perhaps. We must not discount any possibility, however remote."

I nodded slowly. "Not only was the prospect of suicide brought up more than once, but both Signore Aicardi and the Marquesa suggested the possibility of a supernatural explanation."

"That is an excellent point, Doctor. It is as if some of the guests are motivated to get us to latch onto any possibility other than the existence of a murderer within these walls. Signore Aicardi becomes a man of great interest. Anything else?"

I shook my head, unsure of where I had heard any falsehoods uttered. Then one question entered my brain. "Constable, why did you ask Mr. Warburton about his presence on that particular beach?"

"Alexandria's Battery?" Dunkley's eyebrows rose suggestively. "Doctor, do you know what that beach is known for? It is not the Diamond-Back Terrapin, as our naturalist claims. Because of the number of wrecks on the reefs just offshore from it, Alexandria's Battery Beach has the highest concentration of beach glass on this side of Church Bay."

I frowned again. "But I still do not understand how the beach glass relates at all to Dumas' murder? It wasn't even in his room!"

"That is very true, and yet its presence remains a mystery. Furthermore, when I gave Mr. Warburton a chance to explain why he was at Alexandria's Battery, he said nothing of beach glass. It is suspicious, and anything suspicious must be considered."

I nodded in agreement, and then another thought occurred to me. "I think the Marquesa may be lying to us."

"Why do you say that, Doctor?"

"I have not examined her, of course, but it is my medical opinion that the Marquesa is likely suffering from consumption."

Dunkley was astonished. "I will admit, Doctor, that she does not look well, but how can you know the cause of her illness without an examination?"

"Do you recall where she lived prior to her time in Madrid?"

"Somewhere in Switzerland, I think," replied Dunkley.

"Indeed. It was Davos Platz, the locale of one of the most famous sanatoriums in the world. The crisp mountain air does wonders for patients with consumption."

Dunkley nodded slowly. "But she freely admitted that she had been there."

"Indeed, but she also reported that she was travelling to Florida. I have yet to visit that part of the United States, but from what I have read about it, the climate of Florida is similar to that of Bermuda. Its summers are noted for their great heat and extreme humidity, the exact opposite of the airs of Davos Platz. Someone with consumption would not last long in Florida."

Dunkley stared at me for a moment, clearly trying to process how this information could assist in determining the murderer of Gustave Dumas. "Perhaps she is better?"

I shook my head. "Absolutely not. Although it can be a painful and lingering disease for many years, the signs are clear. She is certainly in the last stage. And there is one more thing. Who was present when we determined the number of bullets with which Mr. Dumas had been shot?"

Dunkley considered this. "Just you and I."

"Exactly! Then how did the Marquesa know that he had been shot seven times? I certainly did not tell her!"

"Nor I," said Dunkley grimly, pausing to think about the implications. "That is an excellent point, Doctor, but can you explain how the Marquesa exited a room with a barred door?" he asked.

I sat back in dismay over the collapse of my theory. "No, of course not. It is not conceivable that a woman as weak as the Marquesa could have descended that ladder in the midst of such a great storm."

"I agree. The ladder is a critical clue. In my opinion we can discount anyone who could not have navigated it."

"That would include the Marquesa and Mr. Sims," I said. "I also highly doubt whether Madame Dubois or Mrs. Foster could have done such a thing."

"This leaves Mr. Delopolous, his reported lumbago notwithstanding, as our most likely suspect. Mr. Cordeiro, Mr. Warburton, Mr. Bey, Mr. Aicardi, Mr. Dubois, and Dr. Nemcek are less likely possibilities."

"There is also the chance that it could be someone not affiliated with the hotel. Someone who fled into the night?"

"That option must be considered, Doctor, though my instincts tell me that the answer lies within this hotel. There are few places for villains to hide in St. Georges' where I would not have heard rumors about them. In a quiet town, where all gossip is welcome, strangers generally do not pass without remark. And that storm was too great for anyone to leave the confines of the town. There is no place of safety between St. George's and Flatts upon so wild a night. Furthermore, I am convinced that this was not a random slaying. Dumas was targeted for some reason. We have to determine why. Was it his Confederate sympathies? Are there any other observations that you have made that could be of assistance?"

I contemplated this for a moment. I cudgeled my brain in the endeavor to find some suggestive anomaly. And then a thought dawned upon me. "Yes, there is. I have often wondered how the murderer knew that Dumas was going to drink the drugged comet vintage of Mr. Sims. What if he had chosen Senhor Cordeiro's Madeira wine?"

Dunkley nodded slowly. "That is an excellent question, Doctor. I had not thought of that. You said yourself that he went about in mortal fear of some personal attack. He would not have taken such extreme precautions as he did with the liquids that he drank unless he had a specific danger to guard against. But without Dumas being drugged, the murderer could never have gotten close enough to shoot him seven times."

"All we have is Mr. Cordeiro's word that he drank the other bottle. What if he disposed of the wine? I forgot to mention this to you, but I stumbled upon Mr. Boyle removing a dead plant from Mr. Cordeiro's room this morning."

"A plant? What on earth has that to do with anything, Doctor?"

"When I examined the soil, I noted some ruby-colored crystals on the top layer."

From the look in his eyes, it was apparent that Dunkley did not realize the significance of this. "So?"

"I have never before seen such crystals in the soil of a house-plant. However, after imbibing from a well-aged bottle of wine, I have seen something similar in the bottom of my wine glass. "

Dunkley rocked back in his chair. "Good heavens! Are you suggesting that Mr. Cordeiro poured his bottle of wine into the plant in his room, which killed it?"

"I am."

"But he told us that he drank it. Any he would have no reason to lie unless he knew that the bottle was also drugged."

"Precisely," said I, nodding.

"Can you be certain, Doctor, that those crystals were sediment from a wine bottle?"

I shook my head. "No, I am not. It is merely a hypothesis. There may be a way to chemically prove it, if we can recover them from wherever Mr. Boyle was taking the plant, and if an adequate laboratory exists upon the island that could re-solubulize the crystals."

Dunkley exhaled harshly. "I am afraid not, Doctor. Perhaps they could do such a thing in the best hospitals of London, but not here. Damn, it's potentially a fine clue! If we could prove it, it might be sufficient to place our Mr. Cordeiro in the dock, and perhaps even put his head in a noose."

"But there were many other clues in that room, all of which pointed to someone other than Mr. Cordeiro," I protested. "The red paint, the pieces of eight, and the Persian slipper, for example."

Dunkley nodded thoughtfully. "That is very true, Doctor. One might say that we are suffering from a plethora of clues. Perhaps they are red herrings, left behind on purpose solely to confuse us?" said he, shaking his head in exasperation. "We must contemplate this and try to winnow the chaff from the wheat. What are the special points upon which the whole mystery turns?" He held up his palm toward me. "No, don't answer now, Doctor. Let us both try to come to a conclusion, and then we will compare notes." He reached into his coat-pocket and pulled out his cherry-wood pipe, which he filled with tobacco from a little pouch. He leaned back and began to silently emit great puffs of blue smoke as he flipped through his memorandum book.

It was apparent that the constable did not want to be disturbed, so I stood up and quietly walked over to the window. It looked out only upon a plain little alleyway that ran between the Globe Hotel and the building beside it. It was not much of a view, but I soon found that this ordinariness was beneficial for the workings of the mind, as there was little to distract it. What a tissue of mysteries and improbabilities the whole thing was! I contemplated the clues and our conversations with the guests, however, and endeavored to find some explanation which would cover all of these facts. What in the world could be the connection between all of the oddities that we had witnessed? I turned the case over in my mind and found that the list of clues was rapidly building to the point where my mind was no longer able to enumerate and categorize them. Since I had long been in the habit of jotting down little lists on whatever scraps of paper I could find, I decided to make such a document now. I sat back down and fished a pen from my pocket and started jotting on some blue-tinged stationary. I could not help smiling at the document when it was complete. It ran this way:

GUSTAVE DUMAS – ATTRIBUTES OF HIS MURDERER
1. *Possession of Laudanum & Hypodermic Needles. – Leos Nemcek.*
2. *"   " Red Paint. – Dario Aicardi.*
3. *"   " Pieces-of-Eight. – Marquesa Garcia-Ramirez?*
4. *"   " Persian Slippers. – Mehmet Bey?*
5. *"   " the Colt Revolver. – Hector Dubois.*
6. *"   " the Powder-Stained Gloves. – Bruce Sims.*
7. *Able to Silently Climb the Staircase. – Antonio Cordeiro.*
8. *"   " Climb Ladder during a Great Storm. – Aristides Delopolous.*
9. *"   " Collect Sea-Glass. – George Warburton.*
10. *Note Written to Dumas. – Bruce Sims or Mehmet Bey?*
11. *Banks at Cox & Co., Charing Cross. – George Warburton?*

12. Antipathy towards Dumas' Confederate Sympathies. — Lucy Dubois?

The last name was the most difficult to set down. My heart rebelled against the notion that she might be involved in any way in such a brutal slaying. When my list was finally complete, I sat back to contemplate it. I soon realized that it had led me no closer to the truth. Based on the clues so far, a case could be made against virtually any of the guests. And part of me was profoundly ambivalent about finding the answer. As far as I could tell, Monsieur Dumas was a singularly unpleasant individual. I felt no real antipathy to his murderer. If I wanted to admit the truth to myself, it would have to be that I was helping the constable purely for the thrill of the hunt.

Eventually, the constable looked up from his book. He first gazed at his pipe. "I'm afraid that I have smoked this down to its dottle and still do not know how it was done, nor why it was done in such a grotesque fashion. Did you come up with anything, Doctor?"

I shrugged and handed him my list.

After he read it over, he looked up. "You succinctly sum up the difficulties of the situation well, Doctor. I don't like it. If your list is to be believed, none of them fits every clue. Do you think one of them could be mad?"

I shook my head in vexation. "Monomania can be exceedingly difficult to diagnose, Constable, and there are few limits to its possibilities," I answered. "The mad can occasionally appear completely normal, but every word that they say is a falsehood, and they can be capable of horrific outrages. But I am no alienist and have no training in the modern French psychology, so I could be of little help in ferreting out a madman from amongst the guests. And not knowing who it is, we would have to discount all of the testimony that we have heard and proceed with nothing but the clues, which do not lead us very far."

"True enough," said Dunkley, shaking his head sadly. "Perhaps it is the husband of fair Lucy after all."

My eyebrows rose in astonishment. "Monsieur Dubois? Why would you suspect him?"

"It was his gun that did the actual deed. And it is a rare assassin who comes to a job unarmed. Furthermore, he is the only countryman of Dumas in the hotel. Perhaps the Frogs knew each other. It is as close of an association as I am able to come up with."

I contemplated this statement, for a thought had suddenly struck me. "You know, Constable, I am not certain that he is actually French. I think Monsieur Dubois may be Belgian."

"Belgian?" remarked Dunkley, astonished. "Pray tell, what makes you think that?"

I cast my thoughts back two days to the dining room, where the company assembled in the Globe Hotel broke its fast. I described to him what I had witnessed at the Dubois' table. "You see, Constable, a Frenchman would have ordered a crepe, a little pancake that I was surprised that Mrs. Foster knew how to prepare. Instead, Monsieur Dubois ordered a waffle. But the waffle originated in Brussels."

Dunkley shook his head irritably. "But why would he and his wife lie about something like that? Feigning to be French causes him to appear more closely associated with the dead man, not less. It's quite incomprehensible."

My hackles rose at the suggestion that Lucy had lied to us. "His wife might not be party to his falsehood. They are recently wed, and she too may have been fooled by a set of fabricated identification papers, created to replace the ones conveniently lost in his hotel's supposed fire. Perhaps he even set the fire in order to lend authenticity to his tale?" As the words lifted from my tongue, a glimmer of a thought began to percolate in my brain about something I had seen that had implications in the case, something to do with papers.

But this thought was dashed by the constable proceeding with our discussion. "In any case, there are multiple individuals in this hotel who are potentially lying to us." He began to tick them off on his fingers. "Mr. Warburton regarding the beach-glass. The Marquesa regarding her destination. Mr. Cordeiro regarding the fate of the second bottle of wine. Mr. Delopolous regarding his lumbago. And finally, Mr. Dubois and his nationality."

"Why would they all lie to us?" I exclaimed. "They cannot all be involved!"

Dunkley shook his head morosely. "Fear of being questioned by the police induces people to do queer things. Everyone has something to hide, Doctor. Something in their past, or even the present, of which they are ashamed. They do not want the truth being dragged into the harsh light of day, even if it has absolutely no bearing upon this case." He leaned back in his chair and thought for a moment. "If you are correct, Doctor, and if Mr. Dubois is a Belgian, then none of the guests - excepting Dumas, of course - is actually French. A few of them have passed through France, of course, but none have any strong link to the man."

I nodded slowly. "Yes, that is very interesting. How peculiar that we would have such an assorted clientele at this hotel."

"Yes, this week the Globe is aptly named. Mrs. Foster has certainly attracted all sorts of odd guests from almost every corner of the world."

"Especially Europe. We are missing only a German," said I.

The constable frowned. "What about Dr. Nemcek? Surely he spoke in German."

I shook my head. "As a citizen of Austro-Hungary, Dr. Nemcek shares a common tongue with the Germans, but there is a vast difference between the Czechs and the Germans."

Dunkley leaned forward in his chair and slapped his palm down upon the table: "Dash it all, Doctor! All of this talk brings us no closer to the truth. If anything it only serves to confuse us further. Who knows who did it? We might as well draw lots to decide who to arrest!"

With his words, the inextricably puzzled knot that has enwrapped my brain began to disentangle. I stared at him for a moment. "What did you say?"

"I said that there is no utility to further discussion. Let us face the guests. But first, if you would kindly fetch the Persian slipper from your room. I will add it to the rest of the evidence."

I thought I saw a dim glimpse of a possible solution, but every time I tried to wrap my thoughts around it, it slipped from my grasp. In any case, I had my instructions to carry out. The constable and I rose from our seats and moved towards the door. When Dunkley threw it open, we found that the dining room was surprisingly deserted. It was as if each of the guests had decided to spend the remaining minutes before the constable's *dénouement* in the isolation of their own room. Dunkley looked about and then pulled out his pocket-watch to confirm the time. Only ten minutes remained until the time the constable had indicated. He turned to me, shrugged his shoulders and raised his eyebrows in astonishment. "I hope that they haven't all fled the island, Doctor," he said with a wry face.

"No fear of that, Constable," interjected an accented voice. We turned to find Senhor Cordeiro emerging from his room, which lay next to the ladies' parlor that had become our headquarters. "I am certain that the others will be down presently," said he, gravely.

Dunkley turned and nodded to me. I ascended the stairs as quickly as my leg would permit and began to make my way through the twisting corridor back to my room. However, before I could hardly leave the landing, the second door in the corridor opened and Lucy Dubois stepped out, quickly closing the door behind her. I abstractly registered that she had changed into a scarlet gown which, combined with her lustrous hair and impossible loveliness, conferred on her the appearance of one of the seraphim descended to earth. My breath caught in my throat. She did not seem surprised or perturbed to find me at her threshold. Instead, a deep smile spread over her face and alighted in her deep green eyes. There was no possibility that she feigned her pleasure at my presence. I found that all thoughts and words had disappeared from my brain.

"What a stroke of luck to find you here, Doctor!" said she with great feeling. "I have been intending to speak with you – alone – one more time before the constable presented his conclusion to the case. Who knows how much time will be left to us afterwards."

"I seem to see dimly what you are hinting at, Madame," I stammered. "Do you fear that the constable intends to charge you?"

She threw her head back and laughed gaily. "No, do not be absurd, Doctor! But once the guests are free to depart the hotel, I do not know if we will have a chance to repeat our walk in the garden. There are many things that I would like to say to you."

In my inmost heart, I believed that she felt identical emotions to mine. I decided to throw reserve to the winds. "And I to you, Madame. You see, I have had no keener pleasure than the time that we have shared. Since then I have been all off-color. I realize that what I am about to say is ignoble and you would be well within your rights..."

At that moment, the large bulk of Mr. Sims arrived from deeper in the corridor and interrupted our *tête-à tête*. His eyes darted back and forth between Madame Dubois and myself, perhaps wondering why we were blocking his path.

"Good evening," said he, addressing both of us with a polite nod.

My courage fled and I affected a shameful retreat. "Good evening, Mr. Sims. Perhaps later, Madame?" I bowed and fled down the hall. When I reached my door, I paused for a moment and gazed at the final door. It belonged to the murdered man and had proved to be the ingress to a fantastic world where everything was turned on its head. I hardly knew what to do next. Finally, I turned the key in the lock and pushed into my room. I immediately strode over to the dresser where I had discovered the slipper earlier that morn. Pulling open the drawer, I was astonished to find that the drawer was empty. The slipper had vanished like the genii of the *Arabian Nights.*

My overstrung nerves failed me suddenly, and I dropped to the edge of the bed and laughed feverishly. I had reached the end of my tether.

§

CHAPTER XXIII:
A POSSIBLE SOLUTION

Eventually, I brought my surfeit of emotion under control and composed myself. I pulled my handkerchief from my sleeve and wiped it over my brow. I had almost exposed my deepest sentiments to a woman whose hand was already claimed. When she refused me, as I knew she must, my shame would have been profound.

I sighed and stood up. It was time. Ignoring the discomfort in my leg, I made my way out of my room and back down the stairs. At the bottom, I turned and entered the dining room, where I found that I was the last of the guests to arrive. Mrs. Foster, Mr. Boyle, and the entire clientele of the Globe Hotel were anxiously gathered in a great semi-circle around Constable Dunkley. I noted that the women were sitting, as was Monsieur Dubois and Mr. Sims. The other men all stood. I hovered by the door, acutely aware that Lucy Dubois was seated directly opposite from my perch. While the interest of the others was focused on the constable, she alone appeared most intent upon me. Dunkley himself was separated from the assembled company by one of the dining tables. He had an expression of the most reflective gravity upon his face.

"Thank you for joining us, Doctor," he said upon my arrival. He turned his attention to the rest of the room. "Ladies and gentlemen, in one hour I must report to Mayor Hyland and the Justice of the Peace my conclusion to this case. Should anyone care to confess, it would save us much time." He paused but the silence that met this request was absolute. "Very well, I will therefore set out the clues in this case."

Dunkley reached into his brown wide-awake and carefully extracted the various items that he had confiscated from Dumas' person and room. The first object was none other than the Colt revolver that had been used to kill the man, once the property of Monsieur Dubois. The large powder-stained gloves that had been stolen from Mr. Sims were next, followed by the man's silver watch and gold chain, identity papers, money, wax vestas, cheroots, and jade cigar holder. The various receipted accounts from his room were deftly stacked in one corner of the table, with the crudely-scrawled letter from the mysterious 'B' upon the top. The Confederate seal and the two pieces-of-eight were laid next to each other, followed by the inscribed jack-knife, the nine shards of sea-glass, and the burned slipper from the fire-grate. Even the man's green Calvados bottle was set out.

Dunkley turned to me and held out his hand. "The slipper please, Doctor."

My mouth was suddenly dry. "I am afraid that it is no longer in my room," I stammered.

Dunkley frowned at me, as if he could not credit my statement. "I see," he eventually said, following a pregnant pause. "Then pray be seated, Doctor."

Although my legs were taut with emotion, I could not fail to obey his command and I sank into the nearest chair. Glancing at Lucy Dubois, I imagined that I saw a hint of pity in her eyes.

Dunkley shook off this setback. "No matter, there is already too much evidence for my taste. The trick is to recognize, out of a number of clues, which are incidental and which are vital." He waved his hand over the table. "The vast majority of these items have no bearing whatsoever upon what I will term the Globe Hotel Mystery. They are merely distractions from the true reason that Mr. Dumas was murdered. In fact, there are only three items on this table that are of any assistance. The first are these interesting coins." He picked up the silver coins and twirled them between his fingers. "These are coins not commonly seen in Bermuda. In fact, as the Marquesa so helpfully pointed out, these are coins from the days when the great heavily-laden treasure fleets still sailed from the Americas back to Spain. Many of those ships never reached their home shores, but instead lie littered upon the ocean floor after losing their way in one of many terrible storms. And what else comes from those wrecked ships? Why sea-glass! It always bothered me why these bits of glass were left upon the landing table. But the key of the whole matter was this crude note." He reached over, and held it up for the inspection of the crowd. "Due to all of your kindly assistances, I have studied the writing of every man in this room, and I am confident that none of you, no matter how well you might have disguised your hand, could have possibly written this note. And yet the note explains Mr. Dumas' reason for being in St. George's. He was summoned here. Or, to be more precise, he was summoned to 'the place of the barrel.' This strange phrase gave me much pause. And then a statement by Mr. Warburton made it all clear."

I looked over at the English naturalist and noted that he appeared considerably astonished at the constable's words. But Dunkley was not finished. "Mr. Warburton informed me that the unfortunate Mr. Dumas was highly interested in the art of dowsing. There is only one locale on Bermuda that might be referred to as 'the place of the barrel.' That is Cooper's Island. Cooper's Island lays very close to here on the other side of St. David's, the large island just across the harbor from where we stand. If you will be so kind as to listen, I will now tell you the tale of Cooper's Island and Christopher Carter."

He paused and nodded in my direction. "Four days ago, the Doctor and I were fortunate enough to witness the recovery of a great lump of ambergris. At that time, I related to him the story of the Three Kings of Bermuda. With his permission, I will repeat it now." He glanced over at me, and I gave him a silent assenting nod. The account that he proceeded to relate to the assembled company did not differ from the one I had recently heard. However, once it was complete he continued to describe what occurred after the confiscation of the men's ambergris. "Rumors differ about what happened next. It is most probable that Carter betrayed his fellows Waters and Chard and gave evidence that they were solely responsible for the crimes committed. While the latter two may have been deported in chains, it is clear that Carter was allowed to remain on Bermuda, becoming its first permanent citizen. Furthermore, it was decided that Carter would be compensated for his share of the ambergris. It may be hard to fathom today with so many people crowded upon these isles, but in 1612 he was reportedly offered the entirety of massive St. David's Island! Even more difficult to conceive, Carter supposedly rejected St. David's in favor of the far smaller Cooper's Island, which was readily granted to him. It is said that he spent the remainder of his days digging on that island. But what could he have been digging for?"

Dunkley raised his eyebrows suggestively. "The answer is obvious, of course. The treasure fleets had been returning from the New World since shortly after its discovery in 1492. There is definitive evidence that either the Spanish, or the Portuguese," here his gaze swung over to Senhor Cordeiro, "landed upon Bermuda as early as 1543, for they carved it into the rugged surface of a rock over in Smith's Parish. And it is said that on Cooper's Island there were obvious signs of previous brief visitations. Most notable of these were a triangular pile of stones, too unnatural to be anything but the work of men, and a large inscribed metal plate affixed to one of the smooth-barked yellow-wood trees that once grew in the rocky woodlands of the isles. A plate that was not hung by English hands. Only two years later, two Spanish ships were spotted by Governor Moore approaching the east of the island – where Cooper's lies, mark you – only to be repulsed by the garrison that he had established on Castle Island. The garrison had fired its very last shot when the Spanish finally turned their tails and fled, a fortunate occurrence or this island might today be known as *Las Bermudas* and answer to a different monarch," he nodded with mock regret at the Marquesa as he said these words. "It was clear in everyone's minds that the Spanish ships were returning for one thing only – to reclaim their previously buried treasure, which they had marked with the stones and plate. These legends were enhanced when an old white-bearded Spanish sailor was interviewed in England. He told a tale of how he and his companions had brought ashore gold and treasure, burying it under repurposed wooden ship's hatches between two sandy bays in a valley of what would become known as Ireland Island, where the Royal Navy's Dockyard now resides. On certain days of the year when the sun rose unimpeded by clouds, the cross that was raised on the island across from this horde was clearly intended to point towards the repose of this still un-located fortune. And if you were to discount these tales as nothing but baseless rumors, you would be mistaken, for parts of the treasure have been unearthed! This was first proven in 1709, when a man named John Hilton dug up a hundred and fifty ounces of Spanish Silver not far from here. And then, in 1726 a Spanish jar came to light on Cooper's Island, its innards stuffed with gold plate, golden tankards, and doubloons. Is there more to be discovered? Only time will tell."

The assembled company stared at Constable Dunkley intently when he completed this extraordinary narrative. There was little sound in the room, as if the group was holding its collective breath, wondering what came next. The constable studied them for a moment, and then continued. "Therefore, ladies and gentlemen, it is my belief that Mr. Dumas came to our island in order to search for the remainder of the great Spanish Treasure Trove. This explains why he was staying in out-of-the-way St. George's, rather than the more central comforts of Hamilton. In order to avoid the heavy taxes imposed by the government on any recovered loot, any treasure recovery would have necessitated great secrecy. There are still plenty of men here who recall the great wealth that blockade running once provided, and who would not be much perturbed to risk some clandestine treasure-hunting. Some of them are former wreckers, and no better than out-and-out pirates. Clearly, Mr. Dumas contacted some of these men, one whose name begins with a 'B.' Unfortunately for his future health, he eventually must have had a falling out with the gang of thieves, quarreling over the division of some of the recovered treasure. This explains the grotesque placement of the Spanish coins upon his eyes. It was obviously intended to serve as a warning to others not to betray the group over monetary disputes. One of the infernal rogues must have set the ladder up against the house, an event unlikely to be noticed under the cover of the distracting storm."

Although I had been entranced by the almost mythical quality of Dunkley's tale there were many parts that bothered me, and I finally decided to speak up. "But how did they drug the wine?"

Dunkley turned to me and nodded sagely. "Clearly one of the gang must have entered the hotel earlier that day, once it became apparent that a great storm was brewing, and had been in hiding ever since. I suspect that he must have slipped into the upstairs W.C. Any guest attempting to utilize it during the day would have naturally assumed that it was occupied by another guest at the moment, and would have repaired to the one by the kitchen instead. This man must have been an expert in picking locks, for he absconded with the hypodermic syringe of Dr. Nemcek, one of Mr. Dubois' pistols, and some of Mr. Aicardi's paints. He then fled via the previously arranged ladder into the garden, clambered over the low wall, and took refuge in a bolt hole prepared by one of his fellow thieves."

I shook my head. "That would have taken more than a cool hand and an iron nerve. It would have taken extraordinary luck. Surely such excursions would have been noted by someone?" I protested.

"Not if they occurred while the guests were assembled below. Did you not say that everyone gathered to listen to Mrs. Dubois playing the violin? What better time to carry out his schemes?"

"And the sea-glass? What part did it play?"

Dunkley shook his head. "I cannot say for certain. But I will tell you my theory. I think it was sent to Dumas earlier that day as a final warning to play fair with the rest of the gang. That is something that secret societies are wont to do. And he would have recognized the implications of the sea-glass due to the locale of the treasure. One of the overwhelming arguments against the continued existence of Spanish treasure upon Bermuda is the question of the location of its whereabouts. So much of the isles have been exhaustively explored, especially Cooper's. One possibility is that it is secreted in a cave. We know that at least a few exist on the isles, especially in the porous limestone that comprises much of Hamilton Parish, and there are continued rumors that others remain to be found. So what reason could exist why a cave might remain undiscovered to this day? What if it was submerged?" He said triumphantly.

"But if it was submerged, how could they recover any treasure from it?"

"Ah, that is why the men here required a foreign partner. Or to be more precise, why they needed a French partner. You see, Doctor, last night I carefully examined the receipted accounts that we found in the murdered man's room. Most of them did not appear to have any bearing upon this case, but one puzzled me. It was a reference to a book published by a Frenchman named Bert and entitled *La Pression Barométrique*. I had little idea what the book was about, but I sent this information to my chief, Superintendent Clarke, and he made inquiries amongst the learned in Hamilton. Imagine my surprise to learn that this book dealt with a method of how to safely pump air through a hose into a transparent helmet so that a man could operate for an extended period of time underwater. It then all became clear. The local villains can barely read English. They would have needed someone to translate the book without questioning how they intended to employ their newfound knowledge."

The assembled company was silent as they appeared to ponder this. After a span of about a minute, Mr. Sims finally ventured to ask a question. "Constable, who do you then intend to charge for the crime?"

Dunkley shrugged. "I will round up the usual rogue's gallery of ne'er-do-wells. With the proper pressure, it is exceedingly possible that one of them will crack like a nut and spill all, implicating his collaborators in the hopes of sparing his own miserable hide. If not, then I will have to recommend to the jury that they bring a verdict of murder by persons unknown."

As if a spigot had been turned and a great pressure released, the room erupted in a great babble of conversation. Each man turned to the fellow next to him with a flurry of laughs and handshakes. Even the dour Marquesa appeared to crack a sardonic grin. I alone sat quietly, unhappy with this explanation. I must confess that I was out of my depths. It was still all dark to me, but I felt that the constable had failed to provide a spark to illuminate the murky quagmire of Dumas' murder. It was then that someone new arrived upon the scene, with a banging upon the front door. To my great surprise, when Mrs. Foster opened it, she encountered Lieutenant Thurston with a telegram in his hand. He eagerly scanned the room until his gaze alighted upon me.

"Ah, Doctor," exclaimed the soldier, breathlessly. "Your brother sent me here in all haste, as he was certain that you would want to see this wire from Dockyard." He handed it to me, and I read it eagerly. The text was short. It ran: *'The symbol you describe in conjunction with the suggestive initials can only pertain to one entity, the* Légion étrangère, *better known in the Queen's tongue as the French Foreign Legion. I hope this may be of assistance with your inquiry. I remain your obedient servant, etc. etc. Dr. Edward Lewton Penny.'*

I recalled some newspaper stories that I had read when I was but a young lad that detailed one of the many great undertakings of the Legion. I recalled what I knew of the last days of an Austrian nobleman who had been unwillingly thrust upon the world's stage, his tragic end in a far-off land. As all of this knowledge began to percolate into my brain, a new possibility precipitously dawned upon me. It was as if the clouds had lifted and the light of truth was breaking through. I looked up from the page, and found that most of the room had not remarked on Thurston's appearance. Only the attention of Lucy Dubois was riveted upon me, and I thought that something like fear suddenly sprang up in her eyes. As I stared back at her, the facts of the case darted like lightning before my eyes. The mystery suddenly cleared away as this new discovery furnished the missing link which led me to the complete truth.

Before I deigned to do anything with my sudden knowledge, I turned to Thurston and bade him wait. Patting my breast pockets, I quickly located a pen and a scrap of paper. I hurriedly jotted down another questioning telegram, this time to be sent to another locale entirely. Thurston raised his eyebrows speculatively when he saw my enquiry, but he kept his tongue and tipped his hat before departing.

I am afraid that I barely bid him leave, as I was too busy reviewing the threads of the affair which were now all in my hands. I finally understood the whole of that remarkable chain of events. Why all of the surviving guests, save only Lucy and the Marquesa, were of a similar age. Why so many of the men stood with such an erect posture and carried their handkerchief in their sleeves. Why Mr. Warburton was so eager to get to Bermuda by a certain date. Why Mrs. Foster had been so put out by my appearance at the hotel. Why Mr. Sims appeared so familiar with several of the other guests, and the true meaning of his overheard conversation with Signore Aicardi. How Signore Aicardi knew that Lucy played the violin. Why Mrs. Foster knew how to make crepes and why Mr. Sims used a French expression. Why the Marquesa travelled without a maid, and how she knew about the Mexican herb Jimson weed. How Mr. Sims developed the habit of chewing coca leaves, and how Senhor Cordeiro knew to pour out his invaluable bottle of wine. How Monsieur Dubois' pistol, Dr. Nemcek's hypodermic needle, and Signore Aicardi's paint were so easily extracted from their rooms. Why Mr. Sims' gloves had been used, and why the Persian slippers had been worn. Why there were no footprints in the garden at the base of the ladder. How Mr. Delopolous and Mr. Bey were able to share a room, despite the hereditary hatred that existed between their nations. Why there was no German guest and no Frenchman other than Dumas. Why Dumas feared for his life and vainly sought to preserve it. Where Dumas had obtained a jade cigar-holder, and what the bank receipts suggested. Why he had been marked with the coins and the paint. Why the pistol that had taken Dumas' life had been reloaded, and the reason for the nine shards of sea-glass. Heavens forbid, I even understood why Lucy's heroine was Boudica, the Briton queen who long ago had enacted her bloody revenge upon the traitorous Romans. But I also found a glimmer of hope, sprung from a violet ink spot upon her sleeve that perhaps explained the actual reason why Monsieur Dumas showed such displeasure at sharing a room with his wife. I then recalled a quote that she had previously recited from Shakespeare's *The Tempest*. But I recalled it in full. 'Alas, the storm is come again! My best way is to creep under his gabardine; there is no other shelter hereabouts: *misery acquaints a man with strange bed-fellows*. I will here shroud till the dregs of the storm be past.'

"Oh, what an ass I have been!" I exclaimed as I sprang to my feet, all thoughts of discomfort in my leg forgotten. "Constable," I called out over the excited din of the crowd. "I have two final questions to ask that may have a very direct and vital bearing upon this mystery." A morbid silence settled over the assembled company as they turned their attention upon me.

The constable looked confused, but shrugged amiably. "Pray continue, Doctor."

I first turned to the supposed Frenchman. "I have a simple question for you, Monsieur Dubois."

"But of course," said he, shrugging gallantly.

"Monsieur Dubois, are there any common French surnames that begin with the letter 'E?'"

If I had thought that the room had drawn quiet at my initial interjection, it was nothing compared to the utter silence that met this question. Dubois' eyes flickered across the room, not resting on any one person, before they refocused upon mine. Finally, he spoke. "*D'accord.* There is one. Etienne."

"Thank you," said I with a nod. "The second question is of paramount importance. It is for Signore Aicardi," I turned to the Italian painter. "Will you, on your word as a gentleman, respond with honesty?"

The man stiffened and he looked me in the eyes. "I am your servant, sir. I will answer your question."

"After Constable Dunkley and I questioned you, upon your departure you murmured something in Italian. Would you please repeat it?"

His face showed the greatest consternation at this obviously unexpected question. He passed his tongue over what I imagined to be parched lips before answering. "I believe that I said '*E quindi uscimmo a riveder le stelle.*"

"And what exactly does that mean?"

"A translation in English might run something to the effect of *'and then we emerged again to see the stars.'*"

Although I thought I knew the answer, I asked the question regardless. "And is that a quotation from somewhere?"

Aicardi nodded slowly. "It is the final line from the *Inferno* of Dante Alighieri."

I turned towards the Australian rugby-player, "Did you know, Mr. Sims, that the great American poet Henry Wadsworth Longfellow, in collaboration with some friends, which included your acquaintance Dr. Oliver Wendell Holmes, published an excellent translation of the *Inferno* about a decade ago?"

Sims frowned and rose stiffly from his chair. "I was not aware of that, Doctor. I was never much of a reader."

"That is a great shame, sir, for it is simply remarkable what you can learn from books. I happened to read Mr. Longfellow's translation when I was at university, and the final line comes after Dante and Virgil have just emerged from the final, deepest circle of Hell. And do you know what they had encountered in that last circle?"

"I do not," said he, tersely.

"They saw the devil himself gnawing upon the souls of Judas, Brutus, and Cassius. And why were these three, out of all of the great villains of history, punished so severely? What was their common crime? I will tell you. They were traitors. And one, Judas, had sold himself for thirty pieces of silver. Thirty pieces might be too great to leave upon a dead man's corpse, but two fit upon the eyes quite nicely."

I turned to the constable. "What you related about a gang of treasure hunters is a plausible explanation, Constable Dunkley. It is certainly what we were intended to believe. However, would you kindly permit me to propose an alternate theory?"

"Of course, Doctor," said he, in a perplexed tone.

"If you would suffer me to expound upon my notion, I will ask you to come away with me for a time, far from the Globe Hotel of St. George's, Bermuda. Far also from this year when we all gathered unto this unlikely place, a sojourn which ended with the strange murder of the man known as Gustave Dumas. I wish you to journey back thirteen years in time, and westward some hundreds of miles in locale, so that I may lay before you the singular and terrible narrative of a man who is no longer with us. Once I have detailed these distant events, perhaps we shall have solved this mystery of the past."

§

CHAPTER XIV:
AN EXTRAORDINARY TALE

In the southern portion of the great North American Continent lies a land as varied and as changeable as its inhabitants. From the arid and repulsive deserts of the north, to the vast, teeming jungles of the south, it is a region where a man has great barriers to finding peace. The terrible silences of the desert are balanced by the unrelenting cacophony of the jungle, all of which conspire to drive a man towards madness and despair. A smattering of villages are scattered about, breaking the monotony of the enormous lonely stretches, but even those are filled with inhabitants whose bearing and language are all but incomprehensible, so as to provide little relief from a slow descent into hopelessness. Furthermore, all parts of the land share the common characteristics of inhospitality, misery, and ultimately death, either by a shriveled, parched end or a rotting, decaying finale.

One small part of that great land contained within its borders all of the diversity of the country as a whole. The Sierra Gorda was infamous for being extremely rugged, with high steep arid mountains and deep lush canyons. But the most dangerous part of all was the abundance of pit caves that had eroded over thousands of years through the limestone. Their edges were often hidden by foliage, such that a man cutting his way through the region must be ever cautious of his footing, for one wrong step could send him plummeting to a dark and abandoned doom.

Gazing over this very scene, there sat upon the sixteenth of March, eighteen hundred and sixty-seven, a man whose countenance betrayed weighty concerns. Although he was relatively short, he had powerful shoulders and a round, clean-shaven face, lightly freckled. His green eyes were arresting, they bespoke of an intense inward life, so bright were they, so alert, so responsive to every change of thought. They were the eyes of a man who had experienced much more than his thirty-two years would

213

suggest. Although the sun had barely begun to shine over the mountain peaks and filter through the trees of the forest, his forever-rumpled fiery red hair was already protected by a great cream-colored circular hat, which some might term a *sombrero*. He wore a blue coat, with a yellow collar and epaulettes. Its brass buttons were still shiny despite a week of marching through the forest. His red leggings were trimmed by a blue stripe and tapered to white spats over black boots. A rifle and ammunition-containing satchel lay immediately to his side.

His eyes had risen in response to a faintly detected sound, but nothing followed it, and he concluded that it must have been one of the various nameless mammals that inhabited this forest. His gaze was drawn back to the letter he held, hoping for an explanation that he had missed during one of the first dozen times that his eyes had traversed the pages scribbled in a crabbed foreign hand. Despite being signed by one of his superior officers, Lieutenant-Colonel Moreau, the motives behind the instructions within were still inscrutable.

"Commandant," said a voice softly. "Are you ready to move out?" From the soft Spanish accent, Iain Harrier recognized the approach of his second-in-command.

He looked up and saw a man dressed in an identical fashion as him, albeit with one less bar on his shoulder insignia. Despite the similarity in dress, the two men otherwise differed greatly. The second man was tall and lithe, with immaculately- flowing black hair and a perfectly waxed moustache. In another world, outside of a soldier's uniform, the man might have been mistaken for a Latin dandy. But standing warily in the dappled shade of the forest, his rifle cradled in his arms, his dark eyes gleamed with a dangerous intelligence.

"Tell me, Diego, do you ever question your decision?"

Capitaine Diego Garcia Ramirez brows knitted in response to this query. "To what decision do you refer, Commandant?"

"The Legion, *Capitaine*, the *Légion étrangère*. Do you ever think that you should not be here, sweltering in the mountains of Mexico, fighting the war of a country not your own? You are a Marquis, born and bred to command your own countrymen, and yet here you stand, taking orders directly from an unlettered American, and ultimately from unseen men in the gilded salons of Paris."

The *Capitaine* smiled grimly. "You are not so unlettered as you imagine, sir. Not everything can be taught in *l'ecole*, some things can only be learned through experience. And your experience is far greater than most men with whom I am familiar. The men and I trust your judgment implicitly."

Harrier looked down at the camp, where his men were slowly stirring. The rising sun's rays filtered through the trees sufficiently to illuminate the scene. A few of the men were breaking down the tents, while others prepared a simple gruel over a low fire. He nodded slowly. "Have I ever spoken of that morning, *Capitaine*?"

Garcia Ramirez's manicured eyebrows rose appreciably. "Antietam? Never," said he, shaking his head. "I did not want to pry..."

"It was a September morn, the corn in the fields high and the weather temperate. Even the humidity seemed tolerable when we emerged from our tents before the dawn even broke. Though, of course, all of that was to change. Twelve hours later, we knew the fields near Dunkers Church as simply a 'hot place.'" His gaze turned distant as he remembered the events of five years earlier. "The night before, it seemed like we were invincible. General McClellan discovered that Lee had secretly divided his army and driven north. Our forces, eighty thousand men strong, had intercepted a force less than half our size at a place that none of us from the west had ever heard of... Antietam Creek. Of course, that name is forever seared in our memories now, at least in those of us fortunate enough to walk away with our life and limbs. I was stationed atop a gentle crest, across from the center of Lee's thin grey line. My bayonet was fixed, but little good it would do me when the rebels were entrenched in an ancient farm trail, sunken beneath the ground around it by years of horse carts. As we charged down that crest and across the field, two thousand riflemen poured lead into us furiously. It seemed as if with every step that I took a man beside me fell. But there were too many of us and we fell upon them in wave after wave. For every unlucky soul, there was another like myself that made it across the field of death miraculously unscathed. And when we reached the end of their line, we found that we could fire along the length of the sunken road into a mass of closely-packed Confederates. You cannot imagine the intimate terror on their faces. There was nowhere for them to hide in that 'Bloody Lane,' except perhaps under the bodies of their fallen brothers and comrades. There lay so many dead rebels that they formed a line which one might have walked upon as far as a man could see.

"Elsewhere, the Federal army was not so successful. Late in the day, when men could barely hold their rifles, Rebel reinforcements arrived from Harper's Ferry and drove us back from where we had advanced. By nightfall, it was over. To many it must have seemed like a stalemate. Both sides held much the same ground that we had when we awoke that morn. But to those of us that could see past the carnage of the bloodied bodies and imagine the larger picture, we knew that this vast slaughterhouse tolled the beginning of the end for the Rebels. The losses on both sides were unimaginable. Some say over seven thousand fell and were pitched into mass graves over the next few days. We could absorb those losses, but to the undermanned Rebels, it was staggering. From there, the march to Appomattox was inevitable." He paused for a moment to remove his hat and run his fingers through his hair. "I've never been back to Antietam. I think that, even should I be fortunate enough to die an old man in my bed, I never will have the courage to face those fields again. But they were verdant even then. I suspect that they produce an absolute abundance of crops now, as long as one does not mind tilling up a bone every once in a while."

"Sir," said the *Capitaine* gently. "Let us move on. Once we take ship, we can complete this mission, and then you are free to do what you will. You can return to that home of which you speak so fondly, nestled in the hills overlooking the city of San Francisco rising through the fog. You will feel the arms of your wife around you and raise your daughter up onto your shoulders."

"It was a morning much like this one. Not the weather or the environs, of course," said Harrier, waving his arm around the camp. "But the smell in the air. If you take careful note, you can taste it on the breeze. It is the smell of iron. It is as if the earth itself knows that blood is about to be spilt." He seemed to return to the present and fixed his gaze on the Spaniard. "Diego, I want you to do me a favor. If I don't make it out of Mexico, I want you to deliver a letter for me to Julianne and Lucy."

Capitaine Garcia Ramirez smiled grimly. "Better you ask Hector, sir. He will take your letter to your wife and daughter. If you fall, I will be at your side."

Harrier nodded slowly. "Perhaps you are right, Diego. Come, let us finish this mad mission." He rose from his perch upon the rocks and made his way down to the camp, with the *Capitaine* following closely behind. As he entered the circle of men, they all rose. There were no salutes, as Harrier ran a battalion too relaxed for such formalities, especially here in the mountain forests of Mexico. Most of his battalion had been sent onto Veracruz by the direct route and only this elite section commanded by Lieutenant Ralph Foster was ordered to proceed by a more obtuse track. The Bermudian was the only other officer present, though in Harrier's opinion every man present was worth two normal officers. Of their sixteen men, only eight were presently in the camp, the others were off standing picquet duty. The gigantic Australian *Sergent Chef* nodded his respects as Harrier passed.

"Sims, are the men ready to move out?" asked Harrier of the *Sergent*.

"Yes, sir, they are. If I may sir..." Sims waited for a confirmatory nod from Harrier before continuing. He spat out a wad of the coca leaves that he had taken up chewing during his time in South America. "We are all wondering why we are moving through this god-forsaken forest, rather than making a direct line towards Veracruz?" observed Sims thoughtfully.

Harrier had wondered the same thing himself. He reflected back seven days the day when this mad mission had begun.

§

Harrier was sitting in the shade of some elaborate Mudéjar arches in the courtyard of the opulent residence that had been commandeered as the headquarters for his battalion while encamped in Santiago de Querétaro. He was studying maps of both the city and its surrounding environs in hopes of visualizing how the Republican forces might try to attack. Harrier had spoken to numerous local residents, so he was well aware of the history of the town. It dated back over two hundred years to the Conquistador era, when they were battling the local tribes for control of the region. During one critical battle, the numerically-superior local tribes were on the verge of annihilating the Spaniards when suddenly a total eclipse of the sun occurred. The Spaniards went on to claim that they also saw an image in the sky of Saint James Matamoros riding a white horse carrying a rose-colored cross, and this vision caused the natives to surrender. Harrier valued his first officer too highly to ever insult the Spaniard's patron saint, but after the horrors he saw committed on both sides during the American Civil War, he privately held grave doubts whether any army could truly claim to possess divine favor. He suspected that the natives were simply stricken dumb in awe of the eclipse. The current inhabitants of Santiago's city seemed divided in their predictions for the future. The landed gentry appeared to take strength from the fanciful legend. Although the Republican forces of Benito Juárez, the elected president of Mexico, appeared to possess greater numbers, the more wealthy locals seemed to believe that Santiago was on the side of the Emperor and he would turn the upcoming battle in Maximilian's favor. The poorer classes, on the other hand, appeared to believe that Juarez was a manifestation of Santiago himself.

Officially, Harrier's battalion had been left behind in an advisory capacity, though he knew that unofficially it was intended that he would directly support the loyalist Mexican Army in any engagements with Juárez's forces. Thus, Harrier continued to attempt to envision how Juarez would attempt to attack. However, his attention was soon distracted by the arrival of a horse outside the villa. Within seconds, a dusty *Sous-Lieutenant* appeared. Harrier recognized the man as one that was attached to the staff of General Bazaine, currently headquartered in Veracruz.

Despite his significantly inferior rank, the *Sous-Lieutenant* barely saluted Harrier, who idly wondered if this arrogance was born of the man's proximity to General Bazaine, or if it was the typical disdain of the officers seconded from the French Army for those rare foreigners who were promoted from the ranks, as Harrier had been. He handed Harrier a sealed note, and then turned to depart, again with a lack of acknowledgment bordering upon insolence. Once the man had left, Harrier opened the note and, as he read it, his eyebrows quickly rose in surprise. As an American, born in a land free of heredity nobility, despite commanding an entire battalion of the French Foreign Legion he was one of the few officers who had never been summoned to appear before the Emperor. Until now.

Harrier rapidly rose and strode to his room in order to change from his daily uniform to his finest dress regalia. As he checked his appearance in a tarnished silver mirror, his thoughts turned to the history of the Emperor Maximilian. He was the younger brother of Francis Joseph, who had ascended to the throne of Austria-Hungary in 1848. As the second son, Ferdinand Maximilian Joseph had spent his childhood knowing that he was not meant for a throne, and his inherent curiosity had led him to study the natural sciences, especially botany. Of course, he spent the required time in the Austrian Navy, but after he married Carlota, daughter of King Leopold of Belgium in 1857, the happy couple retired to a life of leisure and study. But in 1863, their lives were forever altered when Napoleon III of France begged Maximilian to take the throne of Mexico, recently conquered from its democratically elected leader Benito Juárez under the pretext of safeguarding foreign investments. Maximilian was hesitant, but after both the Mexican exiles in Europe and the Vatican also interceded, Maximilian and Carlota acquiesced. Unfortunately, the idealistic young nobles were not aware of the ulterior motives of all three groups, who planned to use them as pawns to further their status in the great game of international power.

Not long after Maximilian was installed as Emperor, it became clear that his honesty and integrity would prevent him from acceding to the unjust demands of the landed proprietors and clergy. He even refused to make the state of Mexico fund the upkeep of his palace, rather paying for it from his own personal income. As his support began to dwindle, the forces of Juarez began to regroup. Shortly thereafter, the War Between the States drew to an end in May 1865. Once the United States had caught its breath from four years of brutal conflict, it suddenly realized that French troops were encamped in the country directly below its borders. The government immediately protested that the French presence contravened the Monroe Doctrine, which in 1823 stated that further efforts by

European nations to colonize land or interfere with states in North or South America would be viewed as acts of aggression requiring intervention by the armed forces of the United States. Federal troops began to amass at the Texan border.

Harrier was personally conflicted by where his choices had led him. After Antietam, he had continued to serve in the Union Army, and took part in Sherman's March to the Sea. After Lee's surrender at Appomattox in April 1865, Harrier had found himself a skilled soldier with no other appreciable skills. Harrier considered attempting to settle into a peacetime appointment, but whenever he lay down at night, faces of the men that he had slain upon the battlefield visited him in the darkness. Only when he was exhausted from a day full of military exercises did the faces fail to appear. And so he took ship to the one country where they freely accepted soldiers from other countries.

Before he knew what had happened, he found his battalion back on a ship across the Atlantic. If Harrier had ever heard of the Monroe Doctrine, he had long since forgotten it, so that he was unconcerned that the Legion would ever come into conflict with the forces of his native land. Harrier arrived too late to participate in the Legion's defense of Hacienda Camarón, already legendary throughout the globe. But he distinguished himself in innumerable other skirmishes with the Republican forces and soon found himself being rapidly promoted through the ranks.

§

Harrier was expected at the Casas Reales y Cárceles, the combination palace and jail that served as the Emperor's headquarters, and he was rapidly escorted though a series of passageways into an ornate room. The thick walls kept out the afternoon heat, but also cast the room in perpetual gloom. Most of the light emanated from an extravagant candelabrum.

When Harrier entered the room, his gaze was immediately drawn to the man behind the desk. He was about Harrier's age, but the cares of ruling a country had erased most of the hair from the top of his pate, with only some brown tufts persisted above his ears and running into an enormous splayed beard topped by an elaborate handlebar moustache. His eyes were a soft blue and his mouth possessed a sensitive character. All in all, it was an unusual face to rise out of the Imperial uniform that he wore, his shoulders draped with worked golden chains.

Harrier was not surprised to find Maximilian flanked by the white-haired and bearded Generals Miguel Miramon and Tomás Mejía, both legendarily loyal to the Emperor. Two other men made up the remainder of Maximilian's entourage. The first Harrier knew to be the suave Colonel

Miguel Lopez. The Colonel had a pleasant cultured smooth face, high-nosed and pale, with something perhaps of petulance about the mouth. He had a steady eye and a brisk manner. His hair was grizzled round the edges, and thin upon the top. All three men were part of the loyalist Mexican Army. The final man was unfamiliar to Harrier, despite the fact that he was the only man to share his French uniform. The man had a sallow face, scored with deep lines and eyes that bordered on bilious, making it difficult to place his age, but nearer to fifty than forty. He had thinning black hair that receded from his high forehead, and his little pointed beard was touched with a hint of grey. He was rail-thin, but his bowed shoulders suggested weakness rather than lithe strength. His nose was thin and projecting, reminding Harrier of one of the buzzards that circled the skies of this land. His eyes were brown, and the candlelight reflected a calculated look. The shoulder insignia near his epaulets made clear that he was a Lieutenant-Colonel, one rank higher than Harrier.

Harrier saluted the five men and remained at attention, in deference to the Emperor. Colonel Lopez opened the introduction. "Commandant Harrier. At ease. Do you know, Colonel Moreau?"

Once he heard the name, Harrier realized that he did know the Frenchman by reputation. The man was descended from an honorable stock, but rumors had circulated about some questionable actions. However, Harrier's silence was taken as a negative by Colonel Lopez, who continued. "No? Well, he brings grim tidings from General Bazaine at Veracruz."

The Frenchman stepped forward, "As you know, Commandant, the French Army is withdrawing from Mexico. That now includes your battalion of the Legion, Commandant." He fell silent, clearly awaiting a response from Harrier.

A great wave of relief washed over Harrier, and the expression clearly must have showed on his face.

General Mejía spoke up sharply. "You look pleased, Commandant." His tone made clear that his fury was barely contained.

"I am most sorry about this news, General, for it plainly means that the Emperor must now withdraw as well. But personally, I would not be telling the truth if I did not admit that I am glad that I do not have to face my countrymen on the field of battle. I killed my fellow Americans for almost four years, more of them than I care to remember. I would prefer to never do so again."

"I am not abdicating, Commandant," the voice was pleasant, the words precise despite the Germanic accent. It was the voice of a scholar, not an Emperor. "I may not have been born in Mexico, but I have come to love this land and its people. I have served them to the best of my abilities, and this is my adopted country now. Despite what Napoleon III urges, I will not abandon them. I have asked them if they want me to abdicate and the answer was clear. They want me here, and I will stay."

Harrier was silent. The Emperor's proclamation did not require an answer. But the Emperor appeared to see the hint of a question in his eyes.

"Do you have an observation, Commandant?" the Emperor asked. "Feel free to speak your mind."

"Forgive me, Your Imperial Majesty, your devotion is not in question. Nor is the bravery of the Imperial Mexican Army. But without the French forces, your men will be hopelessly outnumbered by the Republican forces of Juárez. You have only about eight thousand men."

The Emperor smiled grimly and shook his head. "You are not wrong, Commandant. But Santiago de Querétaro will not be easy to take, no matter how many men Juárez has. We can hold out until reinforcements come."

Harrier frowned in incomprehension. "Reinforcements, Your Imperial Majesty?"

"As much as I would like to think that all men fight for honor or loyalty, the reality is that there will always be men who are willing to fight for monetary gain. As long as I can buy their loyalty, this war can still be won. But my resources here in Mexico are finite. I need someone to travel to Europe and raise capital to use for funds. That is why you are here, Commandant."

If possible, Harrier's frown deepened further. "Sire?"

"General Miramon here has asked questions, Commandant. He has sought a vast number of opinions as to who is the most honest man in the French forces. Imagine his surprise, Commandant, when he discovered that the most honest Frenchman was actually an American! The men were unanimous in choosing you, Commandant."

Harrier shook his head vigorously. "I am not worthy of such an appraisal, Sire."

"It is not a matter of debate, Commandant. Your superior officer, Colonel Moreau has agreed that you and a section of your choosing will be temporarily seconded to the Mexican Army. But you will not fight in the siege of Santiago de Querétaro. Nor will you withdraw with the main French forces, which are likely to be harried by Juárez all of the way to Veracruz, and who will therefore move slowly. Instead, your squadron will move like the wind towards the sea. You will take this coffer to Paris and place it into the hands of Napoleon III himself. He owes me as much, since he failed to aid my dear Carlota."

"They are all cowards!" General Mejía spoke with disdain. General Miramon raised a hand to try to stay Mejía's outburst, but the rash General would not be stopped. "No! Forgive me, my Emperor, but I will speak my mind! Napoleon! Bah, that fat fool isn't fit to carry the name of his illustrious uncle." Lieutenant-Colonel Moreau stiffened at these words, but General Mejía plowed on. "Your brother is equally useless, quivering in Vienna after being slapped about by Bismarck. Even Pius IX proved to be nothing but a greedy little Italian coward. None of them deserve to call themselves gentlemen after turning away the supplications of the Empress Carlota herself!"

Harrier thought the Emperor would be upset at these vicious insults of the great leaders of Europe, as well as the Pope himself. Not that Harrier disagreed with General Mejía's opinions, but he would never dare to voice them aloud. The Emperor only laughed, as if he had heard this a hundred times before. "Come, come, General. Let us not upset these fine officers of the French Legion by besmirching the name of their Emperor. Napoleon's concerns are valid. Between the United States Army encamped upon our northern borders, and Bismarck's Prussians amassing upon his eastern frontier, Napoleon III's forces are spread too thin. There is no shame in his withdrawal. As for my brother and the Pope, however, you may have a point."

Harrier licked his lips with an atypical nervousness. "Your Imperial Majesty, may I ask what is inside the coffer?"

The Emperor nodded. "Of course. A man should understand the reason why he is risking his life. You may know, Commandant, that before I was called to lead this great nation, I made some inquiries into the natural sciences. As part of that pursuit, in 1860 I undertook a voyage to the rain forests of Brazil. There I was given the opportunity to purchase a few gemstones of a remarkable size and clarity from all about the South American continent. These are what I wish Napoleon to sell for me." He took a key from a silken cord about his neck and turned it in the coffer's lock. As Maximilian threw open the lid, the lights of the candles reflected upon a collection of gems that Harrier had never thought to lay eyes upon outside of a drawing from the Arabian Nights.

"At the bottom of the stones, Commandant, there is a detailed list of what the coffer contains, sealed by my hand, so that no stone can disappear or be substituted with a lesser one. There are two hundred and twelve diamonds of the first water from the Gran Sabana region of Venezuela, including the magnificent thirty-three carat greenish-yellow Carlota Diamond, now named after my consort. There are three hundred and four yellow topazes from the Ouro Preto mine in Brazil, two hundred and forty-two aquamarine beryls from Aracuaí, Brazil, ninety red garnets from Lavra Navegadora, Brazil, a hundred and twenty three opals from the Sierra Gorda, seventy agates, half from Brazil and half the fabled Cyclops agate of Mexico, and eighty-eight turquoises from Chuquicamata in northern Chile. But the pride of the collection is the unparalleled *émeraudes* from the Muzo and Cosquez mines of Columbia. There are two hundred and fifty-seven common emeralds, including an emerald and diamond necklace that is of inestimable value. There are two emeralds of particular note. The first has become known as the Maximilian Emerald. It is twenty-one carats in size and a deep grass-green color. It was cut and set for me into a golden ring, and it alone is worth a small duchy. Finally, there is another stone, known as the Empress Emerald, which at two-hundred and thirty carats is the second largest emerald in existence, even larger than the Moghul Emerald. The largest, of course, was the Queen Isabella Emerald, however, in 1757 the ship carrying it to Spain mysteriously caught fire and burnt somewhere in the strange waters between Florida and Bermuda. The Queen Isabella will never be seen again and so the Empress Emerald, named after my wife, has now claimed the premier spot on that exclusive list." Maximilian plucked the Empress Emerald from its berth in the coffer and held it up to the light. It was cut into a multitude of facets, which made it appear to be almost a perfect dark green sphere the size of a child's fist. "But this emerald was not purchased on my trip to the Amazon," the Emperor continued. "The Empress Emerald was given to me by the grateful inhabitants of my new home. For this emerald once belonged to Cuauhtémoc, the last king of the Aztecs. In 1521, Cuauhtémoc was captured by the Conquistadors trying to cross Lake Texcoco in disguise while fleeing from the eighty-day siege of Tenochtitlan. Hernán Cortés tortured him for four years trying to get the king to divulge the whereabouts of his hidden treasures.

"Cortés was a monster, of course, his greed insatiable. Upon his arrival he had been handed the Stone of Judgment, later called the Isabella Emerald, by Montezuma himself. It was thought to be the most powerful instrument of the Aztec culture, destined to be reclaimed by Quetzalcoatl upon his return, as prophesied in the Aztec Codex. There was a legend that when the Stone of Judgment is reunited with twelve crystal skulls, the secrets of the universe will be revealed to its bearer. But it now lies in the waters of the Atlantic. Cortés was not satisfied with owning this great stone. He wanted more, and he was aware of another legend that spoke of an emerald called the Stone of Life, able to impart eternal youth to its bearer. It was said that Cortés desired this mystical stone more than anything in the world, but Cuauhtémoc valiantly refused to lead him to it. Finally, in a fury Cortés had the king executed, ensuring that the Conquistadors would never learn the stone's hidden whereabouts. But over three hundred years later my grateful people presented it to me when they realized that I came here to lead this nation to greatness, not despoil its riches like so many before me. Its value is inestimable and it pains me deeply to send it from this land, where it belongs. But someday, when there is peace in the land, we will reclaim it. Though," he paused, finally smiling sadly, the lines of care worn deep into his brow, "I am afraid that it has not shed any years from this face."

"Your Imperial Majesty," protested Harrier. "Surely you must keep something back. You cannot send away all of your wealth."

The Emperor smiled again. "You are a wise soldier, Commandant. I see how you have risen so far. Do not fear. I will keep one stone in reserve." He patted a small satchel that hung from his neck. "Now, your Colonel Moreau has devised a route for you. At the end you will find a ship waiting for you that is manned by my adherents." Moreau moved forward and handed Harrier a sealed letter. "Once you reach Paris, you must insist that Napoleon III acts with great haste in disposing of the jewels. He should not accept less than half-a-million sterling for them. We can hold out here for several months, but we must be reinforced before the summer." The rest of the conversation with the Emperor and his advisors was spent in strategizing how Harrier was to help supervise the recruitment of mercenaries for the Emperor's cause.

§

Harrier's focus came back to the present. He turned to the huge man that served as his *Sergent Chef*. The twenty-seven year-old Australian was one of the men that he trusted with his life, and he was a natural leader of the more junior soldiers. "I am wondering the same thing myself, *Sergent* Sims. But our orders are clear. I've read the letter a dozen times and there is no question." He turned to one of the junior soldiers. "Speaking of letters, Hector, I have one that I would like you to deliver for me."

The *Legionnaire de Deuxieme Classe* saluted Harrier. "It would be my honor, sir."

Harrier smiled. Hector Dubois was a good kid, the youngest in the section at just a few months past his eighteenth birthday. With his fine intellect and passion for debate, Dubois could have easily studied law. He was knife-sharp, and Harrier suspected that he might go far if he ever returned to his home country of Belgium. Harrier often wondered what had driven Dubois from his homeland, as he did for the other members of the section. But it was an unspoken rule in the Legion never to pry into a man's reason for joining.

The other *Legionnaires de Deuxieme Classe* were also fine young men, and only a few years Dubois' senior. Aristides Delopolous was clearly born and bred on a boat, back on one of the Greek Isles. But he followed orders precisely and was one of the best riflemen in the entire battalion. Mehmet Nazim Bey was his opposite in almost every way, intellectual rather than athletic, Turkish rather than Greek. But in some odd fashion, the two men had become the closest of friends, each covering for the other's deficiencies, and bringing out the best in the other man. Legionnaire Bey had a natural skill for all things mechanical and Harrier suspected that he might train as an engineer someday.

The *Legionnaires de Premiere Classe* were also some of the best soldiers that Harrier had ever served with. Both the Portuguese Antonio Cordeiro and the Englishman George Warburton were young men, but impressively skilled in tracking and shooting. The Bohemian Leos Nemcek was the least natural soldier under his command, but he had distinguished himself by becoming an unofficial assistant to the regimental army officer. Harrier hoped that the bright young man might someday attend medical school once he was discharged from the Legion. The Italian Dario Aicardi served as the section's Corporal, and with his artist's precision he rivaled Delopolous for accuracy with a rifle.

The officers were as strong as the men that they led. Lieutenant Ralph Foster hailed from a tiny island in the midst of the Atlantic, and though he dreamed of acting, some unexplained impulse had led him to join the Legion. But his natural good-humor and relaxed leadership style made him immensely popular amongst the men. He spoke often of returning to his home isle and opening an inn with his beautiful bride Elizabeth, whose photograph he was often fond of showing to the other men as proof of how fortunate he had been. *Capitaine* Diego Garcia Ramirez was his opposite, formal and stiff whenever Foster was relaxed and jovial. But the Spaniard was deeply respected, for every man knew that his word was stronger than steel, and that he was a man of both boundless loyalty to his friends and implacable hatred to his enemies. Although *Capitaine* Garcia Ramirez was not known for his humor, Harrier thought that the man must be joking when he said that his wife back in Spain was twice as hard as himself.

In sum, it was an elite section and Harrier was proud to command it. It was little wonder why they were chosen for this delicate mission, but Harrier was still puzzled by the orders found in the letter of Lieutenant-Colonel Moreau. He had no more time to ponder the oddities, however, for as soon as he had handed his letter to Mr. Dubois, a branch cracked in the neighboring woods. The men turned as one, all reaching for their rifles which were never far from hand. But before they could raise their arms into position, a band of disheveled men stepped from the woods, all with rifles trained upon Harrier and his men. Although the men wore peasant dress and had unshaven cheeks, the rifles in their hands appeared new and free of any rust or wear that might impede their accuracy.

Harrier was stunned. "What?" he stammered. "How did you get past the picquets?"

"Your men are dead, Commandant," said a large man harshly. He had skin bronzed by the tropical sun, and greasy dark hair tied in a loose knot behind his head. In age he appeared a little over thirty, but his hard eyes spoke to a life lived roughly. "The same will happen to you if you fail to obey me. Throw down your guns and put your hands behind your heads."

Harrier tried to place the man's accent. It was not Mexican or even Spanish. Nor was it French, not entirely. But it was maddingly familiar. None of his men had moved. Harrier's eyes flickered around the camp, attempting to count how many men were arrayed against him. There were at least six in his immediate field of view, which meant at least another six behind him, and likely a few more concealed in the trees in reserve. If the man was telling the truth, which seemed likely since they had made their way into the camp itself, then Harrier was down to just eight men in addition to himself and the other two officers. The odds were stacked against them. "Do as he says," said Harrier finally. "Throw down your guns."

"Sir?" said Ralph Foster questioningly.

In a flash, the man that appeared to be the leader of the ruffians turned his gun on Foster and shot him in the shoulder. Foster collapsed to the ground and the rest of Harrier's section seemed about to jump into action. "Stop!" Harrier cried out before the rest of his men were gunned down, for he knew that there was no way they could bring their arms to bear before the bandits fired.

The bandit leader growled, "That is what happens to anyone who disobeys me!"

"You heard the man!" Harrier ordered. "Drop your weapons, and hands behind your head. You too, Mr. Sims!" With a clatter of metal upon the hard ground, his men quickly obeyed his order.

"Excellent," growled the bandit. "Now, Commandant, give me the key."

Harrier frowned. "Key?"

"Do not play games with me, Harrier! I can take it from your dead body just as easily as from your live hands."

Harrier's mind was moving as fast as a race horse. It was possible that the man had deduced his rank by the number of bars on his shoulder insignia next to the green and red epaulettes. But how could the man have known his name? And how could he have known about the key that Harrier carried? And then the man's accent clicked. He had known men with the same tone on their tongue during McClellan's push towards Richmond.

"You are far from home, Creole," Harrier finally replied.

The man's response was to backhand Harrier across the mouth. "Shut up! You have one more chance to hand over that key before I send you to hell."

"Of course," replied Harrier evenly. But his mind continued to race. He decided that after these men found the Emperor's gems, there was little chance that they would let he and his men live. If Harrier made a move it was likely that many of his men would die, but some might live. As Harrier slipped the silken cord from about his neck, he glanced over at Sims and gave the *Sergent* a minuscule nod.

The Creole roughly took the key from Harrier and immediately strode over to the Commandant's tent. Kneeling down, he pulled out the Emperor's coffer and fitted the key into the lock. In seconds, he was rising and turning about with the Empress Emerald held aloft in his hand. The attention of the other bandits was distracted for a moment, which was all the time that Sims needed. In a flash, an enormous bowie knife emerged from a sheath nestled along his spine, and erupted from the chest of the bandit across from him. He and the other Legionnaires dove for their guns and some form of cover, while the stunned bandits began a ragged fire.

Despite the element of surprise, Harrier was still not confident about their odds. He cared more about the lives of his men than he did the Emperor's gems. "To the woods!" he cried. His men reacted like the disciplined soldiers that they were. He was proud to see Legionnaire Nemcek dragging the fallen Foster after him into the deeper forest. The section took up shelter behind tree trunks and began to return fire towards the bandits in the clearing. For a moment, Harrier thought that the tide was turning and that they might prevail despite their wounded man and numerical inferiority.

Then, to his immediate right, he saw *Capitaine* Garcia Ramirez take a bullet directly through his eye. The man fell with barely a sound and Harrier felt a pang at the loss of such a good friend. As he continued to return fire, his mind still tried to puzzle out how the Creole had found them, and how he knew about the treasure that they were carrying. Surely, the soldiers of the Mexican Army were loyal to the Emperor and would have wanted to see this mission succeed. Only one other man knew about the mission, and that was the man that gave them the orders for their route through the Sierra Gorda. *Moreau, that damned traitor*, thought Harrier.

The gunfire from the Creole's men appeared to be tapering off, until Harrier heard a final shot ring out. He noted this one much more clearly than any other gunshot that he had ever heard before. The name echoed in his brain. *Moreau. Moreau.* And then he felt an agonizing pain, sharper than any prior hurt. He couldn't localize the pain; it seemed to be coming from everywhere. But it was soon washed away by an embracing darkness. *Moreau. Moreau.* And then a final thought...*Lucy....*

§

CHAPTER XXV:
THE CONSTABLE'S DILEMMA

The silence of the room when I finished my tale was deep and profound. Everyone had listened spellbound to this fantastic narrative. Only the creaking wheels of a cart being driven down Duke of York Street punctuated the stillness. Excepting only the incredulous constable, the faces of the men surrounding me were grim, while the women's faces were fixed into emotionless masques. But I thought I detected a hint of tears forming in the corners of Lucy's eyes.

"You have a lively imagination, Doctor," said Sims finally, a firm and even tone to his voice. "That is a cock-and-bull story if I've ever heard one."

"Perhaps," I admitted. "It is all conjecture and surmise. I don't insist that every detail is exact. But I think I have aimed close to the mark. It has at least an answer for everything. It is too monstrous a coincidence to suppose that a group of individuals, all with military attributes or connections, could have come together in this tiny hotel by chance alone. I think that less than half of your section made it out of that forest alive, Ralph Foster with enough lead in his chest that it would trouble his health for the shortened remainder of his life. If they had appeared in Europe without the Emperor's jewels, with which they had been entrusted, the survivors would have been looked upon with the greatest suspicion. They likely decided never to rejoin the Legion, but rather to make their own way in the world. However, before they separated I suspect that the survivors of that ambush agreed to hunt down and extract revenge upon the man who betrayed their mission, regardless how far across the globe he tried to flee. Without Harrier's letter from Moreau, it likely took the survivors many years to learn the exact identity of who stood to profit from such a perfidy. Many of them took other professions in order to survive, but the common yearning for justice never died in anyone's heart. For those surviving men of the *Légion étrangère* were avenging more than just the deaths of their friends and leaders. They were avenging the death of Emperor Maximilian himself. Despite braving a three month siege, perhaps always hoping that the jewels that he sent with Commandant Harrier would soon purchase succor, Maximilian was finally captured by the forces of Benito Juarez. A travesty of a court-martial sentenced him to death. Despite telegrams of protest from the leaders of Europe, and even the great French writer Victor Hugo, a firing-squad soon ended the Emperor's life, as well as those of Generals Miramon and Mejia. The Empress Carlota has never admitted that her husband was dead, and she has been in seclusion near Trieste since that time. So, in a way, they were avenging her as well. Moreau got away out of Mexico and carried himself and the memory of his abhorrent crime to some land beyond the seas. But danger was dogging his footsteps. The survivors knew that any vengeance would have to come from outside the pale of the law. I suspect that the mercenaries who carried out the ambush were eliminated first. It was reading the news of the Creole's death that likely drove Colonel Moreau to hide his identity under that of the investor Dumas. And yet he was drawn out of hiding by his own un-slacked greed. Although Moreau had received the lion's share of the magnificent jewels stolen from Harrier's tent, he had to share at least part of the spoils with the mercenaries that had actually carried out the despicable deed. And Moreau lost heavily dabbling in stocks. He was ready to do anything on earth to regain his ill-gotten fortune. And so a great plan was concocted to lure him to Bermuda, to the very hotel run by the widow of one of the ambushed men, with the pretense of hunting for treasure. And there the sword of justice fell upon him."

Constable Dunkley interjected. "But Doctor, we have handwriting samples from every man in this room. I've examined them to the minutest detail. I am confident that none of them wrote the note that we found in Dumas' room."

I nodded grimly. "I agree, Constable. None of the guests wrote that note. But we do not have a handwriting sample from every man in this room, do we, Mr. Boyle?" I turned to the innkeeper's assistant, my eyebrows raised.

The livid flush that rose on his cheeks was a sufficient answer. His gaze darted around the room, before settling upon the constable. "Harry, you know that I never properly learned my letters. How could I have written that?"

The constable looked puzzled, but I continued. "The note we found was crudely written," I agreed, "much like something written by a man just learning, but whose words were being dictated by someone far more trained. Someone who masterminded this entire revenge. Someone like an *avocat*, Monsieur Dubois."

Dubois' only response was a haughty silence.

"But Doctor, what is your proof?" asked the constable, his eyebrows drawn low in intense thought.

"I freely admit that I have little proof. However, according to this wire that I just received from Dr. Penny," I held up the telegram, "it is an undisputed fact that the knife possessed by Colonel Moreau, or Monsieur Dumas if you will, carries the symbol of the *Légion étrangère*."

"He could have bought that somewhere," protested Dr. Nemcek, "it is not proof that the murdered man once belonged in the ranks of the illustrious French Foreign Legion!"

"True enough, and yet it explains much. Dumas believed that you were on his track and he was always on his guard against you. He feared that he was at the center of a monstrous conspiracy, and he was correct! Dumas always had the look of a man who had spent too long a residence in the tropics. His jade pipe stem must have hailed from Central America. And it explains why there is no German in this hotel, for years of rising tension that eventually led to the unhappy Franco-Prussian War have made it impossible for a German to be allowed to join the Legion. And it explains why Monsieur Dubois wished to be thought of as a Frenchman, when in fact, he is a Belgian. For he did not wish to draw attention to Moreau's nationality, which might have made us consider exactly where a Frenchman would interact with such an assorted crew."

As Constable Dunkley and the guests pondered this, a tremulous voice broke through the silence. "There are many such places, Doctor," said the Marquesa, "where the French interact with other nationalities. Their tentacles are far-reaching. I do not see why you have to invent such a preposterous tale."

"I apologize if I have pained you, Marquesa. I intended no dishonor to your husband. And yet, you yourself failed to deny that he fell in battle. I know your sadness must be profound, but I suspect that your fury is even greater. A woman of Spanish blood does not lightly condone such a treacherous act. When passions flagged, when new careers developed and distractions arose, who pressed the men to carry on for the final years of the last thirteen? I believe that you were not being completely honest with us, Marquesa, when you told us your reason for your maid's dismissal. You are not going to Florida, are you? Bermuda is equally on the route to Mexico, I think."

Her eyes flashed at me, and her head was raised proudly. Then it sank to her chest. "You know my fate as well as I, Doctor. I have only a little

CRAIG JANACEK

time left and I would not have stranded Beryl in the New World. But I will lie with my Diego again very soon." Her chest sobbed.

Lucy went to her aid with a handkerchief and glare of anger for me, all thought of her natural reserve apparently lost in her over-powering excitement and concern for the Marquesa. But the Marquesa stiffened and thrust out a defiant chin before waving her away gently. Nonetheless, Lucy turned to the constable heatedly. "Constable, you have only the Doctor's words to support this farcical tale. But have you considered the possibility that he may not be entirely well? He has just been through a horrific battle and was terribly wounded. Perhaps that is why he sees enemy soldiers everywhere, and envisions conflicts that never occurred? He has also been voraciously reading mystery novels. Perhaps that is why he perceives conspiracies where none exists? He has even imagined that a Persian slipper has been appearing and disappearing from his room!"

I was stunned by this accusation against my competence, especially arising from one that I held in such high esteem. For an instant I could have sworn that the faintest shadow of a smile flickered over her lips. Dunkley turned to me with a shadow of doubt having risen in his eyes. But despite my bitterness I pressed on. "There is one other little item, but it is a suggestive one. In England, a jury is composed of twelve men. Tell me, Monsieur Dubois, do you happen to know the composition of the tribunal for a court-martial in the French Foreign Legion?"

Dubois nodded slowly, as if pondering whether he would be found out in the event of him uttering a falsehood. "I believe that a military tribunal in the French Foreign Legion is presided over by a Judge Advocate, with as few as three and as many as seven officers who pass final judgment."

"If I count correctly, excluding myself, there are nine guests remaining in this hotel. The addition of Mrs. Foster makes ten. One man must have served as the Judge Advocate. Perhaps the highest ranking soldier left alive from the company? But that man could still play a role, such as drinking heavily from a drugged bottle of comet vintage Sauternes in order to allay the nervous victim's fears? And the remaining nine would have to draw lots to determine which of the seven were allowed to pass judgment. Constable, how many shards of sea glass did you find?"

"Nine."

"That's correct. Seven that were green and two that were blue. The perfect tools with which to draw lots. And how many bullet holes did we find in the dead man?"

"Seven," said the constable, his voice a barely audible croak.

"You wondered, Constable, why the gun was reloaded and another bullet fired? There is your answer. You see, Constable, there is no single murderer. That was their *coup de maître*, their masterstroke. Everyone in this hotel had a hand in his death."

Sims turned to Dunkley and trained the full force of his powerful gaze upon the befuddled man. "Constable, enough of this rigamarole! I believe that the time has come to decide which tale provides the most likely explanation for the murder of Monsieur Dumas: your splendid, straightforward theory of a vicious fall-out between desperate pirates, or the Doctor's convoluted fairy-tale of revenge across the years? The magnificent fair-play of the British criminal law is in your hands."

Dunkley looked plagued with irresolution. The ripple of emotions across his face was clear, and his response was slow in coming. "The Justice of the Peace in Hamilton is not noted for the leniency of his sentences from the bench." He turned to me pleadingly. "You must help me decide, Doctor. I have never met a man who was more eminently suited to represent a British Jury than you. Does everyone agree?"

I looked about the room. My eyes caught the gaze of each of the guests, who I had come to know so well over the last few days. But I mainly wished to look into the eyes of Lucy, to try to gauge what thoughts were foremost in her mind.

Lucy was the first to speak. "The Doctor is a gentleman to whose mercy I should be entirely willing to trust," said she with great solemnity.

I gazed at her, befuddled. Was she simply trying to manipulate me? I could not be certain the veracity of her feelings. And then I realized that her prior outburst, rather than an attack upon my character, was actually an attempt to provide me with an escape from the predicament of being correct. Terribly correct. But Sims must have taken my hesitation for an internal debate about what course of action. "You realize, Doctor, that without the stone, you cannot prove it," said the former *Sergent-Chef.*

I took a deep breath and found my equanimity. I looked at him and nodded. "What does the law of England care for blood shed many years ago in far off Mexico, or for the great treasure which this man has allegedly stolen? They are like crimes committed on some other planet, and any sequelae that have rippled out from the first offense are equally inconsequential. It is not our responsibility to police a justifiable private revenge. Clearly the first solution, the Constable's solution, is the correct one. Mine was nothing but the phantasm of an overwrought imagination."

With that pronouncement, Lucy smiled broadly and the room once again broke into a happy buzzing of conversation. Tears sprang to her eyes and she nodded at me before turning away. I watched her for a moment, until the constable clapped his hand upon my shoulder.

"Tell me, Doctor," he said warmly. "Do you really believe that? Are we commuting a felony?"

I thought about this for a moment. "It's not about what I believe, Constable. It's not even about what I could prove, which is very little. It's about what is right. The sword of justice has fallen, albeit far from the scene of the original crime and long after the loot has been dispersed. But fallen it has, and no one would doubt that its aim was true. There was always only one criminal in this hotel, and he is dead. All that remains is men - and women - who have lost someone dear to them. But is that not every man's story? We are not so different from them. In the same situation, we may have trod a similar path."

Dunkley nodded slowly. "Thank you, Doctor, for all of your assistance."

"But I've done nothing!" I protested.

"That's not true, Doctor. You have told a wonderful story, despite all its evil memories. And there is great power in stories. You have a gift, Doctor, which I would encourage you to develop. Even if this tale can never leave this room, everyone who heard it knows the truth. I will call upon you tomorrow."

He shook my hand, and moved over to the table where the assembled clues lay. He started to put them back into his satchel, one by one. Just then, the little negress serving girl entered and tugged upon my sleeve to obtain my attention. She wordlessly handed me a wire. Tearing the envelope open, I found that Thurston had been speedy in carrying out my inquiry. I now understood everything. I was about to confront Lucy when my attention was suddenly drawn to the one object upon the table that was out of place. The one object that should never have been in the murdered man's room. I began to see dimly the answer to another mystery. "Constable!" I called out. The company quieted and turned as one to try to ascertain the meaning for my sudden excitement. "I have one last request."

Dunkley shrugged. "Name it, Doctor."

"The clues in the case," I motioned to the table, "do you have any use for them?"

Dunkley appeared to ponder this. "We have been unable to locate either a will or any relatives of the deceased, so there is no clear inheritor of the man's property. However, I doubt that the magistrate would look kindly if I gave you his silver watch," said he, dryly.

"What about the Calvados bottle?" said I, with as much nonchalance as I could muster.

Dunkley looked at me shrewdly, perhaps wondering if I planned to drink the entire bottle myself. He finally shrugged. "I can't imagine that this inconsequential bottle will be much missed. Take it, Doctor."

"Thank you, Constable," said I, simply. I waited for him to finish packing his satchel and, with a final glance at the crowd and a shake of his head, he finally departed the hotel. Once the front door had closed behind him, I turned back to the assembled crowd, who were again watching me warily.

"It seems to me that the murdered man, whatever be his name, was not completely bereft of his ill-gotten fortune, for he was flush with both cash as well as some expensive personal items." I turned to the naturalist. "Mr. Warburton, do you think that he had any remaining jewels?"

The Englishman studied me for a moment. "If he did, I have no doubt that they are secreted away in a series of banks so that no single man should ever know exactly what he has."

"Like Cox and Company?" I interjected.

He smiled and shrugged. "Perhaps. Or possibly Holder & Stevenson of Threadneedle Street? There are many fine banks in London. Or, since he was French, perhaps the Bank of France or the Credit Lyonnais? He was in Prussia once, so perhaps the Deutsche Bank? It little matters. If he died without a legal heir, they may lay there forever, gathering dust. No one in this room is likely to ever lay eyes upon anything. Which was never the point."

"And the Empress Emerald? Would he have entrusted that to any bank? Banks can be robbed."

Warburton licked his lips. "I thought we agreed that the Emerald was a figment of your imagination. You surely did not find it in the room of Mor... I mean, Dumas."

My lips curled up at his slip. "I would ask that you humor me, sir." I turned to the Italian. "I ask you, Signore Aicardi. You are an artist. If you had a great treasure to hide, where would you do so?"

Aicardi narrowed his eyes and peered at me. "The best place to hide something is in plain sight, but intermixed with other items of great similarity."

"Exactly! And thus, I ask you, Mr. Sims: if the man we knew as Dumas did not drink fortified spirits, as you and I learned that evening that he drank with us, then why did he have a bottle of Calvados in his room?"

Sims frowned. But before he could reply, I did something rash. To his probable astonishment, I suddenly tossed the bottle of Calvados towards him. But I deliberately underthrew it. I knew with his injured knee that Sims stood little chance of ever catching it, and though he instinctually lunged for it, the bottle instead shattered upon the ground into a hundred pieces of green glass. Amber liquid splashed everywhere, wetting the shoes of the nearest men.

"Have you gone mad, mate?" Senhor Cordeiro roared. "That's a damn fine bottle to waste like that!"

But I paid him no need. Instead I bent down to where the remnant of the base lay. "I think you might find this perhaps a tad rarer than the Calvados, Senhor." I held up the bottom of the bottle, which was now obviously oddly shaped. For there was no punt dimpling upwards. Instead, I popped a brilliantly scintillating round green stone free from the encasing glass. It was similar to a golf ball in size, and of such a purity and radiance that it twinkled like the aurora borealis in the hollow of my hand.

"Ladies and gentlemen," said I, "I present to you the legendary Empress Emerald." The wonder on their faces told me that they truly did not know that it was hidden under their noses the entire time. They had done the deed solely for the sake of revenge, not for material gain. Lucy's eyes in particular were shining, almost to the point of tears, and her cheeks were tinged with color. "Of course, its existence cannot be made known to Constable Dunkley, for it would irrevocably alter his decision. But what is to be done with it? Maximilian is long in his grave, and no amount of emerald-derived funds will bring him back. Carlota is irretrievably stricken with brain-fever. It will do her little good. Perhaps it should now belong to the heir of the man who gave his life trying to protect it?" I walked over to Lucy and held it out to her. "Perhaps it should belong to Lucy Harrier?"

She gasped and her hand rose to her lips. Gazing intently at me, her eyes never leaving mine, she reached out and took the Emerald from my hand. "How did you know?"

"When Mr. Boyle was unable to resist the coercion of my brother and gave me a room at the hotel, against the better judgment of Mrs. Foster, your company was suddenly short a room. That explains why Monsieur Dubois was so upset. He did not wish to stain your honor, but there was no other way to keep you all under one roof. And so, you quickly had new papers made with your false name. I believe that there is a printing press here in St. George's? I imagine that is where you accidently acquired the violet ink spot that blemished your glove on the day when we first conversed in the garden. A wire to the registry office in Hamilton where you disembarked merely confirmed my suspicion of your true last name."

Her eyes finally broke from mine and dropped to her palm, the famous *Émeraude* coruscating in the lamplight. "And what should I do with this, Doctor?"

I shrugged as carelessly as I could manage. "That is up to you. You have your whole life before you. There is no one left in need of punishment. It is a *fait accompli*. Your father can finally rest," I threw a meaningful glance over at Mr. Sims. "The world is your oyster."

She shook her head, her eyes troubled. "It is not a pearl, Doctor. Nor is it that simple. I've not known anything else."

"It is never too late to reinvent yourself."

She nodded slowly, but her eyes did not rise again to meet mine.

§

I made desultory conversation for a few moments with the other guests until I eventually decided that it would be best if I repaired to my room and allowed them to reflect upon the culmination of their combined adventure. Mr. Boyle was good enough to deliver my supper to my room upon a tray, along with a message from my brother that a ship was leaving tomorrow afternoon for England if I was ready to depart. After a moment's consideration I asked Boyle to reply in the affirmative. I ate in a reflective silence, hardly tasting what I put into my mouth.

When I put out the light, I soon found that I could not sleep. After struggling against it for what seemed like several hours, I felt that it was quite hopeless. So I rose and looked out of the window into the garden below. The night was fine and clear. The stars shone cold and bright above us, while the moon bathed the whole scene in a soft, uncertain light. Broad bars of golden light from the lower windows stretched out interrupting the darkness, as if to provide a glimmer of hope for the ambiguous future. I finally turned away and lit the candle. I glanced at my watch and was surprised to find it was not even one o'clock in the morning. I pulled on my flannel dressing gown, with the intention of continuing Dickens' *Drood*. The book, however, had been left in the billiard room. I strode to the door and flung it open. What I found there produced what I can only assume was an ever-growing astonishment upon my face. For standing outside my door, her hand raised as if she were about to knock, was Ms. Lucy Harrier, clad only in a sheer chiffon white nightgown, barely obscuring the glories that lay beneath.

Her face lit up with a brilliant smile. "Ah, Doctor, I am so happy that you are awake. I fear that I could not sleep. We owe you a thousand apologies for our myriad of deceptions, and I hope that you will absolve me. We have used you most cruelly."

"Not at all," said I, futilely crossing my arms over my chest, for it was quite beyond my power to resist the light shining from her brilliant green eyes.

She reached out and laid her hand upon one of my arms. Her touch sent an electric shock up to the very hairs upon my head. "Doctor, please. It is true. We even placed the slipper in your room for you to find, and then stole it again in order to induce the constable to doubt your veracity.

We worried that you were drawing too close to the truth." She stepped closer to me, crossing the threshold of my room.

"Ah," I stammered.

Perhaps seeing the look of incredulity upon my face, she pressed on. "Calm yourself, Doctor. You know your Shakespeare. The tempest has passed. There is no more need for us to take 'strange-bedfellows.' The sea is calm around this little isle now. And my bounty is as boundless as the sea..." Her whole face shone with an inward light.

"Romeo ends tragically, Ms. Harrier," I managed to say, shaking my head.

"Does it have to? Can Shakespeare not be wrong, from time to time? No more moments should be lost. Now that we no longer have to maintain the illusion that Hector and I are a couple, I am free to sleep where I wish." She closed the door behind her, and stepped forward again until there was absolutely nothing between us. A sudden flood of joy, amazement, and incredulity utterly submerged my mind. The rest of the night was spent in a realm where words did not matter.

§

EPILOGUE:
THE *ORONTES*

A nd so concludes my sojourn upon the Isle of Devils. I shall be brief, and yet exact, in the little which remains for me to tell. A duty devolves upon me to omit no detail and not retain in my hands any factors in the mystery, so that some day when we are all beyond the reach of human law, the truth may be known.

When I awoke alone the following morn, it was with a curiously empty feeling, as if I was missing some crucial element from my life, akin I thought to the sensation that wounded soldiers occasionally report after the battlefield loss of a limb. I dressed slowly in my finest uniform. I knew that I simply had to embark upon a new boat, but it felt as if I had a funeral to attend. Packing my valise, I gazed about the room, suspecting that I was forgetting something. But there was nothing there, excepting only the specters of the past.

I made my way along the twisting coconut-matted hall and down the creaking staircase one last time. At the bottom of the stairs, in the hotel's entryway, I found Constable Dunkley awaiting me.

"Good morning, Doctor," said he, warmly.

"And to you, Constable."

"Please call me Harry, my friend. I am not on duty this morning. I have been given a brief leave as a recompense for the successful conclusion of the Globe Hotel Case."

A half-smile touched my face. "I congratulate you, Harry."

"I wanted to thank you personally for the invaluable assistance that you provided on the case of Mr. Dumas." He cleared his throat self-consciously. "Although the explanation that you provided ultimately proved to be no more than a fantastic product of your imagination, I think that the other solution we arrived at is more than satisfactory. The brutes that shot Dumas must have fled Bermuda long ago in a private boat. The villains got clean away and will likely never be caught. I am afraid that we must consider the case closed."

I nodded in acceptance of this explanation. "Justice has been done here. I am as certain of that as I am of the rise of tomorrow's sun. There never was an Etienne Moreau."

He shrugged and wryly grinned at me. "Not on this island. The dead man's papers state his name quite clearly, and I've not heard any convincing proof to the contrary. By the way, Doctor, since the case is closed, all of the evidence pertaining to it must be destroyed. As you are about to depart from us, would you be so kind as to dispose of this in the deepest trenches of the Atlantic?" He reached into his ever-present wide-awake and pulled out the jack-knife, with its no longer mysterious initials 'L.E.' and the well-worn flaming ring symbol.

I took the knife from him and hefted it in my palm. "It's a well-made blade, Harry. It would be a shame to discard it simply because of the crimes of its previous owner."

"It would be an equal shame if that knife remained upon the island and stirred up questions that are best left buried," said he, with raised eyebrows and a significant look.

"I understand," I smiled at him. "No one will ever know the origin or the fate of this blade." I paused for a moment and slipped it into my valise.

"Thank you, Harry," I said, holding out my hand.

He shook it warmly. "No, thank you, Doctor. Now, if you would be so kind as to depart through the side entrance, I believe that there are a few others that might like a word with you." He directed me into the dining room.

There, to my vast surprise, I found the guests of the Globe Hotel assembled *en bloc,* awaiting me. The first was the long-widowed Mrs. Elizabeth Foster, with Graham Boyle standing loyally by her side.

"Safe travels, Doctor," said the proprietress kindly. "May your next repose be more welcoming and restful than this one proved to be when you descended upon me unawares six days ago."

I returned her smile. "Thank you, Mrs. Foster. I assure you that there are no hard feelings. I completely understand. And Mr. Boyle," I said, turning to the sturdy man, "are congratulations in order?" I looked back at Mrs. Foster significantly.

He glanced down at her and smiled. "I believe that they are, Doctor. I assure you that when you receive your invitation, it will be written out by a better hand than mine."

"I wish I could attend, sir," I replied, with sincere disappointment in my voice. "But I regretfully suspect that it may be a few years before I make my way back to Bermuda."

"If you do, sir, I guarantee that the Walker Room will always be ready for you."

"Yes, I think that I would prefer that to the one next door."

"It may be a while before we are able to let that one out again," Mrs. Foster interjected. "Though there are always some with macabre tendencies who seek out such rooms, hoping to commune better with the departed." She shook her head, as if she could not fathom such a thing.

I made my final leave-taking with the happy pair and moved to the next guest. The Marquesa Garcia-Ramirez sat majestically in her chair, still appearing to dominate the room from the force of her will alone, despite her humble position.

"*Buen viaje*, Marquesa," I said with a formal bow. "May the airs of Mexico agree with you."

A sardonic grin cracked her pale face. "You know as well as I, Doctor, that I am not long for this world. We shall not meet again on this side of the veil. But I am content. My husband is avenged and I will be with him soon. My only regret is that he never got a chance to meet you, Doctor. He always appreciated an honorable man."

I silently nodded my gratitude at this undue praise and moved on to the next guest, Mr. Warburton. He held out his hand, which I took. "Thank you, Doctor. The Marquesa is correct. There are many clever physicians and there are many compassionate physicians. But it is a rarity to find one that is both. I would hope that someday you might find it acceptable to visit me at my father's estate. There have been many eminent Harley Street specialists, even heads of prestigious medical schools, who have departed our house in a huff, unsuccessful at solving the colonel's problem. But I think that you of all people might be the one to help."

I nodded my head. "I will think on it, sir." I moved on to the next guest, Doctor Nemcek.

He spoke first. "As one medical man to another, I know the agony of a long voyage without something to stimulate the mind. Do you have something to read on the boat, Doctor?"

I shook my head. "No, I have left the copy of Dickens with Mrs. Foster. I think I have had enough of mysteries and detectives for the time being."

"Well then, let me give you a parting gift," said he, holding out a small package wrapped in a common brown paper and tied with a string.

My indignation reared up. "I cannot accept..."

"Hush, Doctor. This is no bribe. It is merely something by which to remember us."

I took the package from him and unwrapped it. Inside I found a small book. It was a copy of Henri Murger's *Vie de Boheme.*

I looked up in surprise, only to find him smiling at me. "I am confident that this may further your education on the different types of Bohemians."

I nodded my acceptance. "Thank you, sir. I promise you that I will read it closely."

Senhor Cordeiro smiled at me as I approached him. "Farewell, mate," said the Portuguese wine-merchant, stretching out his hand.

I took it and replied, "I never imagined what troubles would follow when we picked you up at that dock in Hamilton, Senhor Cordeiro."

He nodded with a mock contriteness. "You never know what fate has in store for you, Doctor. Sometimes you must trust yourself to its winds and hope that it lands you in a safe harbor. Often times, I find that things work out for the best. Do you not agree?"

I reflected upon this. "Yes, I suppose that I do. I have certainly learned a great deal upon these isles. Though I doubt that I will have much use for my new-found investigative skills after my return to England."

"I certainly hope not, Doctor!" he laughed. "I will try to visit you some day, and I expect to find a man of your great talents securely ensconced in a lucrative medical practice in the finest district in London. If I do come, I assure you that I will bring with me my finest bottle of *vinho da roda* Madeira, since you never did get a chance to taste it."

"I trust that this time, should I partake, I shall actually awaken the following morn?"

"You may count upon that, Doctor," said he, with a final smile and nod.

I moved on to Mr. Delopolous. The short but powerful man gave me a quick bow. "*Afaristo*, Doctor. You are a good man. I am sorry about lying to you about my lumbago."

"And a few other things, I think?" said I, raising one eyebrow.

"Perhaps, though I tried to stay as close to the truth as possible, for I have never enjoyed deceiving those that I respect. And you have that, Doctor."

"Thank you, sir," I replied, as he wrung me by the hand, touched by the man's simple words.

The next guest in the line was Mr. Bey. The little engineer smiled at me. "My friend," he said. "May I presume to give you a final memento of your time in the Globe Hotel?" He handed me a square black morocco case, which I reluctantly took. When I lifted off the lid, inside I found the missing Persian slipper. "It was once found amongst your items, was it not? So I thought that perhaps it should be yours again?" he concluded.

A half-smile curled up the right side of my mouth. "I'm not certain what use I will find for a single Persian slipper."

He shook his head. "You never know, Doctor, you never know."

I slipped this too into my valise. Turning, I found that the next guest was Signore Aicardi. He pressed my hand in his strong, warm grasp. "*Ciao, Dottore.* It has been a pleasure meeting you."

"And you as well, sir," I replied. "I hope to see your works exhibited in the galleries of London someday soon."

"Ah," he waved his hand airily, "perhaps, *Dottore,* perhaps, though an artist creates because there is something inside of him that needs to be set free. Whether the world appreciates it or not is beside the point. Art exists solely to ease the yearning of the artist. I will give you an example from the realm of literature, by the greatest poet of my homeland. Since you gleaned so much knowledge from one little line of Dante's *Inferno,* let me leave you with the last line that he ever wrote: '*Ma già volgeva il mio disio e 'l velle, sì come rota ch'igualmente è mossa, l'amor che move il sole e l'altre stelle.*'"

"I recognize the word 'stars' again, Signore, but I freely admit ignorance of the rest."

"It is from the *Paradiso, Dottore.* At the very end, Dante was instructing us how to live, weaving a pattern from the lessons of his own life. I hope that someday you will understand what he meant. If I were to translate the words into your harsh English tongue, it might go something like this: 'But now was turning my desire and will, even as a wheel that equally is moved, for we have shared the love that moves the sun and the other stars.'"

I stared at him intently, wondering what he knew of my feelings for Lucy. But there were no answers in the dark depths of his eyes. "Thank you, Signore, I will consider what you have said."

The next man was none other than Lucy's mythical husband, now revealed as the Belgian Monsieur Dubois, who grinned and nodded at me. He took my hand and held onto it tightly, looking me in the eyes. "You know, Doctor, when a good man dies, those that care deeply for him will sometimes take up his cares and responsibilities?"

I nodded slowly, unsure of what he meant. "I have heard of such things."

"Then rest assured that Iain's daughter is well cared for by eight fathers and two mothers. And yet, all we really desire is that she finally finds happiness after so many years of misery. If she were to meet a man who could accomplish that, a man with a great nobility of spirit, however humble his situation, he would have our blessing."

I nodded, unable to answer him through the tightness in my throat. He pulled me into a half-embrace. Finally, I stepped back and he let go of my hand.

I moved on to what appeared to be the last guest, Mr. Sims. The gigantic man smiled and nodded down at me. He stretched out his hand for me to shake. "It has been a pleasure knowing you, Doctor. Mayhaps we will meet in a scrum someday, once our respective injuries have fully healed?"

I absently rubbed my left shoulder and shook my head dejectedly. "I am not certain that will ever happen, Mr. Sims."

"I am sorry to hear that, Doctor, for I am certain that you would have been a worthy opponent. And furthermore, if that is truly the case, the English Army has lost a fine soldier. I would have been honored to serve under you."

I shook my head again. "I was only a regimental medical officer, Mr. Sims. I never commanded men in the line of fire."

"Their loss, Doctor. As you have certainly learned by now, not all officers are worthy of the command entrusted to them. And some, despite their apparent lack of command, are born to be true leaders of men." He stiffened and saluted me.

I silently returned his salute, and then turned to the door. I found that I had indeed reached the end of the guests. I looked about for a final time, but the one person that I had devoutly wished to see was not present in the room, and it became increasingly clear to me that she was not going to make an appearance. This realization caused my heart to sink to the point where I almost lost control in front of this indomitable group of former soldiers, and it took all of my strength to walk out the door with my head high and my face dry.

§

When I stepped foot out of the hotel into the blazing sunlight I found Henry awaiting me in Mr. Robinson's one-horse trap. He leapt down to silently shake my hand and help me load my valise. We then both alighted and Robinson lightly flicked the horses to spur them into action.

"That was a strange business you found yourself mixed up in, brother," said Henry finally.

"Indeed," was all that I could muster.

Henry glanced over at me, as if to determine the etiology of my clipped comments. "You seem down, brother, which I can certainly appreciate. Others have reported similar emotions when they have finally been required to depart the salubrious climate of Bermuda. And it is never easy to leave loved ones, even those as poor as me!"

His efforts managed to elicit from me a half-smile. "Yes, I think that must be it."

Henry appeared to contemplate things for a minute before he continued. "You know, brother, there is another being as forlorn as yourself at your departure. Not I, of course, for we will see each other again! But Gladstone, our bull-pup, now whines that you are not around. What did you do to prompt such loyalty?" He shook his head in wonderment. "Once you establish yourself in London, presuming your situation allows it, I think I will have to send him to you."

"I would very much like that, brother," I replied simply.

We lapsed into silence and the trap clipped along, passing on our right the garden where I first spoke with Lucy. As we travelled back along the same route over the hill and down to Fort St. Catherine that I had taken upon my initial arrival to St. George's, I felt as if the clock was winding backwards. Every yard that we covered seemed to erase another moment of the last few days, and it seemed as if by the time I reached Dockyard, the remarkable happenstances of the Globe Hotel would be nothing more than passing will-o-the-wisps of my imagination. It was not a pleasant sensation.

When we arrived at the pier below the Fort's mighty ramparts we found the same small sloop, the *Caliber*, awaiting us. Henry helped me with my valise and we tumbled into the boat.

"We are travelling straight to Dockyard, correct, Captain Smith? No detours to Hamilton this time, I trust?" Henry called to the skipper.

"Right you are, sir, and Bob's your uncle," replied the man through teeth clenching his brier-root pipe.

Henry turned to me. "I have secured you a berth on another troopship, brother, very similar to the *Malabar*. It is called the *Orontes*, after the river near Antioch."

"Thank you, Henry, I am certain that it will be more than adequate."

The conversation again flagged and I was free to look out at the passing shores of the island, the wind whipping through my hair. As we progressed along the northern shore back to the far western tip of the isle, my eyes were continually drawn back to the east, where I knew that St. George's lay over the hill beyond my gaze. A poet once claimed that when he left a certain joyful place, his heart remained behind. I had never understood the truth of those profound words until now.

Several times Henry leaned over as if he were about to hazard a remark, but each time he drew back and left me to my silent musings. Eventually, as I knew it must, the journey came to its end on the same rough pier from which we had first innocently cast off towards St. George's six days prior.

I clambered out of the boat as well as my leg would allow, and I stood by while Henry instructed Captain Smith to await his return. Henry then turned to me with a considering look in his eyes. "You've changed, Ham," he said.

"What do you mean?" said I, frowning.

"The boy I once knew is gone, I think, only to be replaced by the man that I see before me."

"War will do that."

He shook his head. "No, it is more than that. Even in this short time I've watched you become more thoughtful and introspective."

I frowned. "Are you saying that I've become aloof?"

"Not at all. Call it a gift, a grand gift. I think that you have gained experience, the knowledge of which will ensure your reputation of being excellent company for the remainder of your existence."

I nodded ruefully. "I suppose that the circumstances of my stay on Bermuda have made a deep impression upon me."

With that said, we then proceeded up the ramp and through the gate into Dockyard proper. Heading back along the quay, my eyes were involuntarily drawn to the massive floating dock. Its impressive bulk effectively distracted me from my other thoughts. Finally, we were almost past it and I looked forward to try to find my new ship. The task was simple, as it lay in the same place from where I had disembarked from the *Malabar*. But I had no eyes for the ship. For there was a tall, slender figure standing a stone's throw off from the gangplank, and when she turned her freckled cheeks lit up in rosy elation at my approach. My brain was confused by her presence, but some warm glow of hope began to return to my heart.

Henry would have had to be a blind man to not notice Lucy, for her fiery hair and emerald green dress was enough to draw attention away from the sun itself. He followed the track of her gaze back to me, and then nodded in understanding. "Ah, Ham, I will just go make certain that everything is arranged. You will be alright here for a few minutes, will you not?"

As I was unable to form a coherent word, he must have taken my silence for agreement, and he picked up his stride leaving me in his wake. I stood rooted to the ground, unsure of what my next action should be, my nerves worked up to the highest pitch of tension.

She hurried forward to meet me with a face which spoke of her joy. "Hello, Doctor. I think that I forgot to tell you that you were scintillating last evening."

"Please, Mademoiselle," I stammered, "I would be named if you would call me by my real honor."

She laughed gaily. "Your wish is my command. What is that your friends call you... ah yes, 'Hamish?' Tell me, Doctor, the name 'Hamish' means 'James' in Scottish, does it not?"

"Indeed," I replied, the word catching in my throat.

"Then I think that this will be my pet name for you," she reached out and took my hand in hers. "I will always remember you as my brave James."

I had no reply for this, and merely gazed into her green eyes. I had never known anyone so vitally alive. She lived intensely, every fiber of her being fully participating in her actions. She smiled back at me. "Oh, poor James, your honest face is twitching with anxiety. You look like a man who wishes to ask a question."

"No," I stammered, "nothing comes to mind." I dropped my gaze to the rough wooden planks of the quay.

I could sense her smile deepening in the tone of her voice. "You are a poor fibber, James."

I looked up from my inspection of the ground and studied her. "Perhaps I am," I finally replied. "In fact, I have two."

She raised her eyebrows. "There is no time like the present."

I considered my position. "If you insist."

"I do."

"About Monsieur Dubois..."

"Hector?" said she, frowning. "What of him?"

"Ah, well, it is just that you shared three nights with him..." I stammered.

Her eyebrows rose archly. "Did you count, Doctor?" she replied, smiling impishly.

"Well, you see..."

She forestalled my discomfiture. "You need not be concerned, James. Hector's inclinations in such matters lie in a different direction entirely. I assure you that my honor is quite intact. Or, at least, it was, until last night." Her smile told me that she had no regrets for what had passed between us. "But you said that you had two questions?"

"What color glass did you draw on that night? Blue or green?"

She pursed her lips and gazed into my eyes. "I see. I had perhaps expected another question." She nodded her head slowly. "And are you certain that you want to know the answer?"

"No," I shook my head. "I am not."

"Then perhaps it is better not to know. For regardless of the color shard, I was fully prepared to go forward with what was required of me.

And I cannot say that it is likely to weigh very heavily upon my conscience. He was an animal concealed in a human body." She hung her head for a moment, and then looked up at me again. "Does that alter your feelings toward me?"

I searched my soul for an answer and realized that, in fact, I did not care. "No, I do not think that anything could change how I feel about you. I'm yours to the rattle."

As I spoke, a smile erupted on her face that kindled a joy in my soul. "That is very sweet of you to say. I am most happy to hear that, James." She reached into her handbag, and drew forth the ink-stained glove that she had worn during our first walk in the park. "I wish you to have this, as a remembrance and as a gage, for you seem to me like a knight errant of old." She pulled my hand to her breast and then leaned in to kiss me on my cheek. As she did so, I breathed in her scent and felt the warmth of her lips. It was a memory that I knew would stay with me for many years to come. A final whisper carried on it the words that I had been longing to hear. A great shadow seemed to pass from my soul.

Before I could reply in turn, she pulled away. I began to open my mouth, but she raised her fingers to my lips and stilled my voice. "No, James, do not speak. I could not bear to hear it. Know this... I wish that we had met under different circumstances. Your destiny awaits you in London, where I know that your star will rise high. And I must return to San Francisco, at least temporarily. But if you ever find yourself in my fair city, I would be most happy if you would call upon me. Do not lose heart, James. As a wise man once said, 'journeys end in lovers meeting.' This is not an *adieu*. Instead I will say only *à bientôt*." She dropped my hand and turned away from me. I watched her walking briskly down the quay until her vivid scarlet hair was but a speck in the somber distance. But she never turned to look at me again. I felt as if a void had been created in my heart, and I wondered how I would possibly fill it.

§

After Lucy had quitted my vision, Henry quietly rejoined me. He gave me a questioning glance, but otherwise held his peace. We walked the rest of the way to the gangplank in silence. There we were met by a short, thick man with a chinchilla beard growing out of the creases of his double chin, and wearing the typical dress of the English sailor. He was clearly the ship's purser.

I gave him my name, which he checked again a list that he held. Finally locating it, he looked up with a pleasant smile. "Welcome aboard the *Orontes*, Dr. Watson. We will have you on a Portsmouth jetty in less than a month. You will have plenty of time before the holidays and the New Year."

Before I could board, however, Henry enfolded me in a brotherly embrace. Finally stepping back, he allowed me to start up the ramp. When I reached the midway point, I heard his voice call after me one final time. "Whatever shall you do once you get to London, brother?"

I turned about to look him in the eyes, and shook my head. "I shall have to take lodging, though to be honest, Henry, with my limited funds I suspect that I may need to find a roommate. Given the state of my nerves, someone studious and quiet I hope."

§

POSTSCRIPT: A LETTER

The Fourth of December, 1880

My dear Henry,

You will be happy to know that my time onboard the Orontes was most pleasant. I spent a considerable time conversing with a new acquaintance, a retired naval officer turned globetrotter, named Sir Montague Brown. He listened to my adventures upon the Isle of Devils and encouraged me to set down the facts while they were still quite recent and before my recollections faded. Knowing your passion for fantastic stories, I thought I should entrust you with this extract of reminiscences from my journal, in which you will finally understand what transpired at the Globe Hotel and the reasons for my reticence when we parted. Perhaps inspired by Mr. Tom Moore, who found the climate of Bermuda so conducive to writing, this tale has expanded to a length approaching that of a novel. It implicates so many people that, for many years, it will be impossible to make it public without the case becoming a cause célèbre. Please keep it safe for me. Perhaps someday, when the principal protagonists have had their frail threads snapped by Clothis, the truth can finally be brought to light. To do so now would be an unthinkable breach of confidence. Until we meet again, brother, I remain, affectionately,

John Hamish Watson, M.D.
Late Army Medical Department
Mailed from Portsmouth, England

§

LITERARY AGENT'S NOTES

What are we to make of this remarkable document? The sixty unquestioned cases that comprise the Sherlock Holmes Canon demonstrate but four examples of episodes where Holmes solves a case without the assistance of Dr. John H. Watson, two solved before he met Watson (*The "Gloria Scott"*, 1874, & *The Musgrave Ritual*, 1879), and two narrated by Holmes when either Watson had deserted him for a wife (*The Adventure of the Blanched Soldier*, 1903), or during Holmes' retirement upon the Sussex Downs (*The Adventure of the Lion's Mane*, 1907).

However, there are no known authentic examples of Watson solving a case without Holmes. The closest thing we have is when Holmes would send Watson to be his representative / understudy on a mission. In 1889, Watson was dispatched to accompany Sir Henry Baskerville to Dartmoor, where he would write up reports of his inquiries to Holmes, who ostensibly remained behind in order to attempt to stop a "disastrous scandal" from occurring in London (Chapters VI through XI, *The Hound of the Baskervilles*). However, Watson's activities were later revealed to be intended as a distraction while Holmes carried out the true investigation from his lair beneath the Vixen Tor. In 1895, Holmes claimed to be too busy with "important research" to investigate the case of Violet Smith, so he sent Watson to observe the facts for himself (*The Adventure of the Solitary Cyclist*). Perhaps the most pure example occurred in 1899 when Holmes was too occupied with the case of the two Coptic Patriarchs to go out to Lewisham himself, so he sent Watson to gather the details of Mr. Josiah Amberley's house (*The Adventure of the Retired Colourman*). And finally, in 1901 Holmes sent Watson to Lausanne, Switzerland to determine the fate of Lady Frances Carfax, though he failed to trust Watson to accomplish this task himself and followed him in the disguise of a French working-man (*The Disappearance of Lady Frances Carfax*).

However, Watson admits that during Holmes absence known as the Great Hiatus (1891-1894) he attempted "more than once" to solve "various problems which came before the public," albeit "with indifferent success" (*The Adventure of the Empty House*).

Can we thus believe that Watson was embroiled in a murder mystery as fantastic as that set down in the preceding pages now known as the Bermuda Manuscript? Even if it is a genuine product of Watson's hand, as our research clearly supports, perhaps this tale of treasure and revenge is more the product of a feverish imagination after having read one too many tale of Poe and Collins? And yet, we know that Watson seemed to attract law-breakers. Holmes once called him "the stormy petrel of crime" (*The Naval Treaty*). Besides the case of Percy Phelps, Watson also provided Holmes a convenient personal introduction to Robert Ferguson (*The Adventure of the Sussex Vampire*), and furthermore, he brought to Holmes' notice the cases of both Victor Hatherley and Colonel Warburton, the latter of which was never fully documented (*The Adventure of the Engineer's Thumb*).

Therefore, perhaps there is an element of truth to this tale, which would solve one of the great mysteries of Doctor Watson's background. What happened to the missing five months between the Battle of Maiwand (July 27, 1880) and the fateful meeting of Holmes and Watson at St. Bart's (the date is never exactly specified, but it is commonly supposed by the noted Sherlockian scholar Christopher Morley to have occurred on January 1, 1881), given that the typical sea voyage between India and England lasted only about one month? Are we to believe Watson when he reports that he spent all of that time in the base hospital at Peshawar (Chapter I, *A Study in Scarlet*)? A clue perhaps exists in the mention of the HMS *Orontes*, which was a troopship intended for carrying men to the British colonies in Southern Africa and the West Indies, unlike the HMS *Serapis*, which plied the route to India. If Watson accurately reported that he disembarked the *Orontes* on a Portsmouth jetty, then it can likely be concluded that he did not come directly from India.

Some readers may suggest that elements of the tale contained in the Bermuda Manuscript appear to borrow rather too heavily from other Holmes and Watson stories (and even fictional mysteries concocted by other writers) to be authentic. And yet, as the Master Detective himself tells us: "The old wheel turns and the same spoke comes up. It's all been done before, and will be again" (Chapter II, *The Valley of Fear*). Perceived unoriginality, I am afraid, cannot solely be used to fashion an assertion of forgery. And what about claims that parts of the manuscript simply do not sound like Watson? Admittedly, there were fragments of the manuscript that were too water-damaged to interpret, and these small sections required some careful extrapolation. I had considered bracketing these sections for the sake of complete transparency, but ultimately decided it was too distracting from the main thrust of the tale. Scholars who must know exactly which portions I was forced to invent may contact me for clarification. Any other sections of the Bermuda Manuscript that do not appear to have an authentic Watsonian voice can only be explained by the fact that this was his first foray into the world of literature, and it is perhaps not surprising that he had not yet found the mature tone that characterizes such later masterpieces as *The Adventure of the Speckled Band* or *The Hound of the Baskervilles*. I freely admit only to creating the somewhat fantastic title, as Watson clearly had not intended these notes for publication, and thus he never bothered to name them. However, I believe that given the titles employed for his other four novellas, *The Isle of Devils* has a certain faithfulness of which the good doctor would have likely approved.

Finally, Watson had many outstanding attributes that vastly contributed to the success of his partnership with Holmes. We all know of his famous "grand gift of silence" (*The Man with the Twisted Lip*). Holmes calls him "scintillating" (*The Adventure of the Missing Three-Quarter*) and that he has a "native shrewdness" and "innate cunning" (Chapter I, *The Valley of Fear*). But one of his greatest strengths was his immense modesty. He preferred to be the reflector of Holmes' undisputed brilliance. But by so doing, he unfortunately left his readers with the false impression that he was lost without Holmes. And yet, Holmes himself says in 1903 that "Watson has some remarkable characteristics of his own, to which in his honesty he has given small attention amid his exaggerated estimates of my own performances" (*The Adventure of the Blanched Soldier*). And in 1896, Holmes admitted that "I never get your limits, Watson. There are unexpected possibilities about you" *(The Adventure of Sussex Vampire)*. Perhaps this tale is one of those unexpected possibilities? It may finally set the record straight about the true nature of John Hamish Watson, MD.

PREFACE: THE BERMUDA MANUSCRIPT

- Foolscap is a traditional paper size from the British Commonwealth that was cut to the size of 8.5 × 13.5 inches, as opposed to the now standard A4 paper size of 8 x 13 inches. Watson was well known to have written on foolscap folio (Chapter I, *The Valley of Fear* and *The Adventures of the Bruce-Partington Plans & Norwood Builder*). The effects upon writing while travelling in a moving vessel (a train, specifically) were carefully noted by Holmes (*The Adventure of the*

Norwood Builder), but this likely also applies to writing on ocean-going ships of the day.

- There are, of course, sixty stories that make up the official Sherlock Holmes Canon, however, two were written by Holmes himself (*The Adventures of the Blanched Soldier & the Lion's Mane*), while two were told in a third-person voice, presumably that of Sir Arthur Conan Doyle, Watson's first literary agent (*The Adventure of the Mazarin Stone & His Last Bow*). As such, those four manuscripts are obviously not in Watson's distinctive handwriting, and are of no use when attempting to confirm the authenticity of this report.

- The Houghton Library of Harvard University is the repository for the manuscript of *The Adventure of the Three Students*. The Berg Collection of the New York Public Library possesses *The Adventure of the Norwood Builder,* Chapter XI of *The Hound of the Baskervilles,* as well as the aforementioned *The Adventure of the Blanched Soldier,* the latter of which we did not bother to consult. Haverford College in Pennsylvania is the proud owner of *The Adventure of the Second Stain,* having been bequeathed it by the estate of the author Christopher D. Morley (1890-1957), Haverford class of 1910. The Lilly Library at Indiana University holds the manuscript for *The Adventure of the Red Circle.* The Bibliotheca Boderiana in Cologny/Geneva preserves *The Adventure of the Abbey Grange.* The British Library is fortunate to have two genuine Watson manuscripts, *The Adventures of the Missing Three-Quarter & the Retired Colourman.* The Richard Lancelyn Green Bequest at the Portsmouth City Museum acquired *The Adventure of the Creeping Man* in 2009. Finally, the skeptics at the National Library of Scotland possess the manuscript for *The Adventure of the Illustrious Client.* It should be noted that this is one of the last Holmes stories published (only four genuine adventures followed it). Although the events therein took place in 1902, the story was not released until 1924, and it is therefore unclear exactly when Watson would have set it down in pen (certainly no sooner than 1912, since he asked Holmes' permission "for the tenth time in as many years"). Therefore the comparative manuscript was written at least thirty-two (and possibly as many as forty-four) years after the events recorded in the Bermuda Manuscript. It would not be an enormous conjecture to hypothesize that a man's handwriting might evolve somewhat from that of a robust man of eight and twenty years, to that of a more mature man of sixty or seventy odd years, especially if his health had begun to decline. Watson's date of death is unclear, though it has been reported to have occurred as early as 1929 (when he would have been seventy-seven years of age).

CHAPTER I: THE *SERAPIS*

- If Watson's dates are to be believed, the following would be a reasonable timeline of his movements during the year 1880 (most dates approximate):
  - July 27: Battle of Maiwand; Wounded in shoulder and leg
  - August 10: Completion of 535 mile retreat to base hospital in Peshawar
  - August 29: Recuperation nearly complete; Struck down by Enteric Fever
  - October 18: Departs Karachi on board the *Serapis*
  - November 2: Transfers to the *Malabar* at Cape Town
  - November 20: Embarks at Dockyard
  - November 26: Departs Bermuda on board the *Orontes*
  - December 4: Embarks at Portsmouth, stays for "some time" at a private hotel in the Strand
  - January 1, 1881: Introduced to Holmes by Stamford
- Watson continued to maintain a diary at least through the year 1889, when he mentioned it again during his adventure on Dartmoor (Chapter X, *The Hound of the Baskervilles*).
- Watson presents a similar recollection of the Battle of Maiwand in his first work intended for publication (Chapters I & V, *A Study in Scarlet*). General Roberts was a recipient of the V.C., which stands for the Victoria Cross, England's highest honor for gallantry in the face of the enemy. Amazingly, despite Holmes and Watson bravely serving England as espionage agents during the Great War (*His Last Bow*), neither man is recorded as ever being decorated with the V.C. Perhaps the records were suppressed, or perhaps they refused it, as Holmes once did with a knighthood (*The Adventure of the Three Garridebs*)?
- Watson recalls his war wounds multiple times in the Canon (Chapter I, *A Study in Scarlet* & Chapter I, *The Sign of the Four*), recalling that he brought home a residual Jezail bullet, the "relic of [his] Afghan campaign" (*The Adventure of the Noble Bachelor*). Watson also makes clear that his *tendo Achilles* was damaged as a result of his military duties (Chapter VII, *The Sign of the Four*), such that the 'two wound' hypothesis becomes the only possible explanation for his described ailments, and this is finally confirmed by the Bermuda Manuscript.

- Since they were both Companions of the Bath, Major General Sir Neville Devere, C.B., was likely familiar with Sir Augustus Moran, C.B., former British Minister to Persia and unhappy father to Colonel Sebastian Moran (*The Adventure of the Empty House*). Either Violet Devere misspoke or Watson's memory erred, for we are unable to find any record of a Major-General Devere in charge of the Third Buffs. Of course, the Third Buffs (or the Royal Munsters) were not even stationed in Peshawar or the Khyber Pass in the late summer of 1880, so perhaps Watson was deliberately obscuring the truth in order to protect the confidence and feelings of a lady, as we know he was wont to do? On the other hand, if Watson was not using a pseudonym for the lady, one wonders if she and the general were related to Lord Robert Walsingham *de Vere* St. Simon (*The Adventure of the Noble Bachelor*)?

- Although we know that Watson had a "grand gift of silence" (*The Man with the Twisted Lip*), one wonders about what actually occurred during the lengthening moments of 'exquisite silence' that Watson records occurring on the hospital's darkened verandah. We know from Watson's own words that by 1888 he had "an experience of women which extend[ed] over many nations and three separate continents (Chapter II, *The Sign of the Four*). Was Violet Devere counted in that tally? Interestingly, the name Violet appears more times in the Canon than would normally be encountered for a name of its prevalence during that era (*The Adventures of the Copper Beeches, the Solitary Cyclist, the Illustrious Client*, and *the Bruce-Partington Plans*). Perhaps Watson continued to utilize this name subconsciously whenever he was searching for a pseudonym to hide one of Holmes' clients' true identities? Although it is crystal clear that Watson marries Ms. Mary Morstan in 1888, she also tragically died by c.1892, so that Watson was at liberty to return to Baker Street by the time of Holmes' miraculous return from the Great Hiatus. However, Watson remarried sometime around 1902. The name of this fortunate lady was never divulged, but it is tempting to speculate that Watson may have finally been reunited with Ms. Violet Devere after a twenty-two year separation, both older and wiser, but perhaps still aware of their once strong feelings for each other.

- History does not record what became of Watson's Penang lawyer. It is possible that by 1888 Watson simply stopped calling it by that slightly absurd name, and this was the "stick" that he carried while he and Holmes and Toby hunted Tonga through the streets of London (Chapter VII, *The Sign of the Four*). We also now understand how Watson immediately recognized Benares metal-work when he saw the chest that once contained the Agra treasure (Chapter XI, *The Sign of the Four*, 1888), since there is no evidence that he ever visited Benares himself.

- Outbreaks of erysipelas would continue for many years until Sir Alexander Fleming discovered penicillin in 1928. Watson read a report of an outbreak in the London evening papers in 1902 (*The Adventure of the Illustrious Client*).

- St. Vitus Dance, also known as Sydenham's chorea, is a disease characterized by rapid, uncoordinated jerking movements affecting primarily the face, feet and hands which typically results from an untreated childhood infection with Group A beta-hemolytic Streptococcus. Common in the days before Fleming's discovery of penicillin (1928), it is now very rare.

- Watson clearly decided to take Jackson up on his offer, though possibly not for as long as another nine years, when he bought the practice from Farquhar "shortly after [his] marriage." It may be that he was waiting to fully recuperate from his war wounds, since he believed that "the public not unnaturally goes on the principle that he who would heal others must himself be whole" (*The Stock-Broker's Clerk*). Jackson (*The Crooked Man*) and Anstruther (*The Boscombe Valley Mystery*) would accommodatingly cover for Watson's absence from his practice while assisting Holmes in cases (*The Final Problem*). Watson relayed that his thriving practice was initially located "no very great distance" from Paddington Station (*The Adventure of the Engineer's Thumb*, 1889), though its exact location is never specified in the Canon. Crawford Place, as mentioned herein by Jackson, is between Paddington Station and Baker Street, near St. Mary's Hospital, as would be expected for residence of a general practitioner. Most suggestive of the accuracy of the account in the Bermuda Manuscript is the name of the short lane leading off it: '*Watson's Mews.*'

CHAPTER II: THE *MALABAR*

- As an interesting aside, Watson's first literary agent Sir Arthur Conan Doyle wrote a story in 1903 entitled *The Last Adventure of the Brigadier (How Etienne Gerard Said Goodbye to His Master)*, which chronicled an unsuccessful attempt to rescue Napoleon from St. Helena. One wonders if Sir Arthur got the idea from Watson?

- Of course, Master Billy was not the only spirited British boy upon the high seas. Master Jacky Ferguson was sent out for a year as well at Holmes recommendation (*The Adventure of the Sussex Vampire*). Watson never records what became of Master Billy after he grew out of the role of cabin boy aboard the *Malabar*. It is perhaps tempting to imagine that, on Watson's recommendation, he acquired a job as a page at 221B Baker Street (*The Problem of Thor Bridge*). Billy's tenure at Baker Street was a long one, lasting from no later than 1888 (Chapter I, *The Valley of Fear*) to at least 1903 (*The Mazarin Stone*).

- Watson's quotation from *The Rime of the Ancient Mariner* (1817) is the only indication that we have that Watson was familiar with the works of Samuel Taylor Coleridge (1772-1834). Coleridge was indisputably an opium addict, even admitting that he dreamt up the poem *Kubla Khan* (1816) under its influence.

- That Watson was a voracious reader is self-evident from a perusal of the Canon. The list of books that he has reported reading is long and varied. Watson clearly enjoyed *The Wreck of the Grosvenor* (1877) enough to continue to read the author's other works, for by early 1885 he was "deep in one of Clark Russell's fine sea stories'" (*The Five Orange Pips*). Sensational novels bound in vividly illustrated yellow boards and originally intended for railway travelers, were always referred to by Watson as "yellow-backed novels" (*The Boscombe Valley Mystery*). Even before his fateful meeting with Sherlock Holmes Watson was extremely fond of mysteries: "'Oh! A mystery is it?' [he] cried, rubbing [his] hands" (Chapter I, *A Study in Scarlet*). Wilkie Collins' (1824-1889) classic *The Moonstone* (1868) is considered the first detective novel (as opposed to Poe' short stories) written in English, and certainly Watson would have read it.

- Lomax's quote 'But dearly was that conquest bought' was from the opera *The Americans* (1811) by John Braham, with words by S.J. Arnold. Very popular in its day, Sherlock Holmes would later quote from a later part of the same passage ('For England, home and beauty') (*His Last Bow*).

- Watson's allusion to a 'modern Alexander' refers to Alexander the Great of Macedonia, who legendarily slept with a copy of *The Iliad* under his pillow.

- It is not clear how much of Watson's list of ships is accurate. It is well documented that the HMS *Northampton* was at Bermuda in 1880, where its generator-powered electric lights were a 'brilliant display" and "most splendid" (the Bermuda *Royal Gazette*). The HMS *Warrior* certainly undertook a voyage to Bermuda in 1869, but it is less clear that it would have been spotted there by Watson in 1880. Fortunately, the ship is still intact and can be visited in the historic dockyard of Portsmouth, England. Both the *Irresistible* and the *Scorpion* were definitely stationed in Bermuda during that time, as was the *Vixen*, which was deliberately scuttled in 1896 off the western shore of Bermuda and can be reached by scuba divers today. There does not appear to be good evidence that the *Achilles* was in Bermuda in 1880. While it is possible that the cutter *Alicia* would have been spotted in Bermuda waters, it is odd that a ship of the same name was mentioned by him twenty years later to have mysteriously disappeared (*The Problem of Thor Bridge*). As it is not an uncommon name, it may be a coincidence.

CHAPTER III: THE ISLE OF DEVILS

- The Llandoger Trow pub on King Street is supposedly the meeting place of Daniel Defoe and the historical inspiration for 'Robinson Crusoe', Alexander Selkirk. It is also rumored to be where Robert Louis Stevenson got the idea for the Admiral Benbow pub at the beginning of his great work, *Treasure Island* (1883). The pub is a 17th-century Grade II listed building that still stands in Bristol.

- Unfortunately for Mr. Brewis, although he would eventually return to Bristol temporarily and marry his sweet barmaid, she would later prove to be unfaithful to him when he was sent back to Bermuda, taking her pleasures with Mr. James McCarthy (*The Boscombe Valley Mystery*). This is the only mention of Bermuda in the Canon, suggesting that Watson may have had painful or unpleasant memories of his sojourn there.

- The Floating Dock nobly served its purpose until 1906, when the new generation warships were too large to fit in its constraints. It was then sold to a German company for scrap metal. After partially dismantling it, the Dock was being towed away when it fell into a gale and broke loose. It then got stuck upon a reef near Spanish Point, where multiple attempts to remove it have failed. Even today you can see a large chunk of rusted iron lying on the water, all that remains of the greatest floating dock in history. No other shipyard appears in the Canon of Sherlock Holmes, though one does make a memorable appearance in the 2009 eponymous film.

- From 1880 to 1885, Dr. Edward Lewton Penny was the Dockyard parson, schoolmaster and librarian. His complaints about life on Bermuda were legendary.

- Ironically, a train was eventually installed in Bermuda in 1931, but Henry was right. It was a mad idea, crushed by the rapidly advancing onslaught of the automobile. The Bermuda Railway stopped operations only seventeen years later, leaving only a pleasant foot trail and the ruins of several bridges. Watson was very familiar with the injuries suffered by railway-men (*The Adventure of the Engineer's Thumb*).

- Oddly, many of the ships reported by Watson in Hamilton Harbor seem familiar to scholars of the Canon. The brig *Hotspur* makes its first appearance in the recollection of James Armitage, talking about a ship he was picked up by in 1855 (*The "Gloria Scott"*). One of the ships sounds very similar to the *Gloria Scott*, though it must have been a sister ship, for she was blown-up thirty-five years earlier. The British barque *Sophy Anderson* was lost in approximately 1887, though the facts surrounding the case have never been fully elucidated (*The Five Orange Pips*). The barque *Lone Star* was lost in the equinoctial gales of the Atlantic in 1887 (*The Five Orange Pips*). The ill-fated steamer *Norah Creina* was also lost with all hands off Oporto in 1887 (*The Resident Patient*). At least two ships in Hamilton Harbor survived that grim year, including the steamer *Esmeralda*, which was still sailing in 1888 (Chapter XI, *The Sign of the Four*), and the SS *Palmyra*, which often sailed a route from Cape Town to England, though it was the site of a great tragedy when Jack Douglas was pushed overboard from it upon the orders of Moriarty (Epilogue, *The Valley of Fear*). Perhaps it is too much of a coincidence that all of the vessels that Watson spies in Hamilton Harbor would later play a role in his tales of Holmes and he may have changed the names of some of the ships involved in the later cases, and took the names from this experience?

- The Hamilton Hotel was the first of the grand hotels that would eventually become the cornerstone of the Bermuda tourist industry. It was finished in 1852, and was extended and modernized at the beginning of the twentieth century to attempt to keep up with competitors such as the famous pink Hamilton Princess. Sadly, it was destroyed by fire on 23 December 1955, and was never rebuilt. It stood where the City Hall car park is now located.

CHAPTER IV: THE GLOBE HOTEL

- Sadly, little remains today of the North Shore sights pointed out by Henry. Admiralty House would go on to serve an important function in the Battle of the Atlantic in World War II, intercepting U Boat signals, but later fell into disrepair. The Black Watch Well was eventually abandoned and capped off by a featureless slab of concrete. The name of the regiment lives on however, in the excavated Black Watch Pass road that links the North Shore to the city of Hamilton.

- In 1888, the most exclusive hotels in London charged eight shillings for a room (*The Adventure of the Noble Bachelor*), so five shillings a night is rather expensive.

- Henry was right about Bermuda's forts. British Bermuda would never be successfully invaded, other than a little-known episode in 1777 by some pesky Americans.
- The interior dividing walls and twisting corridor described by Boyle (and later mapped out by Mrs. Foster) as being installed by Mr. Foster when he acquired the building for the purpose of turning it into a hotel are no longer present in the modern-day iteration of the property (now the Bermuda National Trust Museum). Despite exhaustive efforts, I have been unable to locate any other historical floor-plans of the building that would either support or refute the authenticity of the Bermuda Manuscript.
- At the Globe Hotel the four-poster bed in which Georgiana Walker gave birth to her fourth child, was still on display in the 1950s. The bed's canopy was in fact a Confederate Naval Jack. What happened to the bed after that is a mystery.

CHAPTER V: ST. GEORGE'S

- Five thousand pounds in 1880 would be the equivalent of at least $600,000 today! Not bad for a hunk of whale biliary secretion! Bermuda would become known as manufacturer of fine perfumes in 1928, when the Perfumery was opened. This moved its operations to historic Stewart Hall in St. George's in 2004.
- Washington Irving (1783–1859) wrote a tale entitled 'The Three Kings of Bermuda' which detailed the adventures of Misters Carter, Waters, and Chard.
- In 1867, the house that would become the Globe Hotel was rented to Ralph Foster, the first of many proprietors. He died the following year at the age of thirty-three, but his widow continued to run the hotel and bar with billiard room for another fourteen years. It would have been hard for Mr. Foster to stride the timber of the Globe Theater, considering it burned down in 1613. A second theater of that name was built on the same site by 1614, however this iteration was closed in 1642 and vanished under the expanding morass of London. It wasn't until 1997 that the new Globe rose from the ashes near its original site. It is true that the wreck of the *Sea Venture* almost certainly could not have served as the model for *The Tempest*. However, that does not mean that the author of that play could not have been inspired by the Isle of Devils, whose existence was well known to well-educated Elizabethans, having first been discovered in 1511 by the Spanish. Doubts regarding the authorship of the "Shakespeare" plays have existed since at least 1848, and the great American essayist Ralph Waldo Emerson (1803–1882) was indeed a skeptic of the merchant of

Stratford's authenticity. Emerson and Watson may have doubted the authorship of the plays, but it is unlikely that they ever backed the most likely contender, Sir Edward de Vere, the 17th Earl of Oxford, as his candidacy was not proposed until 1920.

CHAPTER VI: THE HEART OF THE ISLAND

- Tycho Brahe (1546–1601) did indeed have a golden nose (or perhaps copper), having lost the original in a duel. And the eccentric scientist not only kept a tame moose (or elk) at his castle, but he fed it beer. The unfortunate creature one night had a bit too much to drink, fell down the stairs and died. True story.

- The irony of course, is that the church of St. George's ran into difficulties in 1894 and was never completed. The ruins today are known by the poetic name "The Unfinished Church."

- Watson's admiration for General Charles George Gordon (1833–1885) continued to grow, such that sometime after the General's death at the hands of the Mahdists Watson acquired a "newly framed picture" of him for the walls of 221B Baker Street (*The Cardboard Box*). Gordon's "Ever-Victorious Army" was a sort of a French Foreign Legion in reverse.

- Boudica, the queen of the British Iceni tribe who led an uprising against the Romans in c.60 CE, was very popular amongst the Victorians, who saw Queen Victoria as a sort of second coming of the ancient queen. Alfred, Lord Tennyson (1809–1892), the Poet Laureate, wrote an eponymous poem about her in 1865. Later, in 1905, London would see the erection of a great bronze statue of Boudica atop her war chariot next to Westminster Bridge and across from Big Ben.

- Watson quotes a famous line from a poem of John Milton (1608–1674), *On His Blindness* (c.1655): "We also serve who only stand and wait."

- It is generally accepted that Watson was born in 1852. His birthplace is less certain, but there does appear to be a hint of the Scottish in various aspects of his history, such as his middle name and even his surname, so it is certainly plausible that the Bermuda Manuscript is accurate in its claim for Edinburgh.

- It is possible that the Watson family traveled on the *Rock of Gibraltar*, since the Adelaide-Southampton line's new ship the *Bass Rock*, was not completed until near 1897. Watson's father was fortunate to arrive in Australia by 1853, as the boom was largely over by 1854, plunging towns like Melbourne into severe depressions.

- Watson's early background (before he attends the University of London) is relatively obscure. One of the few certainties is that he attended boarding school in England with Percy "Tadpole" Phelps, who was two classes ahead of him (*The Naval Treaty*). Although not explicitly stated, it stands to reason that Watson would have known Phelps best if his older brother Henry was also in Phelps' class. But it is even debated exactly which school Watson and Phelps attended. The two major candidates include Winchester College, Hampshire and Wellington College, Berkshire. If the Bermuda Manuscript is authentic, the issue may have been solved. Watson's old school number would stick in his brain for many years, as he continues to use it as a memory device as late as 1899 (*The Adventure of the Retired Colourman*).

- The exact timetable of Watson's sojourn on the Indian subcontinent is a bit muddled. At first, he appears to suggest that he spent almost no time in India before proceeding to Afghanistan (Chapter I, *A Study in Scarlet*), but he later refers to his service in India (*The Cardboard Box & The Problem of Thor Bridge*), implying that some adventures must have taken place there as well. The issue may never be made clear, unless we are so fortunate as to discover another preserved manuscript from Watson's early days.

- Although considered by Holmes to be an expert on the ways of women (*The Adventure of the Second Stain*), when around a women to whom he is significantly attracted, Watson had a funny tendency to get extremely nervous and reverse objects in his sentences (Chapters III & IV, *The Sign of the Four*).

- Some herpetologists have made the unequivocal statement that there is no such snake as a "swamp adder." However, in an age when new species are still being discovered in the far corners of the world over one hundred and forty years after Holmes and Watson first embarked on their adventures together, this seems like an overly bold statement..

- A reader might suspect Watson of boasting about his experience with women, as he makes such a claim again (Chapter II, *The Sign of the Four*). However, since eight years have passed, we will be generous and assume that the doctor has forgotten. Much has been made of exactly which three continents Watson was referring. Clearly Europe must be one, likely with an unrecorded sweetheart of his days at the University of London. Asia is certainly the second, with the aforementioned Miss Violet Devere finally being revealed as the source of his knowledge. While some scholars have assumed Australia, it seems likely that Watson was sent back to England for boarding school at far too young of an age to have acquired any significant "experience of women." Now we realize that he must have been referring to the Americas, further strengthening the plausibility of the Bermuda Manuscript.

CHAPTER VII: PIERCING THE VEIL

- Prussic acid was the common name for hydrogen cyanide. It was a common poison of the Victorian era and beyond, used both for murderous purposes as well as a preferred method of suicide. *Aqua tofana* was an arsenic-based poison that originated from southern Italy. Fowler's solution was a tonic of potassium arsenite invented by Dr. Thomas Fowler of Stafford, England in 1786 for treating a wide range of ailments, including malaria and syphilis. It was still in use until the 1950's.

CHAPTER VIII: A DARKENING SKY

- One method by which we attempted to prove the authenticity of the Bermuda Manuscript was to try to match up the hurricane described with Watson with those known to have affected Bermuda during the year 1880. We almost determined the manuscript was a fake when it became clear that the only hurricane to hit the island that year occurred on 29 August. This storm was accompanied by winds of 'appalling violence,' destroyed numerous homes and four churches, and ruined the local fruit crop. Since Watson clearly must have still been recuperating in the Peshawar base hospital on that day, this seemed an insurmountable problem. However, it was later pointed out that we have only Mr. Boyle's word that the storm on that night was a true 'hurricane.' It may have simply been a very intense tropical storm, and the relatively inexperienced Watson would have had no frame of reference to determine otherwise. Thus, the 'hurricane argument' has little bearing on the potential authenticity of the Bermuda Manuscript.
- The irony is that Watson would never discover the identity of the murderer in the *Mystery of Edwin Drood*, since Dickens died before he could finish it. Of course, it is possible that Watson was reading the 'James version' of the novel. In 1873, a young American by the name of Thomas James published a version of *Drood* which he claimed had been 'ghost-written' by Dickens' spirit speaking through him. This created a great sensation and mixed reviews, but some critics, including Watson's first literary agent Sir Arthur Conan Doyle, praised this version for its similarity in style to Dickens' work.

CHAPTER IX: MURDER

- As an experienced army physician, Watson sadly would have had far too much experience with the effects of *rigor mortis*, the knowledge of which was also applied in the cases of Bartholomew Sholto (Chapter VI, *The Sign of the Four*) and the so-called Blessington, actually the bank robber Sutton (*The Resident Patient*).

CHAPTER X: A TANGLED SKEIN

- The translucent emerald-green jadeite derives primarily from two sources: Burma and Guatemala. While Watson was more likely to be familiar with the Burmese jade exported into China, in retrospect this was a missed clue that Dumas had spent time in Mesoamerica.
- Twenty gold sovereigns corresponded to twenty pounds sterling. Since twenty shillings equaled one pound, this translated to four hundred shillings, or almost thirty-five days of half-pay (eleven shillings, six pence) for Watson. This was quite a bit of money to be carrying around, since in 2010 terms, twenty pounds was the equivalent of approximately £8400 ($13,250). The twenty fifty-pound notes was an almost inconceivable amount of money (£420000 or $660,000).
- Watson never makes clear exactly which brass replica of the Great Seal of the Confederacy was in the possession of Mr. Dumas. While the embossing press and brass replica die were made in London, they never made their way to Richmond due to the naval blockade between Bermuda and America. Did Dumas purchase the die while in Bermuda? Where was he taking it? We may never know the answer. It appears likely that after Dumas' death this die was returned to its Bermuda caretakers, and it can now be found in the National Trust Museum within the Globe Hotel, St. George's, Bermuda.

CHAPTER XI: THE EVIDENCE OF THE PROPRIETRESS

- The Canon has several examples of maps reproduced for the reader's enlightenment. Like Mrs. Foster's maps, two were drawn by others, one by Percy Phelps (*The Naval Treaty*), and the other by Stanley Hopkins (*The Adventure of the Golden Pince-Nez*). Only one map was definitively drawn by John H. Watson, since he signed it (*The Adventure of the Priory School*). The maps reproduced herein are digital re-creations, as the original versions found with the manuscript (presumably the ones drawn by Mrs. Foster) were so water-damaged as to be almost unreadable.
- Mrs. Foster and Constable Dunkley give an accurate representation of the activities of Major Walker and his wife during their sojourn in St. George's.

- It is not clear from the historical records if Ralph Foster ever left the island of Bermuda, nor is it recorded why he chose the Globe name for his hotel. It is plausible that the account found in the Bermuda Manuscript is accurate in this regard.

CHAPTER XII: THE EVIDENCE OF THE AUSTRALIAN RUGBY-PLAYER

- The practice of transporting English criminals to Australia in order to decrease the burden of the English prisons began in 1788 and continued through 1850 in New South Wales and as late as 1868 in other parts of the continent.

- Upon first reading the Bermuda Manuscript, I assumed that I had discovered proof that it was a modern forgery when I read what I thought to be an obvious anachronism: 'three sheets to the wind.' Imagine my surprise when I found that this phrase goes back in printed form to at least 1821. Robert Louis Stevenson placed a version of this phase three years later into the mouth of Long John Silver in his masterpiece *Treasure Island*.

- The first known international Australian Rugby tour took place in 1899, when the teams from New South Wales and Queensland played a four match series against a team from Britain. The first known international tour for the Australian Rugby team was in 1908, when a squad of players travelled nine months through United Kingdom, Ireland and North America, even winning the gold medal in the 1908 London Olympic Games. Assuming the authenticity of the Bermuda Manuscript, either an Australian Rugby team actually blazed that trail twenty-eight years prior to the official records, or Sims was lying through his teeth about what he was doing in Cambridge, Massachusetts when he injured his knee.

- Oliver Wendell Holmes, Sr. (1809–1894) was an American physician, poet, professor, lecturer, and author. He was regarded by his peers as one of the best writers of the nineteenth century, and was great friends with Longfellow and other giants of American letters. His most famous prose work was *The Autocrat of the Breakfast-Table* (1858). He was on the faculty of Harvard Medical School and was also recognized as an important medical reformer. Since he measured only 'five feet three inches when standing in a pair of substantial boots' and was pushing seventy-one years of age by the time that Sims met him, Sims' description is likely a fair one. Watson never mentions O.W. Holmes again in his writings, but the inspiration of a medical-man-turned-author upon Watson's later literary pursuits is crystal clear, though the shared name with Sherlock Holmes can only be a coincidence.

- The proverbial 'drop that made the cup run over' is from the French: '*c'est la goutte d'eau qui fait déborder le vase.*' A more typical English expression would be: 'the straw that broke the camel's back,' which dates back to the works of none other than Charles Dickens (*Dombey and Son*, 1848), though he clearly found it in an earlier work, as the proverb is originally Arabic.

- The coca leaves that Sims chews are directly related, albeit in a much weaker form, to the infamous seven-per-cent solution that Holmes was wont to utilize when he felt the stagnation of the mind (Chapter I, *The Sign of the Four*).

CHAPTER XIII: THE EVIDENCE OF THE PORTUGUESE WINE-MERCHANT

- In 1876, lawn tennis, a game devised by Major Walter Clopton Wingfield a year earlier and originally called '*Sphairistike*' (ancient Greek for 'the art of playing ball'), was added to the activities of the All England Croquet Club in Wimbledon. In the spring of 1877, the club was re-titled 'The All England Croquet and Lawn Tennis Club' and signaled its change of name by instituting the first Lawn Tennis Championship. A new code of laws (replacing the code until then administered by the Marylebone Cricket Club) was drawn up for the event. Today's rules are similar except for details such as the height of the net and posts and the distance of the service line from the net. The only event held in 1877 was the Gentlemen's Singles, which was won by Spencer Gore, from a field of twenty-two. Gore lost to Frank Hadow in 1878. There are no records of an Antonio Cordeiro participating in the early tournaments, so he was either lying or perhaps played under an assumed name to hide his foreign origin?

CHAPTER XIV: THE EVIDENCE OF THE BOHEMIAN PHYSICIAN

- *The Lancet* is one of the world's oldest general medical journals, founded in 1823 by Thomas Wakley, an English surgeon. It is hardly surprising to find Dr. Nemcek reading it.
- Watson was clearly conversant in German, as he had no problems when Holmes quoted from Goethe (Chapters VI & XII, *The Sign of the Four*). "*Mit der dummheit kämpfen götter selbst vergebens,*" which indeed translates as "against stupidity the gods themselves contend in vain," is from *The Maid of Orleans* (1801) a play by the other great German romantic poet Johann Christoph Friedrich von

Schiller (1759–1805), most famous for his *Ode to Joy* later utilized by Beethoven.

- Barring a monstrous coincidence, when Dr. Nemcek refers to Antonín Dvořák, it seems likely that this is actually the same as 'Mr. A. Dorak,' Professor Lowenstein's London agent (*The Adventure of the Creeping Man*). As the surname 'Dorak' is actually of Turkish origin (from the town of the same name on the shores of Lake Apolyont with some royal tombs of an age near to that of fabled Troy), it is obvious that either Watson or the printer John Murray made a spelling mistake, and the man's "curious," "Slavonic" name was actually meant to be 'Dvořák.' Dr. Nemcek was thirty-three years of age in 1880 (when the events of the Bermuda Manuscript unfolded), and Dr. Watson was not to hear the name 'Dorak' again until 1903.
- Dr. Nemcek was correct about the word 'pistol' being the only word in the English language derived from the Czech. However, this singularity lasted only for another forty years, until the word 'robot' was introduced to the public by the Czech writer Karel Čapek in his play *R.U.R. (Rossum's Universal Robots*, 1920).
- *'Si vis pacem para bellum,'* translates to 'If you wish for peace, prepare for war.' Any physician of the Victorian era would be very well acquainted with Latin. Watson was able to recognize it whenever Holmes tossed out a Latin saying (e.g. Chapter VII, *A Study in Scarlet*).
- The Hippocratic Oath, which may or may not have actually been written by Hippocrates, was first spoken as part of the modern graduation ceremony of new physicians in Wittenberg, Germany, in 1508. The version that Watson paraphrases from is now considered rather antiquated and has been updated by modern medical schools.

CHAPTER XV: THE EVIDENCE OF THE TURKISH ENGINEER

- It is highly appropriate that Mr. Bey would smoke a meerschaum pipe, as Turkey is the main source of that soft mineral. Although commonly depicted as such, there is no evidence in the Canon that Holmes ever smoked such a pipe (clay and cherry-wood were the two undisputed descriptions of Holmes' pipes).
- Sadly, the cruel Abdul-Hamid would not be deposed for another twenty-nine years (1909). Surprisingly, in 1903 Holmes would admit to taking a commission from him (*The Adventure of the Blanched Soldier*). There may have been extenuating circumstances to explain

this lapse in moral judgment, or perhaps Holmes was actually working as a double agent for the forces of the Young Turks opposed to the Sultan?

- George Stephenson (1781–1848) was the English engineer who built the first public railway line in the world to use steam locomotives, and was renowned as being the "Father of Railways."

- Bey's reference to Gioachino Rossini's opera *La Cenerentola* (1817) is a confusing one, since the opera does not utilize the plot device of the fitted slipper, but instead has a pair of bracelets. Bey must have been thinking of Charles Perrault's version of the tale (1697).

- The reference to the Turkish or Persian slipper brings to mind the one owned by Holmes. It only appears three times in the Canon (*The Musgrave Ritual & The Adventures of the Naval Treaty & The Empty House*), but its fame as the repository for his shag tobacco far eclipses those few mentions.

CHAPTER XVI: THE EVIDENCE OF THE GREEK PUGILIST

- Despite recurring revolts from 1866 onwards, Crete would only achieve partial independence in 1897, and would not fully join Greece until the end of the Balkan Wars in 1913.

- It is interesting to speculate whether Mr. Delopolous' unnamed mother was somehow related to Paul and Sophy Kratides, both of whom hailed from Athens (*The Greek Interpreter*). Paul and Sophy both appeared to be young when they attracted the attention of Sherlock Holmes in 1888. Based on the timing of these cases, it seems plausible that Mr. Delopolous could be either their first cousin once removed or their second cousin.

- The Marquess of Queensbury rules were drafted in 1867. As for Delopolous' claim that the Greeks invented boxing, there is certainly some truth there, though the Sumerians and Egyptians can also make a case. The earliest use of gloves is depicted in the great frescos of the Minoan palaces of Crete and Santorini. However these sites were not excavated until after 1880. The boxing match in the *Iliad* was won by Epeios, son of Panopeus, a minor character. Although the first modern international Olympic Games took place in Athens in 1896, precursor events also occurred in 1870 and 1875, to which Delopolous clearly must have been referring.

- At the time of Watson's Bermuda adventure, a fine Chianti likely hailed from the vineyards of the Baron Ricasoli. Their name has been linked to wine production since 1141 and it is reputed to be the second oldest winery in the world. In 1872, Baron Bettino Ricasoli wrote the formula for Chianti Classico wine, which he developed after more than a decade of research. He called for a mixture of 70% Sangiovese, 15% Canaiolo, 10% Malvasia (later amended to include Trebbiano) and 5% other local red varieties. In 1967, the Denominazione di origine controllata (DOC) regulation set by the Italian government firmly established the "Ricasoli formula" of a Sangiovese-based blend with 10-30% Malvasia and Trebbiano. However, recent modifications have moved today's Chianti further away from the blend that Watson and his brother would have enjoyed. Since 1996 the blend for Chianti Classico has been 75-100% Sangiovese, up to 10% Canaiolo, and up to 20% of any other approved red grape variety. such as Cabernet Sauvignon, Merlot or Syrah. In the greatest of ironies, since 2006, the use of white grape varieties such as Malvasia and Trebbiano have been prohibited in Chianti Classico. The Iron Baron would have shuddered at this deviation from his formula.

- Telegrams were frequently used by Holmes and Watson throughout London and beyond, but at first glance this appeared to be an anachronism that might call into question the authenticity of the Bermuda Manuscript, for Bermuda was not linked to the outside world by telegraph until the completion of the Bermuda-Halifax Cable undersea cable in 1890. However, on further review it appears that the Royal Engineers had at least erected an intra-isle system to connect the strategic forts and Dockyard, which replaced the flag signals that had worked across the islands since the 1820s. In 1863, the No 5 Company of Royal Engineers had constructed a single overhead, roadside iron wire from the Central Signal Station at Fort George above St George's eleven miles west to the Governor's Residence at Mount Langton. In 1864, the civil government contributed for its extension with a branch from Mount Langton to the Post Office in the capital of Hamilton. By 1866, the line had been extended two miles westwards to Spanish Point and the Admiral's House opposite Dockyard on Ireland Island. It was completed in 1868 by the laying of an over two mile submarine cable to Dockyard, with a grand total of eleven military telegraph offices on the Bermudas. Clearly this is the system that Watson must have utilized.

CHAPTER XVII: THE EVIDENCE OF THE ENGLISH NATURALIST

- The Langham, London opened in 1865 and was one of the Grand Hotels of Victorian high society with opulent comforts and luxuries.

- Warburton's story regarding his father appears to be falsified. There is no record of a Trelawney Warburton serving in the 17th Lancers during the Charge of the Light Brigade. The Lancers were in fact commanded by Captain William Morris, and while three members of the 17th did receive a V.C. for their gallantry, none were named Warburton. However, it seems odd that Warburton would pick such a famous battle in which to set a fictional account of his father's exploits, when more obscure ones were available. So perhaps the historical records are incomplete?

- Warburton's enthusiasm for re-discovering the presumably extinct Cahow was ahead of his time. Seventy-one years later, in 1951, the Cahow would be dramatically rediscovered on islets in Castle Harbor.

CHAPTER XVIII: THE EVIDENCE OF THE ITALIAN PAINTER

- By careful analysis of Aicardi's description it appears that he is referring to the painting entitled *Boating* (1874, Metropolitan Museum of Art, New York) by Édouard Manet (1832–1883). Manet's *The Suicide* (Foundation E.G. Bührle, Zurich, Switzerland) is believed to have been completed between 1877 and 1881, though Aicardi's reference here argues against the latter date.

- It is not clear exactly to which Vernet Signore Aicardi refers. There was Claude Joseph Vernet (1714–1789), his son Antoine Charles Horace Vernet (1758–1835), and his son Émile Jean-Horace Vernet (1789 – 1863), all of whom were painters. The Italian Aicardi's love of the French school is likely attributable to his time in the *Légion étrangère.*

- It is difficult to reconcile Aicardi's tale about a serialized novel by Wilkie Collins with the reported dates of the Bermuda Manuscript, since his *The Policeman & the Cook* was not released until 1881. However, Aicardi was also lying about the nature of his conversation with Sims. Was it just a coincidence that Aicardi mentioned Beeton's Christmas Annual or Lippincott's Monthly Magazine while discussing the optimal way to publish a story? These represent the first (*A Study in Scarlet*) and second (*The Sign of the Four*) places that Watson directed his first literary agent, Sir Arthur Conan Doyle, to publish his early cases with Holmes, and perhaps he got the idea from Aicardi?

- For a translation of "*E quindi uscimmo a riveder le stelle*" see the notes to Chapter XXIII.

- Presuming that Aicardi was being honest when he claimed Milano as his home, the constable's suggestion that he might be involved with either the Mafia (originated from Sicily), or the Carbonari or Camorra (both begun in Naples) seems to divulge a lack of knowledge about the geopolitical factions of the early Italian state.

CHAPTER XIX: THE EVIDENCE OF THE SPANISH MARQUESA

- Davos Platz was the site of a famous tuberculosis sanatorium.
- Francisco José de Goya y Lucientes (1746–1828) was a Spanish painter during the Napoleonic invasion of the Iberian Peninsula. He painted both horrific depictions of war (a series known as *Los Desastres de la Guerra*), and a magnificent portrait of the English hero of the Peninsular War, The Duke of Wellington, now to be found in the National Gallery, London. Presumably the Marquesa possessed a copy of this portrait and not the original Goya.
- Keeping Jimson weed in the house to ward off ghosts was an Aztec practice, which the Marquesa most likely would have learned of only by residing in Mexico!

CHAPTER XX: THE EVIDENCE OF THE AMERICAN LADY

- Lucy's quote, "Alas, the storm is come again!... I will here shroud till the dregs of the storm be past" is derived from *The Tempest*, Act Two, Scene Two.

CHAPTER XXI: THE EVIDENCE OF THE FRENCH LAWYER

- It is clear from the Canon that Watson is fluent in French, as he has no problem following along and reporting Holmes' not infrequent use of French phrases. It is most evident near when Watson reports in 1881 that he was reading a French novel, *Vie de Boheme*, that was not translated into English until 1888 (Chapter V, *A Study in Scarlet*). Dubois' comment, '*L'homme n'est rien, l'oeuvre tout,*' translates as 'the man is nothing, the work is everything.' Watson's retort, '*Battre le fer pendant qu'il est chaud,*' translates as 'To strike when the iron is hot.'
- We can find no evidence that there was a fire at the Palace Hotel, San Francisco in 1880. It is highly probable that Dubois is lying. If Dubois actually stayed at the Palace, built in 1875, he was clearly flush for money, for it was at the time one of the largest and most expensive hotels in the world.
- Watson's first literary agent, Sir Arthur Conan Doyle, once accused Watson of "never show(ing) one gleam of humour or mak(ing) a

single joke" in his book *Memories and Adventures*. This only goes to show how little Sir Arthur actually read Watson's words, for Holmes clearly states that Watson has a "certain unexpected vein of pawky humour" (Chapter I, *The Valley of Fear*).

CHAPTER XXII: THE LIST OF EVIDENCE

- The Mayor of St. George's in 1880 was William C.J. Hyland (1817–1892), a post which he ably served, since on the 3rd of October 1892, he was elected unanimously for the twelfth time in a row!
- This literary agent has not attempted to verify Watson's claim that a bottle of Madeira poured into an orchid would result in the death of the plant within forty-eight hours. I did not wish to purposefully murder an orchid (which in my experience die handily enough on their own) and I certainly did not wish to waste a fine Madeira!
- The *Arabian Nights*, more properly known as *One Thousand and One Nights*, was probably first encountered by Watson in the form of the c.1840 sanitized translation of Edward William Lane. The more famous eroticized version of Sir Richard Francis Burton was not available until c.1888.

CHAPTER XXIII: A POSSIBLE SOLUTION

- All of the tales of treasure recounted by Constable Dunkley are verifiable Bermudian legends. Dunkley's prediction that more Spanish treasure will be found in Bermuda will come true, thanks in large part to the work of the diver Teddy Tucker. His most famous find is considered one of the most valuable pieces of sunken treasure ever found. The emerald-studded 22-karat gold Tucker Cross was discovered in 1955. It is believed to have come from 'San Pedro', a Spanish galleon which was lost on the reefs in 1594.
- Dunkley's envisioning of how the sea-glass played into the mystery must have drawn on knowledge about the activities of a local branch of the KKK, perhaps remnants of Confederate sympathizers after the war? It is similar to how other branches utilized warnings "sent to the marked man in some fantastic but generally recognizable shape – a sprig of oak-leaves in some parts, melon seeds or orange pips in others" (*The Five Orange Pips*).
- Dunkley's prediction that more caves remained to be found in Bermuda also came true. The most famous one, Crystal Caves, was discovered in 1905, when two young teenagers named Carl Gibbons and Edgar Hollis were engaged in a spirited game of cricket and lost their ball down a hole. Exploring further led to a previously hidden natural wonder.

- Paul Bert published *La Pression Barométrique*, providing the first systematic understanding of the causes of decompression sickness in 1878.
- Longfellow's translation of *The Inferno* was published in 1867. His actual translation of the final line was 'Thence we came forth to rebehold the stars.' While Longfellow's version in general is quite beautiful, that particular line sounds a bit odd to modern ears.
- The astute reader will recognize echoes herein of Watson's introduction to "Part 2 – The Scowrers" (Chapter VII, *The Valley of Fear*). Much of what follows in Chapter XXIV reads like a prototype to the full novellas that serve as interludes and explanations for the mysteries of *A Study in Scarlet* and *The Valley of Fear*.

CHAPTER XXIV: AN EXTRAORDINARY TALE

- Watson's telling of the final hours in the life of Commandant Iain Harrier are far too detailed for it to be conceivable that he could have simply dreamt up all of these details. It seems likely that he misrepresented his reminiscences here with an amalgam of what he actually said on that night at the Globe Hotel supplemented with details that must have been admitted by Lucy later that evening.
- Harrier's recollection of the French intervention in Mexico and the brief reign of Emperor Maximilian are essentially accurate. The French Foreign Legion became part of the world consciousness due to their defensive stand at the Battle of Camarón (1863), in which sixty-five men held off a force of over two thousand for an entire day, until only two unwounded survivors remained. Like Thermopylae (480 BCE), the Alamo (1836), and many others before it, there is something mythical about a doomed stand.
- Generals Miramon and Mejía never abandoned their loyalty to Maximilian. They died seconds after him, executed by the same firing squad, the last words on their tongues, "Long live the Emperor!" Colonel Lopez, on the other hand, proved less trustworthy. In May 1867, Lopez was bribed by the Republican Army to open a gate into Santiago de Querétaro, albeit after first obtaining their agreement that Maximilian would be allowed to escape. Of course, the Republicans failed to hold their side of this devil's bargain after the city fell. Maximilian's attempt to break through the Republican lines via a cavalry charge led by Felix Salm-Salm failed, and Maximilian was captured.
- Maximilian's emerald and diamond necklace and the twenty-one carat Maximilian Emerald Ring eventually made their way into the possession of the American heiress Marjorie Merriweather Post

(1887-1993) by unclear means. She was a great collector and art connoisseur and it seems likely that she obtained them in Paris, where she had the ring's emerald reset by Cartier into a new ring flanked by baguette diamonds. She eventually donated both items, plus many others, to the Smithsonian Institute's Museum of Natural History.

- The story of the Queen Isabella Emerald is much as Watson described it herein. Hernán Cortés was presented the nine-hundred sixty-four carat Stone of Judgment by King Montezuma in 1520, perhaps mistaking the conquistador for the return of Quetzalcoatl. The stone remained in Mexico for several hundred years in the possession of Cortés' descendants until it was dispatched back to Spain. The ship's manifest noted that it contained a hundred chests of emeralds, including the mystical Isabella Emerald, gold idols, gold and jade death masks of Aztec emperors, and crystal skulls. The ship was then lost in an accident, but contrary to Maximilian's prediction, the Queen Isabella Emerald and an almost unbelievable amount of accompanying treasure were discovered in 1993 twelve miles off the coast of Florida. The emerald is still not on public display.

CHAPTER XXV: THE CONSTABLE'S DILEMMA

- At his final moments, Maximilian spoke only in Spanish and gave his executioners a portion of gold not to shoot him in the head, so that his mother could see his face. His last words were, "I forgive everyone, and I ask everyone to forgive me. May my blood which is about to be shed be for the good of the country. Viva Mexico, viva la independencia!" Despite having taken the money, the Juarista firing squad shot him in the face. After Maximilian's execution, in a small satchel around his neck, they discovered the almost near colorless forty-two carat ""Emperor Maximilian Diamond." This diamond was returned to his widow, and was eventually sold to pay her medical expenses. It passed through many other hands, and its current location is unknown.

- The 'Execution of Emperor Maximilian' is now one of the most famous paintings of Édouard Manet. It was painted in 1868 and is in the possession of the Kunsthalle Mannheim.

- Where did Watson witness the aurora borealis, commonly known as the Northern Lights? Although we tend to think of them as being associated with the Scandinavian countries, the northernmost tip of Scotland has a geomagnetic latitude similar to that of Oslo, Stockholm, and Helsinki, and aurora sightings are not uncommon there. Perhaps Watson visited during one of his breaks from medical school?

- Watson's suspicion that there was a printing press in St. George's was correct. It can still be visited in Featherbed Alley, though one wonders if it was originally located on Printer's Alley?
- Like so many other phrases in the English language, 'The world is your oyster' was coined by Shakespeare in Act II, Scene II of *The Merry Wives of Windsor*. And of course, Lucy's quote 'My bounty is as boundless as the sea' is from Act II, Scene II of *Romeo and Juliet*.

EPILOGUE: *THE ORONTES*

- Elizabeth Foster would sell the Globe Hotel in 1882. Perhaps she received a sufficient portion of the proceeds from the sale of the Empress Emerald to enable her to retire?
- When Watson first met Holmes in the laboratory of St. Bart's, he admitted to Holmes that he kept a "bull pup" (Chapter I, *A Study in Scarlet*). This utterance was made more mysterious by the complete absence in the rest of the Canon of any reference to a dog ever living at 221B Baker Street. Perhaps Watson was anticipating receiving Gladstone from his brother, but something ultimately prevented this reunion?
- Here we have some confirmation of the theory of Dorothy L. Sayers, who claimed that the fact that Watson's wife once called him 'James' was an affectionate spin on his middle name Hamish, which means James in Scottish Gaelic (*The Man with The Twisted Lip*). This was a common Victorian practice, as seen in the case of Mrs. Effie Munro, who calls her husband Grant by his nickname 'Jack' (*The Yellow Face*) and Miss Presbury who calls Mr. Trevor Bennett by the same pet-name 'Jack' (*The Adventure of the Creeping Man*).
- 'Journeys end in lovers meeting' is of course from Act II, Scene III of Shakespeare's *Twelfth Night*. The French have many ways of saying goodbye, each with a subtle shade of difference. *Adieu* is used for true goodbyes in the sense of you are either unsure whether or not you will see the person again, or, if you do see him again, it will be a very long time, while *à bientôt* means 'see you soon.'
- Tradition holds that Watson met Holmes at St. Bart's Hospital on 1 January, 1881.
- Unfortunately, Watson would not see his brother again. Although when they parted Henry was left with good prospects of advancement in the British Army, he threw away his chances by sheer carelessness. His was drummed out of the 99th Regiment, and washed up in America to live for some time in poverty, with occasional short

intervals of prosperity. Eventually, however, he took to drink and died around early 1887 (Chapter I, *The Sign of the Four*).

- According to an apocryphal play, Watson's acquaintance onboard the *Orontes*, Sir Montague Brown, the aristocratic English globetrotter would apparently meet up with Watson again on the streets of San Francisco (see notes below).

- Because Watson apparently mailed the account of the Bermuda Manuscript to his brother shortly after landing on a Portsmouth jetty, it is unclear whether he ever reunited with Ms. Lucy Harrier. However, in 2001, a long-suppressed play was unveiled that might throw some light upon the subject. That play was entitled *Angels of Darkness* and was apparently written by Watson's first literary agent, Sir Arthur Conan Doyle. Although the exact genesis of the play is unclear, it seems likely that Conan Doyle wrote it during a period of great personal turmoil, for it is filled with historical inaccuracies about his friend John H. Watson, M.D. And yet portions of that manuscript feel as if they contain hints of the truth. In the play, Watson travels to San Francisco around 1884 and there woos a young woman, returning with her to England in order to wed. In the play, her name is given as Lucy Ferrier. That is patently absurd since the real Lucy Ferrier unfortunately is known to have died in Salt Lake City around 1860 (Part II, Chapter V, *A Study in Scarlet*). It seems much more likely that Conan Doyle heard the name wrong, and Watson instead journeyed to San Francisco to reunite with Lucy *Harrier*. If so, then tragically she must have died before 1888, when Watson encountered Ms. Mary Morstan (*The Sign of the Four*). But if their marriage lasted but only a few short years, in the absence of any of Watson's other early writings coming to light, we can simply imagine that Watson and Lucy might have found great happiness together, however brief.

§

ABOUT THE AUTHOR

In the year 1998 CRAIG JANACEK took his degree of Doctor of Medicine of Vanderbilt University, and proceeded to Stanford to go through the training prescribed for pediatricians in practice. Having completed his studies there, he was duly attached to the University of California, San Francisco as Associate Professor. The author of over eighty medical monographs upon a variety of obscure lesions, his travel-worn and battered tin dispatch-box is crammed with papers, nearly all of which are records of his fictional works. These include several collections of the further adventures of Sherlock Holmes (*Light in the Darkness, The Assassination of Sherlock Holmes*, and the forthcoming *Treasure Trove Indeed!*), two Dr. Watson novels (*The Isle of Devils,* and the forthcoming *The Gate of Gold*), and two non-Holmes novels (*The Oxford Deception & The Anger of Achilles Peterson*). His short stories have been published in the *MX Book of New Sherlock Holmes Stories, Part I* (October 2015), the *MX Book of New Sherlock Holmes Stories, 2016 Annual* (May 2016), the *MX Book of New Sherlock Holmes Stories, 2017 Annual* (coming spring 2017), and *Holmes Away From Holmes: Tales of the Great Hiatus* (December 2016). He lives near San Francisco with his wife and two children, where he is at work on his next story. Craig Janacek is a *nom-de-plume.*

ABOUT THE TYPE

This book is set in Baskerville Old Face, a transitional serif typeface designed in 1757 by John Baskerville (1706–1775) in Birmingham, England. The typeface was designed to reflect Baskerville's ideals of perfection, for which he chose simplicity and quiet refinement.

It is unclear whether this John Baskerville is, in fact, one of the two sons of Hugo, who in 1742 set down the curious, old-world narrative of his eponym ancestor known as the Curse of the Baskervilles.

74642194R00172

Made in the USA
Middletown, DE
28 May 2018